Pedro Calderón de la Barca, Denis Florence MacCarthy

Three Dramas of Calderón

from the Spanish

Pedro Calderón de la Barca, Denis Florence MacCarthy

Three Dramas of Calderón
from the Spanish

ISBN/EAN: 9783337382780

Printed in Europe, USA, Canada, Australia, Japan

Cover: Foto ©Andreas Hilbeck / pixelio.de

More available books at **www.hansebooks.com**

CALDERON'S DRAMAS AND AUTOS,

Translated into English Verse

BY DENIS FLORENCE MAC-CARTHY.

From Ticknor's *History of Spanish Literature*. London: 1863.

"Denis Florence M'Carthy published in London (in 1861) translations of two plays, and an *auto* of Calderon, under the title of 'Love, the greatest Enchantment; the Sorceries of Sin; the Devotion of the Cross, from the Spanish of Calderon, attempted strictly in English Asonante, and other imitative Verse', printing, at the same time, a carefully corrected text of the originals, page by page, opposite to his translations. It is, I think, one of the boldest attempts ever made in English verse. It is, too, as it seems to me, remarkably successful. Not that *asonantes* can be made fluent or graceful in English, or easily perceptible to an English ear, but that the Spanish air and character of Calderon are so happily preserved. Mr. M'Carthy, in 1853, had published two volumes of translations from Calderon, to which I have already referred; and, besides this, he has rendered excellent service to the cause of Spanish literature in other ways. But in the present volume he has far surpassed all he had previously done; for Calderon is a poet who, whenever he is translated, should have his very excesses, both in thought and manner, fully produced, in order to give a faithful idea of what is grandest and most distinctive in his genius. Mr. M'Carthy has done this, I conceive, to a degree which I had previously considered impossible. Nothing, I think, in the English language will give us so true an impression of what is most characteristic of the Spanish drama; perhaps I ought to say, of what is most characteristic of Spanish poetry generally".—tom. iii. pp. 461, 462.

From "Blätter für Literarische Unter-

haltung". 1862. Erster Baube, 479 Leipzig, F. A. Brockhaus.

"Erwähnenswerth ist folgender Kühne versuch einer Nachbildung Calderon'scher stücke in Englischen Assonanzen.

"Love, the greatest enchantment; The Sorceries of Sin; The Devotion of the Cross, from the Spanish of Calderon, attempted strictly in English Asonante, and other imitative verse. By Denis Florence Mac-Carthy".

Diese Uebersetzung ist bem Verfasser ber "History of Spanish Literature", George Ticknor, zugeeignet, ber in einem Schreiber au ben Uebersetzer bie Arbeit "marvellous" nennt unb bam fortfährt:

"Nicht baß sie bie Assonanzen bem englischen Ohr so hörbar gemacht hätten, wie bies mit ben Spanischen ber Fall ist; unsere wiberhaarigen consonanten machen bies unmöglich; baß Wunberbare ist nur, baß sie bieselben überhaupt hörbar gemacht haben. Meiner Meinung nach nehme ich Ihre Assonanzen so beutlich wahr, wil bie Von August Schlegel ober Gries unb mehr als biejenigen Friebrich Schlegel's. Aber bieser war ber erste, ber ben versuch bazu machte, unb ausserbem bin ich Kein Deutscher. Wurbe es nicht lustig sein, wenn man einmal ein solches Experiment in französchicher Sprache wolte?"

"Ohne zweifel würbe MacCarthy Ohne ben vorgaug beutscher Nachbilbner bes Calberon ebenso wenig barauf gekommen sein englische Assonanzen zu versuchen, als man ohne bas ermunternbe Beispiel beutscher Dichter unb Uebersetzer barauf gekommen sein wurbe, in Uebersetzungen unb originalbichtungen unter welchen letztern wol besonbers Longfellow's "Evangeline", zu nennen ist, englische Herameter zu versuchen, was in letzter zeit gar nicht selten geschehen ist'.

From "*Boletin de Ferro-Carriles*". Cadiz: 1862.

"La novedad que nos comunica de

la existencia de traducciones tan acabadas de nuestro grande é inimitable Calderon, ostendando, hasta cierto punto,
las galas y formas del original, estamos
seguros será acogida con favor, si no
con entusiasmo, per los verdaderos amantes de las letras españolas. A ellos
nos dirijimos, recomendándoles el último trabajo del Señor Mac-Carthy,
seguros de que participaran del mismo
placer que nosotros hemos experimentado al examinar su fiel, al par que
brillante traduccion; y en cuanto á la
dificil tentativa de los asonantes ingleses, nos sorpende que el Señor Mac-
Carthy haya podido sacar tanto parido, si se considera la indole peculiar
de los dos idiomas".

Extracts from Letters addressed to the Author.

From Henry Wadsworth Longfellow, Esq.

Cambridge, near Boston,
America, April 29,
1862.

"I thank you very much for your
new work in the vast and flowery fields
of Calderon. It is, I think, admirable;
and presents the old Spanish dramatist
before the English reader in a very attractive light.

"Particularly in the most poetical
passages you are excellent; as, for instance, in the fine description of the
gerfalcon and the heron in 'El Mayor
Encanto'.—11 *Jor.*

"Your previous volumes I have long
possessed and highly prized; and I
hope you mean to add more and more,
so as to make the translation as nearly
complete as a single life will permit.
It seems rather appalling to undertake
the whole of so voluminous a writer.
Nevertheless, I hope you will do it.
Having proved that you can, perhaps
you ought to do it. This may be your
appointed work. It is a noble one.

"With much regard, I am, etc.,
"HENRY W. LONGFELLOW.
"Denis Florence Mac-Carthy, Esq".

From the Same.

Nahant, near Boston,
August 10, 1857.

"MY DEAR SIR,
"Before leaving Cambridge to come
down here to the sea-side, I had the
pleasure of receiving your precious
volume of 'Mysteries of Corpus Christi'; and should have thanked you
sooner for your kindness in sending it
to me, had I not been very busy at the
time in getting out my last volume of
Dante.

"I at once read your work, with eagerness and delight—that peculiar and
strange delight which Calderon gives
his admirers, as peculiar and distinct
as the flavour of an olive from that
of all other fruits.

"You are doing this work admirably,
and seem to gain new strength and
sweetness as you go on. It seems as if
Calderon himself were behind you
whispering and suggesting. And what
better work could you do in your
bright hours or in your dark hours
than just this, which seems to have
been put providentially into your
hands!

"The extracts from the 'Sacred Parnassus' in the *Chronicle*, which reached
me yesterday, are also excellent.

"For this and all, many and many
thanks.

"Yours faithfully,
"HENRY W. LONGFELLOW.
"Denis Florence Mac-Carthy, Esq.".

From George Ticknor, Esq., the Historian of Spanish Literature.

"Boston, 16th December, 1861.

"In this point of view, your volume
seems to me little less than marvellous.
If I had not read it—indeed, if I had
not carefully gone through with the
Devocion de la Cruz, I should not
have believed it possible to do what you
have done. Titian, they say, and some
others of the old masters, laid on
colours for their groundwork wholly
different from those they used afterwards, but which they counted upon to
shine through, and contribute materially to the grand results they produced. So in your translations, the
Spanish seems to come through to the
surface; the original air is always perceptible in your variations. It is like
a family likeness coming out in the
next generation, yet with the freshness
of originality.

"But the rhyme is as remarkable as
the verse and the translation; not that
you have made the asonante as perceptible to the English ear as it is to the
Spanish; our cumbersome consonants
make that impossible. But the wonder

is, that you have made it perceptible at all. I think I perceive your asonantes much as I do those of August Schlegel or Gries, and more than I do those of Friederich Schlegel. But he was the first who tried them, and, besides, I am not a German. Would it not be amusing to have the experiment tried in French?"

From the Same.
"Boston, March 20, 1867.

"The world has claims on you which you ought not to evade; and, if the path in which you walk of preference, leads to no wide popularity or brilliant profits, it is, at least, one you have much to yourself, and cannot fail to enjoy. You have chosen it from faithful love, and will always love it; I suspect partly because it is your own choice, because it is peculiarly your own".

From the Same.
"Boston, July 3, 1867.

"Considered from this point of view, I think that in your present volume ["Mysteries of Corpus Christi", or "Autos Sacramentales" of Calderon] you are always as successful as you were in your previous publications of the same sort, and sometimes more so; easier, I mean, freer, and more happily expressive. If I were to pick out my first preference, I should take your fragment of the 'Veneno y Triaca', at the end; but I think the whole volume is more fluent, pleasing, and attractive than even its predecessors".

From the first of English religious painters.
April 24, 1867.

"I cannot resist the impulse I have of offering you my most grateful thanks for the greatest intellectual treat I have ever experienced in my life, and which you have afforded me in the magnificent translations of the divine Calderon; for, surely, of all the poets the world ever saw, he alone is worthy of standing beside the author of the Book of Job and of the Psalms, and entrusted, like them, with the noble mission of commending to the hearts of others all that belongs to the beautiful and true, ever directing the thoughtful reader through the love of the beautiful veil, to the great Author of all perfection.

"I cannot conceive a nation can receive a greater boon than being helped to a love of such works as the religious dramas of this Prince of Poets. I have for years felt this, and as your translations appeared, have read them with the greatest possible interest. I knew not of the publication of the last, and it was to an accidental, yet, with me, habitual outburst of praise of Calderon, as the antidote and cure for the trifling literature of the day, that my friend (*the*) D— made me aware of its being out".

[The work especially referred to in the latter part of this interesting letter is the following: "Mysteries of Corpus Christi (*Autos acramentales*), from the Spanish of Calderon, by Denis Florence Mac-Carthy". Duffy, Dublin and London, 1867.]

Extracts from American and Canadian Journals.

From an eloquent article in the " Boston Courier", March 18, 1862, written by George Stillman Hillard, Esq., the author of " Six Months in Italy"—a delightful book, worthy of the beautiful country it so beautifully describes.

"Calderon is one of the three greatest names in Spanish literature, Lope de Vega and Cervantes being the other two. He is also a great name in the universal realm of letters, though out of Spain he is little more than a great name, except in Germany, that land so hospitable to famous wits, and where, to readers and critics of a mystical and transcendental turn, his peculiar genius strongly commended him. To form a notion of what manner of man Calderon was, we must imagine a writer hardly inferior to Shakespeare in fertility of invention and dramatic insight, inspired by a religious fervour like that of Donne or Crashaw, and endowed with the wild and ethereal imagination of Shelley. But the religious fervour is Catholic, not Protestant, Southern, not Northern: it is intense, mystical, and ecstatic: like a tongue of upward-darting flame, it burns and trembles with impassioned impulse to mingle with empyrean fire. The imagination, too, is not merely southern, but with an oriental element shining through it. like the ruddy heart of an opal". . .

"But our purpose is not to speak of Calderon, but of his translator Mr. MacCarthy; and to make our readers acquainted with his very successful effort to reproduce in English some of the most characteristic productions of the genius of Spain, retaining even one of the peculiarities in the structure of the verse which has hardly ever been transplanted from the soil of the peninsula". . . .

"Mr. MacCarthy's translations strike us as among the most successful experiments which have been made to represent in our language the characteristic beauties of the finest productions of other nations. They are sufficiently faithful, as may be readily seen by the Spanish scholar, as the translator has the courage to print the original and his version side by side. The rich, imaginative passages of Calderon are reproduced in language of such grace and flexibility as shows in Mr. Mac-Carthy no inconsiderable amount of poetical power. The measures of Calderon are retained; the rhymed passages are translated into rhyme, and what is more noticeable still, Mr. Mac-Carthy has done what no writer in English has ever before essayed, except to a very limited extent—he has copied the *asonantes* of the original". . . .

"We take leave of Mr. MacCarthy with hearty acknowledgments for the pleasure we have had in reading his excellent translations, which have given us a sense of Calderon's various and brilliant genius such as we never before had, and no analysis of his dramas, however full and careful, could bestow".

From a Review of "Love the Greatest Enchantment", etc., in the "New York Tablet", July 19, 1862, written by the gifted and ill-fated Hon. Thomas D'Arcy M'Gee, of Montreal.

"This beautiful volume before us—like virtue's self, fair within and without—is Mr. Mac-Carthy's second contribution to the Herculean task which Longfellow cheers him on to continue—the translation into English of the complete works of Calderon. Two experimental volumes, containing six dramas of the same author, appeared n 1853, winning the well-merited en-comium of every person of true taste into whose hands they happened to fall. The Translator was encouraged, if not by the general chorus of popular applause, by the precious and emphatic approbation of those best entitled by knowledge and accomplishments to pronounce judgment. So here, after an interval of seven years, we have right worthily presented to us three of those famous *Autos*, which for two centuries drew together all the multitude of the Madrilenos, on the annual return of the great feast of Corpus Christi. On that same self-same festival, in a northern land, under a gray and clouded sky, in the heart of a city most unlike gay, garden-hued, out-of-door Madrid, we have spent the long hours over these resurrected dramas, and the spell of both the poets is still upon us, as we unite together, in dutiful juxtaposition, the names of Calderon and Mac-Carthy.

"How richly gifted was this Spanish priest-poet! this pious playwright! this moral mechanist! this devout dramatist! How rare his experience! how broad the contrasts of his career, and of his observation. . . . . Happy poet! blessed with such fecundity! Happy Christian! blessed with such fidelity to the divine teachings of the Cross. . . .

"Very highly do we reverence Calderon, and very highly value his translator; yet, if it be not presumptuous to say so, we venture to suggest that Mac-Carthy might find nearer home another work still worthier of his genius than these translations. Now that he has got the imperial ear by bringing his costly wares from afar, are there not laurels to be gathered as well in Ireland as in Spain? The author of 'The Bell-Founder', of 'St. Brendan's Voyage', of 'The Foray of Con O'Donnell', and 'The Pillar Towers', needs no prompting to discern what abundant materials for a new department of English poetry are to be found almost unused on Irish ground. May we not hope that in that field or forest he may find his appointed work, adding to the glory of first worthily introducing Calderon to the English readers of this century, the still higher glory of doing for the neglected history of his fatherland what he has chivalrously done for the illustrious Spaniard".

Three Dramas of Calderon,

From the Spanish.

LOVE THE GREATEST ENCHANTMENT,

THE SORCERIES OF SIN, AND THE

DEVOTION OF THE CROSS.

BY DENIS FLORENCE MAC-CARTHY.

DUBLIN: W. B. KELLY, 8 GRAFTON STREET.
1870.

LOVE THE GREATEST ENCHANTMENT:

THE SORCERIES OF SIN:

THE DEVOTION OF THE CROSS.

FROM THE SPANISH OF CALDERON.

ATTEMPTED STRICTLY IN ENGLISH ASONANTE AND

OTHER IMITATIVE VERSE,

BY DENIS FLORENCE MAC-CARTHY, M.R.I.A.

WITH AN INTRODUCTION TO EACH DRAMA, AND NOTES BY THE TRANSLATOR, AND THE

SPANISH TEXT FROM THE EDITIONS OF HARTZENBUSCH,

KEIL, AND APONTES.

LONDON:

LONGMAN, GREEN, LONGMAN AND ROBERTS.

1861.

TO

GEORGE TICKNOR, ESQ.

THE HISTORIAN OF SPANISH LITERATURE,

This Volume

IS INSCRIBED IN GRATEFUL REMEMBRANCE OF INFORMATION

LIBERALLY COMMUNICATED,

AND PRAISE GENEROUSLY BESTOWED.

PREFACE.

N 1853 I publifhed two volumes of tranflations from the Spanifh of Calderon, which contained the firft (as it ftill continues to be the only) complete verfion of any of his plays that has ever been prefented to the Englifh reader.* This attempt met with as much fuccefs as I could have reafonably anticipated for it, confidering the circumftances under which the work grew up, as detailed in the preface, and the timidity with which I fhrunk from the whole metrical difficulties of my tafk—difficulties which then appeared to me to be fo infurmountable, that, had I the time, I fcarcely would have had the courage to try and overcome. A forced leifure, however, of many months, occurring at irregular intervals, but extending through the whole of the intervening period,

* The dramas contained in thofe volumes are the following :—*The Purgatory of Saint Patrick, The Conftant Prince, The Scarf and the Flower, The Phyfician of his own Honour, The Secret in Words*, and *Love after Death*.   The remark in the text is by no means meant to difparage Mr. Fitzgerald's *Six Plays of Calderon freely tranflated*, London, 1853, the nervous blank verfe of which, though I think unfuited to Calderon, I greatly admire; but furely a tranflator who confeffes that he has "funk, reduced, altered, and replaced" whatever did not feem to him particularly "fine" in his author, can fcarcely be taken as a fatisfactory interpreter of a poet whofe very defects and extravagances are as characteriftic of his genius as are his beauties.

having again induced me to refume my labours upon Calderon, I felt the very difficulties, which before I had left unattempted, an attraction and an incentive, as fupplying a more laborious occupation, and a more engroffing diftraction.   I felt, too, a fincere artiftic conviction that I was bound to do my beft for a poet whom I had been, to fome extent, inftrumental in introducing to a foreign audience, and a determination that he fhould not fuffer in their eftimation by any wilful omiffion or neglect on the part of him at whofe invitation he had appeared before them. Two things I fet before me at the beginning of my renewed tafk, which, I truft, I have pretty faithfully obferved to the end; namely, in the firft place, to give the meaning of my author exactly, and in its integrity, neither departing from it through diffufenefs, nor cramping it through condenfation; and, fecondly, to exprefs it ftrictly in the form of the original, or not to exprefs it at all.

It is by no means my intention to enter into the oft-debated queftion as to the principles which fhould guide or coerce the tranflator in his tafk.   As far as the tranflator is concerned, it is a much eafier thing to produce a popular and flowing verfion of any foreign poem or play, than a faithful and exact one; and the effect to be produced will fo depend upon the capacity and culture of the reader,—whether, in a word, he will have his German or Spanifh fo thoroughly " done into Englifh," as to have every particle of its original nature eliminated out of it, or will have it faithfully prefented to him, with all its native peculiarities preferved,—is fo much a matter of tafte, that no definite rule can ever be arrived at in the matter.   What Mr. Newman has faid upon this fubject fo entirely agrees with my own impreffions, that I print his obfervations here, the more readily, that I have been actuated independently by the fame convictions long before I was aware that they were fhared by him.   Mr. Newman, alluding to fome of his own critics, who had laid down, as axioms, certain principles which he confiders to be utterly falfe and ruinous to tranflation, thus proceeds :—" One of thefe is, that the reader ought, if poffible, to forget that it is a tranflation at all, and be lulled into the illufion that he is reading an original work. Of courfe, a neceffary inference from fuch a dogma is, that whatever has a foreign colour is undefirable, and is even a grave defect. The tranflator, it feems, muft carefully obliterate all that is characteriftic of the original, unlefs it happens to be identical in fpirit to fomething already familiar in Englifh. From fuch a notion I cannot too ftrongly exprefs my intenfe diffent. I aim at precifely the oppofite ;—to retain every peculiarity of the original, as far as I am able, *with the greater care, the more foreign it may happen to be,* whether it be matter of tafte, of intellect, or of morals."[*]

On this principle I have acted throughout the entire of this volume, with what fuccefs, however, of courfe remains to be feen.

The peculiar feature, then, of this Tranflation is its rigid adherence to the metres of the original, and particularly to that efpecial Spanifh one, the *afonante* vowel rhyme, of which but a few fcattered fpecimens exift in Englifh, and thefe rather as famples of what our language was incapable of producing to any confiderable extent, than of what it could achieve. This metre is fo very peculiar, and fo oppofed to anything that bears the femblance of rhyme in Englifh, that I have known feveral perfons, who were able to read in the original a romance, or a fcene from a Spanifh play, and who, notwithftanding, never perceived the delicate and moft elaborate form of verfification they had been enjoying, until their attention was drawn to it ; when once feen or heard, however, the difcovery is hailed with delight, and we look or liften for the ever-recurring fimilarity of cadence or conftruction, " the manifold wild chimes" of the Spanifh afonance, with pleafure and furprife. The numerous examples of it throughout this volume will fhow the reader

---

[*] *The Iliad of Homer, faithfully tranflated into unrhymed Englifh Metre,* by F. W. Newman. (London, 1856.) Preface, p. xv.

what it is more clearly, perhaps, than any explanation; and yet some
definition of it may not be inappropriate in this place. "The Spanish
asonante,"* says the late Lord Holland, "is a word which resembles
another in the *vowel* on which the last accent falls, as well as the vowel,
or vowels, that follow it; but every consonant after the accented vowel
must be different from that in the corresponding syllable. Thus: *tòs*
and *amòr*, *orìlla* and *delìra*, *àlamo* and *pàxaro*, are all *asonantes*." † This
definition, though, perhaps, a little too limited for the boundless variety
and freedom of the asonance, may be considered tolerably satisfactory.
The rhyme, such as it is, is not confined, as in all other languages, to a
few repetitions, of which those in the octave stanza are, perhaps, the
most frequent; but in Spanish, the *same* asonance, that is, the same
recurring similarity of vowel, or vowels, in the last accented syllable, or
syllables, of every second line is kept up unchanged, however long may
be the ballad or the scene in which it is commenced. In Spanish, from
the open sound of the vowels, and from the copiousness of the language,
this is easy. In fact, it is said that the difficulty lies not in producing
the *asonante* where it is required, but in avoiding it in the intermediate
lines, where it is superfluous. But in English the case is very different;
from the comparative weakness of the vowel sounds,‡ from the rare
possibility of combining them, and, what is still more, from their per-

---

* This, word is generally written *assonant* in English. For a thing so entirely
Spanish, perhaps the Spanish form is the more appropriate one, and I have therefore
followed Lord Holland and Mr. Ticknor in calling it by its original name.

† *Life of Lope de Vega*, vol. II. p. 215.

‡ Mr. Newman has a remark, in the Preface from which I have already quoted,
which seems to be applicable here, especially in reference to the general objection made
against the introduction of the asonance into northern languages, namely, its insuffici-
ency and incompleteness of *sound*. "An accentual metre," he says, "in a language
loaded with consonants, cannot have the *same sort* of sounding beauty, as a quantitative
metre in a highly vocalized language. It is not audible sameness of metre, but a likeness of *moral genius* which is to be arrived at." P. xvii.

petual variation in quantity, anything like producing the fame effect as
in the Spanish is impossible.   Yet this " ghost of a rhyme," as Dean
Trench calls it,* is better than none at all; and I have found, from my
own experience, that an inflexible determination to reproduce it, at
whatever trouble, even though with imperfect fuccefs, enables the tranflator more clofely to render the meaning of the original, and faves him
from the danger of being tempted into diffufenefs by the facilities of
expanfion which even the unrhymed trochaic, *without the afonante*, too
readily fupplies.   Tranflators who have felt the weight of too much
liberty might find within the reftricted limits of the *afonance* the fame
falutary reftraints which Wordfworth difcovered

> " Within the fonnet's fcanty plot of ground "—

it is to be hoped with fome flight portion of the fame fuccefs.
    With regard to the dramas and *auto* felected for tranflation in this

---

* In his charming little book on Calderon (*Life's a Dream, &c.* London, 1856),
Dean Trench has the merit of being the firft to attempt the tranflation of any portion
of Calderon into equivalent Englifh *afonantes:* his tranflations having been made, as
I infer from his preface, about eighteen years before they were publifhed.

I may fupply here an omiffion in the Preface to my *Dramas from Calderon*, when
noticing the contributions to a knowledge of the Spanifh Drama which our early
Englifh literature fupplies, an omiffion alfo noticeable in that part of Dean Trench's
Effay which goes over the fame ground.   I was not aware at the time that Preface
was written that Sir Richard Fanfhaw, the tranflator of Guarini and Camoëns, had
given, in 1649, a very pleafing verfion in fhort lyrical lines, almoft Spanifh in their fe-
licity and grace, of Antonio de Mendoza's long and fingular drama, *Querer por Solo
Querer* (" To Love for Love's Sake").   This is the drama which took Charles Lamb
three " well-wafted hours" to read, and, according to him, nine days to reprefent.
(See the *Extracts from the Garrick Plays* in his *Specimens of Englifh Dramatic Poets*,
Bohn's Ed. 1854, p. 476.)   " Five or fix mortal hours," however, are the limits which
Don Ramon de Mefoneros Romanos in the *Apuntes Biográficos* prefixed to his *Dramaticos Contemporaneos de Lope de Vega*, t. ii. p. 28, puts to the patience of the
audience in liftening to the fix thoufand four hundred verfes of whch the original drama
confifts.

volume, little requires to be faid in this place, as I have prefixed to each of them fuch introductory remarks as feemed neceffary for the proper underftanding of the time and circumftances of their production. They all may be confidered reprefentative pieces—pieces that convey a fair idea of the clafs of drama, whether *Fiefta, Comedia,* or *Auto,* to which they belong. The firft, *Love the Greateft Enchantment,* which is the ftory of Circe and Ulyffes, is a favourable fpecimen of the dramas which Calderon founded upon claffical or mythological fubjects. Of thefe he wrote altogether eighteen, and though they have been greatly admired, not alone in Germany, but in England, for the freedom with which the poet entered into poffeffion of thefe ancient fables, ufing them for his own purpofes with a frefhnefs of invention ever new and ever delightful, but one only out of the eighteen has ever been even analyfed in Englifh with anything like completenefs or precifion.*

The next piece, *The Sorceries of Sin,* is even ftill more interefting and more wonderful. It is an *auto,* and therefore, though dealing with the fame ftory as its foundation, is as different from the preceding play as fpirit is to matter, or the foul to the body. In fact, the long dramatic fpectacle in which the ancient Hellenic fable ftarts into new life, in an-other climate, and at a different era, beneath the power of a new creator, feems to be worthlefs in the poet's eyes, unlefs he can deduce from it its *moral,* namely, the power of Man to refift, or, at leaft, to triumph over temptation, if he will only liften to the voice of his own foul, and the filent whifperings of repentance and of grace. This he has done in *The Sorceries of Sin.* In the introductory remarks which I have pre-fixed to it the reader will find fome moft interefting and valuable biblio-graphical notes by Mr. Ticknor, relative to the firft publication of the

---

* The drama alluded to is *Los Tres Mayores Prodigios,* on which there is a good paper in *Frazer's Magazine* for Auguft 1849. *Eco y Narcifo* is referred to with great praife in the *Weftminfter Review* for January 1851, pp. 295-307.

autos, taken from communications which he has had the kindnefs to addrefs to me upon the fubject. Upon the general character of the *autos* I cannot do better than refer the reader to the third part of Dean Trench's effay, to which I have previoufly made allufion.

The celebrity of the third piece which this volume contains, *The Devotion of the Crofs*, and the mifconceptions which exift as to its real character, will be, I truft, fufficient excufe for my having tranflated it. As in the other cafes, I refer the reader to the introductory remarks prefixed to this tragedy, which Dean Trench characterizes as, " defpite of all its perverfity, a wonderful and terrible drama."*

The Spanifh text, which I have printed for the convenience of the reader, is founded, as far as the *comedias* are concerned, partly on the edition of Keil, and partly on that of Hartzenbufch. The *fcenes* are altogether taken from the latter edition. Where any important difference exifts between the text of the two editions, I have generally drawn attention to it in a foot-note. The *auto*, with the exception of a few flight corrections, is printed verbatim from the edition by Apontes (*Autos Sacramentales*, 6 vols. 4to. Madrid, 1759-60, vol. vi. p. 109).†

* For a fupplementary note to *The Devotion of the Crofs* fee next page.

† In addition to what has been faid in the note to p. xi. relative to Sir Richard Fanfhaw's tranflation of *Querer por Solo Querer*, it may be mentioned that he alfo tranf- lated another dramatic fpectacle from the Spanifh, called *Fieftas de Aranjuez.* See *The Companion to the Play-houfe*, London, 1764, v. ii., under letter F, where it is erro- neoufly attributed to Mendoza. This is doubtlefs the mafque written, by the unfortu- nate Count of Villa-Mediana, for the birth-day feftivities of Philip IV. in 1622. See Ticknor, v. ii. p. 172, n.; fee alfo Madame d'Aulnoy's *Relation du Voyage d'Efpagne*, t. ii. pp. 20, 21. (La Haye, 1715,) for a very curious account of the exhibition of this fpectacle, and for the author's premeditated act of daring gallantry towards the Queen, which, it is fuppofed, led to his immediate affaffination.

Summerfield, Dalkey,
   September, 1861.

SUPPLEMENTARY NOTE TO THE DEVOTION
OF THE CROSS.

IN the Introduction to *The Devotion of the Cross*, and at p. 284 of the Tranflation, I have ftated that *La Devocion de la Cruz* was firft printed at Huefca, in 1634, under the title of *La Cruz en la Sepultura*, and as the work of Lope de Vega. This miftake, in a volume forming a portion of a collection containing the dramas of various authors, is perhaps not to be wondered at; but it feems ftrange that the fame error fhould be repeated fix years later, in a volume of the collection devoted exclufively to the dramas of Lope himfelf, in the twenty-fourth part or volume of which (Madrid, 1640) *La Cruz en la Sepultura* is again given as the work of Lope de Vega.* In a note to the exceedingly valuable catalogue of all the Comedias and Autos of Lope de Vega, compiled with fuch care and labour by the diftinguifhed Spanifh fcholar Mr. J. R. Chorley, of London, and prefented by him with fo much liberality to Señor Hartzenbufch for his fourth volume of Lope's *Comedias Efcogidas* (Madrid, 1853-60), it is ftated that this twenty-fourth part is the only one out of the twenty-five to which the collection of Lope's comedias extended (1604-47), which is wanting to complete the copy in the Spanifh Library of Lord Taunton, at Stoke Park, near London. It is preferved, however, with the others in the National Library of Madrid. Mr. Chorley alfo mentions that according to Mr. Ticknor (under date October 1857), the edition of Huefca, 1634, is to be found in the Library of the Arfenal at Paris, and in the Library of the Vatican at Rome. A volume of the collection of feparately-printed Spanifh plays, brought from Spain by Lord Arlington in the reign of Charles the Second, and now preferved in the Library of the Britifh Mufeum, contains, according to Mr. Chorley, two of Calderon's dramas (one of them being *La Cruz en la Sepultura*), which are both attributed to Lope de Vega.†

---

* See Schack's *Gefchichte der Dramatifchen Literatur und Kunft in Spanien*, b. ii. p. 696, Lord Holland's *Life of Lope de Vega*, vol. ii. p. 151, and Mr. Chorley's *Catalogo de Comedias y Autos de Frey Lope Felix de Vega Carpio*, referred to above.

† *Catalogo de Comedias, &c.* p. 542. I may add that the fecond, *Amor, Honor, y Poder* is alfo given under another name in the twenty-fourth of Lope's Comedias above mentioned. The volume publifhed at Huefca in 1634 contains, in addition to thefe, a third of Calderon's dramas, erroneoufly attributed to Lope, namely *Un Cafligo en Tres Venganzas*. See Hartzenbufch's *Catalogo Cronologico, Comedias de Calderon*, t. iv. p. 669.

LOVE THE GREATEST ENCHANTMENT.

FROM THE SPANISH OF CALDERON.

INTRODUCTION.

THE Homeric Circe, previous to her becoming the heroine of this drama of Calderon, had figured under various names, and with various adventures, in the romances and romantic poetry of Europe, and we recognize her as the fame perfon, whether called Morgana, as in Launcelot du Lac, and in Boiardo, Alcina, as in Ariofto, or Armida, as in Taffo. To thefe may be added the Dueffa of Spenfer, in 1590, and in 1634 (the year preceding the firft performance of Calderon's drama) a male reproduction of the character in the " Comus" of Milton. Under her original name, Lope de Vega had devoted upwards of three thoufand lines to her adventures in his " Circe," a poem in octave ftanzas, which he publifhed in 1624. The ground-work of Calderon's Circe is to be found in Homer, *Odyffey*, B. x. from line 135 to 574, and B. xii. from line 8 to 141. But he was under great obligations both to Ariofto and to Taffo, the former of whom, in the Sixth Canto of the Orlando, and the latter, to a ftill greater degree, in the Sixteenth Canto of the " Gerufalemme," fupply him with many of his moft interefting incidents. Indeed the thirty-feventh ftanza of the Sixteenth Canto of the latter poem may be taken as the key-note of his entire compofition, and as fuch I introduce it here in the quaint verfion of Fairfax, although the concluding couplet of the original—

> Lafcia gl' incanti, e vuol provar fe vaga
> E fupplice beltà fia miglior maga—

more clearly expreffes the meaning of Calderon :—

> All what the witches of Theffalia land
> With lips unpure yet ever faid or fpake,
> Words that could make heaven's rolling circles ftand,
> And draw the damned ghofts from Limbo lake,
> All well fhe knew, but yet no time fhe fand
> To ufe her knowledge or her charms to make,
> But left her arts, and forth fhe ran to prove
> If fingle beauty were beft charm for love.

The experiment of recalling Ulyffes to his martial taftes and duties, by placing before him the long-unufed armour of Achilles, is probably fuggefted by the fimilar ftratagem which gave Rinaldo courage to break from the enchantments of Armida; but both, no doubt, founded upon one of the later traditions of Achilles himfelf, who, when concealed in the court of Lycomedes of Scyros, under the difguife of a maiden, was difcovered by Odyffeus through a fomewhat fimilar ftratagem. The conduct of Armida herfelf upon her defertion alfo prefents refemblances to the cataftrophe in *El Mayor Encanto Amor*, detracting nothing, however, from the merits of Calderon's work, in which every incident of the ancient claffical myth is recaft, reborn, as it were, in the creative mind of the poet with a frefhnefs (fays Schack, from whom I have derived fome of the foregoing references) which, while preferving all the charms of the old Hellenic Legend, impreffes upon it the diftinctive and not lefs delightful character of modern romance.*

The following curious paper I have tranflated from a document firft publifhed by Don Cafiano Pellicer, in the fecond volume of his *Tratado Hiftorico fobre el Origen y Progrefos de la Comedia en Efpaña*, and introduced

---

* *Gefchichte der dramatifchen Literatur und Kunft in Spanien*, B. III. p. 190.

as a preface to this play by Hartzenbufch in his edition of Calderon.*
It is interefting as well for fhowing the labour which the great poet took
in working upon the plan of the machinift, and in what refpects he
departed from it, as for the very remarkable proof which it gives of the
mechanical refources of the theatre in the reign of Philip the Fourth,
and the unequalled magnificence with which this and fimilar royal
pageants were produced at the court of Madrid. The Mafques of Ben
Jonfon,† which were about the fame period the delight of "our James,"
are the only productions which can be compared with thefe dramatic
fpectacles of fplendour and ingenuity; and while, in their united labours
as dramatift and machinift, the palm for poetical excellence muft be given
to Calderon, it will be perceived that, in productions of this kind, the
great Englifh architect had no mean rival in the lefs widely known, but
ftill famous Italian artift, who had the honour of being Calderon's fellow-
labourer in thefe magnificent fhows.

"CIRCE,

"*A Dramatic Spectacle which was reprefented on the great pond of the
Retiro,‡ the invention of Cofme·Lotti, at the requeft of her moft excellent
Ladyfhip, the Countefs of Olivarez, Duchefs of San Lucar la Mayor, on
the night of St. John [June 24, A.D. 1635].*

"There will be formed in the middle of the pond a ftationary ifland,
raifed feven feet above the furface of the water, with a winding afcent,
terminating at the entrance into the ifland, which will be furrounded by
a parapet of loofe ftones, adorned with corals and other curiofities of the

---

* *Biblioteca de Autores Efpañoles*, T. VII. p. 385. Madrid, 1848. *Tratado Hiftorico fobre el Origen y Progrefos de la Comedia y del Hiftrionifmo en Efpaña*, por D.
Cafiano Pellicer. *Parte Segunda*, p. 146. Madrid, 1804.

† *Chloridia*, which he produced in conjunction with Inigo Jones in 1630, coft
3000*l.* for decorations.

‡ The celebrated palace of the *Buen Retiro*.

fea, fuch as pearls and fhells of different colours, with waterfalls and fimilar decorations. In the midft of this ifland will be fituated a very lofty mountain of rugged afcent, with precipices, and caverns, furrounded by a thick and darkfome wood of tall trees, fome of which will be feen to exhibit the appearance of the human form covered with a rough bark, from the heads and arms of which will iffue green boughs and branches, having fufpended from them various trophies of war and of the chafe, the theatre during this opening fcene being fcantily lit with concealed lights : and, to make a beginning of the feftival, a murmuring and a rippling noife of water having been heard, a great and magnificent car will be feen to advance along the pond, plated over with filver, and drawn by two monftrous fifhes, from whofe mouths will continually iffue great jets of water, the light of the theatre increafing according as they advance ; and on the fummit of it will be feen feated in great pomp and majefty the goddefs Aqua, from whofe head and curious vefture will iffue an infinite abundance of little conduits of water ; and at the fame time will be feen another great fupply flowing from an urn which the goddefs will hold reverfed ; and which, filled with a variety of fifhes, that, leaping and playing in the torrent as it defcends, and gliding over all the car, will fall at length into the pond. This admirable machine is to be accompanied by a choir of twenty nymphs of rivulets and fountains, who will advance, finging and playing, along the furface of the water : and, when this beautiful piece of mechanifm ftops in the prefence of His Majefty, the goddefs Aqua will commence the fcene by reprefenting the Loa.* This being finifhed, the found of various inftruments will be heard, and the proceffion will retire from the theatre in the fame order, and with

---

* The *Loa* here mentioned is probably that which precedes the *Auto, Los Encantos de la Culpa* (*The Sorceries of Sin*), which is alfo founded on the ftory of Ulyffes and Circe, and a tranflation of which forms the fecond portion of this volume. This *Loa* has no connection with the incidents of either drama or auto, being merely a glorification of Madrid. In it, however, the goddefs Aqua makes her appearance, which fhe does not do in either *Love the Greateft Enchantment*, or in *The Sorceries of Sin*, her

the same musical accompaniment as it entered.   Scarcely has it disappeared, when a stirring sound of clarions and trumpets will burst forth, with discharges of musketry and cannon, and the cry of *Land! Land!* will be heard from within: and a great and beauteous gilded bark will be discovered, adorned with streamers, pendants, banneroles, and flags, which, with swelling sails, will come to harbour, furling her sails, and dropping her anchors and cables; and on her deck will be seen Ulysses and his companions, who, returning thanks to the gods for having reached land, will speak of their past misfortunes and their present necessities, none of them having the daring to disembark even to seek refreshment, fearing the dangers that might ensue; on which account, lots being drawn, eighteen of them will be compelled to enter the long-boat, and to make the attempt: and they having tremblingly leaped on the island, a great number of various animals, such as lions, tigers, dragons, bears, and others, will place themselves before them, who, astonished and full of terror, will form themselves into a body for their defence; but the animals, with human intelligence, will approach them caressingly, at which moment will be heard a sad, but melodious strain of music, proceeding from the trees and plants, which with human forms have been there metamorphosed, at which musical wail, the animals, in their various ways, will perform an extraordinary dance, and while this is kept up and continued, a terrible earthquake, with agitation of the air, will be felt, which, awakening flashes and peals of thunder, will dart forth a forked bolt, that, striking the top and summit of the mountain, will so loose and shatter it, that it will fall to pieces in various parts of the theatre, at which event the animals will disappear, and the music will cease, and the mariners will remain full of terror and amazement,

---

place in the car being filled, in the former, by the nymph Galatea, and in the latter by the personification of Penance.   The car itself seems to have been used in other of these gorgeous spectacle-plays of Calderon.   In his *Phaeton*, for instance, which was also acted on the pond of the Retiro a few years later, there are two references to its having been seen by the audience on several previous occasions.—TRANSLATOR.

feeing, in the place where the mountain ftood, a fplendid palace appear, inlaid with precious ftones of various colours, of a rich and well-defigned architecture, with columns of agate and cryftal, having bafes, capitals, and cornices of gold, and ftatues of bronze and of marble, all arranged in their proper places. And the frightful and horrible wood will at the fame·time be transformed into a fair and delicious garden, enclofing a lofty edifice of fpherical form, with corridors and porticos; and in the midft of each delightful compartment will be feen fountains of running water, covered alleys, and numbers of domeftic animals paffing to and fro; and, at the appearance of this new wonder, the theatre will be illuminated by a brilliancy fo great, that it will feem as if the fun miniftered its light, which will proceed from and be the refult of the reflection which the jewels of this rich and fumptuous palace will make, and from two fplendid ftars which, with fingular and remarkable brilliancy, will iffue from the waves and waters of the pond; and, in front of the porticos and corridors in the centre of the crefcent, Circe will be feen feated on a majeftic throne, dreffed magnificently in flower-embroidered robes of filk, attended by many ladies and damfels, fome of whom will go about gathering herbs and flowers, which they will place in golden bafkets, and others will collect in cryftal vafes waters of various kinds, for the ufe and convenience of the forcerefs and her enchantments; and Circe, with a grave and compofed countenance, holding a golden wand in one hand, and in the other a book, from which fhe reads, (the timid companions of Ulyffes being prefent, and beholding with wonder what has happened,) fhe will direct one of her ladies to encourage and to lead them to her prefence, when, with an agreeable and deceitful countenance, fhe will afk them who they are, and for what object they have approached that ifland. To which they will give anfwer, referring to the events of the fiege of Troy, and the fubfequent misfortunes that had befallen them fince its fall; and they will implore pity and fuccour for themfelves and their difmantled and ill-provided veffel: and fhe, feigning compaffion for their mifery and misfortune, will promife them affiftance, and, defcending from her throne, on which, up to this time, fhe has been feated, fhe will ftrike the earth with her golden wand, and at the inftant a fplendidly-furnifhed table will arife, at which banquet a potion in a golden cup will be adminiftered to them which will transform them into fwine, with the exception of one, who, flying a fimilar metamorphofis, and the treacherous hofpitality of the forcerefs, will re-enter the boat, ftill lying by the fhore, and will relate this new adventure to Ulyffes: and fhe, enraged at the flight of their companion, will beat the feeming fwine with her wand, ordering them away to the fty, at which much amufement will arife from their grunting; and fhe will make one of them, who appears of a humorous turn, to ftand upright, and fpeak naturally as a man: and this one, ferving as the *graciofo*, will make entertaining jefts and comic buffooneries with the ladies, endeavouring to fit in their laps, and imitating the playfulnefs of a lap-dog: and, taking a fancy for one of them, he will fall in love with her, whom Circe will transform into a monkey, through anger and jealoufy that the appearance of any lady fhould appear to the fwine more beautiful and attractive than her own: from which will refult a pleafant and entertaining allegory, for the lady feeing herfelf transformed into a monkey, and great difcord on this account enfuing between her and the fwine, will under this metaphor point out the punifhment which follows the vices and fenfuality of men; and on the other hand a like allegory, under the metaphor and transfor- mation of the lady into a monkey, the degradations which follow thofe of women. In the meanwhile, the cavalier who fled the dangers and deceits of Circe, having come to the prefence of Ulyffes, and having related the mournful fate of his companions, will move him to fuch pity, that he will inftantly go to their relief; and, making the land in his boat, he will hear a voice, without knowing from whom it proceedeth, and feeking the fource of this voice, it will be found to proceed from one of thofe cavaliers who, clothed in rugged bark, have been transformed into trees, who will exhort him not to proceed farther, nor expofe himfelf to the certain danger that threatens him, but that he fhould fly the enchantments of that ifland, originating in the deceptions of Circe, and in her magic and impure loves : at which Ulyffes, wondering, will afk him who he is, and what was the occafion of fo cruel an enchantment. To whom he with deep forrow will anfwer that he was one of the companions of King Picus, and will relate the tragic and mournful fate which had overtaken them and their king, all being, as their final misfortune, either transformed into trees, or condemned to wander, in the fhape of various animals, through the woods. At which Ulyffes, compaffionate and confufed, will refolve to undertake their reftoration as a part of the conqueft he was about undertaking; and fcarcely will he have proceeded to put it into execution, when Mercury will be feen coming through the air, dazzling with various colours and reflexions, who, as ambaffador from Jupiter, will prefent him with a flower, by means of which he will be able to come triumphant out of the adventure which he had vowed, and from the fnares and enchantments of Circe : to whom Ulyffes will fcarcely have given thanks, when from his prefence, cleaving the air, he will return to heaven : and Ulyffes, recovering his breath, and thus fecure of fuccefs, will with frefh courage come in fight of the beautiful palace, in which will be feen new wonders, fince at the difappearance of the throne on which Circe had been feated, under an arch in the middle of the porticos and corridors, will be difcovered a moft beautiful open portal, through which will be feen long and deep perfpeXives, exciting great admiration; and while Ulyffes ftands in fufpenfe during the carrying out of this prodigy, that follower of his who, changed into a fwine, aXts the part of the *graciofo*, will come before him, and recognizing him, will ftrive to embrace him, and with his filthy fnout attempt to kifs him, calling to his companions, who, grunting in a comic way, will furround him, making altogether a grotefque tableau; and he, compaffionating their mifery, will carefs them, afking the talking fwine to introduce him to the enchantrefs Circe; and they then, fearing greater evil, perceiving her prefence, will fly away, leaving Ulyffes alone with her, whom, in an affable manner, the enchantrefs will receive, inviting him to drink, and offering him the fame cup which had been prefented to his companions. Ulyffes will excufe himfelf, threatening her, in order that fhe fhould give them their liberty; and fhe, refufing, will fo provoke the anger and fury of Ulyffes, that he will put his hand to his fword; but, feeing that his threats are of no avail, and his fword equally ineffectual, he will change his anger and fury into flatteries and careffes; and, pretending to be enamoured, will offer to dwell with her, and to comply with all her wifhes and defires, provided that fhe will reftore his companions to their original fhape, which Circe offers to do, and, enamoured of him, embraces him; and, conducting him to his companions, fhe will make them wafh in a beautiful fountain, the waters of which will reftore them to their original fhape of men, all except the *graciofo*, who, for their greater pleafure and entertainment, will remain transformed, gaining nothing from his ablutions but a ftill longer fnout, and the fudden acquifition of a pair of afs's ears; at which, haraffed and enraged, he will indulge in various comic and amufing expreffions, and will implore Circe to reftore him, and of Ulyffes he will afk it, and of his companions in like manner: which fhe will promife to do when he has done penance in that fhape for having been attracted more by the beauty of the lady transformed into a monkey, than by hers. And, matters being thus arranged, there will appear in the pond fix barks or floops, commanded and fteered by fix cupids, in which Circe will caufe the companions of Ulyffes to enter, affigning to each one the lady to whom he is to pay court, and to the graciofo-fwine the lady that was transformed into a monkey: and fhe herfelf will enter with Ulyffes into hers; and, finging to the found of various inftruments, they will go through the pond, fifhing with rods for frefh fifh, which, wherever the tackle is thrown into the water, will nibble at the fly, and, being caught by the hook, will be raifed up, plunging and bounding; but the fwine-transformed graciofo, in place of catching frefh fifh, will only draw up thofe that are falted and dried, fuch as dog-fifh and hake; and after this comic diverfion the little fleet will form a crefcent, the bark of Circe and Ulyſſes being in the centre, ſhe will command the ſea, in order to give pleaſure to her new lover, to bring forth and exhibit on its waves the diverſity of fiſhes and marine monſters which it contains in its womb : at which precept and command the pond will be ſeen filled with a variety of fiſhes, great and ſmall, which, playing with each other, will force up through their mouths and noſtrils frequent jets of odoriferous water, which, ſcattered in fragrant ſhowers upon the ſpectators, will diffuſe a ſweet and agreeable odour around.   And at this time will come and appear ſuddenly upon the pond VIRTUE, diſguiſed under the form and figure of a female magician, ſeated upon a great ſea-tortoiſe, and ſeeming to Circe (in conſequence of her aſſumed diſguiſe of a magician) a great friend of hers, ſhe will be rejoiced to ſee her, and will compliment her on her arrival, at which they will all diſembark upon a flowery lawn in front of the palace, where they will ſit down ; and then, converſing on various matters, and being much pleaſed at the viſit of her friend, Circe, to entertain her, will introduce a groteſque aſſemblage of ſirens and tritons, who, on the water of the pond, will perform a wonderful ſort of dance, the like of which has never been ſeen or heard of : at the end of which, they having diſappeared, and Circe, Virtue, and Ulyſſes having reſumed their converſation and diſcourſe, Circe will aſk Virtue the reaſon that has moved her to leave her ſtudies and magical purſuits to come and viſit her : and ſhe will anſwer, that the object of her coming is her love for Ulyſſes, whom, from the moment of his birth, ſhe had deſtined for herſelf, having experienced from him ſuch tender reſpect and attention, which have obliged her to ſeek him, and to come for him, in order to withdraw him from her hands, becauſe her great love allowed her no reſt, nor confidence in her ancient friendſhip with Circe.   And the companions of Ulyſſes, hearing this explanation, wondering and confuſed at what had happened, will be aſtoniſhed, and not knowing Virtue under the diſguiſe of a magician, will believe her to be mad ; but Circe, laughing, and treating what her friend had ſaid to her as a jeſt, will treat her with raillery, notwithſtanding which she, through jealousy, and to reassure herself, will make Ulysses and his companions perform a mimic tournament on foot, the tilting enclosure suddenly appearing for the occasion : scarcely has this begun, when Virtue, praising the shape, the graceful deportment, the activity and courage of Ulysses, will cause great jealousy to Circe, who will suspend the tournament, causing the lists to disappear, and commanding Virtue on the instant to depart the island ; but she will not do so, unless she can take Ulysses with her ; at which Circe, angry and enraged, will make great incantations, shapes, spectres, and enchantments to overcome her and to drive her thence, which will produce in the air and on the island great prodigies and wonderful appearances, which will do no injury to Virtue, who will conquer them all ; and Circe, finding that she is powerless to subdue her, will go away in wrath, leaving Virtue alone with Ulysses, who will reveal herself to him, rebuking him for his way of life, and censuring him for his effeminacy, asking him if it was he that she had conducted out of Greece, and had made victorious over the Trojans, and recalling the other glorious achievements of Ulysses. He, grateful, and with his memory restored, will repent, and will promise to follow her, abandoning his vices, which, till then, had held him in forgetfulness, at which she will lead him to the fountain, where, beholding himself as in a mirror, he will see himself so different from what he was in the days of his valour, that, with a fixed determination, he will resolve to leave Circe. At which there will appear in the theatre a very old and deformed giant, wearing a venerable beard, dressed in the habit of a hermit, and with a staff in his hand, whose presence will compel Ulysses to inquire of Virtue who he is, and what was his business with him ; to whom she will give answer: " This is he whom thou art to follow, and whom thou oughtest to congratulate in order to rise from the abyss of vices into which thou hast fallen." With that Ulysses will turn to the giant, and ask him to give him his protection, and to tell him who he is : and the other will assure him of it, saying that he is called the Buen Retiro, (the Happy Retreat,*) and telling Ulysses that what is necessary to obtain for him a place in the temple of eternity, and to make his name famous, illustrating it with glorious actions, is to follow him, the Happy Retreat, because unless he followed that, he would not be able to renounce vice and love virtue, which could only be done by retiring from all that could divert him from her.   With that Ulysses, determining to follow the Happy Retreat, will embrace Virtue, and being embraced by her, Circe will return in despair, and, seeing Ulysses embraced by Virtue, will ask him if these were the attentions, the fond vows, the promises and flatteries, on account of which she relied upon his steadfastness and fidelity : and she will ask him not to leave her, availing herself for that purpose of great threats, mingled with caresses, at which, mocking her, Virtue will say, that not only is she powerless to subjugate Ulysses, but that, for his greater triumph, he will take with him all whom that enchanted isle contains, and, for the carrying out of this, it will be so arranged, that the trees will then burst asunder, and from their trunks and cavities all will issue forth who have been there confined.''

Love the Greatest Enchantment was first printed, in the year 1641, in the second volume of the poet's dramas, published by his brother.   It is thus described :—

"*El Mayor Encanto Amor,* a *fiesta* which was represented before his Majesty on the night of St. John, in the year 1635, on the pond of the royal palace of the Buen Retiro." (*Segunda parte de Comedias de Calderon.*   Collected by Don José Calderon, his brother.   Madrid, 1641.)

Previous to its representation, however, in 1635, a still earlier play on the same subject had been produced, to which the date of 1634 has been assigned, from an allusion to it in the first act of *Love the Greatest Enchantment,* to which I have more particularly referred where the passage

---

* "*El Buen Retiro,*" a pun, doubtless, on the name of the palace in the gardens of which this spectacle was to be exhibited.   In the phraseology of the " Pilgrim's Progress," perhaps it might be translated " Giant Good-path."—TRANSLATOR.

occurs. This drama was called *Polyphemus and Circe*, and was the united work of Mira de Mefcua, Perez de Montalvan, and Calderon. It is fuppofed to have been printed at Madrid in 1652, in the *fecond part* of the collection of *Comedias de varios Autores*,* as would appear from the MS. index, by Don Juan Ifidro Fajardo, of all the plays printed in Spain to the year 1716, which is preferved in the National Library of Madrid. Of this *fecond part*, however, there feems to have been two diftinct impreffions, the one above mentioned, in 1652, and another in 1653. Of thefe impreffions, no copy of the edition of 1652 is known to exift, and that of 1653 does not contain the drama of *Polyphemus and Circe*. A copy, however, has been made up by Señor Hartzenbufch from two manufcripts kindly placed at his difpofal by Señor Duran, (the editor of the moft complete *Romancero* that has yet been given to the world,) and publifhed by him in the fourth volume of his edition of Calderon.† In addition to the curious paper juft given, it may be interefting to give an analyfis of this hitherto unknown drama, as a further evidence of the care and deliberation with which Calderon

---

* It is fingular, as Mr. Ticknor remarks, that of this collection of the old dramas of Spain, which at leaft extended to forty-three volumes, (from the lift of Fajardo, above mentioned, it would appear there were forty-feven,) fo little fhould now be known. Of thefe volumes, at the date of the publication of his " Hiftory of Spanifh Literature" (1849), Mr. Ticknor himfelf poffeffed three, namely, the twenty-fifth (Sara-goffa, 1633), the thirty-firft (Barcelona, 1638), and the forty-third (Saragoffa, 1650). He mentions two others, which he had not feen, namely, the twenty-ninth (Valencia, 1636), and the thirty-fecond (Saragoffa, 1640). In addition to the twenty-fifth (a copy of which, as has been already mentioned, is in the poffeffion of Mr. Ticknor), Señor Hartzenbufch mentions four others, the twenty-eighth (Huefca, 1634), the thirtieth (Saragoffa, 1636), the thirty-third (Valencia, 1642), and the part above defcribed as wanting the *Polifemo y Circe*. It is from the thirtieth volume of this collection he has taken the firft fketch of Calderon's *Armas de la Hermofura*, namely, *El Privilegio de las Mujeres*, which he wrote in conjunction with Montalvan and Antonio Coello. It is given in vol. iv. p. 397, of his edition. Madrid, 1848-50. TR.

† *Comedias de Calderon.* Por Don Juan Eugenio Hartzenbufch, vol. iv. p. 413.

elaborated thofe dramas, the fubjects of which feem to have been favourites with himfelf.

POLYPHEMUS AND CIRCE.

Written by Doctor Mira de Mefcua, Doctor Juan Perez de Montalvan, and Don Pedro Calderon de la Barca.

The firft act is by Mira de Mefcua. The opening fcene, in the pofition of the fhip, &c. refembles the correfponding one in *Love the Greateft Enchantment*. It is a faint outline of the complete picture painted by Calderon.

In the tenth fcene Polyphemus quotes Gongora, and feems well read in Spanifh poetry.*

> " Un poeta me dijo que en la luna,
> Defde la cumbre defte monte, puedo
> Efcribir mis defdichas con el dedo."—Pp. 416-17.

The lines of Gongora referred to are—

> " Y en los cielos defde efta roca puedo
> Efcribir mis defdichas con el dedo ?"
>
> *Fabula de Polifemo y Galatea*, Stanza 49.†

The firft act ends with a ftruggle between *Love* and *War* for the poffeffion of Ulyffes, as in Calderon's play. The fong in favour of the former is fung by the firens, the call to the latter is given by one of the Greeks called Turfelino. The refrain is the fame in both plays : Ulyffes yields to Love, and is overcome with fleep, as in *Love the Greateft Enchantment*. The experiment which Circe makes ufe of as a teft of his

---

* In Montalvan's fpecial Auto on the fame fubject, Polyphemus plays on a guitar. This Auto of *Polifemo*, which Montalvan fubfequently publifhed in his *Para Todos*, is fuppofed to have been written as early as 1619.

† *Poetas Liricas de Siglos* 16 *y* 17, in Biblioteca de Autores Efpañoles, vol. xxxii. p. 462.

affection, is to affume the appearance of a ftatue while he fleeps. Ulyffes awakes, and, feeing his miftrefs turned to marble, bewails his lofs, and declares that there is nothing now in the palace of Circe that can detain him. He rufhes towards the fea, determined to embark; Circe follows, declaring fhe is ftill alive, and rejoiced in her heart at the fuccefs of her experiment.

The fecond act is by Montalvan.

In this act Montalvan introduces fome harmonious verfes, in octave ftanzas, taken from his earlier *Auto* of *Polifemo*, which, as I have faid, was probably written before 1619, but not publifhed till 1632; or, as Señor Hartzenbufch fays, 1633, in the edition of his *Para Todos*, which appeared at Huefca in that year. Thefe verfes are followed by a very fpirited fcene between Polyphemus and Galatea. The dialogue is kept up with great livelinefs, each party fcarcely ufing more than one line—a rhetorical forbearance very unufual in Spanifh plays.

The third act is by Calderon. Ulyffes relates that in confequence of his having preferred Irene, one of Circe's ladies, to the enchantrefs herfelf, for no other reafon, he would have us believe, but her refemblance to the abfent Penelope, the jealous and indignant Circe had taken a very fummary way to put an end to that flirtation, by caufing palace, ladies and all, to difappear. Indeed, at the end of the fecond act, the grated window at which Ulyffes and Irene had been converfing at the moment of this cataftrophe, and of which the thoughtful lady advifed her lover to lay hold, is reprefented as flying away, with the hero himfelf hanging on. The ftory of Polyphemus then proceeds in the ufual way. In this play, the difenthralment of Ulyffes is effected by an appeal from Acis (the cataftrophe connected with whom and Galatea takes place in the fecond act), who comes forth bleeding from the rock which Polyphemus had flung upon him, and at whofe fountain Ulyffes was about to drink. At the departure of the hero from the ifland, Circe makes the fame appeal that is given in *Love the Greateft En-chantment*, occafionally in the fame words. At the end the indulgence

of the audience is aſked for the three poets who had joined in its com-
poſition.

It only remains to add that the reſemblance, which every one will
perceive exiſts between the opening ſcene of *Love the Greateſt Enchantment* and *The Tempeſt,* in the poſition of the ſhip, the nautical phraſe-
ology uſed by the ſeamen, and the jokes of the *graciofos* and clowns,
ſeems to be purely accidental.   If Calderon were acquainted with the
works of his great Engliſh predeceſſor, and he might eaſily have been ſo,
as he was but twenty-three years of age when the firſt folio was publiſhed; and from the intercourſe then exiſting between Spain and England,
it would not be at all ſurpriſing that the volume had found its way to
the Peninſula; he would ſcarcely have confined his imitations to this
one paſſage, and perhaps another in his *Saber del mal y del bien* (To
know good and evil), where the idea conveyed in Shakeſpeare's famous
lines—

> " All the world's a ſtage,
> And all the men and women merely players,"

is expreſſed by Calderon with almoſt equal power in the well-known
reflection commencing,—

> *" En el teatro del mundo*
> *Todos ſon repreſentantes."*

PERSONS REPRESENTED.

ULÍSES.	ULYSSES.
ANTÍSTES.	ANTISTES.
ARQUELAO.	ARCHELAUS.
POLIDORO.	POLYDORUS.
TIMÁNTES.	TIMANTES. } _Companions of Ulysses._
FLORO.	FLORUS.
LEBREL.	LEBREL.
CLARIN.	CLARIN.
LÍSIDAS.	LYSIDAS, _Prince of Tuscany._
ARSIDAS.	ARSIDAS, _Prince of Sicily._
BRUTAMONTE, _gigante._	BRUTAMONTE, _a giant._
AQUÍLES.	SHADE OF ACHILLES.
CIRCE.	CIRCE.
CASANDRA.	CASSANDRA.
CLORI.	CHLORIS.
TISBE.	THISBE. } _Her ladies._
SIRENE.	SIRENE.
FLÉRIDA.	FLERIDA.
ASTREA.	ASTREA. } _Her attendants._
LIBIA.	LIBIA.
La Ninfa IRIS.	IRIS. } _Nymphs._
GALATEA.	GALATEA.
Griegos, Soldados de Arsidas, Tritones, Sirenas.	_Greek and Sicilian Soldiers, Tritons, Sirens._

SCENE, _Sicily._

LOVE THE GREATEST ENCHANTMENT.

<table>
<tr><td>

JORNADA I.

</td><td>

ACT THE FIRST.

</td></tr>
<tr><td>

*Suena un clarin, y defcúbrefe un navío,
y en él* Ulíses, Antístes, Arquelao,
Lebrel, Polidoro, Timántes, Floro,
Clarin *y otros Griegos.*

</td><td>

The Sea and Coast of Sicily.

*A fhip is difcovered ftruggling with the
waves: in it are* Ulysses, Antistes,
Archelaus, Polydorus, Timantes,
Florus, Lebrel, Clarin, *and others.*

</td></tr>
</table>

<table>
<tr><td>

Antíftes.

N vano forcejamos,
 Cuando rendidos á la fuerte
  eftamos,
 Contra los elementos.
   Arquelao.
Homicidas los mares y los vientos,
Hoy ferán nueftra ruina.

   Timántes.
Iza el trinquete.
   Polidoro.
  Larga la bolina.
   Floro.
Grande tormenta el huracan promete.
   Antíftes.
¡ Hola, iza !

</td><td>

Antíftes.

E ftrive in vain,
 Fate frowns averfe, and drives
  us o'er the main
 Before the elements : —
   Archelaus.
Death wings the wind, and the wild
 waves immenfe
Will be our graves to day.
   Timantes.
Brace up the forefail.
   Polydorus.
  Give the bow-line way.
   Florus.
The rifing wind a hurricane doth blow.
   Antíftes.
Hoift !

</td></tr>
</table>

Lebrel.
A la efcota!
Clarin.
          Al chafaldete!
Ulifes.
Júpiter foberano,
Que efte golfo en efpumas dejas cano,
Yo voto á tu deidad aras y altares,
Si la cólera templas deftos mares.

Antiftes.
¿Sagrado Dios Neptuno,
Griegos ofendes á pefar de Juno?

Arquelao.
Caufando eftá defmayos
El cielo con relámpagos y rayos.

Clarin.
¡Piedad, Baco divino!
No muera en agua el que ha vivido en
     vino.
Lebrel.
¡Piedad, Momo fagrado!
No el que carne vivió, muera pefcado.

Timántes.
Monumentos de hielos
Hoy ferán eftas ondas.

Todos.
          Piedad, cielos!
Polidoro.
Parece que han oido
Nueftro lamento y mífero gemido,

Lebrel.
To the mainfheet! —
Clarin.
          Let the clew-lines go! —
Ulyffes.
O Sovereign Jove!
Thou who this gulf in mountainous
     foam doft move,
Altars and facrifice to thee I vow,
If thou wilt tame thefe angry waters now.
Antiftes.
God of the Sea, great Neptune! in def-
     pite
Of Juno's care, why thus the Greeks
     affright?
Archelaus.
And fee, the kindling Heavens are all
     ablaze,
With angry bolts and lightning-wingèd
     rays.
Clarin.
Son of Silenus, truly called *divine!*
Save from a watery death thefe lips
     that lived on wine!
Lebrel.
Let not, O Momus! 'tis his lateft wifh,
A man who lived as flefh now die as
     fifh! —
Timantes.
This day, thefe waves that round about
     us rife
Will be our icy tombs: —
All.
          Have pity, O ye fkies! —
Polydorus.
It feems that they have liften'd to our
     prayer—
Our wild lament that pierced the dark-
     fome air—

Pues calmaron los vientos.

Arquelao.
Paces publican ya los elementos.
Antiftes.
Y para mas fortuna,
(Que la buena y la mala nunca es una)
Ya en aquefte horizonte
Tierra enfeña la cima de aquel monte
Corona de efa fierra.

Timántes.
Celages fe defcubren.
Todos.
Tierra, tierra !
Ulifes.
Pon en aquella punta,
Que el mar y el cielo, hecho bifagra, junta,
La proa.

Polidoro.
Ya toca el efpolon la playa.
Antiftes.
Vaya toda la gente á tierra.
Todos.
Vaya;
Antiftes.
Del mar cefó la guerra.

Ulifes.
Vencimos el naufragio.
Todos.
A tierra, á tierra !
[*Llega el bajel y defembarcan todos.*

Ulifes.
Saluda el peregrino,
Que en falado criftal abrió camino,

Since fuddenly the winds begin to
    ceafe.
Archelaus.
Yes, all the elements proclaim a peace :—
Antiftes.
And for our greater happinefs,
(Since good and evil on each other prefs)
See, on the far horizon's verge
The golden fummits of the hills emerge
From out the mift that fhrouds the
    lowlier ftrand.
Timantes.
The clouds are fcatter'd now;
All.
The land ! the land !
Ulyffes.
Beneath this promontory, which doth
    lie
A link of ftone betwixt the fea and fky,
Turn the tired prow :
Polydorus.
The rock bends beetling o'er :—
Antiftes.
All hands defcend on fhore :—
All.
All hands on fhore !
Antiftes.
After the war of waves the air grows
    bland : —
Ulyffes.
Shipwreck we have fubdued.
All.
To land ! to land !
[*The veffel anchors and all the
    crew difembark.*
Ulyffes.
Salute this hofpitable land,
Whofe curving fhores like fheltering arms
    expand

La tierra donde llega,
Cuando inconſtante y náufrago ſe niega
Del mar á la inconſtancia proceloſa.

Antiſtes.
¡Salve, y ſalve otra vez, madre piadoſa!

Arquelao.
Con rendidos deſpojos
Los labios te apellidan, y los ojos.

Clarin.
Del mar vengo enfadado;
Que no es gracioſo el mar, aunque es
   ſalado.
Lebrel.
No es aqueſo forzoſo
Que yo no ſoy ſalado, y ſoy gracioſo.

Uliſes.
¿ Qué tierra ſerá eſta ?

Timántes.
¿ Quién quieres que á tu duda dé reſ-
   pueſta,
Si, ſiempre derrotados,
Mares remotos, climas apartados
Habemos tantos años diſcurrido,
El rumbo, el norte y el iman perdido ?

Polidoro.
Pues no nueſtras deſdichas han ceſado;
Que el monte, donde ahora has arribado,
No parece habitable

To claſp us to its breaſt:—
Storm-tofs'd and ſhip-wreck'd we awhile
   may reſt
Nor dread the ſea's wild rage, the ſtorm-
   wind's wilder mirth !
Antiſtes.
Hail! and thrice hail, O holy mother
   Earth !—
Archelaus.
To thee O land! our grateful tears and
   ſighs
Breathe from our lips, and tremble from
   our eyes :—
Clarin.
Loathing the tireſome ſea, I turn from
   it,—
So much of ſalt and yet ſo little wit !—
Lebrel.
That does not follow, ſince the ſalt ſea
   can
Make a good merman of a merry-man !—
Ulyſſes.
What land is this, what ſhore, what
   ſheltering creek ?
Timantes.
Which of us all can anſwer what you
   ſeek ?
Since ever driven along the watery waſte
Through diſtant ſeas and climes aſunder
   placed,
We for ſo many years have now been
   toſt—
Our route, our polar ſtar, our compaſs loſt?
Polydorus.
I fear new trials threaten us again ;
Since from this hill where we have ſhelter
   ta'en,
The place looks all deſerted—hillocks
   piled

En lo inculto, intrincado y formidable.

Antíſtes.
En él las mas pequeñas
Ruinas, de gente humana no dan ſeñas.

Arquelao.
Solo ſe vé de arroyos mil ſurcado,
Cuyo turbio criſtal deſentonado
Parece, á lo que creo,
Deſperdiciado aborto del Leteo.

Lebrel.
Que habemos dado, temo,
En otro mayor mal, que el Polifemo.

Floro.
Quejas ſon laſtimoſas y ſeveras,
Cuantas ſe eſcuchan, de robuſtas fieras,

Timántes.
Y ſi las copas rúſticas miramos
Deſtos funeſtos ramos,
No pájaros ſuaves
Vemos, nocturnas ſí, agoreras aves.

Arquelao.
Y entre ſus ramos rotos y quebrados
Trofeos de guerra y caza eſtán colgados.

Polidoro.
Todo el ſitio es rigor.
Floro.
          Todos es eſpanto.
Antíſtes.
Todo horror.

On woody plains, and heaths untrodden
  rude and wild.
Antiſtes.
From this I cannot ſee the ſlighteſt trace
Of human dwellings in this loneſome
  place.
Archelaus.
'Tis furrow'd by a thouſand tiny ſtreams
Whoſe troubled tide ſo hoarſe and ſlimy
  ſeems,
That one could almoſt think
It burſt and ſtray'd away from Lethe's
  leaden brink.
Lebrel.
Worſe than the cave of Polyphemus,
  here
A greater evil threatens us I fear :—
Florus.
And hark! that diſtant ſound appears
  the howl
Of famiſh'd beaſts that through the
  foreſts prowl;
Timantes.
And if we turn our eyes
Unto the darkſome boughs that hide us
  from the ſkies,
No gentle ſongſters warble from the trees,
But hoarſe nocturnal birds of fatal
  auguries.
Archelaus.
Suſpended from the boughs, methinks
  I trace   [chaſe.
Some broken trophies of the war and
Polydorus.
All here is gloomy.
Florus.
                    All is full of fear.
Antiſtes.
Horror!

Arquelao.
Todo afombro.
          Timántes.
                    Todo encanto.
     Lebrel.
Abforto de mirar fus feñas quedo.
¿ Creeráfmé una verdad, que tengo
     miedo ?
          Clarin.
Sí creeré, fi es que arguyo,
Que por mi corazon fe juzga el tuyo.
     [*Vanfe todos, y quedan Ulifes y Clarin.*

     Ulifes.
Pues los dos nos quedamos,
Por efta parte penetrando vamos.
¡ Qué bofque es de confufion tan rara
Aquefte que pifamos !
          Clarin.
                    Y aun no para
En efo, pues del trifte obfcuro centro
Suyo, miro falirnos al encuentro
Un efcuadron de fieras,
Bárbara inculta huefte, que en hileras
Mal formadas embifte
A los dos.

          Ulifes.
               Defendámonos (ay trifte !)
El uno al otro.—Pero cómo es efto ?
No folo á nueftra ofenfa fe han difpuefto,
Pero humildes, poftrados y vencidos,
Los pechos por la tierra eftan rendidos.
     [*Salen animales, y hacen lo que fe va
          diciendo.*
Y el Rey de todos ellos,

Archelaus.
And terror !
          Timantes.
               And enchantments drear !
     Lebrel.
At all thefe figns I ftand and gape dif-
     may'd—
Can you believe it true that I'm afraid ?—
          Clarin.
Eafily, truly, and for this alone,
I judge your heart and courage by my
     own.
     [*Exeunt all but Ulyffes and Clarin.*

     Ulyffes.
Since we alone of all our comrades ftay,
Let us attempt to penetrate this way :
What tangled wood with thorny thickets
Is this we tread ?   [blind,
          Clarin.
               And worfe remains behind,
For from its central fad obfcurity,
My frighten'd eyes a fearful fquadron fee
Of banded wild-beafts iffuing through
     the gloom ;
Hither the favage hoft appears to come,
In broken ranks the dreadful foe flocks
     nigh
To attack us two !—
               Ulyffes.
               O woe ! then let us die
Defending one another !—Stranger ftill,
They do not feem difpofed to do us ill :
But humbled, vanquifh'd, crowd around,
And with their proftrate breafts falute
     the ground.
[*The Animals enter and act as they are
     defcribed.*
And fee the King of all the train—

El leon, coronado de cabellos,
En pie puefto, una vez hácia las peñas,
Y otra hácia el mar, cortes nos hace
    feñas.
O generofo bruto,
Rey de tanta república abfoluto,
¿Qué me quieres decir, cuando á la
    playa
Senalas? ¿que me vaya,
Y que no tale mas el bofque, donde
Tienes tu imperio? A todo me re-
    fponde,
Inclinada la tefta,
Con halagos firmando la refpuefta.
Creamos pues al hado ;
Que un bruto no mintiera coronado.—
Convoca á gritos fieros
A nueftros compañeros,
Para que al mar volvamos,
Y agradecidos el peligro huyamos.

Clarin.
Compañeros de Ulífes,
Que difcurris los bárbaros paifes
Defte encantado monte,
Defamparad fu bárbaro horizonte.
    Ulífes.
Al mar volved, al mar, que triftemente
Con halago las fieras obediente,
Cuando fus voces nueftras gentes llaman,
Quieren quejarfe, y por quejarfe, braman.

Clarin.
Todas con manfo eftruendo,

The lordly Lion crown'd with his own
    mane—
Standing erect, doth beckon courteoufly,
Now to the rocks, and now unto the
O generous and noble brute,   [fea.
Of thine own realm fole monarch abfo-
    lute !   [to fhow
What wouldft thou fay by feeming thus
My way to the ftrand ? Is it that I
    fhould go,
Nor feek to penetrate this myftic wood,
Where thou doft hold thy court ? Oh !
    I am underftood !   [imperial eye,
He bends his fovereign head, his proud
And with careffes ftrengthens his
    reply :—
On fate and on his word let us rely,
A King—even though of beafts—can
    never lie !
With hurried cries of hope and fear
Convoke our fcatter'd comrades here,
That to the fea we may return once
    more,   [fhore.
And grateful fly the dangers of this
    Clarin (*calling*).
Companions of Ulyffes, who
Roam this favage region through,
Come, leave this land by fiends poffeft,
Come, fly this mountain's magic breaft !
    Ulyffes.
To fea ! to fea ! with what a fad affent
The wild beafts' voices with our cries
    are blent !
With us they call our people o'er and
    o'er,   [ing roar !
They wifh to warn them, and in warn-
    Clarin.
With gentle clamour through the woods
    they flee,

Repitiendo las señas, van huyendo.
     Ulíses.
Mucho es mi asombro.
      Clarin.
       Y mi tristeza es mucha.
      Ulíses.
Dioses, ¿ qué tierra es esta ?
     Sale huyendo ANTISTES.
      Antistes.
        Atiende, escucha :
  Entramos en ese monte,
  Ulíses, tus compañeros,
  A examinar sus entrañas.
  A solicitar su centro,
  Cuando á las varias fortunas
  Del mar pensamos que el cielo
  Nos habia dado amparo,
  Nos habia dado puerto.
  Mas ay triste ! que el peligro
  Es de mar y tierra dueño ;
  Porque en la tierra y el mar
  Tiene el peligro su imperio.
  Digalo alli, coronado
  De tantos naufragios ciertos,
  Y aqui lo diga, ceñido
  De tantos precisos riesgos :
  Aunque ni el mar, ni la tierra
  No tienen la culpa dellos,
  Pues el hombre en tierra y mar
  Lleva el peligro en sí mesmo.
  Por diversos laberintos,
  Que labró, artífice diestro
  Sin estudio y sin cuidado,
  El desaliño del tiempo,
  Discurrimos ese monte,
  Hasta que hallándonos dentro,
  Vimos un rico palacio.
  Tan vanamente soberbio,
  Que embarazando los aires,

Still making signs and pointing to the sea.
     Ulysses.
Great is my wonder.
      Clarin.
       Great my mournful fear.
      Ulysses.
What is this land, ye Gods ?—
      [ANTISTES *rushes in.*
      Antistes.
     Oh ! listen, thou shalt hear :—
We, Ulysses, thy companions,
Dared this mountain wild to enter,
Its interior to examine,
To explore its inmost centre,
For we thought the fickle fortune
Of the sea at length had ended,
And that heaven had given us favour,
And the earth a welcome shelter ;
But, alas ! doth Danger lord it
Over land and sea for ever,
Sea and land th' eternal kingdom
Ruled by Danger's deathless sceptre ;
There his gloomy throne is builded
Of unnumber'd shipwreck'd vessels,
Here his widening realm is bounded
By a ring of risks unended,
Though nor land nor sea should justly
Bear the blame of these excesses,
Since on both, the seeds of danger
Man within his own breast beareth ;
Through the labyrinthine passes,
Which with careless hand Time cleav-
  eth—
Time the cunning craftsman making
Most of that which he neglecteth,
Without seeming toil or effort,—
In through these the mount we enter'd,
And advanced, until with wonder
A rich palace we beheld there,

Y los montes afligiendo,
Era para aquellos nube,
Y peñafco para eftos,
Porque fe daba la mano
Con uno y con otro extremo :
Pero aunque viciofos eran,
La virtud no eftaba en medio.
Saludamos fus umbrales
Cortefanamente atentos,
Y apenas de nueftras voces
La mitad nos hurtó el eco,
Cuando de Ninfas hermofas
Un tejido coro bello
Las puertas abrió, moftrando
Apacible y lifonjero,
Que habia de fer fu agafajo
De nueftros males confuelo,
De nueftras penas alivio,
De nueftras tormentas puerto.
Mintió el defeo ; ¿ mas cuándo
Dijo verdad el defeo?
Detras de todas venia,
Bien como el dorado Febo,
Acompañado de eftrellas,
Y cercado de luceros,
Una muger tan hermofa,
Que nos perfuadimos ciegos,
Que era, a envidia de Diana,
La diofa deftos defiertos.
Efta pues nos preguntó,
Quiénes eramos; y habiendo
Informádofe de pafo
De los infortunios nueftros,
Cautelofamente humana,
Mandó fervir al momento
A fus Damas las bebidas
Mas generofas, haciendo
Con urbanas ceremonias
Político el cumplimiento.

So fuperbly proud and haughty,
That embarraffing the zephyrs
And the mountains' fides oppreffing,
It to thofe a vaft cloud feemeth,
And to thefe a rock as mighty :—
Since at once to earth and heaven
Each of its extreme ends reaches ;
But unlike the extremes of vices,
In its midft no virtue dwelleth.
We, its threfholds fair faluted,
Courteoufly approaching nearer,
And the fwift thief Echo fcarce
Half our ftolen words repeated,
When a linkèd choir of nymphs
Wide its ample doors extended,
Showing in their fmiling looks
Such a fweet and gracious prefence,
That we thought at length had come,
After all our toils, refrefhment,
After all our evils, good,
And a haven after tempefts :—
Falfely fpoke our wifhes thus ;
But, ah ! when have wifhes ever
Spoke the truth ? Behind them all,
Like the golden fun attended
By the morning ftars, and girt
Round with rofy eaftern ether,
Came a woman, ah ! fo fair,
That our dazzled eyes believed her
(To Diana's envy fure)
The fole goddefs of thofe deferts :—
She inquired of us, at length,
Who we were: and when was ended
The brief outline of our woes,
She, with purpofe well diffembled,
Order'd her attendant dames
To fupply us with whatever
Generous and refrefhing drinks
We in our condition needed,

Apenas de fus licores
El veneno admitió el pecho,
Cuando corrió al corazon,
Y en un inftante, un momento,
A delirar empezaron,
De todos los que bebieron,
Los fentidos, tan mudados
De lo que fueron primero,
Que no folo la embriaguez
Entorpeció el fentimiento
Del juicio, porcion del alma,
Sino tambien la del cuerpo ;
Pues poco á poco extinguidos
Los proporcionados miembros,
Fueron mudando las formas.
¿ Quién vió tan raro portento ?
¿ Quién vió tan extraño hechizo ?
¿ Quién vió prodigio tan nuevo ?
¿ Y quién vió, que, fiendo hermofa
Una muger con extremo,
Para hacer los hombres brutos,
Ufafe de otros remedios,
Pues deftas transformaciones
Es la hermofura el veneno ?
Cual era ya racional
Bruto, de pieles cubierto ;
Cual, de manchas falpicado
Fiera con entendimiento ;
Cual fierpe armada de conchas,
Cual de agudas puntas lleno,
Cual animal mas immundo :
Y todos al fin á un tiempo
Articulaban gemidos,
Penfando que éran acentos.
La mágica entonces dijo :
" Hoy vereis, cobardes Griegos,
De la manera que Circe
Trata cuantos pafageros
Aqueftos umbrales tocan."—

Greeting us the while with all
Courteous geftures and addreffes.
Scarcely of thefe poifon'd drinks
Had the mouth received the effence,
When it reach'd the very heart ;
So that quickly, in my prefence,
Strange delirium feized on all ·
Who had drunk what they prefented,
So that the fwift drunkennefs
Not alone benumb'd the fenfes,
Or obfcured the reafon, part
Of the immortal foul, but even
Reach'd the very frame itfelf ;
So that the well-moulded members
Gradually began to lofe
Their fix'd outline and prefentment.
Who e'er faw fo ftrange a portent ?
Who bewitchment fo demented ?
Who a prodigy fo new ?—
And who faw too this extremer
Wonder, that a woman deck'd
With fuch charms as fhe poffeffes,
If fhe wifh'd to make men brutes,
Should have other means invented,
When fo well for fuch transformings
Beauty's poifonous power fucceedeth ?
One, though keeping reafon ftill,
Seem'd a rough-fkinn'd beaft untether'd ;
One, with ftain'd and fpotted hide,
Seem'd a brute with human fenfes ;
This a ferpent arm'd with fcales,
That by prickly ftings protefted ;
This became an animal
Moft unclean, and all together
Utter'd howls and cries, believing
They were words that they accented.
Then the fair magician faid,
" Coward Greeks, this day's experience
Teacheth you how Circe treats

Yo, que por ſer el que haciendo
Eſtaba la relacion
De nueſtros varios ſucefos,
Aun no habia al labio dado
El vaſo, el peligro viendo,
Sin que reparara en mí
Circe, corrí; que en efecto,
El que ſe ſabe librar
De los venenos mas fieros
De una hermoſura, es quien ſolo
Niega los labios á ellos.
Eſto en fin me ha ſucedido,
Y vengo à aviſarte dello,
Porque deſta Esfinge huyamos.
¿ Pero dónde podrá el cielo
Librarnos de una muger
Con belleza y con ingenio ?

Uliſes.
¿ Cuándo vengada eſtarás,
O injuſta deidad de Vénus !
De Grecia ? ¿ cuándo tendrán
Divinas cóleras medio?
Antiſtes.
No en laſtimoſos gemidos
La ocaſion embaracemos,
Que tenemos de librarnos :
Al mar volvamos huyendo.
Uliſes.
¿ Cómo, habemos de dejar
Aſi á nueſtros compañeros?
Clarin.
Perdernos, ſeñor, noſotros,
No es alivio para ellos.
Uliſes.
Juno, ſi en deſprecio tuyo
Vénus ofende á los Griegos,
¿ Cómo tú no los defiendes,

Every traveller who ſteppeth
From his ſhip upon theſe ſhores."
I, that I might be the bearer
Of this newer, ſtranger phaſe
Of the fate that dogs us ever,
Though the cup was at my lips,
Seeing what a danger threaten'd,
Fled ere Circe was aware.
For in truth the only ſecret
Antidote by which to eſcape
Beauty's poiſon'd influences,
Is to never truſt the lips
Even to touch what ſhe preſenteth.
This is my unhappy tale,
And of this I come to tell thee,
That we may this fair Sphinx fly.
But fly whither ? ſince the heavens
Scarce can ſave us from a woman,
Ah ! ſo lovely and ſo clever !
Ulyſſes.
Venus, cruel goddeſs fair,
When wilt thou enough avenge thee
Upon Greece ? Ah ! when will be
Thy divine diſpleaſure leſſen'd ?
Antiſtes.
Let us not in mournful ſighs
Loſe the occaſion chance preſenteth
Of effecting our eſcape :—
Better ſeek the ſea's rude ſhelter.
Ulyſſes.
How ! and can we leave them here,
Our companions thus deſerted ?
Clarin.
But to loſe ourſelves, my lord,
Will, methinks, but little ſerve them.
Ulyſſes.
Juno, if through ſcorn of thee
Venus thus the Greeks oppreſſes ;
Why, reſenting this her ſcorn,

Quejofa de tu defprecio?
Acuérdate, que, ofendida
De Páris, á nueſtro acero
Le fiaſte tu venganza:
Acuérdate, que fangrientos
Por tí abrafamos á Troya,
Cuyo no apagado incendio
Hoy en padrones de humo
Eſtá en cenizas ardiendo.
Si, por haberte vengado,
Tantos males padecemos,
Remédianos, Juno bella,
Contra la deidad de Vénus.

[*Tocan chirimías, y fale en un arco la Ninfa* IRIS, *y canta la Múfica dentro.*

.*Múfica.*
    Iris, Ninfa de los aires,
    El arco defpliega bello,
    Y menfagera de Juno,
    Rafga los azules velos.
      Iris (canta).
    Ya la obedezco,
    Y batiendo las alas,
    Rompo los vientos.
      Ulifes.
Línea de púrpura y nieve,
Nube de rofa y de fuego,
Verde, roja y amarilla,
Nos deſlumbran a fus reflejos.
      Antiſtes.
¿ Qué hermofo rafgo corrido
En el papel de los cielos,
Bandera es de paz?
      Ulifes.
         Y en él
Eſtá la Ninfa pendiendo,
Embajatriz de las diofas,
Reina de dos elementos.—

Doſt thou not in turn defend them?
Oh! remember when thou wert
Wroth with Paris, to avenge thee,
Thou didſt truſt thee to our fwords:—
And that bloody deed remember,
How it was for thee we burn'd
Ilium down, whofe living embers
Raife red monuments of fmoke
O'er its afhes ſtill unquenchèd;
If for wreaking thy revenge,
Such unnumber'd ills have centred
All in us, O Juno fair,
Againſt Venus be our helper!

[*A found of clarions is heard, and the nymph* IRIS *appears in a rainbow, voices are heard finging within.*
      Song within.
Iris, lovely nymph of air,
Now her beauteous bow extendeth,
And, fwift meffenger of Juno,
Rends the azure veil of heaven.
      Iris (fings).
I, the glad-obeying bearer
Of good tidings, float along,
Parting with my wings the ether.
      Ulyſſes.
Curved lines of purpled fnow,
Clouds of fire and rofe-hues blended,
Green and red, and golden yellow,
Dazzle us with their reflexes.
      Antiſtes.
What fair ſtreak of light is this,
That, from heaven's blue walls projeƈted,
Seems the flag of peace?
      Ulyſſes.
         And, lo!
In it is the nymph fufpended,
She who is embaffadrefs
From the Goddeffes, and regent

Iris, bellísima Ninfa,
Si tu respuesta merezco,
¿ Qué, dichosa, vas buscando ?
¿ Qué, infelice, vas huyendo ?

Iris (canta).
A tus fortunas atenta,
O nunca vencido Griego,
Juno tu amparo dispone,
Y yo de su parte vengo.
Este ramo, que te traigo,
De varias flores cubierto,
Hoy contra Circe será
Triaca de sus venenos.
　　　　[*Deja caer un ramillete.*
Toca con él sus hechizos,
Desvaneceránse luego,
Como al amor no te rindas :
Que con avisarte desto,
Ya la obedezco,
Y batiendo las alas,
Rompo los vientos.
　　　Toda la Música.
Y batiendo las alas,
Rompo los vientos.

　　[*Tocan chirimías, y desaparece
　　　el arco y la Ninfa.*
　　　　Ulises.
Hermoso aliento de Juno,
No desvanezcas tan presto
Tanto aparato de estrellas,
Tanta pompa de luceros.
Espera, detente, aguarda,
Que te sacrifique el pecho
Estas lágrimas, que lleves
En señal de rendimiento.
　　　　Clarin.
Ya las esparcidas luces

Of two separate elements :—
Iris, lovely nymph, if ever
I thy answer have deserved,
Say, O happy, whom thou seekest ?
Say, unhappy, whom thou fleest ?
　　　　Iris (sings).
O thou never conquer'd Greek !
Thou whose fate is ever present
To great Juno's thoughtful care,
Unto thee she now has sent me.
See this floral branch I bear
Gemm'd with buds that Flora tended,
It will be the antidote
Against Circe's poison'd secrets,—
　　　[*She lets fall a bunch of flowers.*
Touch with it her magic spells,
They will vanish, if thou yieldest
Not to love's more potent charm :—
With this parting hint I leave thee,
I, the glad-obeying bearer
Of good tidings, float along,
Parting with my wings the ether.
　　　Chorus of voices within.
See ! the glad-obeying bearer
Of good tidings floats along,
Parting with her wings the ether,
　　[*The clarions sound, and the rainbow
　　　and Nymph disappear.*
　　　　Ulysses.
Sweet-sent breath from Juno's lips,
Ah ! do not so soon dismember
Such a glorious gleam of stars,
Such a crimson cloud of cressets,
Oh ! detain thee, listen, stay,
Till at least my breast present thee
With these sacrificial tears,
Of my feelings the mute emblems.
　　　　Clarin.
See, the scatter'd lights retire,

Va doblando y recogiendo,
Haſtaperderſe de viſta,
Por las campañas del viento.
Ulíſes.
Ya no hay que temer de Circe
Los encantos, pues ya veo
Tan de mi parte los hados,
Tan en mi favor los cielos.
A ſus palacias me guia,
Veráſme vencer en ellos
Sus hechizos, y librar
A todos mis compañeros.
Antiſtes.
No es meneſter que te guie
A ſus ojos ; que ella, haciendo
Salva á tus peligros, ſale
Al ſon de mil inſtrumentos.
Aparece el Palacio de Circe.
Salen los Múſicos cantando, y deſpues
    Circe, Casandra, Tisbe, Clori
    y Astrea, *que trae un vaſo en una*
    ſalvilla, y Libia *una toalla.*

Múſica.
En hora dichoſa venga
A los palacios de Circe
El ſiempre invencible Griego,
El nunca vencido Ulíſes.
Circe.
En hora dichoſa venga
Hoy á eſta palacio hermoſo
El Griego mas generoſo,
Que vió el ſol, donde prevenga
Blando albergue, y donde tenga
Dulce hoſpedage, y atento
A ſus fortunas, contento
Pueda en la tierra triunfar
De la cólera del mar,
Y de la ſaña del viento.

Now outgleaming, now condensèd
Till they wholly fade away
On the far-off plains of heaven !
Ulyſſes.
Now I have no cauſe to fear
Circe's magic rites, defended
As I am by friendly fates,
And by favouring ſkies proteſted.
To her palace lead the way,
Thou wilt ſee me there defend me
'Gainſt her ſorceries, and ſet free
My companions from their fetters.
Antiſtes.
Need there's none that I ſhould lead thee
To her preſence, ſince ſhe entereth
Here herſelf, with thouſand cymbals
Greeting thee and thy diſtreſſes.
The Palace of Circe appears.
Muſicians enter ſinging and playing, fol-
    lowed by Circe, Cassandra, Thisbe,
    Chloris, Astrea, *who carries a gob-*
    let on a ſalver, and Libia, *bearing a*
    napkin.

Song.
Be the hour propitious when
To the palace-halls of Circe
Comes the ever-viſtor Greek,
The invincible Ulyſſes.
Circe.
Be the hour propitious when
To this beauteous palace here
Comes the nobleſt Greek that e'er
Has the ſun ſeen amongſt men ;
Here ſhall he enjoy again
Sweet repoſe, and rapture find,
And attention the moſt kind,
Since in triumph cometh he
From the anger of the ſea,
And the raging of the wind.

Felice pues fuese el dia,	May the day thrice happy shine
Que estos piélagos sulcó,	When he plough'd these waves around,
Felice fuese el que halló	Be it happy when he found
Abrigo en la patria mia,	Shelter in this realm of mine :
Y felice la osadía,	Be that courage call'd divine,
Con que ya vencer presuma	With which he in peace doth come
En tranquila paz, en suma	Now to taste the joys of home,
Felicidad inmortal,	He who lately hath subdued
Ese monstruo de cristal,	This cruel crystal monster rude,
Sierpe escamada de espuma.	This azure serpent scaled with foam.
Que yo al cielo agradecida,	Gratefully, with glowing breast,
Pues ya mis venturas sé,	Do I thank the Gods for this,
De tanto huésped daré	That they crown my life with bliss,
Parabienes á mi vida;	Giving me so great a guest :—
Y así, á tus plantas rendida,	Therefore have I hither prest
Con aplausos diferentes,	Thus to throw me at thy feet,
Vengo á recibir tus gentes,	Thus melodiously to greet
Hurtando en ecos suaves	Thy approach with songs, whose words
Las cláusulas á las aves,	Seem the notes of warbling birds,
Los compases á las fuentes.	Or the fountains' murmurings sweet.
Y porque al que en mar vivió,	And since dwellers on the sea
Lo que mas en él le obliga	'Mid each moment's misery,
A sentir, es la fatiga	Feel of all their ills the worst
De la sed, que padeció,	Is the oppressive pang of thirst—
(¿Quién sed en tanta agua vió?)	(Can thirst 'mid so much water be?)
A traerte aqui se atreven	Hither to the ocean's brink—
Los aplausos, que me mueven,	(By this zeal, O wanderer, think
(En señal de cuan piadoso	How I value thy surviving!)
Es mi afecto) el generoso	Have I brought thee the reviving
Néctar, que los dioses beben.	Nectar that the great Gods drink.
Bebe, y sin pavor alguno	Drink, and without any fear
Brinda á la gran magestad	Pledge the sovereign sacredness
De Júpiter, la beldad	Of high Jove, the loveliness
De Vénus, ciencias de Juno,	Of fair Venus, Neptune's sphere,
De Marte armas, de Neptuno	Juno's knowledge, the severe
Ondas, de Diana honor,	Huntress Nymph who rules the grove,
Flores de Flora, esplendor	Flora's flowers, the beams that move
De Apolo; y por varios modos,	Round Apollo's golden throne,
Porque en uno asisten todos,	Or, to blend all praise in one,

Bebe y brinda al dios de Amor.
   Ulíses.
Bellísima cazadora,
Que en este opaco horizonte,
Siendo noche todo el monte,
Todo el monte haces aurora,
Pues no amaneció, hasta ahora
Que te ví, la luz en él,
Admite rendido y fiel
Un peregrino del mar,
Que halló piadoso al pesar,
Que halló á la dicha cruel.
Esa nave derrotada,
Que con tanta sed anhela,
Pez, que por las ondas vuela,
Ave, que en los aires nada,
A tu deidad consagrada,
Víctima ya sin ejemplo,
De tus aras la contemplo,
Pues aqui se ha de quedar
Por trofeo de tu altar,
Por despojo de tu templo.
   [*Llegan* LIBIA *y* ASTREA.
El néctar, con que has brindado
Mi feliz venida, aceto,
Aunque temor y respeto
Me han suspendido y turbado
Tanto, que de recatado,
No me atrevo á tus favores,
Sin que otros labios mejores
Lisonjeen tus agravios :
Y así, antes que con los labios,
Haré la salva con flores.
   [*Mete el ramillete en el vaso,*
    y sale fuego.
   Astrea.
En fuego el agua encendió.
   Libia.
¿ Qué es lo que mis ojos ven ?

Drink and pledge the God of Love.
   Ulysses.
Beauteous huntress, thou that makest
All this black horizon bright,
Flooding all the darksome night
Of this mountain's vault opaquest
With the dawn that thou awakest,
Since thy face its orient is,—
Oh ! receive subdued, submiss,
A poor pilgrim of the sea
Who in grief finds sympathy,
Cruelty in seeming bliss.
Our disrupted bark that there
Gapes with thirst, and stranded lies,
Fish that through the water flies,
Bird that swimmeth through the air,
Consecrated, as it were,
Unto thee, fair nymph divine,
We to-day to thee resign ;
Victim-like it must remain
As a trophy in thy fane,
As a relic at thy shrine.
   [LIBIA *and* ASTREA *advance.*
And this nectar which you drink
To my happy coming here,
I accept, but with a fear
Mingled so with awe, I shrink
But to touch the goblet's brink ;
Terror even my thirst o'erpowers,
Worthier lips than those of ours
Should the draught a goddess sips
Taste, and thus before the lips
I salute it with these flowers.
   [*He applies the flowers to the goblet,*
    from which fire issues.
   Astrea.
Fire from water flaming high !
   Libia.
Can my eyes believe this true ?

Circe.
¿Quién, cielos airados, quién
Mas ha sabido que yo?
      Ulíses.
Quien tus encantos venció
Deidad superior ha sido;
Y pues á tiempo he venido,
Que á tantos vengar espero,
Verás, mágica, este acero
En tu púrpura teñido.
      [*Saca la espada.*
      Circe.
Aunque llego à merecer
La muerte, es bien que te asombre,
Que no es victoria de un hombre
El matar á una muger.
Valor, tan hecho á vencer,
No ha de ser, no, mi homicida.
Rendida tienes mi vida:
Luego de tu acero hoy
Dos veces segura estoy,
Por muger, y por rendida.
      Ulíses.
Por rendida, y por muger
Darte la muerte no quiero;
Vida tienes; mas primero
Que la vaina vuelva á ver
La cuchilla, has de traer
Mis compañeros aqui.
      Circe.
Eso y mas haré por tí.—
Oid, racionales fieras,
En vuestras formas primeras
Trocad las formas que os dí.
      [*Sale cada uno de por sí.*

      Timántes.
¿Qué es lo que me ha sucedido
Este rato que he soñado?

Circe.
Who, O angry heavens! who
Deeper lore has learn'd than I?
      Ulysses.
One, a mightier deity,
Who thy charms hath all subdued;—
By my vengeful arm pursued
Thou the atoning stroke shalt feel,
Sorceress, thou shalt see this steel
With thy crimson blood imbued.
      [*Draws his sword.*
      Circe.
Though by me it is confest
That I merit death from thee,
Still to a man, no victory
Is it to pierce a woman's breast!
Valour hath a nobler test
Than the murderous stroke inhuman—
'Tis to spare a prostrate foeman;—
To subdue is not to slay,
Doubly safe am I to-day
In being conquer'd and a woman.
      Ulysses.
Then for being thus o'erpower'd,
Likewise for the form you wear,
I consent your life to spare,
But before I sheathe my sword,
On the spot must be restored
My companions safe and free.
      Circe.
That and more I'll do for thee:—
Reason-bearing wild beasts, hear!
In your proper shapes appear,
Changing those were given by me!
      [*All the followers of* ULYSSES *enter*
        one after the other.
      Timantes.
What a strange delusive dream
Slumbering fancy round me wrought!—

Polidoro.
En un leon transformado
Mi letargo me ha tenido.
    Floro.
¡ Qué ageno de mi sentido
Me ha usurpado un frenesi !
    Arquelao.
¡ Gracias á Dios, que te vi,
O campo azul cristalino !

    Lebrel.
Vive Dios ! que fui cochino,
Y aun me soy lo que me fui.
    Circe.
Ya libres tus gentes ves.
    Ulíses.
Y ya aqui no hay que esperar.—
¡ Alto, amigos, á embarcar !
    Timántes.
A todos nos da tus pies
Por esta ventura.
    Circe.
                Pues
Tan seguro estás de mí,
No te ausentes, no, de aqui,
Sin que llegue á saber yo
Mas despacio, quién venció
Mis encantos.
    Ulíses.
      Oye.
    Circe.
          Di.
    Ulíses.
Si caben tantos sucesos
En el coto de unas voces :
La fértil Grecia es mi patria,
Y Ulíses mi propio nombre ;
Aunque inclinado á las letras,
Militares escuadrones

Polydorus.
In my lethargy methought
That a lion I had been !
    Florus.
What a frenzy came to screen
Reason's light and nature's laws !
    Archelaus.
Thanks to Heaven ! the cloud with-
    draws,
And I see the azure sky !
    Lebrel.
Blest be Jove ! a hog was I,
And I *am* just what I was !
    Circe.
All thy people now are free.
    Ulysses.
Let us hence, my friends, away !
Quick ! embark ; make no delay !
    Timantes.
At thy feet permit that we
Kneel to thank thee.
    Circe.
              Since of me
Now all fear were worse than weak,
Let me ask you not to seek
Yonder wave, until I know
More of him who has laid low
My enchantments.
    Ulysses.
          Listen !
    Circe.
             Speak !
    Ulysses.
If such strange adventure can
By a single voice be spoken :—
Fertile Greece my country is,
As Ulysses there they know me ;
Though inclined to letters first,
Martial camps and crowds I follow'd,

Seguí; que en mí se admiraron
Espada y pluma conformes.
Cerqué á Troya, y rendí á Troya:
No me permitas que torne
A la memoria sus ruinas,
Basta que Vénus las llore.
Heredero de las armas
De Aquíles fui; porque logren,
Si dueño no tan valiente,
Dueño á lo menos tan noble.
Al mar me entregué, pensando
Volver á mi patria, donde
Trocara el bélico estruendo
A regalados favores.
Engañóme mi esperanza,
Mintióme mi amor, burlóme
Mi deseo.   ¡ O cuanto fácil
Su dicha imagina el hombre !
Vénus, del Griego ofendida,
Mis venturas descompone ;
Que es, aunque diosa, muger,
En quien duran los rencores.
La cárcel abrió á los vientos,
Para mi agravio veloces ;
Que para mis esperanzas
Aun fueran los vientos torpes.
Ellos, que airados embisten,
La fragil armada rompen,
Y yo turbado perdí
Con la confusion el norte.
Huésped viví de Neptuno
Seis años, y por salobres
Campañas de agua, sospecho,
Que he dado una vuelta al orbe.
Entre Caríbdis y Scila
Me ví, y á las dulces voces
Del golfo de las Sirenas
Basilisco fui de bronce.
Llegué al pie del Lilibeo,

Since in me the sword and pen
Woke in turn the same responses,—
I laid seige to Troy, by me
Was the Trojan city conquer'd ;
Little need of memory now
To go o'er that famous story ;
'Tis enough its proud walls fell
And that Venus weepeth o'er them.
I became, by public voice,
Of Achilles' arms the owner,
Since they needed a new lord
If not braver, still as noble ;—
Trusting to the sea, I thought
Soon my country to recover,
Where I hoped, instead of steel,
Arms of fondness would enfold me.
Hope deceived me, love spoke falsely,
Fond desire delusive mock'd me.
Oh ! how easily doth man
Dream of joy from doubtfulest omens !
Venus, wrathful with the Greeks,
All my plans, my schemes disorder'd—
Since a goddess though she be,
Woman-like her rage she fondles—
She the prison of the winds
For my quick destruction open'd ;
Swift were they to do me wrong,
For my hopes so dead and torpid,
On my frail armada soon
Burst they forth with rage ungovern'd,
So that I, confused, overwhelm'd
With amazement, lost the pole-star ;
Six years lived I Neptune's guest,
And his salt seas sailing over,
Must in that time I suspect
Have encompassèd the whole earth.
Between Scylla and Charybdis
I beheld me, and a bronzèd
Basilisk grew to the syren's song,

Efe gigante, que opone
Al cielo fus puntas, fiendo
Excelfa pira de flores,
Donde fui de Polifemo
Mífero cautivo, y donde
Con fu muerte refcaté
Mi vida de fus prifiones,
El trágico fin vengando
De Acis, generofo jóven,
Y la hermofa Galatea,
Hija de Nereo y Dóris,
Que, lágrimas de un peñafco,
Al mar en dos fuentes corren,
Cuando . . . . Mas deber no quiero
Tan poco á hazaña tan noble,
Que la defluzca en contarla,
Prefumiendo que la ignores.
Bafta decir, que feguro
De fus caftigos atroces,
Tuvimos por agradables
De los vientos los rigores,
Porque tan airados fueron,
Que nos trajeron adonde
El rigor de una muger
Venciefe al rigor de un hombre;
Pues venimos donde tú
Mágicas transformaciones
Ufas; llorando lo digan
Efas fieras y efos robles.
Y afi, pues tan generofas
Deidades mas fuperiores
Me afeguran, volveré,
Huyendo de tus rigores,

Though they fang their fweeteft, fofteft;
Then I came unto the foot
Of Lilybœum, which oppofes
Its gigantic mountain-peaks
To the heavens, and crown'd with rofes
Seems a pyramid of flowers,
Where I was awhile the hopelefs
Captive thrall of Polyphemus,
Till my prifon-doors I open'd
By his death; and fo preferving
Life and limb, the felf-fame moment
By the felf-fame ftroke avenging
Acis' tragic end, young lover,
And the beauteous Galatea,
Child of Nereus and of Doris,
Who, the fwift tears of a rock,
Roll twin fountains to the ocean ;—
There . . . . but I would wifh to fhow
More refpect to a deed fo noble
Than to fpoil it by relating,
Thinking that it was forgotten.[*]
'Tis enough to fay that fafe
From his dread atrocious torments
We were wafted by the winds,
Pleafant now, but with their former
Anger wing'd, fince us they bore
Where the rigour of a woman
All man's rigour triumphs o'er,
Since we came where thou performeft
Magic metamorphofes :—
Weeping let thefe beaft-fhapes own them,
And the trees of this ftrange foreft.
Now fince more indulgent powers

---

[*] Alluding to the drama of *Polifemo y Circe*, which Calderon wrote in conjunction with Mira de Mefcua and Perez da Montalvan. It is the original draft of *El Mayor Encanto Amor*, and having been acted the year preceding that in which the latter drama was brought out (1635), was ftill in the memory of the audience. See Hartzenbufch's " Calderon," vol. iv. pp. 413 and 669, and, for an analyfis of it, the introduction to this tranflation of *El Mayor Encanto Amor*, p. 16.

A quebrantar los criſtales
De eſe piélago, que ſobre
Sus eſpaldas tantos años
Huéſped me admitió.　Deſcoge
O ſurto delfin, que vuelas,
Varado neblí, que corres,
Las alas, porque otra vez
La plata del agua cortes,
O con la quilla la rices,
O con el buque la entorches.
Torne pues al albedrío
De aire y mar la nave, y torne
A llevarme donde fuere
La voluntad de los dioſes.

Circe.
Retórico Griego, á quien
Eſe eſcollo criſtalino,
Eſe peñaſco de nieve,
Eſa campaña de vidrio
Náufrago huéſped te tuvo
Tantos años, pues, vencidos
Los hados, llegas, trayendo
Aqueſas flores contigo,
Que ſon antidoto hermoſo,
Que ſon conjuro divino
Contra mortales venenos,
Contra mágicos hechizos :
No tan preſto á peinar vuelvas
Al mar los cabellos rizos,
Que canos y ajados ſon
Hermoſos con deſaliño ;
Deja deſcanſar las ondas,
Y eſe bajel, que al abrigo
De dos montes ſurto yace,
Permite, que agradecido

And divinities more potent
Reaſſure me, once again,
Flying from thy deeds of wonder,
I ſhall break the cryſtal glaſs
Of this ſea, upon whoſe ſhoulders
I, an outcaſt, have been carried
Many a year.　Be then unfolded,
Flying dolphin anchor'd there—
Stranded-falcon ſo ſwift-footed,
Thy white wings, for thou once more
Muſt cut through the ſilver-molten
Surface of the ſea, thy prow
Daſhing up the curling foam-wreaths,
And thy keel wave-woven braid.
Give then, give the ſhip the open
Choice of ſea and air, that I
Borne on it may thus diſcover
Where the Gods deſire I go.

Circe.
Eloquent-tongued Greek King whom
Yonder rippling realm of cryſtal,
Yonder liquid hills of ſnow,
Yonder plains of glaſſy glitter,
Have a ſhipwreck'd gueſt detain'd
Such a length of years : ſince hither,
Conquering adverſe fate, thou haſt come,
Bearing theſe divine flowers with thee,
Which are beauteous antidotes,
Which are god-ſent exorciſms,
Againſt deadly poiſon'd draughts,
Againſt magical bewitchments,
Do not fly ſo quickly back
To outcomb the foam-white frizzled
Locks of ocean, which, though toſs'd
To and fro in wild-treſs'd whiteneſs,
Wear a beauteous negligence :—
Let the waves repoſe a little,
And that bark which in the ſhade
Of two hills at anchor lieth,—

A la piedad de los cielos,
De los hados al arbitrio,
Blanda, y no penosamente
Bata las alas de lino,
En tanto que te reparas
De aquel pasado peligro,
Que derrotado te trajo
A aquestos montes altivos.
Y para que sepas cuanto
Asombro es el que has vencido,
Darte relacion de mí
Este instante solicito.
Esa luminar antorcha,
Que desde su plaustro rico
El cielo ilumina á rayos,
El mundo describe á giros,
Ese planeta, que corre
Siempre hermoso, siempre vivo,
Llevándose tras sí el dia,
Fue el luciente padre mio.
Prima nací de Medea
En Tesalia, donde fuimos
Asombro de sus estudios,
Y de sus ciencias prodigio;
Porque enseñadas las dos
De un gran mágico, nos hizo
Docto escándalo del mundo,
Sabio portento del siglo:
Que en fin las mugeres, cuando
Tal vez aplicar se han visto
A las letras, ó á las armas,
Los hombres han excedido.
Y así, ellos envidiosos,
Viendo nuestro ánimo invicto,
Viendo sútil* nuestro ingenio,
Porque no fuera el dominio
Todo nuestro, nos vedaron

* Hartzenbusch reads *agudo*, see his edition,
t. i. p. 304.—Tr.

Grant that, showing thus thy thanks
To the heavens for their late pity,
For their mercy, to the fates,
It may beat its wings of linen
Tranquilly, without fatigue,
Whilst thou dost repair a little
The effects of that late danger
Which had flung thee almost shipwreck'd
At the foot of those tall cliffs.
And, that thou mayst know the mighty
Terror whom thou hast subdued,
I will give to thee this instant
An account of who I am.
Yonder torch of dazzling brightness
Which, from out its car of gold,
Heaven with glorious beams enlightens,
Earth encircles as it rolls;
That great star whose undiminish'd
Power and beauty lead along
Captive day untired, delighted,
Was my splendour-crownèd sire:
Being of Medea's kindred,
I with her, a child, was rear'd
In Thessalia as a sister,
Where we were its school's amazement,
And the wonder of its science;
For being there well taught, we two,
By a greatly-skill'd magician,
We became the learnèd marvel
Of the world, a lore-enlighten'd
Lamp portentous to the age,
For 'tis ascertain'd that women,
When to letters or to arms
They with resolute will apply them,
Oftentimes surpass the men.
Thus it is, by envy blinded,
Fearing our unvanquish'd spirit,
Dreading the result to witness
Of our quick intelligence,

Las espadas y los libros.
No te digo, que estudié
Con generoso motivo
Matemáticas, de quien
La filosofía principio
Fue ; no te digo, que al cielo
Los dos movimientos mido,
Natural y rapto, siendo
Ambos á un tiempo continuos ;
No te digo, que del sol
Los veloces cursos sigo,
Siendo cambiante cuaderno
De tornasoles y visos ;
No, que de la luna observo
Los resplandores mendigos ;
Pues una dádiva suya
Los hace pobres ó ricos ;
No te digo, que los astros,
Bien errantes, ó bien fijos,
En ese papel azul
Son mis letras : solo digo,
Que esto, aunque es estudio noble,
Fue para mi ingenio indigno ;
Pues pasando á mas empeños
La ambicion de mi albedrío,
El canto entiendo á las aves,
Y á las fieras los bramidos,
Siendo para mí patentes
Agüeros ó vaticinios.
Cuantos pájaros al aire
Vuelan, ramilletes vivos,
Dando á entender, que se llevan
La primavera consigo,
Renglones son para mí,
Ni señalados, ni escritos.
La harmonia de las flores,
Que en hermosos laberintos
Parece que es natural,
Sé yo bien que es artificio ;

Lest all empire should be given
Unto us, to us have they
Swords and books alike forbidden.
I say nothing of the zeal,
Truth inspired, with which I studied
Mathematics, on whose base
All philosophy is builded,
Or with what success I measured,
With a scientific niceness,
The two movements of the sky,
Each by days and years divided,
Both continuous at one time.
I say nought of my untirèd
Watching of the sun's swift course,
As it oped its ever-shifted
Gold-emblazon'd book of light,
Or the moon's poor pauper brightness,
Begg'd for from the sun, like alms,
Since its poverty and riches
Are his beams, refused or given.
I say nothing of the fixèd
Or slow-moving orbs on high
Being to me but letters written
On the heaven's cerulean page.
This alone I say, this singly,
That the study of this science,
Noble though it be, seem'd worthless
To my mind that sought the highest,
Since its free flight, soaring ever
In pursuit of new achievements,
Learn'd what meant the birds' sweet
    ditties,
And the howlings of the wild-beasts,
They to me becoming patent
Auguries or prophesyings.
When the rich-plumed birds sweep by me
Like to living nosegays lifted
High in air, the tidings telling
Of the sweet spring they bear with them,

Pues son imprenta,* en que el cielo
Estampa raros avisos.
Por las rayas de la mano
La quiromancía examino,
Cuando en ajadas arrugas
De la piel el fin admiro
Del hombre ; la geomancía
En la tierra, cuando escribo
Mis caractéres en ella ;
Y en ella tambien consigo
La piromancía, cuando
De su centro, de su abismo,
Hago abrirse las entrañas,
Y abortar á mis gemidos
Los difuntos, que responden,
De mi conjuro oprimidos.
¿ Mas qué mucho, si al infierno
Tal vez obediente he visto
Temblar de mí ? ¿ si tal vez
Sus espíritus aflijo ?
¿ Pero para qué te canso ?
¿ Pero para qué repito
Grandezas mias, si todas
En esta sola las cifro ?
Para que mejor pudiese
Entregarme á mis designios,
A Trinacria vine, donde
En este apartado sitio
Del Etna y del Lilibeo,
Estos palacios fabrico,
Deleitosas selvas fundo,
Y montes incultos finjo.
Aqui pues, siendo bandida
Emperatriz de sus riscos,
La vida cobro en tributo
De todos los peregrinos,
Que náufragos en el mar,
A la ley de su destino,

    * Hartzenbusch reads *planas*.—Tʀ.

They to me are secret ciphers,
Legible although unwritten.
Then the harmony of flowers,
In wild beauteous mazes mingled,
Though so natural it seemeth,
Well I know is artificial ;
Since upon their lovely leaves
Rare advices heaven imprinteth.
By the lines upon the hand
Palmistry's strange lore delights me,
When the destiny of man
In the skin's poor wither'd wrinkles
I can see.   And geomancy
On the earth, when I inscribe there
My mysterious characters ;
And with it I also mingle
Pyromancy, when from out
Earth's far centre, its abysses,
I command its womb to ope
And with groans bring forth the buried
Dead, who answer all I ask,
To my magic spells submitted.
And what wonder, when full oft
Hell itself is seen to shiver
With submissive fear before me,
When I question its lost spirits ?
But for what should I fatigue thee ?
But for what should I thus fritter
Time away, my greatness telling,
When this single proof suffices ?
That I might the better work
Out my plans uncheck'd, unwitness'd,
I Trinacria sought, where here,
In this lonely spot, which circle
Ætna and wild Lilybœum,
I these palaces have builded,
These delicious woods have planted
And with harvests clothed these hills here.
Being thus the brigand queen

Cerrado puerto de nieve,
Ofaron abrir caminos.
Y porque fuefe mi imperio
Mas raro y mas exquifito,
Efas fieras y efos troncos
Todos fon vafallos mios ;
Que los troncos y las fieras
Viven aqui con inftinto ;
Pues árboles racionales
Son hombres vegetativos.
Efta foy, y con mirar
El fol á mi voz rendido,
La luna á mi accion atenta,
Obediente á mi fufpiro
Toda la caterva hermofa
De los aftros y los fignos ;
Con faber, que, cuando quiero,
El cielo empaño, que vibro
Los rayos, que de las nubes
Aborto piedra y granizo,
Que hago eftremecer los montes,
Caducar los edificios,
Titubear todo efe mar
Y penetrar los abifmos ;
Y finalmente trocarfe
Los hombres fin albedrío
En varias formas, teniendo
Ya en las peñas obelifcos,
Ya en las cortezas fepulcro,
Y ya en las grutas afilo :
Hoy á tus plantas me poftro,
Hoy á tu valor me rindo,
Y como muger te ruego,
Como feñora té pido,
Como Emperatriz te mando,
Como fabia te fuplico,
No te aufentes, hafta tanto
Que hayas del hado vencido
El rigor, con que te trajo

Of this realm by rocks engirdled,
I as tribute claim the lives
Of all ftrangers who are fhipwreck'd ;
Daring through this lonely fea,
Yielding to a fate forewritten,
A prefumptuous path to cleave
Through this gulf by fnow-foam filver'd.
And, in order that my realm
Should be rareft and uniqueft,
I have made as vaffals mine
All thefe tree-trunks, all thefe wild beafts ;
For the wild beafts and the trees
Here poffefs peculiar inftincts,—
Vegetative men are they,
Trees with human reafon gifted.
This I am.   The fun fubmiffive
At my potent voice inclineth,
At my beck the moon doth liften,
At my breath, in prompt obedience,
All the beauteous troop of ftars,
And the zodiac figns and circles.
With the knowledge then that I
Can, whene'er I choofe, in mift-wreaths
Hide the heavens, can launch the
      lightnings,
Can from out the clouds parturient
Bring forth frozen fleet and ftones ;
That thefe mountains I can fhiver,
Shake to duft thefe edifices,
Cleave afunder the abyffes
Of the fea, and look within them ;
That, in fine, againft their will
I can change men to the likenefs
Of what form I pleafe, fome having
Obelifks of rocks to gird them,
Some their tombs in rough bark finding,
Some in grottoes their afylum ;
Still I throw me at thy feet,
To thy might to-day I yield me,

Derrotado y perſeguipo
A inculcar* aqueſtos mares.
Quédate unos dias conmigo ;
Verás trocado mi extremo
De riguroſo en benigno,
Con el guſto que te hoſpedo,
Con la atencion que te ſirvo ;
Siendo el Flegra deſde hoy,
No ya fiero, no ya eſquivo
Hoſpedage de Saturno,
Siempre en roja ſangre tinto ;
Selva ſí de Amor y Vénus,
Deleitoſo Paraiſo,
Donde ſea todo guſto,
Todo aplauſo, todo alivio,
Todo paz, todo deſcanſo.
Y no quieras mas indicio
De mi piedad, que ſer hoy
El primero que ha venido
A aqueſtos montes, á quien
Con algun afeéto miro,
Con algun agrado eſcucho,
Con algun cuidado aſiſto,
Con algun guſto deſeo,
Y con toda el alma eſtimo.

Uliſes (aparte).
No fuera Uliſes, ſi ya
Que á eſtos montes he venido,
La libertad no trajera
A cuantos aqui cautivos

* Probably a miſprint for *ſulcar*, which
Hartzenbuſch adopts.—Tʀ.

And as ſimple woman aſk thee,
As a lady I deſire thee,
As a ſovereign I command thee,
As a ſage with tears invite thee,
Not to go from this, until
Thou haſt well ſubdued the rigour
Of the fate that hither drove thee,
Toſt, abandon'd, anger-ſmitten,
Through theſe dangerous ſeas to ſteer
    thee.
Here remain ſome few days with me,
And thou'lt ſee my rude behaviour
Change to more exceſſive mildneſs,
In thy joyful entertainment,
In the attention I will give thee.
Phlegra from this day ſhall be
Not that dreadful, not that fiery,
Dwelling-houſe of Saturn which
Ever is with red blood tinted ;
But a grove of Love and Venus,
An elyſium where unmixèd
Joy ſhall reign, a bower of pleaſure,
Full of rapture, full of bliſſes,
Calm repoſe and ſweet refreſhment.
And thou needeſt have no higher
Proof of my good will than this,
That of all who have come hither
To theſe mountains, thou'rt the firſt
Whom I ſee with aught of kindneſs,
Whom I hear with any pleaſure,
Whom I have in aught aſſiſted,
Whom with any joy I wiſh for,
And whom all my ſoul deſireth.
Ulyſſes (aſide).
I were not Ulyſſes if,
Now that 'mid theſe hills I find me,
I did not reſtore to freedom
All thoſe captives whom bewitchment
Holds impriſon'd here.   To-day

Tiene el encanto. Hoy seré
De aquella Esfinge el Edipo.
    Antistes (aparte á el).
Señor, no de sus lisonjas
Te creas, porque es fingido
Su halago.
    Lebrel.
      Huyamos de aqui.
    Circe.
Qué dices, Ulíses?
    Ulíses.
      Digo,
Que no pudiera ser noble
Quien no fuese agradecido,
Y que conmigo he de ser
Cruel, por ser cortes contigo.
    Casandra (aparte).
Ay de tí! porque no sabes
A lo que te has atrevido.
    Circe.
Pídeme pues en albricias
Una merced.
    Ulíses.
      Solo pido,
Que estos dos árboles, que hoy
A lástima me han movido,
Porque fue mi acero causa
De aumentarles su martirio,
En pago de aquesto, sean
A la luz restituidos.
    Circe.
Este árbol Flérida, una

I will prove myself this sphinx's
Œdipus through all her lures.
    Antistes (aside to him).
Ah! my lord, do not confide thee
To her flatteries : her endearments
All are feign'd.
    Lebrel.
      Ah! let us fly hence.
    Circe.
What, Ulysses, say'st thou ?
    Ulysses.
      This,
That *his* nature were unknightly
Who could thankless be for kindness,
And that *I* must be self-cruel,
Thee to treat with due politeness.
    Cassandra (aside).
Woe to thee! thou little knowest
What thy boldness enterpriseth.
    Circe.
Ask me then by way of earnest
For some favour.
    Ulysses.
      I ask simply
That these two trees which to-day
Moved so much my grief and pity,
Since my sword unwittingly
Upon *them* new pain inflicted,*
Shall, in recompense of this,
Back to living light be given.
    Circe.
This tree here was Flerida,

---

* This is not explained. Nothing is said throughout the entire play from which it can be inferred how the sword of Ulysses augmented the suffering which Flerida and Lysidas endured under their transformation into trees. Perhaps in some passage which is suppressed there may have been a theatrical trick or artifice introduced to which this is an allusion; for instance, Ulysses might have struck with his sword these trees, from which blood might have issued—HARTZENBUSCH.

Divina hermofura, ha fido,	Who, with rareft beauty gifted,
Dama mia, y mi privanza.	Was my confidential lady.
Rindió al amor fu albedrío,	She to love her free heart yielded,
Enamorada de un jóven,	Being enamour'd of a youth,
Lífidas en fu apellido,	Lyfidas by name, entitled
Heredero de Tofcana,	To the fair Etrufcan kingdom,
Que de efe mar peregrino	Who upon this fea a pilgrim
Salió á tierra; y porque ofados	Landed here : and for their daring
Profanaron el retiro	To profane the calm retirement
De mi palacio, afi yacen	Of my palace, thus they lie,
En árboles convertidos ;	Into two fair trees transfigured ;
Porque, aunque yo fiera y monftruo,	Since, though monftrous I may feem,
Tan dada foy á los vicios,	Subject to fo many vices,
Solos delitos de amor	Love's offences are by me
Fueron para mí delitos ;	But the fole ones unforgiven ;
Tanto, que Arfidas, valiente	So much fo, that Arfidas,
Jóven y Príncipe invicto	A brave youth, Trinacria's prince here,
De Trinacria, á cuyo imperio	From whofe fceptre thefe proud hills
Eftos montes tiranizo,	I have fever'd and divided,
Con faber que enamorado	Knowing that inflamed with love
De mi hermofura ha venido,	Of my beauty he came hither,
No ha merecido tener	Merited no greater boon
· Mas favor, que volver vivo.	Than to get back with his life hence.
Pero ya que es la primera	But as this is the firft thing
Cofa, que tú me has pedido,	Thou haft afk'd that I fhould give thee,
Flérida y Lífidas rompan	Flerida and Lyfidas,
Las prifiones que han tenido.	Burft the prifon bonds that bind ye.

[Abrenfe dos árboles, y falen
FLÉRIDA y LÍSIDAS.

[The trees open and FLERIDA and
LYSIDAS come forth.

Lífidas.

Lyfidas.

Torpe el difcurfo, atado el penfamiento,	Dull was my mind, embarrafs'd was my thought,
La razon ciega, el ánimo oprimido,	Blind was my reafon, and my mind oppreft,
Sin ufo el alma, el corazon rendido,	Ufelefs my foul, my heart by fear oppreft,
Muda la voz, y tímido el aliento ;	Mute was my voice, and all my brain diftraught ;
Sin voluntad, memoria, entendimiento,	
Vivo cadáver de efte tronco he fido.	
Ya pues, que me quitabas el fentido,	
Quitárafme tambien el fentimiento.	

Si de amar (ay de mí) á Flérida bella,
  Caſtigo fue eſta forma, en vano
    quieres,
  Que yo me olvide, porque vivo en ella.
Los troncos aman : luego mal infieres,
  Que, por ſer tronco, venceré mi
    eſtrella,
  Pues no la vences tú, y mas ſabia eres.

Flérida.
Racional, vegetable y ſenſitiva
  Alma el cielo le dió al ſugeto humano ;
  Vegetable y ſenſible al bruto uſano ;
  Al tronco y á la flor vegetativa.
Tres almas ſon ; ſi de las dos me priva
  Tu voz, porque amo á Liſidas, en
    vano
  Solicitas mi olvido, pues es llano
  Que, aun tronco, alma me dejas con
    que viva.
No de todo mi amor tendrá la palma
  La parte, en que has querido con-
    ſervarme ;
  De aquella ſí, que permitió eſta calma :
Luego mudarme en tronco, no es
    mudarme ;
  Porque ſi no me quitas toda el alma,
  Todo el amor no has de poder qui-
    tarme

Without the power to will or think of
    aught,
  A breathing corſe I lived this ſtrange
    tree's gueſt :
  Ah ! ſince thou took'ſt the feeling
    from my breaſt,
  Why not the pain that all this ſuffering
    wrought ?
If 'twas for loving Flerida the fair
  I thus was puniſh'd, then how vainly
    tries
  Thy wrath to kill the love that lives
    in her ;—
Trees even love ;—the ſtar that rules my
    ſkies
  If thou doſt ſeek to darken, thou doſt
    err,
  Since thou art foil'd although thou art
    more wiſe.

Flerida.
Life, reaſon, feeling, Heaven's all-wiſe
    decree
  Unites commingled in man's heart and
    brain,
  Feeling and life in beaſts that ſcour the
    plain,
  And life alone in budding flower and
    tree.
Theſe are three ſouls : if two out of the
    three
  I loſe for loving Lyſidas, in vain
  Thou ſeek'ſt that I forget him, ſince
    'tis plain
  That, though a tree, a ſoul ſtill dwells
    in me.
Thoſe I have loſt do not contain the
    whole
  Of that fond love that thy dread wrath
    could wake,

H

Circe.
Agradeced vueſtras vidas
Al huéſped, que me ha venido,
Y vivid los dos ſeguros
Por él ya de mis caſtigos,
Como de vueſtros amores
No deis el mas leve indicio.
    Liſidas.
Siempre, Ulíſes, me tendrás
A tus pies agradecido.
    Flérida.
Y ſiempre confeſaré,
Que por cuenta tuya vivo.
    Circe.
Pues porque empiecen á ſer
Deſde hoy aplauſos feſtivos
Todo el monte, todo el valle,
Todo el mar y todo el ſitio,
Volved á cantar, y todos
Con él volved, y conmigo.
    Múſica.
En hora dichoſa venga
A los palacios de Circe
El rayo de los Troyanos,
El diſcreto y fuerte Ulíſes:
En hora diſchoſa venga . . . .

    Sale ARSIDAS.

    Arſidas.
No venga en hora dichoſa,
Felice en deſprecio mio,

The one I keep is free from thy
    control ;
To change me thus doth ſeem a ſtrange
    miſtake,
    Becauſe if thou doſt take not all my
    ſoul,
    All of my love thou haſt not power to
    take.
    Circe.
For your new-recover'd lives
Thank the gueſt who ſtands beſide me,
And be ſure henceforth that I
Shall not with new pains chaſtiſe ye,
If you give not of your loves
Any new hint to remind me.
    Lyſidas.
Ever ſhalt thou ſee me lie
Grateful at thy feet, Ulyſſes.
    Flerida.
And for ever ſhall I own
Thine the life this day thou giv'ſt me.
    Circe.
Then in order that from this
Our glad feſtive notes ſhould circle
Round the mountain, round the valley,
Round the ſea and all it girdles,
Raiſe the ſtrain once more, and lead
Him and me back thus united.
    Song.
Be the hour propitious when
To the palace-halls of Circe
Comes the terror-bolt of Troy
The diſcreet and bold Ulyſſes,—
Bright, propitious be the hour . . . .

    Enter ARSIDAS.

    Arſidas.
Be it not propitious when
He comes here in my deſpiſal,

Ni el que fue sepulcro á tantos,
Hoy á uno solo sea alivio.
Peligre en la tierra quien
Por aquesos mares vino,
En su sombra tropezando,
De un peligro á otro peligro.
Ese acento harmonioso,
Que le saluda benigno,
Airado trueque en endechas
Tristes, fúnebres caistros
Las cláusulas, porque sean
De sus tragedias aviso ;
Que no es justo, no, que un Griego
Extrangero, advenedizo,
De tanto usado rigor
Venga á mudar el estilo.
¿ Desde cuándo, Circe bella,
Con tanto aplauso festivo,
Con tan alegre aparato,
Tanto noble regocijo
Al forastero saludas,
Recibes al peregrino,
Sin que este mar, ó estas peñas
Le sirvan de precipicio,
O ya convertido en fiera,
O ya en árbol convertido,
Tenga en las peñas su estancia,
Tenga en las grutas su asilo?
Príncipe soy de Trinacria :
No derrotado y perdido
Llegué á este puerto, pues vine
De mis afectos traido,
Porque aun aquesto tambien
Debieses á mi albedrío ;
Que no quiso, no, el que solo
Porque le fue fuerza quiso,
Ni es sacrificio, no siendo
Voluntario el sacrificio.
Y en cuanto tiempo estos montes,

Nor the grave-yard of so many
Prove a solace to him singly ;
Let him who these wild seas dared
On the land endure new risks here,
From one danger to another
Ever treading as he flieth.
Let this softly-cadenced strain,
Which saluteth him benignly,
Change to mournful wails of woe,
Hoarsely change to funeral dirges,
Prophesying thus to him
What the tragic future bringeth.
For it is not fit that he,
A Greek stranger, a benighted
Alien, should come here to change
Thine accustom'd form of rigour,
Since what time, O Circe fair !
With such festal songs and timbrels,
With such joyful preparation,
With a proud display so princely,
Dost thou thus salute the stranger,
Thus receive the wretch here driven,
Without making these steep rocks,
Sea-wash'd, be his precipices,
Or transform'd into a tree,
Or transmuted to a wild-beast,
Make him hold 'mid cliffs his dwelling,
Amid grottoes his asylum ?
Of Trinacria Prince am I :—
Not as one nigh lost and ship-wreck'd
Came I to this port, but drawn
By my true love came I hither,
That my heart's free-will should be
Thus a new claim to thy pity :—
Since he loves not, he who only
Loves because some force inciteth,
And if not spontaneous, all
Sacrifice is worse than idle.
And since sight of thee has been

Por folo mirarte, vivo,
No he debido á tu rigor,
Ni á tu crueldad he debido
Una accion, á quien me mueftre
Guftofo, ni agradecido;
Tanto, que aun de tus encantos
Libre, eftos campos afifto,
Porque en tantos fentimientos
No me faltafen fentidos.
Pues dos hombres folamente
Los que nos libramos fuimos,
Ulífes y yo, porque
Todo hoy en defprecio mio
Refulte; pues fi los dos
Nos refervamos, ha fido
Ulífes para gozarlo,
Y Arfidas para fentirlo.

Ulífes.
Si de mi dicha envidiofo,
Si de mi fuerte ofendido . . . .
       Circe.
Calla, Arfidas, fi conoces,
Que la vida te permito,
Porque es la mayor venganza
Que tomo, como tú has dicho,
Dejarte vivir, teniendo
Sentimientos y fentidos.
Quejarte de mí, es decirme,
Que lo que bufco configo;
Y afi, porque tú te quejes,
Yo la caufa no te quito.—
Cantad, cantad, y tú ven,
Ulífes, al lado mio.
     Lebrel (á Clarin).
No fon muy malas las dos
Circecillas de poquito.

'Mid thefe hills my fole exiftence,
I owe little to thy rigour,
To thy cruelty as little,
Nought for which to thee fhould I
Joy or gratitude exhibit,
Only that exempt from all
Thy enchantments, I can vifit
Thefe dread fields, in order that
For the forrows that afflict me
Human fenfes fhould not fail.
Since then but two men are fingled
Out of all the world, to whom
Freedom from thy fpell is given,
This Ulyffes and myfelf,—
Ah! the exemption but inflicteth
A new pang, a frefh defpifal;
Since if we are both preferved,
'Tis with more malign refinement
To give pain to Arfidas,
To give rapture to Ulyffes.
       Ulyffes.
If thou envieft my good fortune,
If my happier fate afflicts thee . . . .
       Circe.
Ceafe, O Arfidas! if thou
Knoweft that I have permitted
Thee to live, fince greater vengeance
I could take not, as admitted
By thyfelf, than with thy life
Feelings and their food to give thee.
To complain is but to tell me
That I have obtain'd my wifhes,
And that thou mayft ftill complain,
I the caufe fhall ftill leave with thee.
Sing, fing, and at my fide
Come unto my court, Ulyffes.
     Lebrel (afide to Clarin).
Not fo very bad thefe two,
Circe's little fervant Circelets.

Clarin (á Lebrel).
No hay que volver á dar cartas ;
Que yo las tomo, y no miro.

Aſtrea (aparte).
Habíanme dicho, que eran
Los Griegos feos y eſquivos,
Y ni eſquivos ſon, ni feos,
Tanto como me habian dicho.
Líſidas.
¡Gracias á Amor, que otra vez,
Flérida hermoſa, te miro !
Flérida.
¡ Gracias, Líſidas, á Amor
Que otra vez á amarte vivo !
Circe (aparte).
Vencerále mi hermoſura,
Pues mi ciencia no ha podido.
Ulíſes (aparte).
Libraré de aquella fiera
A Trinacria, ſi amor finjo.
Arſidas (aparte).
Solo zelos me faltaban,
Ya eſtá todo el mal cumplido.
Muſica.
En hora dichoſa venga, &c.

Clarin (to Lebrel).
Don't mind ſhuffling ; I will take
My chance of trumps and win though
 blinded.
Aſtrea (aſide).
They have told me that the Greeks
All were ſcornful and unſightly ;
But nor ugly nor ſo coy
Are they as they have been libell'd.
Lyſidas.
Thanks to Love, fair Flerida,
That once more thy face I witneſs !
Flerida.
Thanks to Love, I live once more,
Lyſidas, my heart to give thee !
Circe (aſide).
Let my beauty him ſubdue,
Since ſo powerleſs was my ſcience !
Ulyſſes (aſide).
I, by feigning love, may free
Fair Trinacria from this wild-beaſt.
Arſidas (aſide).
I but needed jealouſy
My full cup of woe to embitter.
Song.
Be the hour propitious when
To the palace-halls of Circe
Comes the never-vanquiſh'd Greek,
The invincible Ulyſſes !
[*Exeunt, all ſinging.*

JORNADA II.

Salen Circe, *llorando*, Flerida, Tisbe,
Casandra, Astrea, Libia, *y* Clori.

Libia.

EÑORA, qué llanto es este ?
    Astrea.
    ¿ Qué pena, señora, es esta ?

Clori.
¿ Tú lágrimas en los ojos ?
    Flérida.
¿ Tú suspiros, y tú quejas ?
    Tisbe.
¿ Qué ocasion pudo moverte
A que sentimientos tengas ?
    Casandra.
Los males comunicados,
Si no se vencen, se templan.
    Circe.
¡ Quien tiene de que quejarse,
O cuanto en quejarse yerra !
Que la justicia del llanto
Hace apacibles las penas.
Yo asi mi tristeza quiero,
Que tan poco no me deba,

ACT THE SECOND.

CIRCE'S PALACE.

Enter Circe *in tears, attended by* Flerida, Thisbe, Cassandra, Astrea,
Libia *and* Chloris.

Libia.

LADY, what lament is this ?
    Astrea.
    Ah, my lady, whence this
    sadness ?
    Chloris.
Canst thou fill thine eyes with tears ?
    Flerida.
Sob and sigh like one distracted ?
    Thisbe.
Say what sudden cause of grief
Can thy senses thus have master'd ?
    Cassandra.
The confiding of our ills
If it cures not, mitigates them.
    Circe.
He who for complaint hath cause,
Oh ! how errs he who complaineth !
Since the justice of his plaining
Turns his very grief to gladness.
I so love my source of sorrow,
Feel so much its sweet advantage,

Que en repetirla procure
Hacer menor mi triſteza.
Dejadme ſola.
   Aſtrea (aparte las dos).
    Oyes, Libia ?

   Libia.
Razonablemente, Aſtrea.
    Aſtrea.
¡ Plegue á Amor, que eſtos extremos
Lo que yo pienſo no ſean !
   Libia.
¡ Plegue al Amor, que ſi haga !
Que es lo que plegamos pienſa :
Pues ſi es amor la ocaſion
Dellos, y ella á verſe llega
Enamorada, dará . . . .
    Aſtrea.
Qué ?
   Libia.
   Libertad de conciencia.
    Aſtrea.
Holgaréme de ſalir
De religion tan eſtrecha,
Como es el honor. Veſtales
Vírgenes Diana celebra
Entre gentes, mas noſotras
Entre animales y fieras   ,
Somos vírgenes beſtíales.

   Libia.
Calla, porque no lo entienda.
   [*Vanſe todas las Damas,*
    menos FLERIDA.
   Circe.
Flérida, tú no te auſentes :
Sola conmigo te queda,
Que tengo que hablarte ſola.

That I would not by repeating
Take one ſting from out my ſadneſs.
Leave me here alone.
   Aſtrea (to Libia).
    Canſt hearken,
Libia ?

   Libia.
   Pretty well, Aſtrea.
    Aſtrea.
Love but.grant that theſe exceſſes
Are not what my fear doth fancy !
   Libia.
Love but grant they are, if it
Fancieth what we both ſigh after !
Since if their true ſource be love,
If ſhe has her own heart granted
To love's ſway, ſhe'll give us . . . .
    Aſtrea.
       What ?
   Libia.
Liberty of conſcience, may be.
    Aſtrea.
I indeed were glad to free me
From a worſhip ſo contracted,
And ſo ſtrict as honour is.
Great Diana celebrateth
Among men her feſtal choirs
Of veſtal virgins, but, unhappy !
We poor beſtial virgins ſeem
Among beaſts who growl and chatter.
   Libia.
Silence, left ſhe overhear us !
   [*Exeunt all the ladies and at-*
    tendants but FLERIDA.
   Circe.
Flerida, in the others' abſence
I would ſpeak with thee alone
Of a certain private matter :
Stay thou here with me.

Flérida (aparte).
Sin duda, cielos, que intenta
Darme castigo mayor,
Que el que en la dura corteza
Tuve, porque hablé esta tarde
A Lísidas.

   Circe.
      Oye atenta:
Este Ulíses, este Griego,
Que esa marítima bestia
Sorbió sin duda en el mar,
Para escupirle en la tierra;
Este, que á la discrecion
De los vientos, con deshecha
Fortuna, tan derrotado
Llegó á tocar estas selvas;
Este, que trajo deidad
Superior en su defensa,
Pues, burlando mis encantos,
Les tiraniza la fuerza;
Este pues, que mi hospedage
Cortesanamente acepta,
Adonde hoy tan divertido
Vive, olvidado de Grecia:
Como si fuera mi vida
Troya, ha introducido en ella
Tanto fuego, que en cenizas
No dudo que se resuelva;
Y con razon; porque ya
En callado fuego envuelta,
Cada aliento es un Volcan,
Cada suspiro es un Etna.
Quisiera .... quisiera dije?
Mal empecé; pues si es fuerza
Querer, Flérida, y ya quiero,
Erré en decir, que quisiera.
Quiero, digo; pero quiero
Tanto á mi ambicion atenta,
Que quiero á Ulíses, y no

Flerida (aside).
      O heavens!
Doubtless now her anger planneth
Some new punishment, severer
Than the hard bark that enwrapp'd me,
Since this evening I have spoken
Unto Lysidas.

   Circe.
      Now, mark me;
This Ulysses, this Greek king,
Whom the sea—that mighty kraken—
Doubtless swallow'd on the ocean
To outspew him on the land here;
He who at the wild wind's listing,
So forsaken, so storm-shaken,
Came to anchor by these groves;
He who calleth in his danger
On some mightier god to aid him,
Since despising my enchantments
O'er their power he tyranniseth:
He who courteously hath granted
All my hospitable wishes,
And a glad guest at my table,
Lives forgetful now of Greece.
He it is who in my heart here
(Ah! as if 'twere Troy) hath kindled
Such a fire, that soon in ashes
Doubtless it must be dissolved;
And with reason, since already
Wrapp'd in hidden flames it burns,
Every breath it breathes volcanic,
Every sigh an Ætna seems.
I would love him .... *would* love!—
   badly
I begin in saying " would ;"
Since, if doom'd to love, I madly
Yield to Fate, I err in saying
I *would* love when love hath happen'd.
Him I say I love, but love

Quiero, que Ulíses lo entienda.	With an eye of fuch exactnefs
Ahora te admirarás	To decorum, that I wifh
De que yo, que tan foberbia	He fhould know not my attachment.
Tu amor reñí, te fie el mio ;	Wonder now that I who late
Pero admiraráfte necia ;	Chid thy love with fo much anger,
Porque la caufa mayor,	Should confide to thee my own ;
Porque la ocafion mas cierta	But thy wonder is the vainest,
De incurrir en una culpa,	Since the greateft caufe of all,
Es haber dicho mal della.	The fure fource that never faileth,
Y porque el contar delitos,	Of committing any fault,
A quien es cómplice, cuefta	Is fometimes to reprimand it.
Menos vergüenza, yo quife	And becaufe confeffing crimes
Recatear efta vergüenza,	To an accomplice doth o'ermantle
Y porque me cuefte menos,	The flufh'd face with blufhes lefs,
Decirlos á quien los fepa.	I defire to drive this hardeft
Yo amo en fin, Flérida mia ;	Bargain with my blufhes thus,
Vengada eftás de mi ofenfa.	And to make my heart's crimes ftand me
¡ Pluguiera á Júpiter fanto,	A lefs price, to tell them thee,
Tú trasformarme pudieras	Who fo well can underftand them.
A mí en infenfible planta,	Ah ! my Flerida, I love !—
Que yo te lo agradeciera !	Now thou art avenged with ample
Porque fi fupiera entonces	Juftice for my bygone wrong.
Lo que es amor, mas quifiera	Would that facred Jove might grant thee
Verte enamorada y viva,	Power, through magic transformation,
Que no enamorada y muerta.	To a fenfelefs plant to change me !
Enamorada en efecto	Oh ! how thankful would I be !
Llego, y pues tú á faber llegas.	Since, if at that time, exactly
Qué es amor, de tí pretendo	I knew what was love, enamour'd
Ayudar una cautela ;	I would fee thee living, rather
Y es, que para poder yo	Than enamour'd not and dead.
Hablar con él, fin que él fepa	Since then love is fuperadded
Que foy yo la que le habla,	To my paft experience, and
Tú con ruegos y finezas	'Thou too knoweft love's enthralments,
Le has de enamorar de dia,	In a little ftratagem
Y diciéndole que venga	I expect that thou wilt aid me ;
De noche á hablarte, eftaré	And it is,—that I may fpeak
Yo con tu nombre encubierta,	With him, without any danger
Donde mi altivez, mi honor,	Of his knowing that 'tis I [thee
Mi vanidad, mi foberbia,	Who fpeak *with* him ; thou muft mafk

Mi refpeto, mi decoro
No fe rindan, y . . . .

          Flérida.
                Oye, efpera,
Que quieres hacer en mí
Dos coftofas experiencias.
Yo amo á Lífidas, y tú
Cruel, feñora, me ordenas,
Que difimule el amarle ;
Yo no amo á Ulífes, é intentas,
Que finja amarle. ¿ Pues cómo,
A dos afectos atenta,
Quieres, que olvide á quien quiero,
Y que á quien olvido quiera?
Damas tienes con quien hoy
Partir los afectos puedas ;
A una alma bafta un cuidado.
         Circe.
Y aun la mifma caufa es efa ;
Yo fé, que quien llega á eftar
Enamorada, no deja
Lugar para otro cuidado
En el alma : luego acierta
Quien á ella el fuyo le fia,
Porque no peligra en ella
El riefgo de enamorarfe,
Pues ya lo eftá ; de manera,
Que tú no me darás zelos,
Y otra sí, cuando te vea
Con Ulífes ; pues tu amor
Sanea la contingencia.

So in foft requefts and fmiles,
So by day his heart entangle,
That when thou requir'ft that he
Meet thee nightly in the garden,
I may take thy place, conceal'd
'Neath thy name as 'neath a mantle,
Where my haughtinefs, my honour,
Where the pride on which I trample,
My decorum, felf-refpect
May be fafe from . . . .
          Flerida.
            Hear, oh! hearken :
For thou wouldft attempt on me
Two experiments the hardeft.
I love Lyfidas, and thou,
Lady, fternly wouldft command me
To diffemble that I love him ;
I Ulyffes love not, nathlefs
Thou defireft I fhould feign fo ;
How, by two defires diftracted,
Can I think of the ne'er thought of,
And forget the never abfent?—
Ladies haft thou here with whom
Thou thy feelings thus may parcel ;
To one heart one care's enough.
         Circe.
It is therefore that I afk thee,
Since I know that whofoever
Is in love, can keep vacated
Heart-fpace for no alien care :
Safe then is he who imparteth
His heart's love to fuch an one,
Since in love itfelf, the latter
Runs no danger of becoming
His friend's rival ; in this manner
Thou no jealoufy wilt give me,
Even when I fee thou ftandeft
By Ulyffes fide,—thy love
Bailing the contingent danger.

Efto ha de fer en efecto.—
¿ Mas qué ruido es efe ?
       Flérida.
              Llegan
Dos criados aqui, y traen
Sin duda alguna pendencia.
       Circe.
Retírate ; que no quiero,
Que á todas horas me vean,
Y efcuchemos defde aqui
Lo que tratan en mi aufencia.
           [*Retíranfe.*

    Sale LEBREL *y* CLARIN.
       Lebrel.
Digo, que es la mejor vida,
Que tuve en mi vida, aquefta.
       Clarin.
Efo dices ?
       Lebrel.
       Efto digo ;
Y que en el mundo no hay tierra
Como Trinacria, y que Circe
Es un ángel en belleza
Y condicion.
       Clarin.
      Eftás loco ?
       Lebrel.
Dime, ¿ ella no nos hofpeda
Como á unos reyes ?
       Clarin.
         Es cierto ;
Mas mucho mejor nos fuera,
Que en fus palacios, eftar
En un bodegon de Grecia.
       Lebrel.
¿ No comemos lindamente ?
       Clarin.
No ; que no hay comida buena

This thou muft in fine contrive.—
But what noife is this ?
       Flerida.
            Two valets
Hither come, engaged no doubt
In fome fcolding match or quarrel.
       Circe.
Step a little back, I would not
Have them every moment pafs me,
And we'll hear from this, how they
Treat me when they think me abfent.
           [*They retire.*

    Enter LEBREL *and* CLARIN.
       Lebrel.
I ftill fay, no fweeter life
Have I in my whole life tafted.
       Clarin.
Can you fay fo ?
       Lebrel.
         This I fay,—
That Trinacria is the marvel
Of the whole world, and that Circe
Is in form and face an angel
Of perfection.
       Clarin.
      Art thou mad ?
       Lebrel.
Tell me, are we not here treated
As if we were kings ?
       Clarin.
        'Tis true,
But a better place, I fancy,
For us were a Grecian cook-fhop,
Than thefe palaces of marble.
       Lebrel.
Don't we eat though fumptuoufly ?
       Clarin.
No, 'tis not a pleafant banquet

Adonde no doy bocado,
Que no pienſe, que me deja
Hecho un cochino.
       Lebrel.
           No es eſo
Tan malo como tú pienſas;
Que yo lo fui, y no me hallaba
Mal con ſerlo; de manera,
Que á cuantos cochinos hay
Sin aliño y ſin limpieza,
Diſculpo, porque ſe ahorran
De muchas impertinencias.
Y al caſo, ¿dónde hallarás
Una cama tan compueſta?

      Clarin.
No eſtá el deſcanſo en la cama;
Ni hay pícaro, que no duerma
Sin penas en un pajar
Mejor, que un ſeñor con ellas
En una cama dorada.
      Lebrel.
¿Dónde eſtos jardines vieras?
      Clarin.
¿Para qué quiero jardines?
      Lebrel.
Cogíte: ¿dónde tuvieras
Dos mozas de tan buen aire,
Como ſon Libia y Aſtrea?
      Clarin.
Daréme por concluido
En tocándome eſa tecla;
Pero no confeſaré,
Que Circe no es una fiera,
Nigromante, encantadora,
Energúmena, hechicera,
Súcuba, íncuba; y en fin
Es, por acabar el tema,
Con los demonios demonia,

Where I ſcarce can take a mouthful,
But I think I'm tranſmigrated
To a hog.
      Lebrel.
      That's not ſo bad
By one half as you imagine;
I was one ſome time, and found me
Nought the worſe for what had happen'd;
So that now when I behold
Happy pigs, unkempt, untrammell'd,
Wallowing in the mire, I give them
My forgiveneſs, ſince their manners
Save them from much uſeleſs trouble.
To the point though; where, my maſter,
Have you ſuch a ſoft bed found?
      Clarin.
Reſt comes not from bed or blanket;
Not a beggar but ſleeps better
On his ſcanty ſtraw-ſtrewn pallet,
Free of care, than doth a lord
Rack'd with *his*, upon his grand bed.
      Lebrel.
Where ſuch gardens have you ſeen?
      Clarin.
Gardens? what care I for gardens?
      Lebrel.
Now I have you, tell me where
Have you ſeen two girls, the matches
Of fair Lybia and Aſtrea?
      Clarin.
Well to that there's but one anſwer;
You have touch'd the chord at laſt;
But I won't confeſs ſo gladly,
Circe is not a wild-beaſt,
A demoniac, a witch-charmer,
An hobgoblin, a wild vampire;
And in fine to end our quarrel,
A ſhe-devil among demons,
A duenda among fairies.

Como, con los duendes duenda.
    Circe (aparte á Flérida).
No puedo fufrir ya mas
El efcuchar mis ofenfas.
    Flérida.
No te des por entendida.
    Clarin.
Y es Circe . . . .

    Salen Circe y Flerida.

    Circe.
        Qué es?
    Clarin.
        Una Reina,
Y á quien dijere otra cofa,
Le daré, porque no mienta,
Dos mil palos, como uno.—
        [á Lebrel.
Y á tí, porque no te atrevas
A hablar mal de las feñoras
Doñas Circes en fu aufencia,
Yo te haré . . . .
    Lebrel.
       ¿ Pues quién hablaba
Mal, fino tú ?
    Clarin.
       Buena es efa ;
¿ A mí por los filos ?
    Circe.
       Bafta.
    Lebrel.
Yo . . . .
    Circe.
    Bien eftá.
    Clarin (aparte).
       El cielo quiera,
Que no oyefe lo demas.
    Lebrel.
¡ Que tan gran mentira creas!

    Circe (afide to Flerida).
Oh! I can't endure to let
This infulting fcene go farther.
    Flerida.
Do not feem as if you heard them.
    Clarin.
Circe is . . . .

    Circe *and* Flerida *advance.*

    Circe.
    Pray what?
    Clarin.
        A lady,
And a queen, and who denies it
I will teach him better manners,
By two thoufand blows at leaft.
        [to Lebrel.
As for you becaufe you gabbled
Something naughty of the noble
Lady Circes in their abfence,
I will make . . . .
    Lebrel.
       Why, who fpoke badly
But yourfelf?
    Clarin.
       Well, that is cool!
Would you turn the tables?
    Circe.
        Mark me.
    Lebrel.
I . . . .
    Circe.
    'Tis well.
    Clarin (afide).
       Heaven grant that fhe
Did not hear our tittle-tattle !
    Lebrel.
Who'd believe fo great a liar ?

Circe.
Yo fé bien lo que es verdad.
Vos os falid allá fuera ;
Que yo haré, que mi caftigo
Hoy efcarmiente la lengua,
Que habló mal de mí.
     Clarin.
          Y ferá
Muy jufto.
     Lebrel.
     Que efto fuceda ! [*Vafe.*

     Circe.
A tí, en pago de que afi
Hoy mis acciones defiendas,
Te quiero dar un teforo,
Con que á Grecia rico vuelvas.
De efe monte en lo intrincado
Llamarás con voces fieras
Tres veces á Brutamonte ;
Que él te dará la refpuefta.

     Clarin.
Mil veces tus plantas befo ;
Que bien tu gran valor mueftras.
A toda ley, hablar bien.
¡ Qué haya hombres de mala lengua !
            [*Vafe.*
     Flérida.
¿ Cómo caftigas, feñora,
Al que te defiende, y premias
Al que te ofende ?
     Circe.
         A fu tiempo
Verás el premio que lleva.

     Sale ASTREA.

     Aftrea.
Ulífes defde fu cuarto

Circe.
I know well the truth of the matter.
Go, and wait without : to-day
I fhall make a dread example
Of the faucy tongue that dared
To infult me.
     Clarin.
        And 't will be
Only juft.
     Lebrel.
     That this fhould happen !
            [*Exit.*
     Circe.
As for thee, to pay thy zeal
In defence of the way I act here,
I intend a gift to give thee,
With which rich to Greece thou'lt
    travel :—
Deep within this mountain's thickets,
Thou fhalt call out loud and fharply
Three times upon Brutamonte,
Who will give to thee thy anfwer.
     Clarin.
At thy feet a thoufand kiffes,
Thou, who knoweft to act fo grandly :
Civil fpeaking is my motto,
Oh ! that men fhould ufe bad language !
            [*Exit.*
     Flerida.
How is it thou doft punifh, lady,
Thy defender, and rewardeft
Him who wronged thee ?
     Circe.
          In due time,
Thou'lt perceive why thus I've acted.

     Enter ASTREA.

     Aftrea.
From his quarter comes Ulyffes

Al tuyo pasa.
      Circe.
        Aqui empieza
Del amor y la altivez
La mas cautelosa guerra,
Pues no he de dar por vencida
La que quiero que se venza.
            [*Vanse.*

JARDIN.

Salen ULÍSES, CIRCE, FLÉRIDA, LÍ-
SIDAS, ANTÍSTES, ARQUELAO, LE-
BREL, CLARIN, CASANDRA, *Damas,*
Griegos, Musicos.

     Ulíses (aparte).
Temeroso vengo, ay triste !
A ver á Circe, si es fuerza
Que como sabia la admire,
Y la admire como bella.
¡ Quién no se hubiera fiado
Tanto de sí ! ¡ quién no hubiera
Hecho cautela el quedarse !
Pues ya contra su cautela
Es imposible olvidarla,
Y es imposible quererla.
      Circe.
En este hermoso jardin,
Adonde la primavera
Llamó las flores á cortes,
Para jurar por su reina
A la rosa, que teñida
En sangre de Vénus bella
Púrpura viste real,
Generoso honor de Grecia,
En tanto que de una caza
Boreal el término llega,
Que será luego que el sol
Vaya perdiendo la fuerza,

To wait on thee.
      Circe.
        Here at last then
'Twixt my love and pride commences
The most singular of battles ;
Since I'd wish that one were victor,
Yet the other not be master'd.
           [*Exeunt.*

THE GARDEN.

Enter ULYSSES, CIRCE, FLERIDA, LYSI-
DAS, ANTISTES, ARCHELAUS, LEBREL,
CLARIN, CASSANDRA, *Ladies, Greeks,*
Musicians.

     Ulysses (aside).
Tremblingly I come, O sorrow !
To see Circe, since I'm fated
For her wisdom to admire her,
To adore her for her graces.
Who would not have so far trusted
In himself ? oh ! who that waits here
Would not need a sage's caution ?
Since, despite of all his calmness,
It is hopeless to forget her,
And to love her is but madness.
      Circe.
Here—where Spring has call'd together
In this bright and beauteous garden
Her sweet parliament of flowers
To swear fealty to the fairest,
To their queen, the rose, who wears
Her imperial purple mantle,
Dyed in the blood of Venus fair,—
I await thee, pride and marvel
Of all Greece, until the chase
Circles o'er our northern lands here,
Which will be when sinks the sun
With his burning beams abated.

Con músicas y festines
Te espero, porque la ausencia,
Y memorias de tu patria
Entretenido diviertas.
   Ulíses.
Bellísima Circe, en quien
Por lo hermosa y lo discreta,
O está de mas el ingenio,
O está de mas la belleza,
No es menester, que mi vida
Tantas lisonjas te deba,
Para que rendido siempre
A tus plantas la agradezca;
Que el merecer adorar
Tu hermosura . . . .
   Circe.
     Aguarda, espera;
Que este cortes cumplimiento
No quiero, Ulíses, que sea
Carta de favor, con que
A mi respeto te atrevas;
Que una cosa es hospedarte,
Agradecida á tus prendas,
Y otra es escucharte amores.
   Ulíses.
Ni yo, Circe, me atreviera
A decirlos; que una cosa
Es cortesana fineza,
Y otra fineza amorosa.
   Circe (aparte).
¡Pluguiera á Dios que lo fuera!—
En esta tejida alfombra,
Que de colores diversas
Labró el Abril, á quien sirve
De dosel la copa amena
De un laurel, al sol hagamos
Apacible resistencia.
Vayan tomando lugares
Todos, y tú aqui te sienta.

Here with songs and festive music
I await thee, that the absence
And the memory of thy country,
Thus amused, may not unman thee.
   Ulysses.
Loveliest Circe, thou in whom
Beauty so to sense is added,
That superfluous seems the sense,
Or the beauty seems not wanted.
Needless is it that my life
Owe thee for such liberal largess
Of all kindness, though thus kneeling
Ever at thy feet 'twould thank thee;
Since to merit leave to worship
Thy fair beauty . . . .
   Circe.
     Stay, detain thee;
Since this courteous compliment,
I, Ulysses, would not have thee
Use against me as a licence
To o'erstep respect's exactness.
One thing is a guest's warm welcome,
Such as worth like thine demandeth,
And another, love to list to.
   Ulysses.
Nor would I, fair Circe, ask thee
So to listen; it is one thing
With a courtier's tongue to flatter,
With a lover's is another.
   Circe (aside)
Would to God, he used the latter!—
On this flower-inwoven floor,
Spread as with a coloured carpet
By rich April's hand, beneath
These o'erhanging laurel branches,
Which—a green-leaf'd canopy,
Tremble o'er it—to the ardent
Sun a soft shade let us make.
All take seats, thine here, I ask thee.

Ulíses.
Temo enojarte otra vez.
   Circe (aparte á Flérida).
Flérida, á entabler empieza
Lo que has de fingir.
   [*Van tomando lugares las damas y
     los galanes, y* Ulíses *se asienta
     en medio de* Circe y Flerida.

   Flérida (aparte á Ulíses).
          Aqui
Me siento, porque quisiera
Daros á entender, Ulíses,
Lo que me debeis.
   Lísidas (aparte).
         ¿ Qué llegan
¿ A ver mis ojos ? ay cielos !
¿ Flérida al lado se sienta
De Ulíses, y con él habla ?
¡ Denme los cielos paciencia !
   Antístes (aparte).
¡ Infelices de nosotros,
Si á estas lisonjas se entrega
Ulíses ! pues tarde, ó nunca
Daremos la vuelta á Grecia.   [*Vase.*

   Música.
Solo el silencio testigo
Ha de ser de mi tormento,
Y aun no cabe lo que siento
En todo lo que no digo.

   Sale Arsidas.

   Arsidas (á Circe).
Si para ver sus desdichas
Siempre ha tenido licencia
Un triste, porque el pesar
A nadie cerró las puertas,
No te admires que la tome

Ulysses.
Once again I fear to offend thee.
   Circe (aside to Flerida.)
Flerida, be now enacted
The feign'd part I gave thee.
   [*The ladies and gentlemen take their
     places, so that* Ulysses *has* Circe
     at one side of him, and* Flerida *at
     the other.*
   Flerida.
          Here
I my place select, to make thee
Feel, Ulysses, what thou owest
To my favour.
   Lysidas (aside).
         O unhappy
Eyes of mine, what sight to see !
Can my mistress by this stranger
Sit and whisper in his ear ?—
O ye heavens, full patience grant me !
   Antistes (aside).
Ah ! unhappy we, if now,
By these false fair flatteries dazzled,
Yields Ulysses, late or never
Shall we back to Greece be wafted.
            [*Exit.*

   Song with Music.
Silence only, ah ! I feel
Must be witness of my woe ;
Though my suffering doth outgrow
Even the all that I conceal.

   Enter Arsidas.

   Arsidas (to Circe).
If to see his own misfortunes
Ever hath a wretch free access,
Since the gloomy gates of grief
Shut not out the humblest sadness,
Wonder not that I avail me

Yo, y que á tus jardines venga,
Pues he de mirar mis zelos,
A mirarlos de mas cerca.
       Circe.
Yo no doy fatisfacciones ;
Pero huélgome que feas
Teftigo de efto, porque,
Sin que yo las dé, las tengas.
       Arfidas.
Pues fiendo afi, y que ya Ulífes
Eftá á la mano derecha,
Como efcogido, yo tomo,
Como dejado, la izquierda.
       Circe.
Pues habemos de pafar
Aqui el ardor de la fiefta,
Porque una aguda cueftion
Mas á todos entretenga,
Haz, Flérida, una pregunta,
Y cada uno la defienda.
     Flérida (aparte).
Diré lo que á mí me pafa,
Porque Lífidas lo entienda.—
Danteo ama á Lifis bella,
Y Lifis manda á Danteo
Difimular fu defeo ;
Silvio olvida á Clori, y ella
Manda, que finja querella ;
Danteo, amando, ha de callar ;
Silvio, no amando, moftrar
Que ama : fiendo efto forzofo,
¿ Cuál es mas dificultofo,
Fingir, ó difimular ?
       Ulífes.
Difimular el que amó,
Lo mas difícil ha fido.
       Arfidas.
Fingir el que no ha querido,
Mas difícil juzgo yo.

Of the boon, and feek thy gardens ;
Since if I muft jealoufy fee,
Beft to fee it near and naked.
       Circe.
Satisfaction for fufpicions
I ne'er give, although it glads me
That you witnefs this, fince I
Give them not, and yet you have them.
       Arfidas.
This then being fo, and fince
On thy right hand fits the favour'd
Gueft, Ulyffes, on thy left
Will I feat me, the forfaken.
       Circe.
Since we here intend to pafs
The fiefta's burning ardour,
That fome fubtle play of wit
May amufe us while it lafteth,—
Flerida, a queftion ftart
Which we all in turn muft anfwer.
     Flerida (afide).
What has pafs'd I'll tell, and truft
Lyfidas may underftand me.—
Laon loveth Lyfis fair,
Yet fhe doth of him require
To diffemble his defire ;
Silvio is free as air,
Yet is forced to affect defpair ;
Laon loves, yet hides his pain ;
Silvio's free, yet wears the chain.
Thus coerced the two, I afk,
Which is the feverer tafk,—
To diffemble or to feign ?
       Ulyffes.
The moft difficult muft be
To diffemble where one loves.
       Arfidas.
Feigning when no paffion moves
Seems more difficult to me.

Cafandra.
Efta opinion me agradó.
    Arquelao.
Yo eftotra pienfo feguir.
    Clori.
¿ Quién difimula el fentir?
    Lifidas.
¿ Y quién fingirá el amar ?
    Thifbe.
Lo mas es difimular.
    Timántes.
Lo menos es el fingir.
    Ulifes.
El hombre, que enamorado
Eftá, (quien lo eftá no ignora,
Que efto es afi) á cualquier hora
Trae configo fu cuidado;
El que finge no ; olvidado
Puede eftar, hafta llegar
De fingir tiempo y lugar :
Luego, fi fu afecto es juez,
Uno fiempre, otro tal vez,
Mas cuefta el difimular.
    Arfidas.
La mifma razon ha fido
La que me da la victoria.
Configo trae fu memoria
Quien ama ; quien finge, olvido :
Luego el que ama no ha podido
Olvidarfe de fentir ;
Quien finge sí, pues ha de ir
Tras la ocafion que fe pierde,
Sin que nadie fe lo acuerde :
Luego mas cuefta el fingir.
    Ulifes.
El fingir fe trae configo
Un cuidado tambien, pues
Batalla es fingir ; mas es
Batalla fin enemigo ;

Caffandra.
That I hold inftinctively.
    Archelaus.
I the other view maintain.
    Chloris.
Who can hide the heart's fond pain ?
    Lyfidas.
Love can have no imitator.
    Thifbe.
To diffemble is the greater.
    Timantes.
'Tis the leffer tafk to feign.
    Ulyffes.
He who loves (it is confefs'd
By all hearts that own Love's power),
Carries with him every hour
Care and trouble in his breaft ;
He who feigneth love's unreft
Feeleth nought that thefe refemble
Till the time and place to tremble
At and in come round ; deciding
'Twixt the fleeting and abiding ;
Then 'tis greater to diffemble.
    Arfidas.
For the reafon you exprefs
I may claim the victory :
He who loves brings memory,
He who feigns, forgetfulnefs ;
One is powerlefs to reprefs
The remembrance of his pain ;
That the other can is plain,
Since 'tis ufed but as a cover,
And forgotten when 'tis over ;
Therefore greater 'tis to feign.
    Ulyffes.
He who feigns muft alfo know
Conftant care, for feigning is
A warfare ; but this war of his
Is a fight without a foe ;

La del que ama no ; teſtigo
Es uno, y otro peſar :
Eſte tiene que triunſar
De muchos afeƈtos ciego ;
Aquel de uno ſolo : luego
Mas es el diſimular.
       Arſidas.
Mayores afeƈtos miente,
Que el que ſiente un mal cruel,
Y le diſimula, aquel
Que le dice, y no le ſiente.
Pruébaſe eſto claramente,
Si un repreſentante á oir
Vamos, porque perſuadir
Nos hace entonces que amó,
Y un enamorado no :
Luego mas es el fingir.
       Uliſes.
Yo ſiento eſto.
       Arſidas.
         Eſtotro yo.
      [*Meten mano á la eſpada.*
       Circe.
¿Qué es eſto? ¿pues como aſi
Hablais delante de mí ?
Duelos del ingenio no
El acero los lidió :
Y aſi, para que ſalgamos
De la cueſtion en que eſtamos,
Deſde el empuñado acero
Hoy á la experiencia, quiero,
Que la duda remitamos.
Uliſes no ama, y defiende
Que es mas zelar un ardor ;
Arſidas ama en rigor,
Y que es mas fingirle entiende ;
Y aſi mi ingenio pretende
La cueſtion averiguar :
Los dos la habeis de moſtrar

That the lover's is not ſo,
Witneſs ſorrows that aſſemble,
Witneſs fears that make him tremble
For his leaguer'd hope nigh loſt :
This fights one, but that a hoſt ;
Then 'tis greater to diſſemble.
       Arſidas.
Hard albeit to conceal,
Yet 'tis falſe to ſay one feeleth
Equal heart-pangs who concealeth,
And who feigns but does not feel ;
This I prove by an appeal
To the aƈtor's mimic pain ;
When we liſten to his ſtrain,
We believe his paſſion real,
Though we know 'tis all ideal ;—
Therefore greater 'tis to feign.
       Ulyſſes.
This I feel.
       Arſidas.
       The other I.
    [*They put their hands to their ſwords.*
       Circe.
What is this? and can it be
That you ſpeak thus before *me ?*
With the ſword we ne'er ſhould try
Wit-jouſts to conclude thereby.
Thus that we may pretermit
The diſpute that here is knit,
Without clenching ſwords to aid it,
By a trial I'll evade it,
And refer the doubt to it.
Free of love, Ulyſſes holdeth
Harder 'tis to hide love's fire ;
Arſidas, who's all deſire,
Thinks to feign, more pain enfoldeth.
Of the truth that each upholdeth
Thus I mean to manifeſt :—
Let the two be put to teſt

Hoy conmigo; y fin reñir,
Tú, Ulífes, has de fingir,
Tú, Arfidas, difimular.
Y el que en la experiencia hiciere
Primera demoſtracion,
Por premio de la cueſtion
Una rica joya efpere.
          Arfidas.
Mi amor aceptar no quiere
El partido, pues la llama
Ha de ocultar que le inflama;
Y Ulífes no ha de fingir,
Pues nada finge en decir
Que te ama, fi te ama.
          Circe.
Sofpechas fon de tus zelos,
Y eſto ha de fer.
          Ulífes.
                    Defde aqui
Finjo fer tu amante.
          Circe (aparte).
                    Afi
Abran camino los cielos,
Para explicar mis defvelos.
          Arfidas.
Yo difimulo, que no
Te quiero, pues me obligó
Tu precepto.
          Circe (aparte).
                    Deſta fuerte
Al uno y al otro advierte
Mi amor lo que defeó.
          Flérida (aparte á Circe).
Si le das á cada uno
Un cuidado, ¿cómo, ay Dios!
Quieres, que yo tenga dos?
Pues en mal tan importuno
Son muchos cuidados uno.

In my perfon; uncomplaining,
Thou, Ulyſſes, play love's feigning;
Arfidas, conceal thy beft.
And who better doth affeét
His affignèd part to-day,
Guerdon of this mimic fray,
A rich jewel may expeét.
          Arfidas.
My true love cannot accept
A partition which concealeth
What my burning heart revealeth.
Light the part Ulyſſes playeth,
Since he feigns not if he fayeth
That he loves, when love he feeleth.
          Circe.
This thy jealous thoughts betray;
Be it fo, howe'er it move thee.
          Ulyſſes.
I henceforth pretend to love thee.

          Circe (afide).
Heaven but point me out a way
That to fhow I dare not fay.

          Arfidas.
I henceforth pretend that I
Love thee not, and thus comply
With thy precept.
          Circe (afide).
                    In this fafhion,
I my heart's new waken'd paffion
Indicate to both thereby.
          Flerida (afide to Circe).
If from thee in feparate fhares
Each a fingle care muſt rue,
Canſt thou wifh that I have two?
Since in haplefs love affairs
One care holds a thoufand cares.

Circe.
¿ Si ambos los has de tener,
Quien te metió, di, en faber
Cual de los dos en rigor
Era cuidado mayor,
Pues no habias de efcoger ?
　　　　　　[*Quiere irfe.*
Arfidas.
Circe fe va, ingrata y bella,
Y aunque fu aufencia fentí,
No la feguiré ; que afi
Difimularé el querella.
Ulifes.
Circe fe aufenta ; tras ella
Iré, aunque mi mal infiero,
Por moftrarla que la quiero.
Circe.
¿ Dónde, Ulifes, vas ?
Ulifes.
　　　　　　Tras tí,
Que eres el fol, de quien fui
Girafol ; vida no efpero,
Aufente tu roficler ;
Y afi tus reflejos figo.
Circe.
Arfidas, ven tú conmigo.
Arfidas.
Tengo otra cofa que hacer ;
Perdona, no puede fer.　　　[*Vafe.*
Circe (aparte).
Bien á los dos confidero
En el combate primero.
¡ O fi efte amor, fi efte olvido,
Uno no fuera fingido,
Y otro fuera verdadero !
　　　[*Vanfe todos, y* FLERIDA *detiene*
　　　　　　á ULÍSES.
Flérida.
¡ Oye, Ulífes !

Circe.
If thou'rt forced the two to hold,
Thou thereby art lefs controll'd ;
What availeth thee to know
Which care works the weightier woe,
Since to choofe thou art not told.
　　　　　　[*She is about retiring.*
Arfidas.
Circe goes, and though my trembling
Heart may for her abfence ache,
I the cruel fair forfake,
Thus my love of her diffembling.
Ulyffes.
Circe goes, and I refembling
One who 'neath fome charm doth move,
Follow her to fhow my love.
Circe.
Whither goeft thou ?
Ulyffes.
　　　　　　After thee,
Sun, whofe fun-flower I muft be ;—
Till thy fweet light from above
Dawns on me no life I know ;
Therefore where thou fhin'ft, I go.
Circe.
Arfidas, come thou with me.
Arfidas.
Pardon me, it cannot be,
I a different duty owe.　　　[*Exit.*
Circe (afide).
In this primal teft the two
Have the fight gone bravely through.
Thus adored, and thus difdain'd,
Would the real love were feign'd !
And the feign'd love were but true !
　　　[*Exeunt all but* FLERIDA, *who*
　　　　　　detains ULYSSES.
Flerida.
Lift, Ulyffes !

Ulíſes.
　¿ Qué me quieres ?
Flérida.
Eſtoy tan agradecida
A la deuda de mi vida,
Que haſta decirte, que eres
Quien hoy en ella prefieres
Sus ſentidos, no tendré
Soſiego en ellos ; porque
Es el agradecimiento
El mas preciſo argumento
Para probar una fe.
Ulíſes.
De tus penas obligado,
Decir puedo, y afligido,
Que antes de haberlas ſabido,
Ya me habian laſtimado.
No debes á mi cuidado
Lo que por tí no hice alli,
Cuando á la luz te volví ;
Porque tú no tienes, no,
Que agradecer lo que yo
No ſupe que hacia por tí.
Ahora sí que debieras
Mi deſeo agradecer,
Pues almas quiſiera ſer,
Para que tú las tuvieras.
Flérida.
Aunque acciones liſonjeras,
Agradezca ſu trofeo
Con mis brazos mi deſeo :—
　　　　[Abrázale.
¡ Yo miſma de mí me admiro !
　　　　　[aparte.
*[Al ir á darſe los brazos ſalen por
　dos puertas* CIRCE *y* LÍSIDAS.
Liſidas (Cada uno aparte).
¿ Qué es eſto, cielos, que miro ?

Ulyſſes.
　　　Call'ſt thou me ?
Flerida.
Ah ! the gratitude I'd ſhow thee
For the debt of life I owe thee
Is ſo great, that, till to thee
I declare it openly,
I can find nor peace nor reſt
In the ſenſes thou haſt bleſt ;
Since a warm acknowledgment
Is the ſtrongeſt argument
Of a true and faithful breaſt.
Ulyſſes.
Though thy pain's unnatural laws
Muſt have moved the flintieſt heart,
I can ſay their bitter ſmart
Pain'd me ere I knew their cauſe.
Then before you thank me, pauſe ;
Thanks to me you do not owe,
Thanks you do not owe me, no,
For reſtoring you to light.
Service can at beſt be ſlight
Given to one we do not know.
Wouldſt thou now my wiſhes meet,
Truſt me, if that debt ſurvives,
If I had a thouſand lives,
I would lay them at thy feet.
Flerida.
Let this flattering act complete
What my words have fail'd to prove,
All my gratitude and love :—
　　　　[Embraces him.
Self-ſurprise amazeth me !
[At the moment of their embracing,
　CIRCE *and* LYSIDAS *appear at
　different doors.*
Lyſidas (aſide.)
What is this, O heavens ! I ſee ?

Circe.
¿ Qué es esto, diofes, que veo ?
Lifidas.
El Griego Ulifes es quien
Darme vida y muerte efpera.
Circe.
Bien que fingiefe quifiera,
No que fingiefe tan bien.
Lifidas.
Muerte mis zelos me den.
Circe.
¿ Mas de qué debo quejarme ?
Lifidas.
¡ La vida intenta quitarme,
Que me ha dado Ulifes, cielos !
Porque darme vida y zelos,
No deja de fer matarme.
Flérida (á Ulifes).
Eftaré, como te digo,
De noche en efe jardin,
Que cae fobre el mar, á fin
De que él folo fea teftigo
Del afecto á que me obligo.
Ulifes.
Flérida, no es groferia
Que refponda la voz mia
Que no te ha de obedecer ;
Pues es mas defaire fer
Amada por cortesía.
Yo he de fingir fer amante
De Circe, y no lo fingiera,
Si otro favor admitiera
Tan poco firme y conftante.
No el defengaño te efpante ;
Que aunque de mi penfamiento
Otro haya fido el intento,
Cefó ; que en el mal que figo,
Solo el filencio teftigo
Ha de fer de mi tormento. [*Vafe.*

Circe (afide).
What a fight ! ye powers above !
Lyfidas (afide).
By the Greek Ulyffes' fpell
Muft I death as life attain ?
Circe (afide).
Though I wifh'd that you fhould feign,
Ah ! you fhould not feign fo well.
Lyfidas (afide).
Jealoufy doth ring my knell !—
Circe (afide).
Wherefore though fhould I complain ?
Lyfidas.
Heavens ! Ulyffes would again
Of that life he gave deprive me !
Since 'tis worfe than death to give me
Life fo link'd with jealous pain.
Flerida to Ulyffes.
I to-night will wait for thee
In the garden o'er the fea,
Since my grateful heart would only,
Of its utterance, have that lonely
Silent fcene its witnefs be.
Ulyffes.
Lady, if my voice replieth
With refufal, it denieth
Not through want of courtefy,
Since affected love to thee
Far lefs courtefy implieth.
I, thou know'ft, muft feign to be
Circe's lover : 'twere not feigning,
If my fuit to her difdaining,
I elfewhere fhould bend the knee ;
Let my candour pain not thee :—
Other homage do I owe,
Other love I fain would fhow,
But unfpoken muft conceal.
Silence only, ah ! I feel,
Muft be witnefs of my woe ! [*Exit.*

Flérida.
No pudiera refponder
Mas á mi contento nada ;
Pues de verme defpreciada,
Soy la primera muger,
Que gufto llegó á tener.
  Lifidas (aparte).
Qué efpero? Mas ay de mí !
Que eftá Circe ingrata alli.
Ocafion efperaré
De quejarme, fi podré.
  Flérida.
¿ Aqui eftás, feñora ?
   Circe.
     Sí.
  Flérida.
¿ Luego ya bien entablado
Lo que me has mandado habrás
Vifto?
   Circe.
   Sí, Flérida, y mas
De lo que te habia mandado.
   Flérida.
Encarecí mi cuidado
Con afecto, ay de mí ! cuanto
Supe.
   Circe.
   Deja afecto tanto,
Flérida, que amando muero ;
Y bien que lo finjas quiero,
Mas no que lo finjas tanto.
Demas, que fi en los primeros
Lances pierdo los fentidos,
No quiero zelos fingidos,
Que fepan á verdaderos.
Tus afectos lifonjeros
Cefen, pues que fu caftigo
Fingido fue tal conmigo,
Que no digo fu tormento ;

Flerida.
A more fortunate reply
Fate could never have devifed !
Since to fee myfelf defpifed
Firft of womankind am I
Who a pleafure feel thereby.
  Lyfidas (afide).
Why delay ? But, dire diftrefs !
Circe's there, the mercilefs.
I a better time muft plan
To expoftulate, if I can.
  Flerida.
Wert thou here, Señora ?
   Circe.
      Yes.
  Flerida.
Saw you then how I expended
All my art in the part I play'd
By your orders ?
   Circe.
   You obey'd
Even more than I intended.
  Flerida.
Woe is me ! I thus offended,
Fancying that you wifh'd for fuch
Feint of fondnefs.
   Circe.
   Ceafe ! Thy touch
Ice-like chill'd my heart and brain ;
Ah ! I die of love !—to feign ?
Yes, but not to feign fo much.
Nay, if thus I fadly rue
This firft feint fo unpropitious,
I defire not by fictitious
Jealoufies to learn the true.
Ceafe then with fond wiles to woo,
Since I pay for thy appeal
With fuch feign'd pain, that I feel
Words are weak to fpeak my woe,

Y aun no cabe lo que siento
En todo lo que no digo.   [*Vase.*
     Flérida.
¿Quién mas necio extremo vió?
¿Hay mas penas, que por mí
Pasen este instante?
     Lísidas.
       Sí;
Que aun ahora falto yo.
No, Flérida hermosa, no
Porque á quejarme me obligo,
Porque para mi castigo,
Que esto hable, que esto vea,
No quiero mas de que sea
Solo el silencio testigo.
     Flérida.
Lísidas, si has escuchado
Lo que á Ulíses dije aqui,
Tambien lo que Circe á mí
Es fuerza que hayas notado.
No lince para el cuidado,
Y ciego para el contento
Estés; que este fingimiento,
Si fue causa de mi engaño,
Tambien, tambien desengaño
Ha de ser de mi tormento.
     Lísidas.
De un triste el rigor es tal,
Que, aunque mal y bien estén
Iguales, duda del bien
El crédito que da al mal.
Uno y otro en mí es mortal;
Y así, al bien y al mal atento,
Flérida, ausentarme intento
De aqueste monte cruel,
Que con ser tan grande, en él
Aun no cabe lo que siento.   [*Vase.*
     Flérida.
Oye, escucha!—Mas ¡ay cielos!

Though my suffering doth outgrow
Even the all that I conceal.   [*Exit.*
     Flerida.
Who has seen more wild conceit?
Can this moment bring excess
Of the pain I suffer?
     Lysidas (*advancing*).
       Yes;
Without me 'twere incomplete:
But I come not to repeat
Vain complaints, alas! not so,
Since, fair Flerida, I know
From the things I hear and see,
Silence only, woe is me!
Must be witness of my woe.
     Flerida.
Lysidas, if audibly
What I told Ulysses floated
To thine ear, thou must have noted
Also Circe's words to me,
Be not then to misery
Lynx-eyed, and to joy but blind:—
If the part to me assign'd
Causes grief by its deceiving
Likewise too in undeceiving
Must I still my torment find.
     Lysidas.
'Tis the torment of the sad,
That though good and evil should
Seem alike, they doubt the good,
And give credence to the bad.
Both a mortal anguish add
To my suffering, I would fain
Flerida forget the twain,
And this cruel mountain flee,
Which however vast it be
Cannot compass all my pain.   [*Exit.*
     Flerida.
Listen! hear me!—But, ah me!

¿ Con qué podrán mis enojos
Detenerle, fi los ojos
No pueden, que en fus defvelos
Rémoras fon de los zelos ?
En vano, ay de mí ! le figo ;
No á explicar mi mal me obligo,
Pues que no cabe, no ignoro,
Aun nada de lo que lloro,
En todo lo que no digo.   [*Vafe.*

MONTE.

Sale CLARIN.

Clarin.

Engañada Circe bella
(Que en efecto las mugeres,
Que faben mas en el mundo,
Se engañan mas fácilmente),
Agradecida me dijo
Que á efte monte me viniefe,
Y que en hallándome folo,
A Brutamonte le diefe
Voces, que al inftante el tal
Brutamonte, fea quien fuere,
Me traeria un gran teforo.
Solo eftoy, ya no hay que efpere.
Brutamonte !—No refponde ;
Brutamonte !—No me entiende ;
A tres irá la vencida :
Brutamonte !

Sale BRUTAMONTE *gigante.*

Brutamonte.
                    Qué me quieres ?
Clarin.
Nada, fi fuere pofible,
Es cuanto puedo quererte.
Brutamonte.
Ya me has llamado, y ya fé

How can all my tears and fighs
Hold him here, when even the eyes
Cannot do fo, though we fee
Oft their light fcares jealoufy.
It is vain, oh ! woe the day !
To purfue him, vain to ftay
Doubts that o'er his heart are creeping,
Let me then in filent weeping
Wail the grief I muft not fay.   [*Exit.*

A MOUNTAIN.

Enter CLARIN.

Clarin.

Circe fair, by me deceived
(Since 'tis eafieft of all women
To impofe on thofe who are
Wifeft in all kinds of knowledge),
Circe fair, as I have faid,
In a grateful moment told me
To this mountain to repair,
And to fhout out Brutamonte
When I found myfelf alone,
And that he upon the moment
Would, whoe'er he be, confer
Some moft precious gift upon me.
I am now alone, why wait ?
Brutamonte !—No refponfes ;
Brutamonte !—No one hears me ;
Third and laft time,—Brutamonte !

Enter BRUTAMONTE, *a giant.*

Brutamonte.
At your fervice, what's your bufinefs ?
Clarin.
Nothing, faith, an it were only
Poffible to get away.
Brutamonte.
You have call'd me, and the object

A lo que vengo; que es este
Recado que traigo.
          Clarin.
                  ¿Y no
La señora Circe tiene
Otros pagecicos mas
Mañeros, que le trajesen?
Porque para mí bastara
Menor seis varas, ó siete.
          Brutamonte.
De mí se sirve, que soy
De Cíclopes descendiente,
Por mas magestad, y espero,
Antes que de aqui se ausenten
Los Griegos, vengar en todos
De Polifemo la muerte.
      [*Sacan una arca dos animales.*
          Clarin.
Poco hay que vengar en mí;
Que yo no le toqué, y siempre
Le tuve, viven los cielos!
Tanto miedo como este;
Que otro hipérbole no sé,
Con que mas encarecerle.

          Brutamonte.
Toma esta caja, que traigo
Para tí.
          Clarin.
     Bien.
          Brutamonte.
               Y agradece
A Circe, que su obediencia
Atadas mis manos tiene,
Para que no te arrebate
De un brazo, y contigo diese
De esotra parte del mar.
          Clarin.
Lindo saque fuera ese;

Of your coming I discover
By the dispatch I carry.
          Clarin.
                  Can
Lady Circe have no other
Little page but you to run
On her errands through the forest?
Quite enough for me were one
Who was six or seven yards shorter.
          Brutamonte.
She makes use of me, who am
From the Cyclops sprung, to show her
Greater grandeur, and I hope,
Ere the Greeks depart these coasts here,
For the death of Polyphemus
To take vengeance on the whole herd.
      [*Two animals draw in a chest.*
          Clarin.
Little need you take on *me:*—
Since I never touch'd him, no then,
But the same fear felt, by Heaven!
Towards him then, that now comes o'er
     me;
I know no hyperbole
Better can my terror show thee.
          Brutamonte.
See this chest I here have brought thee,
Take it.
          Clarin.
     Good.
          Brutamonte.
             And thank the goddess
Circe, that obedient duty
Unto her my strong hand holds here,
So that I do not uplift thee
With one arm, and hurl thee yonder
Far amid the whelming sea-waves.
          Clarin.
What a game of ball, to hop there

Pero, aunque hiciera buen bote,
¿Quién de allá habia de volverme?
      Brutamonte.
Y si esto no hiciera, hiciera
Otra cosa.
      Clarin.
            Cuál?
      Brutamonte.
               Comerte
De un bocado.
      Clarin.
         Y aun no hubiera
Harto para untar un diente.
      Brutamonte.
¡O llegue el dia en que tenga
Esta licencia!
      Clarin.
          ¡O no llegue
Nunca, sino despeado
En el camino se quede!
      Brutamonte.
Toma la caja, y en ella
Hallarás mas que quisieres.
      Clarin.
Un modo de despedirte
Quisiera hallar solamente.
      Brutamonte.
Pues yo me voy.
      Clarin.
         Haces bien.—
¡Qué gigantes tan corteses [*aparte.*
En esta tierra se usan,
Que poquito se detienen
En conversaciones donde
Estorban!

      Brutamonte.
      Y cuantas veces
Me nombrares . . . .

Out so far! But, when I bounded
On the sea, who'd hit me home here?
      Brutamonte.
If I didn't do that, I'd do
Something better.
      Clarin.
         What?
      Brutamonte.
            Just gobble
You up in a bit.
      Clarin.
         'Twould scarcely whet
One of your teeth, so small a morsel.
      Brutamonte.
May the day come soon when I
Have that licence!
      Clarin.
           May it not then
Ever come, but rather founder
On the road before it comes here.
      Brutamonte.
Take the chest, and you will find
In it more than you could covet.
      Clarin.
How to get you to take leave
Is just now my only problem.
      Brutamonte.
Then I go.
      Clarin.
         You do quite right;—
How obliging and how courteous
                [*aside.*
Are the giants of this country,
Who their visitations shorten,
When they find their conversation
Grows a bore!
      Brutamonte.
      And I, as often
As you call me . . . .

Clarin.

    Qué?

Brutamonte.

          Vendré

A eſtos paiſes á verte.   [*Vaſe.*

Clarin.

Yo le ahorraré eſe trabajo
Cuantas veces yo pudiere.—
Fueſe ? Parece que sí,
Aunque aqui no lo parece.
¿ Pero de qué tengo miedo,
Si es humilde y obediente,
Un novicio de gigantes ?
Y pues el teſoro viene,
¿ Quién me mete en diſcurrir?
Tráigale quien le trajere.
¡ Alto pues, abro la caja !
Que la llave en ella tiene.
¿ Quién duda, que habrá diamantes
Como el puño, comó nueces
Perlas, y como las bolas
De los bolos los claveques ?

    [*Abre la caja, y ſale una Dueña.*

Mas, cielos ! qué miro ?

Dueña.

          Miras

A una míſera ſirviente,
Que para ſervir de eſcucha,
Y parlar cuanto dijeres
De Circe, me manda que ande
Contigo acechando ſiempre.
Por eſo en trage de dueña
Me envia, para que aceche.

Clarin.

¡ Lindo teſoro de chiſmes
En la tal arca me viene !
¿ Yo dueña, tras un gigante ?
Aqui falta ſolamente,

Clarin.

    Well ?

Brutamonte.

          Will come

Here to ſee you on the moment. [*Exit.*

Clarin.

Well, that trouble I will ſpare you
Every time I can, good monſter.—
Has he gone ? It ſeems he has,
Though perhaps it ſeems ſo only.
But what need I fear ? He is
Mild and meek in his deportment,
Quite a novice among giants.
Since a treaſure I have gotten,
'Bout the bearer, or the bringer
Why ſhould I diſturb my noddle?
Courage then ! the cheſt I'll open.
With the key that's in the lock here,
Who can doubt that here are diamonds
Bigger than my fiſt, and whole heaps
Of large pearls like nuts, and gems
That like bowls roll o'er each other?

    [*He opens the box, from which a
          Duenna ariſes.*

Heavens ! what's this I ſee ?

Duenna.

          You ſee

A poor wretched ſervant body,
Who to play the part of ſpy,
And to tell what may be ſpoken
Againſt Circe, is commanded
Ever-liſtening to eſcort thee.
Since I'm ſent to liſten, I
Thus duenna-like am clothèd.

Clarin.

What a treaſure-trove of rags
Have I in this cheſt diſcover'd !
Firſt comes giant, then duenna :—
Now the thing that's only wanted

Para que el triunfigurato
De caballeros noveles
Efté cabal, un enano.
   Dueña.
Pues no faltará, fi es efe
El defecto.—Brunelillo!
Sal al punto.

   Sale un Enano.

   Enano.
    ¿Qué me quieres,
Doña Brianda?
   Clarin.
    ¿De dónde
Sales, átomo viviente?
   Enano.
De mi cafa, que lo es
Efta caja, donde fiempre
Acueftas me has de traer.
   Clarin.
¿Pues cómo aqui caber pueden
Un enano y una dueña,
Si cualquiera de ellos fuele
No caber en todo el mundo?
   Dueña.
Brunelillo, gente viene,
Y no es jufto que nos vean.—
Oye, dóblenos, y cierre
La caja.
   Enano.
   Circe lo manda,
Que fiempre al hombro nos lleve,
Y lo que dijere oigamos.
   Dueña.
Y aun mas de lo que dijere.
  [*Métenfe en la caja y cierran.*
   Clarin.
¿Señores, qué es lo que pafa
Por mí? qué teforo es efte?

To make all this transformation
(Like to a knight-errant novel)
Finifh finely, is a dwarf.
   Duenna.
Then if that be fo, no longer
Need you wait.—Here! Brunelillo,
On the inftant.

   A Dwarf comes out.

   Dwarf.
    For what object,
Dame Brianda?
   Clarin.
   Where did you come from,
Living atom, pigmy wonder?
   Dwarf.
From my manfion, which you fee
Is this box, where on your fhoulder
You muft carry me henceforth.
   Clarin.
How I marvel, can this box here
Hold a dwarf and a duenna,
When there's fcarce for either of them
Room enough in all the whole earth?
   Duenna.
Brunelillo, men come yonder,
And 'twere wrong that they fhould fee us.
Hark you! fold us fmooth, and cover
Up the cheft.
   Dwarf.
   Remember, Circe
Bids you bear us on your fhoulder,
And that what you fpeak we'll hear.
   Duenna.
Ay, and more than will be fpoken.
  [*They enter the box, which clofes.*
   Clarin.
What on earth am I to do
With my treafure, good Señores?

Vive Júpiter! que juntos
A su cascara se vuelven.
Aqui hay trampa, vive Dios!
Mas no, en la caja no tienen
Por donde haberse salido.
¿Qué haré en confusion tan fuerte?
Si de Circe no obedezco
El castigo que me ofrece,
Otro mayor me dará,
Si es que otro ser mayor puede
Que levar la caja.   Pues
Ahora veo claramente,
Por qué el gigante la trajo,
Y los animales fuertes;
Porque cosa tan pesada,
Como una dueña, no puede
Sufrirla, sino un gigante
Y dos bestias solamente.—
¿Quién compra dueñas y enanos,
Como peines y alfileres?

Sale LEBREL.

Lebrel (Para sí).
¡ Que tal pensase de mí
Circe, y que á Clarin creyese !
Huyendo vengo á este monte,
Donde á los dioses pluguiese,
Que al castigo, que me espera,
Hallase donde esconderme.
Pondré, que aquesta es la hora,
Que está trazando de hacerme
Sabandija destos montes,
Gusarapo destas fuentes.
Este es Clarin, y aqui dél
Será razon que me vengue.—
Huélgome de haberte hallado,
Clarin.

Clarin.
Por mas que te huelgues,

Jupiter ! my precious gems
In their casket now are cover'd :
Oh ! there must be trap-doors here !
Yet the box contains no open,
Out through which they could have gone.
In such strong fix, how comport me ?
If the punishment rejecting
Which to me hath Circe offer'd,
She a greater one may give me,
If a greater is concocted
Than to bear this box.   I now
Clearly can explain the problem
Why a giant had to draw it,
And two beasts as big as oxen ;
Since such heavy baggage is
A duenna, that the strongest
Giant and two beasts to match him
Must unite them to uphold her.—
Dwarfs ! Duennas ! come, who'll buy ?
Like the man who pins and combs sells.

Enter LEBREL.

Lebrel (soliloquising).
Oh ! that thus could think of me
Circe, and trust Clarin's nonsense !
Flying do I seek this mountain,
And its guardian gods invoke here,
That I may perchance find shelter,
From the wrath impending o'er me.
Now I'll bet she's thinking how
In the best way to transform me
To a beetle of these mountains,
To a wet worm of these ponds here.
Here is Clarin, and here I
Will revenge the wrong he has done me.
Clarin, I'm o'erwhelm'd with joy
To have met thee.

Clarin.
If thy load, then,

No tanto como me pefa.
    Lebrel.
Que vengo á darte la muerte.
    Clarin.
Yo vengo á darte la vida.
    Lebrel.
De qué fuerte ?
     Clarin.
      Defta fuerte :
Circe, obligada de mí,
En efta caja me ofrece
Un teforo, y yo con él
Pretendo fatisfacerte ;
Porque fi del bien hablar
El premio, Lebrel, es efte,
Con dártele á tí, tendrás
El premio, que tú mereces.
¿ Puedes obligarme á mas
De que todo te lo entregue ?
Toma la caja.
    Lebrel.
      No quiero,
Que todo á dármelo llegues,
Sino, pues me defenojas,
Que partamos igualmente.
    Clarin.
Pues llevaráfte la dueña,
Y yo el enano.
    Lebrel.
      ¿ Qué quieres
Decir en efo ?
    Clarin.
      No fé,
Tú lo verás, fi la abrieres.
   [*Pone la caja en otra parte, y*
     ábrela LEBREL.

    Lebrel.
Ponla aqui. Ya abierta eftá.

Is fo great, mine's not lefs weighty.
    Lebrel.
Since to kill thee I'm devoted.
    Clarin.
And to give thee life am I.
    Lebrel.
In what way ?
     Clarin.
      In *this* way, know then.
Circe being obliged to me,
In this cheft to me has offer'd
A great treafure, which as thine
I'm determined to reftore thee ;
Since, if it is the reward,
Friend Lebrel, of the civil-fpoken,
By my giving it thee, thou'lt have
The reward thou'ft won fo nobly.
Can you then oblige me more
Than I do in giving the whole heap ?
Take the cheft.
    Lebrel.
      I do not wifh you
To beftow the whole upon me ;
But fince you've appeafed my wrath,
Be one half to each allotted.
    Clarin.
Then do *you* take the duenna,
And I'll take the dwarf.
    Lebrel.
      You mock me ;
What do you mean ?
    Clarin.
      I do not know ;
But you'll fee all when you open.
   [*He places the cheft in another place,*
     and LEBREL *opens it.*

    Lebrel.
Place it here, 'tis open now.

[Saca LEBREL *todo lo que dice.*

¡ Qué joyas tan excelentes!
        Clarin.
Son muy excelentes joyas . . . .
(Para el diablo, que las lleve.)
                    [aparte.
        Lebrel.
Aquesta cadena escojo,
Y esta para tí se quede.
        Clarin.
Ca . . . . qué?
        Lebrel.
           Cadena; y ahora
Dé diamantes este Fénix
Para mí, y esta Sirena,
Toda de esmeraldas verdes,
Te dejo.
        Clarin (aparte).
        ¡ Viven los cielos,
Que es imposible, que hubiese
Diamantes donde hubo dueñas!
        Lebrel.
Yo no quiero parecerte
Codicioso; esto me basta,
Lo demas es bien te deje.—
¿ Quién no se desenojara   *[aparte.*
Con tesoro como este ?
A buscar á Libia voy,
Y á darla cuanto quisiere.   *[Vase.*

        Clarin.
O yo estoy borracho, ó yo
Sueño cosas diferentes,
O he perdido mi juicio,
O tengo un grande accidente,
O de Circe he hablado mal.
¡ Que joyas hallar pudiese

*[He takes out each article as he
        describes it.*
Oh! what rich gems I behold here !
        Clarin.
Very precious gems they are . . . .
(For the devil himself who bore them.)
                    [aside.
        Lebrel.
I select this pretty chain,
And for you remains this other.
        Clarin.
Pretty what ?
        Lebrel.
           This pretty chain;
Now in turn to me belongeth
This resplendent diamond Phœnix,
And this Siren emerald brooch here,
I leave *thee.*
        Clarin (aside).
        Good gracious heavens !
Can it be that he discovers
Diamonds now where I found dwarfs ?
        Lebrel.
I don't wish that you suppose me
Greedy; so I've had enough :
Of the rest I make thee owner.—
Who would not forego his anger
                    [aside.
For a prize like this I hold here ?
Libia now I go to seek,
And I'll give her what she chooses.
                    [Exit.

        Clarin.
Either I am drunk, or I
Dream now this, and now the other;
Or I have my senses lost,
Or have got some grief in store yet,
Or 'gainst Circe wagg'd my tongue.—
Jewels how could *he* behold here,

Donde yo dueñas y enanos !
Mas yo las ví claramente,
Y supuesto que las hay,
Tomaré las que pudiere.
    [Sale la Dueña no mas del
        medio cuerpo.
    Dueña.
Señor, diga á Brunelillo
Vuesa merced, que me deje
Hacer mi labor.
        [Sale el Enano.
    Enano.
      Señor,
Dígala usted, que no llegue
A lamerme la merienda.
    Dueña.
Tú mientes.
    Enano.
     Tú eres quien miente.
    [Aporréanse y húndense.

    Clarin.
¿ Qué es lo que pasa por mí ?
¡ Valedme, diofes, valedme !
¿ Esta trajo Brutamonte ?

   Sale BRUTAMONTE.
    Brutamonte.
Qué me mandas ?
    Clarin.
        ¡ Qué obediente
Es toda aquesta familia !
¡ Con la presteza que vienen
En llamándolos !—Señor
Brutamonte, á quien profpere
Júpiter con la salud,
Que su gigantez merece,
Yo he visto la caja, y yo
Le ruego, que se la lleve.

Where I faw but dwarfs and damfels ?
But I faw the gems with open
Eyes, and now with open hands too
Shall I make a haul and bolt hence.
    [The Duenna arifes half her
        height in the box.
    Duenna.
Speak to Brunelillo, Sir,
Bid him leave me at my work here
Quietly, your worfhip.
       [The Dwarf rifes up.
    Dwarf.
        Sir,
Tell her not to fpoil my poffet,
Pleafe your worfhip, with her licking.
    Duenna.
Oh ! a lie.
    Dwarf.
    On thy fide only.
    [They beat each other, and
        fink down.
    Clarin.
What, oh ! what fate will befall me ?
Help me ! help me ! all ye Gods here.
Was it this brought Brutamonte ?

   Enter BRUTAMONTE.
    Brutamonte.
What are your commands ?
    Clarin.
        The promptnefs
Of the family's furprifing !
With what quicknefs they all hop here
When you call them !—Brutamonte,
Noble Sir, whom Jove may profper
With fufficiency of health
For your giantfhip's big body,
I have feen the cheft, and I
Afk thee now to take it home hence ;

Quédefe para feñores
Eſto de traſtos vivientes;
Que no he meneſter alhajas,
Que coman, y no aprovechen.
   Brutamonte.
¿ Para efo fe llama á un hombre
Como yo? Eſtoy por hacerle . . . .
   Clarin.
Por defhacerme dirá.
   Brutamonte.
Piezas; y fi le fucede
Llamarme otra vez . . . .
   Clarin.
      No hará.
   Brutamonte.
Por Júpiter ! que le eche
Tan alto de un puntapie,
Que cuando á los cielos llegue,
Ya llegue muerto de hambre ;
Y vuelva, fi acafo vuelve,
De los pájaros comido.
      [Vafe.
   Clarin.
¡ Puntapie bien excelente !
¿ Dónde le hacen puntapies?
No fé, vive Dios ! que hacerme
Entre los tres enemigos
Del cuerpo.

 Salen ASTREA, LIBIA *y* LEBREL.

   Lebrel.
   Un inſtante breve
Habrá, que le dejé aqui
Con las joyas.
   Aſtrea.
    Tiempo es eſte
De bufcarle, que eſtá rico.
Ven, Libia, conmigo á verle.

Living lumber like to this
May be fit for grand feñores,
But fine furniture that eats,
And is ufelefs, I don't covet.
   Brutamonte.
Is't for this, a man like me
Thou dar'ſt call on? I am prompted . . .
   Clarin.
To do fomething pleafant, doubtlefs.
   Brutamonte.
To make bits of thee; another
Time if thou doſt call . . . .
   Clarin.
      I won't then.
   Brutamonte.
By great Jove ! fo high I'll tofs thee
With a kick, that when thou reacheſt
The remote celeſtial bodies,
Thou'lt have long fince died of hunger;
And thou'lt drop, if e'er thou droppeſt,
On the earth, by birds half eaten.
      [Exit.
   Clarin.
Kick fupreme ! of kicks the model !
Where are fuch kicks to be purchafed ?
I know not, as God's above me,
What to do againſt thefe three foes
Of my body.

 Enter ASTREA, LIBIA, *and* LEBREL.

   Lebrel.
    Scarce a moment
Is it fince I left him here
With the jewels.
   Aſtrea.
    Then 'tis proper
That we feek him, fince he is rich.
Libia, come, let's feek our old friend.

Libia.
Aqui está.—Clarin, qué hay?
Lebrel.
De qué fufpiras?
Aftrea.
   Qué tienes?
Clarin.
Tengo dueña, tengo enano,
Y tengo gigante.
Aftrea.
   Vuelve,
Y dinos, qué es efo?
Clarin.
    Es
La dueña, que me atormente,
El enano, que me valga,
Y el gigante, que me lleve.

Aftrea.
Eftás loco?
Clarin.
  A Dios pluguiera!
Aftrea.
¿ Qué modo de hablarme es efe ?
De otra manera Lebrel
A Libia habla, adora y quiere ;
Pues una joya la ha dado,
Y tu ninguna me ofreces
De tantas.
Clarin.
  Déjame, Aftrea,
Y no de joyas me tientes,
Que me harás defefperar,
Si á hablar mas en efo vuelves.
Voces (dentro).
Por acá, por acá !
Circe (dentro).
   Sube,
Remontada garza, á hacerte

Libia.
Here he is.—How goes it, Clarin ?
Lebrel.
Why thus figh?
Aftrea.
   What haft thou got there ?
Clarin.
I've a dwarf here, a duenna,
And a giant alfo.
Aftrea.
   Nonfenfe,
Tell us what it is.
Clarin.
   It is
The duenna who's my torment,
'Tis the dwarf with whom I'm blefs'd
  fo,
'Tis the giant fworn to flog me.
Aftrea.
Are you mad ?
Clarin.
   I would I were fo !
Aftrea.
What a way is this to have fpoken !
In another ftyle Lebrel
Speaks to Libia, worfhips, loves her,
Since a jewel he has given her ;
And to me not one thou'ft offer'd
Of fo many.
Clarin.
  Ceafe, Aftrea !
And on jewels touch no longer,
Since you'll drive me to defpair,
If again you harp upon them.
Voices (within).
Hither ! hither !—
Circe (within).
   Upward ftill,
Soaring heron, and transform thee

Eftrella viva de pluma.
Aftrea.
Circe es efta, que aqui viene ;
Yo no quiero que me vea.
Lebrel.
¡ A Júpiter para fiempre !
[*Vanfe* LIBIA, ASTREA *y* LEBREL.

Sale CIRCE.

Circe.
Por ver fi Ulífes me figue,
Me he perdido de mi gente,
Y dejando á un tronco atado
Efe zéfiro obediente,
Que fatigué, he de efperar
Entre eftos álamos verdes.—
Quién eftá aqui ?
Clarin.
              Un mentecato,
Un fucio, un impertinente,
Un necio, un loco, un menguado,
Y un cuanto vufted quifiere.
Sáqueme, por Dios ! de dueñas,
De hombres largos, y hombres breves,
Aunque me convierta en mona.

Circe.
Yo lo haré, fi efo pretendes.
Clarin.
No me tome la palabra
Tan prefto, fi le parece.
Circe.
Y porque me debas mas
Que otros, que mi voz convierte,
Haré, que tengas tu voz
Y tu entendimiento.   Vete
De aqui.

To a living ftar of plumes !
Aftrea.
Circe's voice ! this way fhe cometh :
Here I would not have her fee me.
Lebrel.
Jove ! nor I upon the whole earth !
      [*Exeunt* LIBIA, ASTREA, *and*
              LEBREL.

Enter CIRCE.

Circe.
To difcover if Ulyffes
Follows, from my train I've loft me,
And unto a tree-trunk tying
My obedient zephyr courfer,
Wearied with the chafe, I'll wait here
Underneath thefe dark green poplars.—
Who is there ?
Clarin.
              A fimple ninny,
A poor moon-calf, a big blockhead,
A born fool, an afs, a madman,
And what elfe your worfhip choofes.
Free me, God's life ! from duennas,
From thefe tall men, from thefe fhort
    men,
Though you make of me a monkey.
Circe.
So I'll do, fince you have told me.
Clarin.
Do not take me at my word
Quite fo quickly, I implore thee.
Circe.
And that you may owe me more
Than the others I transform here,
I will leave to you your fenfes
And your voice.   And now begone
    hence,
Quick !

Clarin.
No lo dije yo
Por tanto.
Circe.
Un punto no efperes.—
Hafta mirarfe á un efpejo,   [*aparte.*
Ya en fu forma no ha de verfe.
Clarin.
Si es que mona me has de hacer,
Solo quiero merecerte,
Que fea mona de lo caro,
Mas que dormilona, alegre.—
Hombres monas, prefto habrá
Otro mas de vueftra efpecie.   [*Vafe.*

Sale ULÍSES.
Ulífes.
Por mas que te he feguido,
Corto el aliento de efe bruto ha fido,
Si bien con harto raftro te feguia,
Pues llevabas por feñas todo el dia.

Circe.
De la caza canfada,
A efte apacible fitio retirada
Me vine.   Qué has volado?
Ulífes.
Un defeo, ay de mí! tan remontado,
Que ofó con alto vuelo
Calarfe entre las nubes de algun cielo,
Donde al fuego vecino,
Con ligereza fuma,
Abrafada la pluma,
Subió defeo, y maripofo vino.

Clarin.
In faith, I didn't mean it
Serioufly.
Circe.
Don't wait a moment.—
Till he looks into a mirror,   [*afide.*
He his own fhape won't recover.
Clarin.
If a monkey you will make me,
Let me for this favour hope then,
That you make a nice ape of me,
Brifk and lively, and no fnorer.—
Monkey-men there, foon you'll have
One more member of your order.
[*Exit.*

Enter ULYSSES.
Ulyſſes.
The quicker was my fpeed,
The quicker fail'd the hot breath of my
fteed,
Following thy track along the devious
way,
Since in thy flight thou haft outftripp'd
the day.
Circe.
Aweary with the chafe,
To this retired and fylvan-fhaded place
I came.   Say, what has rifen?
Ulyſſes.
A fond defire, ah me! from out its
prifon,
Which dared in lofty flight
To pierce the clouds of one fweet hea-
ven fo bright,
That from the glowing fky
Through which it foar'd a paffion-wing'd
defire,
With plumage all afire,

Circe.
¿ De la caza, pregunto, qué has volado ?

Ulises.
En ella te respondo, que un cuidado.
Circe.
¿ Pues cómo á mí en sentido
Equívoco respondes atrevido?
Ulises.
Como pienso que sabes, que esta culpa
Anticipada tiene la disculpa.

Circe.
Ah sí, no me acordaba . . . .
     Ulises (aparte).
           Yo estoy loco.
     Circe.
De la porfía de hoy.
     Ulises (aparte).
          Ni yo tampoco.
     Circe.
Qué dices?

     Ulises.
     Que por ella me atrevia.
     Circe.
Por ella ?

     Ulises.
Sí.
     Circe (aparte).
     ¡ O mal haya la porfía !—
Mas pues fingidos son esos extremos,
Hablemos en la caza sola.

     Ulises.
         Hablemos.
Luego que tú te retiraste de una

Fell back to earth, a flame-singed but-
     terfly.
     Circe.
I spoke of hawking, when I ask'd, What
     rose ?
     Ulysses.
And I replied, a woe of tenderest woes.
     Circe.
Why thus forgetful of my dignity,
Dost thou still make equivocal reply ?
     Ulysses.
Because I thought the task thyself had
     given,
Might have supposed such fault would
     be forgiven.
     Circe.
Ah ! yes, I had forgotten . . . .
         Ulysses (aside).
                 I am mad.
     Circe.
To-day's dispute.
         Ulysses (aside).
          'Twere better that I had.
     Circe.
What do you say ?
         Ulysses.
         'Twas that impell'd my suit.
     Circe.
That only ?

         Ulysses.
         Yes.
         Circe (aside).
         Accursed be the dispute !—
Well, since these feignings but false
     flatteries seek,
Let us speak of the chase alone.
         Ulysses.
         So let us speak :—
You scarce had gone, when near

Guarnecida laguna,
Eſpejo de la hermoſa primavera,
Se remontó una garza, que altanera
Tanto á los cielos ſube,
Que fue á un tiempo aqui pájaro, alli
    mube ;
Y entre el fuego y el viento,
Arbitro igual, (o válgome ſu aliento!)
De ſuerte ſe interpuſo, que las alas
En la diáfana esfera, en la ſuprema,
O las hiela, ó las quema,
Cuando las enarbola, ó las abate,
Tan á compas entre las dos las bate,
Que aqui elevadas é inclinadas luego,
Aqui dan en el aire, alli en el fuego.
Geroglífico era
La garza entre la una y otra esfera
De alguno, que aqui oſado, alli cobarde,
Se hiela á un tiempo, y arde,
Y entre el aire y el fuego ſe embaraza.

        Circe.
Eſo no es de la caza.
        Ulíſes.
Es de la pena mia,
Que es en parte tambien volatería.

        Circe.
Hubiérame ofendido,
Si no ſupiera, Ulíſes, que es fingido.

      Ulíſes (aparte).
¡ A Júpiter pluguiera !

The margin of a lake, that cryſtal-clear
Seem'd a ſmooth mirror for the beauteous
    Spring,
A heron roſe, ſo ſudden its quick wing
Bore it amid the ſky elate and proud,
That at one moment it was bird and
    cloud,
And 'twixt the wind and fire,
(Would that ſuch courage had my heart's
    deſire !)
So interpoſed itſelf, that its bold wings
Wheeling alternate near,
Now the diaphanous, now the higher
    ſphere,
Were burnt or froze,
As down they ſank or upward ſoaring
    roſe,
In all the fickleneſs of fond deſire,
Now in the air and now amid the fire.
An emblem as it were,
This heron was, betwixt each oppoſite
    ſphere,
Of one who is both cowardly and bold,
Can burn with paſſion, and yet freeze
    with cold,
And 'twixt the air and fire ſtill doubts
    his place.
        Circe.
You ſpeak not of the chaſe.
        Ulyſſes.
I ſpeak of my heart's care,
Which ſeems a quarry for each fond
    deſpair.
        Circe.
This would have offended me again,
Did I not know, Ulyſſes, that you
    feign.
      Ulyſſes (aſide).
Ah ! would to Jupiter, 'twere ſo.

N

Circe (aparte).

¡ Pluguiera al cielo, ay Dios ! que no
    lo fuera !
Y pues que folo eftás aqui conmigo,
No finjas, y profigue.

Ulifes.
            Ya profigo.
Atomo ya la garza apenas era,
Cuando, defenhetrada la cimera
Que el capirote enlaza,
Mi mano un gerifalte defembraza,
A quien, porque en prifion no fe pre-
    fuma,
La pluma le halagaba con la pluma,
Y él, como hambriento eftaba,
Duro el laton del cafcabel picaba.
Apenas á la luz reftituidos
Se vieron otro y él, cuando atrevidos,
Cuanta eftacion vacía
Paleftra es de los átomos del dia,
Corren los dos por páramos del viento,
Y en una y otra punta,
Efte fe aleja, cuando aquel fe junta ;
Y el bajel ceniciento
(Que bajel ceniciento entonces era
La garza, que velera
Los piélagos fulcó de otro elemento)
Librarfe determina diligente,
Aunque navega fola,
Hechos remos los pies, proa la frente,
La vela el ala, y el timon la cola.
¡ Mífera garza, dije, combatida
De dos contrarios ! bien, bien de mi vida
Imágen eres, pues fitiar la veo
De uno y otro defeo.

Circe (afide).

Ah ! would to Heaven, 'twere other-
    wife I know !—
And fince you're here alone with me,
    you need
Not further feign ; proceed.
Ulyffes.
            I thus proceed :—
Scarce had the heron dwindled to a fpeck
On the far fky, when from about the neck
Of a gerfalcon I unloofed the band
Which held his hood ; a moment on
    my hand
I foothed the impatient captive, his dark
    brown
Proud feathers fmoothing with careffings
    down ;
While he, as if his hunger did furpafs
All bounds, pick'd fharply on his bells
    of brafs.
Scarce were they back reftored to light,
He and another, when in daring flight
They fcaled heaven's vault, the vaft
    void fpace where play
In whirling dance the mote-beams of
    the day,
Then down the deferts of the wind they
    float,
And up and down the fky
One flies away as the other fwoopeth
    nigh ;
And then the afhen-colour'd boat
(An afhen-colour'd boat it furely were,
That heron, that through fhining waves
    of air
Furrow'd its way to fields remote)
Refolving to be free and not to fail,
Although alone it faileth now,
Of feet made oars, of curved beak a prow,

Circe.
Ahora disculparte no has podido,
Pues yerras, si es fingido, ó no es fingido.

Ulises.
Sí puedo; ser tu amante no fingiera,
Si á la primera vez te obedeciera.—
A uno pues, y otro embate,
Coge las alas, ó las velas bate,
Y poniendo debajo de la una
La cabeza, se deja á su fortuna
Venir á pique, cuando
Nos pareció caer revoloteando
Una encarnada estrella,
Y los dos gerifaltes siempre en ella.
Si ejemplo eres, o tú, á mi pensamiento,
Sé tambien escarmiento,
Y no me ofrezcas esperanza alguna,
Si ha de desengañarme tu fortuna.

Circe.
Aunque sea fingido, todavía
Es ya en ofensa mia,
Pues si te habia mandado
Fingir antes de ahora tu cuidado,
Tambien te mandé ahora
A solas no fingirle.

Sails of its wings, and rudder of its tail;—
Poor wretched heron, said I then, thy
    strife
'Gainst two opposing ills, are of my life
Too true an image; since it is to-day
Of two distinct desires the hapless prey.
Circe.
Now thou canst not excuse thee, since
    'tis plain
Thou offendest, whether thou feignest,
    or don't feign.
Ulysses.
I can; thy lover's part I would badly play,
If at thy first command I could obey.—
'Gainst this, 'gainst that, as either doth
    assail,
It furl'd its wing, and droop'd its lan-
    guid sail,
And placing its dazed head beneath the
    one,
Trusting to fortune, like a plummet-stone
Straight down it fell, we looking, from
    afar
Saw it descending, an incarnate star
Through the dark sky,
With the pursuing falcons ever nigh.
O thou! if thou'rt the image of my
    thought,
Be thou a warning too, with wisdom
    fraught,
Let no delusive hope by thee be shown,
If in thy fate I must foresee my own.
Circe.
Though this be feigning, it offends no
    less,
Than if the feigning were all truthfulness;
Since if I bade thee feign,
At another time, the lover's anxious pain,
I also bade thee now not feign again,

Ulíses.
    Pues, señora,
Si tu castigo espero,
Siendo fingido, y siendo verdadero,
De verdadero ya el castigo pido,
Pues solo esto es fingido en ser fingido.

Circe.
¿Cómo, di, tan osado
Respondes?

Ulíses.
   Como estoy desesperado.
Circe.
¿Cómo tan atrevido
Te desvaneces . . . .
    Ulíses.
     Como estoy perdido.
   Circe.
A hablarme desta suerte?
    Ulíses.
Como finjo quererte.
    Circe.
¿Luego aquesto es fingido todavía?
    Ulíses.
No, señora.
   Circe (aparte).
    ¡O bien haya la porfía!—
Ulíses, aunque fuera
Justo, que de escarmiento te sirviera
Tu osadís, conviene
Disimular, porque la gente viene,
Que hasta aqui me ha seguido;
En su fuerza se quede lo fingido.

Since we are here alone.
   Ulysses.
     O Lady! then
If I alike thy chastisement must rue,
Whether my passionate speech be feign'd
  or true;
Then let the true be punish'd or disdain'd,
Since it is only feign'd in being feign'd.
   Circe.
How hast thou, say, such courage as to
  dare
So bold a reply?
    Ulysses.
    Because I must despair.
   Circe.
Why thus presuming to the uttermost,
Venturest thou now again . . . .
    Ulysses.
     Because I am lost.
   Circe.
To speak though I reprove thee?
    Ulysses.
Because I feign I love thee.
   Circe.
Is this then also feign'd as was thy suit?
    Ulysses.
Señora, no.
   Circe (aside).
    Oh! blest be the dispute!—
Ulysses, though it were
But just, that thou shouldst pay by thy
  despair
For thy presumption; still it needs that
  we
Dissemble, since my people seeking me
Have hither come; thus there is no
  resource,
And the command to feign must still
  remain in force.

Salen todos, excepto CLARIN.
   Arfidas (aparte).
Aunque en tantos defvelos
Mis agravios fe valgan de mis zelos,
No darme intentaré por intendido.
¿ Mas cómo difimula un ofendido ?
Volverme es ya moftrar mi fentimiento ;
Defpejo quiero hacer de mi tormento.—
Siguiéndote, feñora, con tu gente
Por la florida márgen defta fuente
Vine, que ella pautada de colores,
Las feñas de tu pie daba con flores.

     Circe.
Hácia efta parte vine,
Porque es donde la cena ahora previne.
     Lebrel.
¡ Qué bien, qué bien me fuena
Efta palabra, cena!
Mas no veo entre ramas, ni entre flores
Mefas, ni aparadores,
Ni ocupada en doméftico trabajo
A la familia de efcalera abajo
Cruzar muy diligente.

     Circe.
Todos os id fentando brevemente,
Porque en el campo todos
Cenemos juntos, y de varios modos
Se firvan las viandas.—
¡ Hola, la mefa !

     Lebrel.
Dime, á quién lo mandas ?

Enter all, except CLARIN.
   Arfidas (afide).
Although thefe watchings bring no eafe
Unto my wrongful pangs but jealoufies,
Still I would feel as if I did not feel them ;
But how can *he* who knows his wrongs
   conceal them ?
Now to turn back would all my wounds
   lay bare,
And fo I'll mafk them with this light-
   fome air.
Lady, I've follow'd with thy people here
Unto this flower-encinctured fountain
   clear,
Whofe margin, colour'd by its cryftal
   fhowers,
Gave us the imprefs of thy feet with
   flowers.
     Circe.
I led unto this fhade,
As here I order'd fupper to be laid.
     Lebrel.
Supper ! delicious word !
Oh ! how my heart by the fweet found
   is ftirr'd !
But beneath the boughs, nor on the lea,
Tables nor fideboards can I fee,
Nor on needful houfe affairs
The family down-ftairs
Buftling about all bufy and all heated.
     Circe.
Here I defire that you would all be feated,
Since in the open field fhall we
Together fup, and with variety
Of meats be ferved ; and fo as time is
   preffing,
The table there !—
     Lebrel.
Now who are you addreffing ?

Circe.

A quien ya me ha entendido.
　[*Por debajo del tablado sale una mesa
　muy compuesta y con luces, y sién-
　tanse* Ulíses, Circe, *y* Arsidas, *y
　los demas en el suelo.*

Lebrel.

Linda mesa, pardiez! nos ha venido.
¿ No me dirás, si desto no te pesa,
Cuanto habrá que sembraron esto mesa ?

Circe.

¡ Hola, cantad ! cantad, y divertido
Uno y otro sentido
Esté con las viandas y las voces,
Que suenen en los zéfiros veloces.
　　　　　[*Canta la Música.*
　　Música.
　Olvidado de su patria,
　En los palacios de Circe
　Vive el mas valiente Griego,
　Si, quien vive amando, vive.

Tocan dentro cojas y sale Libia.
　　Circe.
¿ Pero qué es esto que escucho ?
　　Ulíses.
¿ Pero qué es esto que oigo ?
　　Flérida.
¿ Qué es esto, cielos, que veo ?
　　Arsidas.
¿ Qué es esto, cielos, que noto ?
　　Circe.
¿ Qué bélico estruendo, qué
Marcial ruido, qué alboroto
Deja la luz del sol ciega,

Circe.

One who can understand me, do not fear.
　[*A table rises from the ground, well
　furnished, and with lights.* Circe,
　Ulysses, *and* Arsidas *seat them-
　selves at it, the others on the
　grass.*

Lebrel.

Jove ! what a crop of table springeth
　here !
Will you not tell me though, if you are
　able,
How long it took the sowing of this table ?
　　Circe.
Sing, sing ! and with the influence
Of music please a double sense,
Let voice to voice replying
Blend with the zephyrs o'er our banquet
　flying.　　　　[*Music within.*
　　Song.
Native land and home forgetting,
In the palace-halls of Circe
Lives the bravest Grecian hero ;
If *he* lives, who loving, liveth.

*A sound of drums is heard from within,
　and* Libia *enters.*

　　Circe.
But what noise is this I hear ?
　　Ulysses.
But what sound is this that stirs me ?
　　Flerida.
What, O heavens ! must I behold ?
　　Arsidas.
Heavens ! to what strain must I listen ?
　　Circe.
Say, what warlike clangour, what
Martial noise is this that filleth
Heaven with darkness, blinds the sun,

Y el eco del aire fordo?
       Libia.
Efe fiero Brutamonte,
Efe gigante furiofo,
Que prefo, feñora, tienes,
Por guarda de tus hermofos
Jardines, porque no robe
Nadie fus manzanas de oro,
Ofendido que á los Griegos
Blanda paz y fuave ocio
En tus palacios divierta,
Olvidados de sí propios,
Habiendo fido homicidas
De Polifemo, que afombro
Era monftruo de los hombres,
Y era hombre de los monftruos :
Comunero de tu imperio,
Para vengarfe de todos,
Convocó del Lilibeo
Cuantos Cíclopes famofos,
Efpurios hijos del fol,
Hoy viven de darle enojos;
Y dándoles pafo al Flegra
Brutamonte cautelofo,
Vienen contra tí en efcuadras
Mal ordenadas, de modo,
Que viendo vagar los rifcos,
Difcurrir los promontorios,
Parece que aqueftos montes
Defcienden unos de otros,
A cuyo eftrépito, á cuyas
Voces y fufpiros roncos,
El fol fe turba, y del cielo
Caducan los ejes rotos.

       Circe.
¡ Ay de mí, en qué gran peligro
Eftoy ! en qué grande ahogo !

And the deafen'd echo dinneth?
       Libia.
That ferocious Brutamonte,
That gigantic form of grimnefs,
Whom, a captive, lady, thou
Makeft guardian of the richnefs
Of thy gardens fair, that none
May their golden apples pilfer,
Being offended that the Greeks,
Gentle peace, and reft, and mirth, here
In thy palaces enjoy,
Home-forgetting, and when drifted
Here erewhile, that they had flain
Polyphemus, who was mingled
Man and monfter—man 'mongft
     monfters,
And a monfter 'mong man's kindred,
Now a rebel of thy realm,
In revenge his foes to kill here,
Hath convoked from Lilybœum
All the famous fpurious children
Of the fun, the giant Cyclops,
Who in fpite of thee ftill live here.
By the cunning Brutamonte
They through Phlegra's pafs admitted,
Come againft thee in diforder'd
Squadrons, fo that up the cliffs here
Climbing, o'er the promontories
Striding, each huge bulk uplifted
'Gainft the fky, they look like moun-
     tains
O'er each other roll'd and rifted,
At whofe clamour, at whofe tumult,
Hoarfe halloos, and hollow whifpers,
The fun groweth dark, and downward
Fall heaven's axes crack'd and fhiver'd.
       Circe.
Woe is me ! in what great danger
Am I ! oh ! how I'm afflicted !

Ulíses.
Dadme mis armas, que yo
Saldré á reciberlos folo ; . . . .
    Arfidas.
No temas, que yo á tu lado
Te defenderé de todo ; . . . .
    Ulíses.
Porque para mi valor
Son tantos Cíclopes pocos.
   [Ulíses *va hácia afuera, y* Ar-
      sidas *acude á* Circe.
    Arfidas.
Porque no quiero mas vida,
No, que morir á tus ojos.
    Lebrel.
Como y cordelejo, dicen,
Que es en el mundo uno propio ;
Mas la cena que efperaba
Es cordelejo, y no como.
    Circe.
¡ Deteneos, deteneos !
Que efte aparato ruidofo
Solo ha fido ma experiencia,
Exámen ha fido folo,
Para ver, cual de los dos
En un peligro notorio
Acudia á fus afectos
Mas noble y mas generofo ;
Y afi en campañas del aire
Fantáfticas hueftes formo.
    Arfidas.
Pues fi ha fido efto experiencia,
Yo foy el que me corono
Vencedor, y el que merezco,
Circe, tu favor hermofo,
Ya pue Ulífes, acudiendo
A fus armas tan heróico,
Dejó de moftrarfe amante,
Pues en riefgo tan forzofo,

Ulyffes.
Bring me here my arms, for I
Shall go forth and meet them fingly ; . . . .
    Arfidas.
Do not fear, for at thy fide
I fhall guard thee from all ills here . . . .
    Ulyffes.
Since for valour fuch as mine
All the Cyclops' ftrength feems little.
   [Ulysses *goes to the fide, and* Ar-
      sidas *approaches* Circe.
    Arfidas.
Since I only wifh for life,
That thou may'ft my death here witnefs.
    Lebrel.
Mirth is juft as good as meat,
So they fay, but all within me
Yearneth for the miffing fupper
As the fitter thing to fill me.
    Circe.
Stay ! oh, ftay here ! ftay ! oh, ftay here !
For this feeming found that ftirs thee,
Is but an experiment,
Is but only a flight trial,
To difcover, of the two,
Which of you in dangerous rifks here,
Would more generoufly, more nobly
Show the love that in him liveth ;
Therefore on the fields of air
Have I phantom hofts depicted.
    Arfidas.
Then if this has been a trial,
I am he, who, as the victor,
Crown me, as the one who merits
Thy divineft favour, Circe,
Since Ulyffes when he hurried
Hero-like to his arms fo fwiftly,
Ceafed to fhow himfelf thy lover,
Since in fuch a needful rifk, he

No acudió luego á su dama,
Que en un amante es impropio.
      Ulíses.
Que acudí á las armas mias,
No niego ; pero tampoco
Niego, que de amante ha sido
El afecto mas forzoso ;
Porque si tomo mis armas,
Para defensa las tomo
Suya.
      Arsídas.
      Nunca en un acaso
Está el discurso tan pronto,
Que espere á causa segunda ;
Lo primero es lo mas propio :
A las armas fuiste, luego
Ya perdiste.
      Ulíses.
      De ese modo
Tú tambien ; pues si me acusas
De poco amante, de poco
Fino, porque no acudí
A Circe, con eso propio
Te convenzo, pues que tú
Acudiste á sus enojos,
Y ya te mostraste amante.
      Arsídas.
Si las nobles leyes noto
De caballería, acudir
A las damas es forzoso ;
Y así, como caballero,
No como amante, socorro
A Circe.
      Ulíses.
      En las de milicia
Es ley, siempre que armas oigo,
Acudir á tomar armas ;
Y así, con valor heróico,
Yo, soldado, caballero

Did not hasten to his lady,
As a lover would from instinct !
      Ulysses.
That I hurried to my armour
I admit, but unadmitted
Is it, that in this, my action
From a lover's impulse differ'd,
Since if I took arms, it was
But in her defence I girt me
With them.
      Arsídas.
      Ne'er in sudden need
Can the reason have such quickness
As to think of second causes ;
The first impulse is the fittest.
To your arms you went, and therefore
You've already lost.
      Ulysses.
      In *this* way,
Have you also ; since if *me*
Thou dost charge with showing little
Love-zeal, for my not approaching
Circe, I can now convict thee
On thine own ground, since thou hast
Sought her, though it was forbidden
To avow thyself her lover.
      Arsídas.
If I understand the firmest
Law of knighthood, 'tis to succour
Ladies when some wrong afflicts them,
Therefore it was not as lover,
But as cavalier, that Circe
I thus guarded.
      Ulysses.
      In war's code too,
'Tis the law, that when the first peal
Calls to arms, we then should arm us ;
And thus, valorous, as befits me,
I, as soldier, knight, and lover,

Y amante, he acudido á todo.
       Arſidas.
Ya ſé, que por la elocuencia
Has de quedar ſiempre airoſo ;
Que no heredaras de Aquíles
El grabado arnes de oro,
Si por el valor humbiera
De dárſele á Telamonio.
       Uliſes.
El valor le mereció ;
Y ahora verás ſi es forzoſo,
       [*Saca la eſpada.*
Pues de eſa voz en ofenſa,
El Flegra volará en polvo.

       Arſidas.
Primero arderá en cenizas
Con el fuego de mis ojos,
Porque á los dos de Trinacria
Volcanes ſe añadan otros.
       [*Saca la eſpada.*
       Circe.
Pues qué es eſto ? ¿en mi preſencia
Sacais el acero? cómo?
       Arſidas.
Tu reſpeto me perdone.
       Uliſes.
Perdóneme tu decoro.
       Arſidas.
Que no hay reſpeto con zelos.
       Uliſes.
Ni decoro con oprobios.
       Lebrel.
En mi vida me hallé en cena,
Que no paraſe en lo propio.
       Uliſes.
Aqui de Grecia !
       Arſidas.
       ¡ Y aqui

Wholly have myſelf acquitted.
       Arſidas.
Yes I know, thy eloquence
Ever proveth thee keen-witted,
Elſe thou hadſt not won the golden
Graven armour of Achilles,
Which had been the Telamonian's,
If to valour it were given.
       Ulyſſes.
'Twas by valour it was won,
This thou'lt own when thou doſt wit-
    neſs
Phlegra into duſt down ſhaken
By my voice in anger lifted.
       [*Draws his ſword.*
       Arſidas.
By the fire-flames from mine eyes,
It will firſt be burnt to cinders,
As if two volcanoes more,
With Trinacrias two, were lit here.
       [*Draws his ſword.*
       Circe.
How is this ? and in my preſence
Dar'ſt thou draw thy ſword ? can this be ?
       Arſidas.
May the reſpect that's due thee, pardon.
       Ulyſſes.
May thy due deſerts forgive me.
       Arſidas.
Since reſpect no jealous heart knows.
       Ulyſſes.
No deſert makes inſult ſtingleſs.
       Lebrel.
Never in my life, a ſupper
Have I waited for, like this here.
       Ulyſſes.
Here for Greece !
       Arſidas.
       And here, on my ſide

De Trinacria! Que aunque folo
Me ves, mis vafallos fon
Efos brutos y efos troncos.—
¡ Fieras de Trinacria humanas,
Dad á vueftro Rey focorro !

*Salen todas las fieras, y pónenfe al
lado de* ARSIDAS, *y los Griegos al
lado de* ULÍSES.

Ulífes.

Aunque á tus voces fe muevan
Mejor, que al eco fonoro
De Orfeo, troncos y fieras,
Haciendo en ellas deftrozo,
Apuraré eftas montañas
Bruto á bruto, y tronco á tronco
[*Riñen.*

Sale CLARIN *de mona.*

Clarin.

Entre Griegos y animales
Mal trabadas lides noto.
No fé á cual debo acudir ;
Porque obligado de todos,
Soy por una parte Griego,
Y por otra parte mono.

Circe.

Pues no puedo reportaros
Con mis voces, con mi afombro
Podré.   Los aires cubiertos
De vapor caliginofo,
Segunda noche parezca,
Y á tanto fracafo abfortos,
Del embrion de las nubes
Sean los rayos abortos,
Y el fol y la luna hoy,
Viéndofe vivir tan poco,
Pienfen, que el camino erraron

For Trinacria ! For though fingle
Here you fee me, I as vaffals
Have thefe wild-beafts and thefe fir-trees.
Human wild-herds of Trinacria,
Succour ! fuccour ! to your king here !

*Enter all the animals and place them-
felves befide* ARSIDAS, *and the Greeks
befide* ULYSSES.

Ulyſſes.

Though unto thy accents move,
Better than when Orpheus' fingers
Touch'd the lyre, the woods and wild-
beafts,
Swift deftruction dealing 'midft them,
Brute by brute, and tree by tree now
Shall I purify thefe hills here.
[*They fight.*

Enter CLARIN, *as a monkey.*

Clarin.

'Twixt the Greeks and animals,
I the conflict watch bewilder'd :
Which of them to join I know not.
Since they're both of them my kinfmen,
Being half monkey, and half Greek,
On my outer fide and inner.

Circe.

Since I cannot hold you back
By my words, my dread bewitchments
May be ftronger.   Let the air
Cover'd with a mift's black thicknefs
Seem to fpread a fecond night,
And the clouds, by terror ftricken,
From their wombs in fudden travail
Give the abortive bolts exiftence ;
And the fun and moon to-day
Seeing how their brief life flitted,
Let them think they've loft their way

De ſus celeſtiales tornos,
O que yo deſde la tierra
Apagué ſu luz de un ſoplo.
   [*Truenos y relámpagos, obſcuréceſe
     el teatro, y riñen á obſcuras.*

       Arſidas.
¿ Adónde, Ulíſes, eſtás ?
      Ulíſes.
Con mi acero te reſpondo.
         [*Pelean todos.*
      Floro.
Qué pena !
       Caſandra.
        Qué ciego abiſmo !
      Arquelao.
Qué llanto !
       Chloris.
        Qué triſte enojo !
      Antiſtes.
Qué obſcura noche !
      Clarin.
         Ha ſeñores !
¿ Somos Griegos, ó qué ſomos ?
      Lebrel.
En tanto que todos andan
Tropezando unos con otros . . . .
      Clarin.
En tanto que cada uno
Buſca de eſcaparſe modo . . . .
      Lebrel.
Yo á la meſa me remito.
      Clarin.
Y yo á la cena me acojo.
   [*Suben ſobre la meſa, y abrázanſe
     uno con otro.*
      Lebrel.
Pero qué es eſto ? un leon
Dió conmigo.

'Mid the fix'd celeſtial circles,
Or that I from off the earth
With a breath their light eclipsèd.
   [*Thunder and lightning ; the theatre
     becomes darkened, and in the ob-
     ſcurity the fighting is ſtill continued.*
      Arſidas.
Say, Ulyſſes, ſay, where art thou ?
      Ulyſſes.
Let my ſword an anſwer give thee.
         [*All fight.*
      Florus.
Oh ! what pain !
      Caſſandra.
        What blind abyſm !
      Archelaus.
Oh ! what yells !
      Chloris.
        What mournful ſhrill ſcreams !
      Antiſtes.
What a night !
      Clarin.
        Oh ! are we Greeks,
Or what are we elſe, good miſters ?
      Lebrel.
While they all o'er one another
Tread and trample, hither, thither . . . .
      Clarin.
While each one of them is thinking
Of the ſafeſt way to flit hence . . . .
      Lebrel.
I'll unbend me at the table.
      Clarin.
I'll take refuge 'mong the diſhes.
   [*They leap on the table, and fall
     into each other's arms.*
      Lebrel.
But what's this ? a mighty lion
Seizes me !

Clarin.

Mas qué toco?
Conmigo ha dado un gigante.

Circe.

Húndase este suelo todo,
Y ponga paz la distancia.

Clarin.

Todo se hunde con nosotros.

   [*Húndese la mesa, y los dos graciosos
     sobre ella, y con la batalla y la
     tempestad se van todos.*

Clarin.

What's this that grips me?
I am seized here by a giant!

Circe.

Let the whole ground sink down with
   them,
And let peace spring from their severance.

Clarin.

All things sink, as down we sink here.

   [*The table sinks into the earth, with
     the graciosos upon it, and with the
     cessation of the battle and the tem-
     pest, the scene closes.*

JORNADA III.

Salen ANTÍSTES, ARQUELAO, POLIDORO, FLORO, TIMANTES *y* LEBREL.

Antíſtes.

AUNQUE ya todos ſepais
Lo que repetiros trata
Mi voz, oidme ; que tal vez
En pena, en deſdicha tanta,
Aun mas que noticias propias,
Mueven agenas palabras ;
Porque en efecto ninguno
Es juez en ſu miſma cauſa.
Siempre á la cólera expueſtos,
Siempre expueſtos á la ſaña
De los hados riguroſos,
Deſpues de fortunas varias,
Arraſtrados del deſtino,
Dimos en aqueſta playa
Del Flegra, exentos vaſallos
Del imperio de Trinacria.
Aqui, contra los venenos
De eſa fiera, eſa tirana,
Antídoto nos dió Juno
En las flores de oro y nácar,
Que Iris trajo, deſplegando

ACT THE THIRD.

THE SEA-COAST, AND NEAR IT CIRCE'S GARDENS.

Enter ANTISTES, ARCHELAUS, POLYDORUS, FLORUS, TIMANTES *and* LEBREL.

Antíſtes.

THOUGH ye all perchance may know
What my voice would fain impart ye,
Hear me ſtill : for many a time,
In ſuch pain, in ſuch-like ſadneſs
More than to one's own thoughts even,
To a ſtranger's words we hearken ;
Since no judge in his own cauſe
Can in truth be thought impartial.
Still unto the wrath expoſed,
Still exposèd to the anger
Of the ever-rigorous fates,
After fortune's various chances,
Dragg'd along by deſtiny,
Came we to this Phlegra's ſtrand here,
Free-born and unfetter'd vaſſals
Of the kingdom of Trinacria.
Here againſt the venom'd draughts
Of this tyrant-queen, this adder,
Juno gave us antidotes

Arcos de carmin y gualda.
Libres pues de fus prifiones
Nos vimos, y cuando trata
Ulífes volver al mar,
Que ya tuvimos por patria,
El blando halago de Circe,
Que cuando vé que no baftan
Mortales venenos, ufa
De mas venenofas trazas,
Perfuadió á Ulífes, que aqui
Unos dias fe quedara
A reparar de los vientos
La repetida inconftancia.
El, fiado en fus cautelas,
Perfuadido á que quedaba
A dar libertad á cuantos
En eftas rudas montañas
Bárbara prifion padecen,
Se quedó, donde á la rara
Beldad de Circe rendido
Vive, fin mas efperanzas.
¿ Quién creerá, que, no baftando
Tantos encantos, ni tantas
Ciencias, á vencer fus hados,
Una hermofura baftara?
Mas todos lo creerán, todos,
Pues todos á ver alcanzan,
Que un amor y una hermofura
Son el veneno del alma.
Rendidos pues al amor,
Tanto los dos fe declaran,
Defde la noche que fueron
Argumento las efpadas,
Y pufieron paz las nubes
Denfas, obfcuras y pardas,
Que Arfidas, zelofo y trifté,
Lleno de zelofa rabia,
Se fue á fu corte, quizá
A difponer fu venganza.

In the flowers of gold and nacre,
Which fair Iris brought amid
Arcs of crocus and of carmine.
Free then from her threaten'd chains
We beheld us, and thereafter,
When Ulyffes would to fea—
Which our country we regarded—
Circe with her flatteries foft,
Seeing that her mortal draughts were
Infufficient, had recourfe to
Means whofe venom nought could
    mafter;
Him perfuading, that fome days
Here he would remain at anchor,
To repair the oft-repeated
Ficklenefs of the winds' difafters;
He, confiding in his caution,
Thinking that he could enfranchife
All who in the barbarous prifons
Of thefe rude hills are held captive,
Here remain'd, where he, o'ercome
By the charms, the unexampled
Lovelinefs of Circe, lives
Without hope or aim or plan here.
Who'll believe, that when had fail'd
Every fcience, all enchantments
To fubdue his fate, the beauty
Of one face was more than ample?
But all *will* believe it, all,
Since all hearts this truth have mafter'd
That wild love and woman's beauty
Are to the foul as poifonous afps are.
Thus furrender'd up to love,
Have the two their wild attachment
So avow'd, fince that night when
Swords cut through the word-entangled
Argument, and black clouds brought
Peace 'amid their mifts of darknefs,
That Prince Arfidas, fad, jealous,

Ulíses pues, sin rezelo,
Solo de sus gustos trata,
Siempre en los brazos de Circe,
Y asistido de sus damas,
En academias de amores,
Saraos, festines y danzas.
Yo pues, viéndonos perdidos,
Hoy he pensado una traza,
Con que á su olvido le acuerde
De su honor, y de su fama:
Y es, que pues el otro dia,
Cuando oyó tocar al arma,
Se olvidó de amor, y fue
Tras la trompeta y la caja,
A todas horas estemos
Desde el bajel, que en el agua
Surto está, tocando á guerra,
Como que á Circe hacen salva;
Cuya voz noble recuerdo
Será de su olvido, clara
Sirena, que tras su acento
Los sentidos arrebata.

Polidoro.
Dices bien, y yo el primero
Seré, que esta tarde haga
La experiencia.
      Timántes.
          Pues ahora
Es tiempo; que Ulíses anda
Estos jardines, que hermosos
Narcisos son de esmeralda,
Y enamorados de sí,
Se estan mirando en las aguas.
      Arquelao.
Yo seré el que desde el mar

Driven by jealous rage to madness,
To his Court retired, where he
Doubtless some dread vengeance
     planneth;
Whilst Ulysses, uncontroll'd,
All his time in pleasure passes,
Ever in the arms of Circe,
And assisted by her damsels,
In academies of love
Studieth balls and feasts and dances;
I then, seeing we are lost,
Have to-day devised a plan here,
By whose means to fame and honour
We may wake him from his trances.
This 'tis, since, the other day,
When he heard arms clang and jangle,
He forgot his love, and went
After the drum's and trumpet's rattle,
We at every hour, from out
Yonder bark, that lieth anchor'd
On the shore, will sound a war-charge,
As if to Circe 'twere a salvo;
Whose voice will a noble memory
Of the forgotten glorious past be,
A clear Syren, at whose strain
All his senses will be ravish'd.

      Polydorus.
You speak well, and I'll be first
To attempt the experiment after
Evening closes.
      Timantes.
          Then the present
Is the time; for through the gardens
Walks Ulysses, through the emerald-
Hued Narcissi self-enamour'd,
Gazing on their own soft green
In the water's clear expanses.
      Archelaus.
I will be the one to found

Haré que toquen al arma;
Antístes aqui se quede,
Para prevenir, que es salva,
Que á Circe hace nuestra gente.
    Lebrel.
Si entre tantos votos halla
Lugar un juro, yo juro
A la deidad soberana
De Júpiter, que haceis mal
En prevenir esta traza.
    Floro.
Por qué?
    Lebrel.
      Porque Circe sabe
Mejor lo que aqui se habla,
Que nosotros, y podrá
Tomar de todos venganza.
Escarmentad en Clarin,
Que habló mal della, y airada
Se vengó, pues no sabemos
Qué hay dél, ni por donde anda.
    Floro.
Todo eso es temor.
    Lebrel.
      Es cierto.
    Arquelao.
Dejadle, no le creais nada,
Y vamos á nuestro intento.
    Todos.
Vamos.
    [*Vanse todos, y quédase* LEBREL.
    Lebrel.
      Vuesarcedes vayan,
Que yo me quedo á tratar
Cosas de mas importancia.
De todos los animales,
Que por estos campos andan,
Quisiera coger alguno,
Que á Grecia despues llevara,

From the sea the martial clang then;
Thou, Antístes, here remain,
To explain, it is a salvo
Given to Circe by our people.
    Lebrel.
If there's room, amid so many
Vows, for a good oath, I swear
By great Jove, the sovereign father
Of the Gods, that you do wrong
In attempting what you plan here.
    Florus.
Why?
    Lebrel.
      Because of Circe knowing
Better about what we chat here
Than we do ourselves; and she
Will take vengeance for it, mark me!
On us all. Be warn'd by Clarin
Who spoke ill of her; in anger
She revenged herself, and no one
Knows his fate or what has happen'd.
    Florus.
All this is but fear.
    Lebrel.
      That's certain.
    Archelaus.
Leave him there, don't mind his tattle,
And let's go and try our project.
    All.
Let us go.   [*Exeunt all but* LEBREL.

    Lebrel.
      My worshipful masters,
You may go, but I'll remain
For a more important matter.
Of the many animals
That across these wild plains wander,
I am anxious to catch one,
Which I may to Greece hereafter

Cuando quifieren los diofes
Efcaparnos de Trinacria;
Porque fuera para allá
Importantífima alhaja
Uno dellos, pues á verle
Solamente fe juntara
Toda Grecia, y yo tuviera
Con él fegura ganancia.
Cierta mona aqueftos dias
Siempre cocándome anda
Con geftos y con viafages,
Y á efta quifiera pefcarla,
Para cuyo efecto traigo
Efte cordel con que atarla
Luego que la vea, porque
Es juguetona, y es manfa.

Sale CLARIN *de mona.*

Clarin.

Hácia aqui, fi no me engaño,
Mis compañeros eftaban,
Aunque, defpues que foy mona,
Por donde quiera que vaya,
Hallaré mis compañeros.
Por feñas les diré, que hagan,
Que me dé libertad Circe,
Pues ya lo enmonado bafta.

Lebrel.

Vela aqui; yo quiero echarle
Efte lazo á la garganta.
Ahora es tiempo.   ¿ Qué me eftorba,
Qué me turba, ó qué me efpanta,
Si una mona diz que es fácil
De coger ?* Díganlo tantas
Como cogidas me efcuchan.

---

* *Coger una mona,* literally, to catch a monkey,
means to be intoxicated. I have paraphrafed it
by a fomewhat fimilar expreffion in the tranflation.

Bring back with me, when the Fates
Let us fly free from Trinacria.
One of them would be at home
Quite a treafure, a full harveft
Of fine profit, for all Greece
Would flock round to fee his gambols,
And I'll make of him clear gain
By exhibiting his antics ;
For fome days a certain monkey
Have I feen that grins and chatters
With odd geftures and grimaces ;
'Tis for him I wifh to angle ;
For which purpofe I have brought
This good cord wherewith to catch him
When again I fee him, fince
He's fo playful and fo active.

Enter CLARIN *as a monkey.*

Clarin.

'Twas but now, unlefs I err,
My companions here were gather'd—
Though fince I a monkey grew,
Wherefoe'er I roam or ramble
I can meet with my companions.
By thefe geftures I would afk them
Circe to implore to free me,
Since with monkeyhood I'm fated.

Lebrel.

There he is ! around his throat
I this noofe would like to faften.
Now's the time. But whence this fear ?
What difturbs me ? What unmans me ?
Since fo eafy, as 'tis faid,
Is it to fuck a monkey ?* Mafters,
Ye who hear me, own how eafy :—

---

* " *To fuck the monkey,* to drink at an ale-
houfe at the expenfe of another."—HALLI-
WELL's *Dictionary.*

No escapareis de mis garras.
  [*Echale un cordel al cuello.*
   Clarin.
¡ Ay, que me ahogas, Lebrel !
No en el pescuezo me hagas
La presa.
   Lebrel.
   Por mas que coques,
No te irás.
   Clarin.
    ¿ No es cosa extraña,
Que hable para mi, y discurra
Con sentidos, vida y alma,
Y con los otros no pueda
Articular las palabras ?
Lebrel, mira que soy yo.
   Lebrel.
¡ Como brinca, y como salta !
No puedo llevar á Grecia
Cosa de mas importancia.
Señora mona, desde hoy
Hemos de ser camaradas,
No hay sino tener paciencia,
Y venir conmigo.
   Clarin.
   Basta,
Que no me entiende.
   Lebrel.
    ¡ Qué gestos
Hace, y con qué linda gracia !

  Salen Astrea *y* Libia.

   Libia.
En todo el dia no hay verte,
Lebrel ; dime, dónde andas ?
   Lebrel.
He andado á caza de monas,
Y á fe que no es mala caza,
Y esta he cogido.

But you won't escape my hands here.
  [*Flings the cord round* CLARIN's *neck.*
   Clarin.
Ah ! you're choking me, Lebrel !
I'm your prisoner, but don't catch me
By the throat thus.
   Lebrel.
   Mouth away,
Come you will though.
   Clarin.
    What a marvel !
That I speak to myself, make use of
All my senses, soul and heart have,
Yet I can't articulate words,
To make others understand me.
Ah ! Lebrel, think who I am.
   Lebrel.
How he bounces ! how he dances !
Nothing could I bring to Greece
More important or attractive.
From this day, Sir Monkey, we
Will be comrades in my travels.
Nothing for't but patience, so
Come along.
   Clarin.
   'Tis plain and patent
He don't understand me.
   Lebrel.
    How
Gracefully he grins and chatters !

  Enter Astrea *and* Libia.

   Libia.
Why, Lebrel, I haven't seen you
All the day : what were you after ?
   Lebrel.
I've been after apes and monkeys,
And with good success : this charmer
I have captured.

Libia.
  ¡ Ay, qué linda
Monica !
   Lebrel.
  Cocala, Marta.
   Libia.
¿ Qué pienfas hacer con ella ?
   Lebrel.
Pienfo, Libia mia, llevarla
A Grecia, enfeñarla allá
A tocar una guitarra,
A andar por una maroma,
Y hacer vueltas en las tablas.
   Clarin.
Yo por maroma ? yo vueltas ?
Efto folo me faltaba.
   Aftrea.
Dime, Lebrel, ¿ y Clarin
Dónde eftá ?
   Clarin.
  Aqui.
   Aftrea.
    Allá te aparta !
   Lebrel.
Defde el dia que quedó
Cargado de joyas tantas . . . .
   Clarin.
¡ Tal tengas tú la falud !
   Lebrel.
No le ví, ni fé que fe haya
Hecho.
   Clarin.
  Yo sí.
   Aftrea.
    Su codicia
Le ha efcondido.
   Clarin.
    Hay mayor rabia !

Libia.
  What a pretty
Little monkey !
   Lebrel.
  Jock, grin at her.
   Libia.
What, though, do you purpofe with him ?
   Lebrel.
Him, my Libia, I fhall carry
Back to Greece, and have him taught
To touch lightly the guitar there,
On the tight-rope there to tumble,
And to dance in booths and taverns.
   Clarin.
I a dancer ! I a tumbler !
Only this alone was wanted.
   Aftrea.
Tell me, though, Lebrel, of Clarin,
Where's he gone ?
   Clarin.
   He's here.
   Aftrea.
    Keep back there !
   Lebrel.
Since the day I left him laden
With his jewels, gems, and jafpers . . .
   Clarin.
May you have the like good fortune !
   Lebrel.
I haven't feen him, nor his abfence
Can I account for.
   Clarin.
   I can.
   Aftrea.
    Doubtlefs
Avarice hides him.
   Clarin.
   Oh ! 'tis madnefs !

Libia.
Circe hácia esta parte viene.
Lebrel.
Pues por si acaso se enfada
De que cogiese esta mona,
Me voy.   Ven conmigo, Marta.
Clarin.
Si me ahoga, qué he de hacer ?

Lebrel.
¡ O cómo he de regalarla !   [*Vanse.*

Salen ULÍSES, CIRCE y *todas las Damas.*

Circe.
En esta florida márgen,
Desde cuya verde estancia
Se juzgan de tierra y mar
Las dos vistosas campañas,
Tan contrariamente hermosas,
Y hermosamente contrarias,
Que neutral la vista duda,
Cual es la yerba, ó el agua,
Porque aqui en golfos de flores,
Y alli en selvas de esmeraldas,
Unas mismas ondas hacen
Las espumas y las matas,
A los suspiros del noto,
Y á los alientos del aura,
Puedes descansar, Ulíses,
Las fatigas de la caza
En mis brazos.

Ulíses.
            Dices bien ;
Pues solo en ellos descansa
El alma, porque ellos solos
El centro han sido del alma.

Libia.
Circe comes in this direction.
Lebrel.
Lest perchance she should be angry
With me for my monkey prize here,
Off I go.   Come with me, Massa.
Clarin.
What's to be done though, if he choke
    me ?

Lebrel.
Faith, to hold him I'll be hard set.
                    [*Exeunt all.*

Enter ULYSSES, CIRCE *and her Ladies.*

Circe.
On this flowery margin here,
From whose green slopes softly slanted,
The two lovely level plains
Of the land and sea expand them,
So contrasted in their beauty,
In their beauty so contrasted,
That the neutral vision doubts
Which is grass and which is water,
Since in bright bays here of flowers,
In green groves of emerald glass there,
The same waves together make
Now the foam-wreaths, now the
    branches,
When the sunny south wind sigheth,
When the softer zephyr panteth,
From the labours of the chase
Thou, Ulysses, in mine arms here
Canst refresh thee.
Ulysses.
            Thou speak'st well ;
Since in them alone comes any
Rest unto my soul, for they
Are its centre, its sole magnet.

Circe.
Con todas estas finezas,
Temo, Ulíses, que me engañas.
    Ulíses.
Por qué?
    Circe.
      Por pensar, que dura
Aquella ficcion pasada.
    Ulíses.
Nunca lo fue para mí.
    Circe.
Quién lo asegura?
    Ulíses.
        Mis ansias.
    Circe.
Quién lo dice?
    Ulíses.
      Mis deseos.
    Circe.
Es engaño.
    Ulíses.
    Es verdad clara.
    Circe.
¡ Quién, Ulíses, la supiera !
    Ulíses.
Escucha, Circe, y sabrásla :
  Vengativa deidad, deidad ingrata,
Que á la de Juno y Júpiter se atreve,
Huésped de esa república de nieve,
Vecino de ese piélago de plata,
  Tantos años la patria me dilata,
Y tantos contra mí peligros mueve,
Que, porque fuese mi vivir mas breve,
A tus umbrales derrotarme trata.
  A ellos llegué, seguro y defendido
De escándalo, de horror, de asombro
    tanto,
Como has en tierra y mar introducido.
  Tus encantos vencí, mas no tu llanto;

Circe.
Ah! I fear thou still deceiv'st me,
Howsoe'er thy tongue doth flatter.
    Ulysses.
Why ?
    Circe.
    Because I think that still
That false feint of loving lasteth.
    Ulysses.
False it never was with me.
    Circe.
Who doth make that sure?
    Ulysses.
        My anguish.
    Circe.
Who doth say it ?
    Ulysses.
      My heart's hope.
    Circe.
'Tis deceit.
    Ulysses.
    'Tis truth's own language.
    Circe.
Who, Ulysses, that can know ?
    Ulysses.
Hear me, Circe, and I'll answer :—
  A vengeful goddess, a dread deity,
One who with Jove and Juno dares
    compete,—
An ill-fared guest where snow-white
    breakers meet,
A lonely loiterer on the silver sea,—
  Long from my country had belated me,
And with new tempests every day
    would beat
My struggling ship, to make my fate
    complete
Led me at length unto thy shores and
    thee.

Pudo el amor lo que ellos no han
    podido :
Luego el amor es el mayor encanto.

Circe.

Con toda aquesa fineza,
La que me debes no pagas,
Porque fue mayor la mia.
        Ulises.
De qué suerte ?
        Circe.
      Oye, y sabrásla :
Vengativa y cruel, porque te asombres,
  A pesar de deidades lisonjeras,
  Reina desta república de fieras,
  Señora deste piélago de hombres,
Viví ; y porque mas bárbara me nombres,
  Ninguno abortó el mar á estas riberas,
  Que á mi sangrienta mágica no vieras
  Trocar las formas, y mudar los
    nombres.
Llegaste tú, y queriendo tu homicida
  Ser, burlaste mis ciencias, con espanto,
  Queriéndote vencer, quedé vencida.
Si mi encanto, al mirar asombro tanto,
  Al encanto de amor rindió mi vida,
  Luego el amor es el mayor encanto.
            [*Duérmese* Ulíses.

Hither I came, my fearless path pur-
    suing,
All fears of thee, all horrors raised
    above,
Thy vain enchantments in a trice sub-
    duing,
But not thy tears, which still could
    victor prove,
  Since love could do what they had
    fail'd in doing
  Then is the greatest of enchantments,
    love.
        Circe.
Even with all thy flatteries
Thou thy debt to me canst cancel,
Since still greater far were mine.
        Ulysses.
In what way ?
        Circe.
      Attend, I'll answer :—
Vengeful and cruel (fear-inspiring then)
  Spite of all goddesses of gentler mien,
  Of this wild kingdom of wild beasts
    the queen,
  The mistress of this wilderness of men,
Long lived I here in my enchanted den,
  No one approach'd these shores of
    smiling green
  But by my bloody magic soon was seen
  Transform'd and prison'd in a bestial
    pen :
At length you came, by power still
    mightier shielded,
You laugh'd my spells to scorn, and
    when I strove
To conquer you, the subtler power you
    wielded
  Enmesh'd me in the net-work that I
    wove,

	Since then my life to love's enchantments yielded,
	Then is the greatest of enchantments, love. [ULYSSES *sleeps.*

Sale LIBIA.

Libia.
La música, que has mandado
Prevenir, está, señora,
Esperando.

Circe.
    Por ahora
No canteis; que desvelado
Se da Ulíses por vencido
A la deidad de Morfeo,
A cuyo letal trofeo
Las potencias ha rendido,
Haciendo de todas dueño
Esta macilenta sombra,
Que á un tiempo halaga y asombra,
Pues es descanso, y es sueño.
Infundid, aves y flores,
Para aliviar sus congojas,
Silencio en templadas hojas,
Suspended vuestros amores.
No hagan ruido los cristales
De los arroyos, callando
Corran las fuentes, mostrando
Obedientes y leales
El amor, que en mí se encierra;
Y en retórico silencio
Digan, cuanto reverencio
Su descanso.

Voces (dentro).
    Guerra, guerra!
[*Tocan dentro cajas hácia un lado.*

Enter LIBIA.

Libia.
Lady, as you have desired,
The musicians now are staying
In the ante-room.

Circe.
    Their playing
Must be now postponed, since tired,
Hath Ulysses yielded up
All his senses to the keeping
Of the god of sleep, and sleeping
Tastes the god's lethean cup—
That pale power, death's shadowy brother,
Who a curse or blessing seems,
As he gives sweet rest or dreams
Which the conscience fain would smother;—
Give, ye birds and flowers and groves,
Give, for that light breath he heaves,
Silence 'mid your trembling leaves,
Brief suspension to your loves;
Streamlets, down in soft attrition
Let your crystals glide, ye flowing
Fountains, now be silent, showing
Your obedience and submission
To the love my breast that charms,
And in silent rhetoric say
How you reverence to-day
His repose.

Voices within.
    To arms! to arms!—
[*Drums and trumpets are heard
from the same side.*

Circe.
Qué es efto? ¿cuándo pretendo
Silencio, hay quien le interrompa?
   [*Defpierta* ULÍSES.
  Ulífes.
Guerra publica efta trompa,
Guerra publica efte eftruendo.
¿Pues cómo, ay diofes! afi
Es hoy perezofo el fueño,
De nobles fentidos dueño?
No foy, fin duda, el que fui,
Pues á delicias fuaves
Entregado, ay de mí? eftoy,
Y tras los ecos no voy
Mas belicofos y graves.—
Perdona, Circe, que afi,
Habiendo guerra y furor,
No me ha de tener tu amor.
  Circe.
Detente, efcucha! ay de mí!
¿Quién efe clarin tocó?

  Sale ANTÍSTES.

  Antíftes.
Quien, penfando que feria
Lifonja, la falva hacia,
Cuando defde el mar te vió.
  Ulífes.
Aqui no hay ya que efperar;
La guerra me ha defpertado,
Porque en el alma ha tocado
La firena militar.
  Circe.
Para templar el furor,
Cantad de amor, cantad pues.
  [*La Múfica al otro lado.*
  Múfica.
¿Dónde vas, Ulífes, fi es
El mayor encanto amor?

Circe.
What is this, that thus deftroys
Silence, that fo late I claim'd?
   [ULYSSES *awakes.*
  Ulyffes.
War, that trumpet hath proclaim'd,
War, that clang of martial noife.
But, ye Gods! from what bafe caufe
Is, to-day, dull fleep abhorr'd,
Of my nobler fenfes lord?
Ah! I am not what I was;
Since by its foft fway fubdued,
Woe is me! when bugles vie,
Ah! my heart doth not reply,
Bold, refponfive, as it fhould.
Pardon me, O Circe, fee!
War and woe are in my ear,
And love muft not keep me here.
  Circe.
Liften, ftay! ah! woe is me,
Who produced this wild uproar?

  Enter ANTISTES.

  Antiftes.
We with trumpets long fo mute,
From our fhip did thee falute,
When we faw thee on the fhore.
  Ulyffes.
Here delay difgraceful feems,
Battle leads my fteps afar;
Since the firen fong of war
Wakes my foul from all its dreams.
  Circe.
Sing of love, fing rapturoufly,
Sing, and thus his rage remove.
  [*Mufic and fong from the other fide.*
  Song.
Stay, Ulyffes, ftay, if love
Greateft of enchantments be.

Ulíses.
¿ Qué blandas voces fuaves,
Repetidas en los vientos,
Son con fonoros acentos
Dulce envidia de las aves ?
¡ Qué bien el amor me fuena !
¿ Cómo tu amor me ha podido,
Circe hermofa, haber vencido
Aquella pafada pena ?
Ya me vuelvo á tu favor.
  Griegos (dentro).
Guerra, guerra !
   Ulíses.
    Mas ¿ qué efpero ?
Las armas me llaman, quiero
Seguirlas.
  Múfica (dentro).
   Amor, amor !
  Ulíses.
¡ Qué blanda, qué dulcemente
Suena efta voz repetida !
  Antíftes (aparte).
Aunque me cuefte la vida,
Tengo de hablar claramente.—
Ulíses, invicto Griego,
¿ Cómo, cuando afi te llama
La trompeta de la fama,
En deliciofo fofiego
Sordo yaces ? ¿ Cuánto yerra,
No fabes, el que rendido
A fu amor, labra fu olvido ?
Oye efta voz !
   Griegos (dentro).
    Guerra, guerra !
   Ulíses.
Tienes, Antíftes, razon ;
Torpes mis fentidos tuve,
Ciego eftuve, fordo eftuve ;
Mas ya que eftas voces fon

Ulyffes.
Ah ! what fweet feductive words !
Ah ! what founds are thofe I hear ?
Sounds whofe foften'd echoes clear
Wake the envy of the birds.
Ah ! how fweet to me love's ftrain,
Sweet and with a ftrange power too,
Lovely Circe, to fubdue
All that paft perturbèd pain :—
'Neath thy fway once more I move.
  The Greeks (within).
To arms ! to arms !
   Ulyffes.
    But why delay ?
Battle calls, I muft away
To the combat.
  Song (within).
   Love, fweet love !
  Ulyffes.
Ah ! how fweetly on the wind
Sounds again that warbled figh !
  Antíftes (afide).
Though I lofe my life thereby
Plainly I muft fpeak my mind :—
O Ulyffes, victor Greek !
When the trumpet of thy fame
Calls thee to a loftier aim,
Canft thou, lull'd in luxury, feek
Not to hear it ? Of love's charms
Know'ft thou not the dire effect ?
How they work fad felf-neglect ?
Lift *this* voice.
  The Greeks (within).
    To arms ! to arms !
   Ulyffes.
Yes, Antíftes, thou art right,
Torpor held my fpell-bound mind.
I was deaf, and I was blind,
But my fenfes and my fight

Recuerdos de mi ofadía,
Las prifiones rompere.
   Circe.
¿Tan ingrata prifion fue,
Ulífes, la prifion mia?
¿Cómo, cuando entre mis brazos
Envidia á las flores das,
Tras otro afecto te vas?
¿Tan fáciles fon mis lazos
De romper? ¿Tanto rigor
Premio es de tantos favores?
Efcucha en hojas y en flores
Efta voz.
   Múfica (dentro).
   Amor, amor!
   Antifles.
No calle el marcial furor.
   Circe.
Amor digan mar y tierra.
   Múfica (dentro).
Amor, amor!
   Griegos (dentro).
   Guerra, guerra!
Guerra, guerra!
   Múfica (dentro).
   Amor, amor!
   Ulífes.
Aqui guerra, amor aqui
Oigo, y cuando afi me veo,
Conmigo mifmo peleo;
Defiéndame yo de mí.
   Antifles.
Efto es honor.
   Ulífes.
   Dices bien,
Todo el honor lo atropella.
   Circe.
Efto es gloria.

By thefe voices are reftored;
I fhall break my chains and flee.
   Circe.
To be captive unto me,
Was it thraldom fo abhorr'd?
How, when in my arms thou'ft given
Envy to the lovelieft flowers,
Canft thou figh for ftormier hours?
Can my fweet bonds then be riven
Thus fo lightly? Doft thou prove
Grateful thus for bygone bliffes?
Hear this voice, that as it kiffes
Flowers and leaves, fings—
   Song (within).
   Love, fweet love!
   Antifles.
Ceafe not, founds that warriors move!
   Circe.
Land and fea fing love's foft charms.
   Song (within).
Love, fweet love!
   The Greeks (within).
   To arms! to arms!
To arms! to arms!
   Song (within).
   Love, fweet love!
   Ulyffes.
Love and war falute my ear,
Either would my heart delight with;
'Tis myfelf that I muft fight with,
'Tis myfelf that I muft fear.
   Antifles.
Honour's here.
   Ulyffes.
   Thou fpeakeft true,
All things lie at honour's feet.
   Circe.
Here is rapture.

Ulíses.
　　　¡ Ay Circe bella,
Qué bien dices tú tambien !
　　Circe.
El gusto es dulce pasion.
　　Ulíses.
Razon tienes.
　　　Antístes.
　　　　　La victoria
Es mas aplauso, mas gloria.
　　Ulíses.
Tú tambien tienes razon.
　　　Antístes.
Guerra y amor en rigor
Te llaman, miedos destierra.
　　　Música (dentro).
Amor, amor !
　　　Griegos (dentro).
　　　　Guerra, guerra !
　　Circe.
Quién ha vencido ?
　　Ulíses.
　　　　　El amor ;
Que ¿ cómo pudiera ser,
Que otro afecto me venciera,
Donde tu hermosura viera ?
Esclavo tuyo he de ser.
No hay mas fama para mí
Que adorarte, no hay mas gloria
Que vivir en tu memoria.
Dichoso mil veces fui
El dia, que tu favor
Mereció mi voluntad.
　　Circe.
Venid todas, y cantad :
" El mayor encanto amor."—
Entra tú ; y vosotros, Griegos,
Mas pesares no me deis,
Y agradeced que no os veis,

Ulysses.
　　　Circe sweet,
Ah ! how well thou speakest, too.
　　Circe.
Sweet is passion's rapturous bliss.
　　Ulysses.
Thou art right.
　　　Antístes.
　　　　　But far more glorious
Is the warrior's wreath victorious.
　　Ulysses.
Thou art also right in this.
　　　Antístes.
War and love both call thee ; prove
Now thy wisdom,—hence, alarms !
　　　Song (within).
Love, sweet love !
　　　The Greeks (within).
　　　　　To arms ! to arms !
　　Circe.
Which has conquer'd ?
　　Ulysses.
　　　　　It is love ;
Since, what other power could have
Any chance of victory,
Thou in beauty standing by ?
From this hour I am thy slave ;
To adore thee be my fame,
All my glory, my reward,
But to live in thy regard.
O thrice-happy day ! that came
All my doubtings to remove,
Since it came thy love to bring.
　　Circe.
Come, my maidens, come and sing,
" The greatest of enchantments,
　　love ;"—
Enter thou ; and, O ye Greeks,
Interrupt our bliss no more,

Entre volcanes y fuegos,
De mi cólera abrasados.

Antiftes.
¡ Ay de nofotros ! que afi
Ya moriremos aqui
Cautivos y defterrados ;
Sepulcro ferá efta tierra
De tanto griego valor.   [*Vafe.*

Múfica.
¡ El mayor encanto amor !
     [*Vanfe todos cantando.*

En otra parte tocan armas, y dice
ARSIDAS.

Arfidas (dentro).
Arma, arma ! guerra, guerra !

Vuelve CIRCE *y todas las Damas.*

Circe.
¿ Qué es efto, habiendo mandado
Yo, que temerofos callen
Los repetidos acentos
De baquetas y metales,
Otra vez ofais, villanos,
Otra vez ofais, cobardes,
Que oprimido el bronce gima,
Que herido fe queje el parche ?

Sale FLERIDA.

Flérida.
No efte repetido acento,
Que con idiomas marciales,
Eftremeciendo los montes,
Titubear los ejes hace,
Cautela ha fido de Griegos ;
Mas defdichas, mas pefares,
Mas penas, mas confufiones,

And be thankful that the roar
Of no red volcano breaks
Round you raging, through mine ire.
Antiftes.
Ah ! unhappy we ! fince here,
Exiled from our country dear,
Captives we muft all expire.
Land foredoom'd of fatal charms,
Grecian valour's grave to prove !
        [*Exit.*

Song.
The greateft of enchantments, love !
     [*Exeunt all, finging.*

In a third direction a martial charge
is founded from within.

Arfidas (within).
War ! war ! to arms ! to arms !

CIRCE, *with her train, returns.*

Circe.
How is this ? when I commanded
That the trembling echoes, humbled,
Should no more repeat the rude notes
Of the drum-fticks and the trumpets ;
Dare ye, once again, vile caitiffs,
Cowards, dare ye thus infult me,
Making the forced bronze-tubes groan,
And the wounded parchment mutter ?

Enter FLERIDA.

Flerida.
No, this rude found now repeated,
Which, in martial idiom utter'd,
Makes the mighty mountains quiver,
And their deepeft caverns rumble,
Was not by the Greeks occafion'd ;
Greater griefs, afflictions newer,
Added forrows, worfe confufions,

Mas tormentos y mas males
Son los que quieren los cielos,
Que estos aparatos causen.
Arsidas, que tantos dias
Fue de tu hermosura amante,
A tus desdenes quejoso,
Ofendido á tus desaires,
Desde que ya enamorada
De Ulíses te declaraste,
Cuando de aquella cuestion
Pusieron los rayos paces,
A su corte se fue, donde,
Queriendo el amor que pasen
De extremo á extremo sus penas,
Que esto en los hombres es fácil,
Amenazando estos montes
Viene, infestando esos mares;
Y con razon, pues las ondas,
Gimiendo del peso grave,
Con ambicion de peñascos
Blasonan, cuando arrogantes
Ven por la campaña azul
De sus salobres cristales
Vagar un Volcan deshecho,
Mover un Flegra portátil,
Correr un Etna movible,
E ir una Trinacria errante.
Lísidas, de mí ofendido,
Creyendo que yo mudable
Amaba á Ulíses, (la causa
Con que yo lo fingí sabes)
Le acompaña, porque así
Pretende de aqui sacarme;
Que agravios de amor y zelos
No guardan respeto á nadie.
Yo lo sé, porque sentada
Sobre esa punta, que hace
Corona al mar y á la tierra,
Arbitro de ondas y valles,

Countless ills and woes unnumber'd,
Are, so heaven has wish'd, the causes
Of the sounds at which we shudder.
Arsidas, who was, thou knowest,
Long the lover of thy beauty,
By thy cold disdainings wounded,
Anger'd by thy proud repulses,
From the day that thou declared thee
Openly Ulysses' lover,
When the question's doubtful issue
Closed in lightning and in thunder,
To his court went, where compelling
His late love to change with sudden
Impulse from one point to another
(Men find easy such abruptness),
Now returns, these mountains threaten-
    ing,
Comes oppressing these white surfs here;
And with reason, since the billows
Groaning 'neath so great a burthen,
Thinking that with rocks they wrestle,
Proudly rush exulting up them,
They behold upon the crystal
Salt hills of their azure surface
Float along a loosed volcano,
Flit a Phlegra down the currents,
Hasten by a mobile Ætna,
A Trinacria through the surges.
Lysidas, with me offended,
Thinking that my heart had suffer'd
Love-change for Ulysses (why
So I feign'd, thou knowest, that urged me)
Comes along with him, thus hoping
That from this he may abduct me;
Since nor love nor jealousy
Show respect to aught that's human:—
This I know, because when seated
On that point which crowns the furthest
Headland height o'er earth and water,

Ví, (como entre obscuros lejos
De unos pintados celages,
Suelen pintarnos las sombras,
Ya jardines, ya ciudades)
Una confusa noticia,*
Que era, al perspicaz exámen
De la vista, neutral duda,
Mezcla de nubes y naves.
Cuando† al acercarse al puerto
La gruesa armada que traen,
A los sulcos de las proas
Rizarse ví, y encresparse
Blanca espuma, que al azul
Camelote de aguas hace
Bella guarnicion de plata,
Que sin que al dibujo guarde
El órden, es mas hermoso,
Por ser dibujo sin arte.
Llegaron á nuestro puerto,
Donde sin faenas baten
Las blancas alas de lino,
Negándose al mar, ó al aire
Esos peces, si son peces,
O esas aves, si son aves.
Sin salva á tierra saltaron,
Y fueron en un instante
Griegos caballos, preñados
De aparatos militares,
Pues abortaron sus vientres,
Siendo del agua Volcanes,
Iras y rayos, que luego
Fueron poblando la márgen.
Bien á los dos conocí,
Que armados á tierra salen,
Y en mal pronunciadas voces,
Que embarazó lo distante,

* Hartzenbusch's edition reads *apariencia.*—
Tr.
  † Hartzenbusch reads *luego.*—Tr.

Waves and valleys lying under,
Saw I, (as the far perspectives
Of some painter's glorious sunsets
Give us shadowy outlines, gleaming
Gardens here, and there dark turrets)—
A remarkable confusion,
Which upon my sight resulted
In a splendid maze of mingled
Clouds and ships of loveliest colour.
When approach'd the great armada
To the port, I saw the surf there,
In the furrows of the prows,
Twist itself, and crisp, and curdle
Foam white fair, which on the azure
Camlet of the sea made lovely
Broidery of netted silver,
Which without design resulted
In that perfect grace, which nature
Ever without art produces.
Then our harbour having enter'd,
They, uncorded, let forth flutter
Their white wind-raised wings of linen,
Leaving sea and sky in utter
Doubt if the great keels were fishes,
Or the sails the wings of birds were.
Giving no salute they leap'd forth
On the land; the ships grown subtle
Great Greek horses, all with war-stores
Pregnant to the very gunnel:
For from out their wombs in birth-
    throes,
(Sea-borne forges they of Vulcan,)
Angry bolts were born, which peopled
All the shore round with their thunders.
Well I knew, of those who leap'd forth
Arm'd on land there, two among them,
And in words caught indistinctly,
Which the distance half obstructed,
Heard I Arsidas, who said:—

Oí á Arfidas, que dijo:
Hoy defta mágica acaben
Los encantos, y efte monte,
Que es tiranizado Atlante
De Trinacria, á mi valor
Se poftre.—Yo viendo el grande
Peligro, que te amenaza,
Volando vine á avifarte.
Preven la defenfa pues,
Si es que hay defenfa que bafte
A la fangrienta venganza
De dos zelofos amantes.
      Circe.
¡ Calla, calla, no profigas !
Ni lleguen ecos marciales
A los oidos de Ulífes.
Aqui tengo de dejarle
Sepultado en blando fueño,
Porque el belicofo alarde
No pueda de mi amor nunca
Dividirle, ni olvidarle ;
Que yo con vofotras folas
Saldré á vencer arrogante.
Tú mi caudillo ferás,
Y no temas, que te falten
Gentes ; que aunque fon tan pocos
Los foldados de mi parte,
Yo armadas hueftes pondré
En las campañas del aire,
Que con tropas de caballos,
Con efcuadrones de infantes,
Fantáfticamente lidien,
Y fingidamente marchen.
Y porque entre tantas fombras
Vivas efcuadras no falten,
Todas vofotras, armadas
Con efcudos de diamante,
Galas defnudad de Vénus,
Túnicas veftid de Marte.

On this day at length is number'd
This magician's laft enchantments ;
And this mountain, this ufurper,
Which like Atlas lords Trinacria,
Shall beneath my valour crumble.
I perceiving the great danger
That thus threatens to engulf thee,
Flew to tell thee.—So get ready
All the aid that thou canft mufter,
If aught aid can ftop the bloody
Vengeance of two jealous lovers.

      Circe.
Ceafe, oh ! ceafe, proceed no more !
Nor let martial echoes thunder
In the clofed ears of Ulyffes ;
Buried in a foothing flumber
Him I mean to leave here lying,
That again war's glorious hubbub
His remembrance, his affection,
Never from my love may funder.
I alone with you will go
This proud boafter's pride to humble.
Thou my general wilt be ;
Fear not that no troops will mufter
At thy call ; for though few foldiers
Have I on my fide to fummon,
I can on the fields of air
Show arm'd hofts in countlefs numbers,
Who in companies of horfe,
Who in fquadrons of light foot-men,
Will fantaftically fight,
Will in phantom files manœuvre ;
And that thou may'ft with thefe fhadows
Lack not living hofts among them,
All of you, my maidens, arm'd
With your dazzling diamond bucklers,
Doff the filken robes of Venus,
And put on Mars' martial tunics.

Cafandra.
Eſta vida, y eſte pecho
Te ofrezco yo de mi parte.
    Clori.
Yo, que conozcan los hombres
Cuanto las mugeres valen.
    Sirene.
Hoy el ſol ſerá teſtigo
De mi valor arrogante.
    Tiſbe.
De nueſtro poder haré
Que el mundo ſe defengañe.
    Aſtrea.
A Pálas verás armada
Cada vez que me mirares.
    Libia.
A mí á Vénus, pues verás
A mis pies rendido á Marte.
    Circe.
Pues con eſa confianza,
Toca al arma.
    Cafandra.
        Suene el parche.
    Clori.
Hiera la trompeta el eco.
    Sirene.
El bronce oprimido brame.
    Tiſbe.
El fuego reviente.
    Aſtrea.
        Sea
Toda Trinacria volcanes.
    Libia.
El duro horror de las armas
Cielo, mar y tierra eſpante.
    Flérida.
Y viva Circe, prodigio
Deſtos montes y eſtos mares.

Caſſandra.
I this life, this boſom offer
Thee on my part in thy trouble.
    Chloris.
I that men may know how much
Woman's courage may be truſted.
    Sirene.
On my valour will the ſun
Gaze to-day with looks of wonder.
    Thiſbe.
Of our power the world no more
Shall make light, as is its cuſtom.
    Aſtrea.
I a Pallas ſhall be thought,
Every time in arms I ſtruggle.
    Libia.
I a Venus, ſince thou'lt ſee
Mars beneath my feet made ſubject.
    Circe.
Thus then confident and bold
Sound the charge.
    Caſſandra.
        Ring out the trumpets.
    Chloris.
Let the drums awake the echoes.
    Sirene.
And the bugles blare and bluſter.
    Thiſbe.
Let the fire burſt forth.
    Aſtrea.
           And be
All Trinacria but one furnace.
    Libia.
At the horrid din of arms
Let heaven, earth, and ocean ſhudder.
    Flerida.
And live Circe, of theſe ſeas,
Of theſe mountains, the fair wonder.

Circe.

Porque á los brazos de Uiíses,
Que en mudo letargo yace,
Vuelva rica de defpojos,
Enamorada y conftante.   [*Vanfe.*

MONTE.

Salen ARSÍDAS, LÍSIDAS *y Soldados.*

Arfidas.

Defde efta excelfa cumbre,
Que del fol fe atrevió á tocar la lumbre,
Y altiva y eminente,
Coronada de rayos la alta frente,
Es immenfa coluna
De efe cóncavo alcázar de la luna,
Entre celages de rubí y topacio
De Circe fe defcubre el real palacio.
¡ Ea pues, mis foldados,
Que valientes, intrépidos y ofados,
En favor de los cielos
Manteneis la milicia de mis zelos !
Hoy efte afombro muera,
Perezca hoy la memoria defta fiera,
Que á Trinacria eftos campos tiraniza,
Siendo el Flegra fu hoguera y fu ceniza.
Libremos pues á tantos
Como tienen fus mágicos encantos
Prefos aqui, y cautivos ;
Queden pues ó bien muertos, ó bien
    vivos.
Refcatemos valientes
Nueftra patria de tantos accidentes,
Y dejemos feguro efte camino
Al náufrago piloto, al peregrino,
Que halló, cadáver de eftas grutas hondas,
Mas tormenta en las peñas, que en las
    ondas,

Circe.

That fhe to Ulyffes' arms—
Who lies there in filent numbnefs,
Still enamour'd and ftill conftant—
May, enrich'd with fpoils, return here.
    [*Exeunt.*

A MOUNTAIN.

Enter ARSIDAS, LYSIDAS, *and Soldiers.*

Arfidas.

From this ftupendous height,
Which dares to touch the fun's refplen-
    dent light,
And in its dazzling blaze
Crowns its proud forehead with the
    golden rays ;—
From this proud pillar-top
Which the fair moon's blue palace-dome
    doth prop,
'Twixt topaz clouds and ruby viftas we
The palace halls of Circe now may fee.
Then on, brave foldiers ! bold,
Valiant, intrepid, refolute, enroll'd
By favour of the fkies,
The avenging army of my jealoufies !
To-day muft die this terror of the earth,
This witch's memory fade as if fhe
    ne'er had birth ;
She who Trinacria tramples in the mire,
Its Phlegra fhe, its fount of afhes, fmoke
    and fire.
This day we muft fet free
The many whom by cruel forcery
She holds imprifon'd here in piteous
    ftate,
Whom living we muft loofe, or dead
    avenge their fate.
Let us, brave comrades mine,

Cuando pisó por estos horizontes
Montes de agua y piélagos de montes.
Y tú, Lísidas fuerte,
A cuya voz se retiró la muerte,
Hoy á Flérida libra soberana
De la injusta prision de una tirana,
O véngate hoy en ella,
Si tus zelos te olvidan de querella.

Lísidas.

Arsidas, valeroso
Príncipe de Trinacria, no zeloso
Mi venganza prevengo ;
Que no tengo los zelos que no tengo,
Porque ya sé, que ha sido
Un cauteloso amor, amor fingido,
El que Flérida á Ulíses le mostraba,
Porque ese Esfinge así se lo mandaba.
No zeloso en efecto, enamorado
Sí, que vengo, atrevido y despechado
A rescater á Flérida, que bella
Es de los cielos flor, del campo estrella.
Y así á tu lado juro
Por ese hermoso rosicler, que puro
Mirado, nos deslumbra,
Y no mirado, á todos nos alumbra,
De no dejarte, hasta mirar postrada
Al fuego de tu enojo esta encantada

Save now our country from such plagues
    malign,
And leave this sea-way clear
To ship-wreck'd pilot and lone mariner,
Who found, a cold corse in these hollow
    caves,
More torment 'mid the rocks, than out
    upon the waves,
Though on this wild horizon his frail
    ·home
Had been high mountain waves and
    watery hills of foam.
And thou, brave Lysidas, for whom
Death in indulgent mood re-oped the
    tomb,
Thou wilt to-day fair Flerida set free
From a dread tyrant's dread captivity,
Or else thy vengeance let her prove,
If in thy jealous rage thou canst forget
    thy love.

Lysidas.

Arsidas, valiant knight,
Trinacria's prince, no jealous torch doth
    light
My vengeful path to Circe's bower again,
For I no more, no more, can feel that
    bitter pain,
Knowing, as now I know,
'Twas false, feign'd love, 'twas love's
    deceptive show
That to Ulysses Flerida display'd—
The feint was order'd, and she but
    obey'd.
'Tis not with jealousy I come, but love,
Ardent, devoted, desperate, to remove
From this foul spot fair Flerida, that fair
Flower of the fairest field, and star of
    clearest air ;
And so, beside thee now,

Selva de amor, donde, por mas efpanto,
Es el amor hoy fu mayor encanto,
Aunque en fus campos, que el Abril
　　dibuja,
O brame el auftro, ó la arboleda cruja.

Arfidas.
Guerra de amor y zelos
Pavor pondrá á los cielos.

Voces dentro.
¡ Cierra, Trinacria, cierra !　　　　[*Cajas.*
Lífidas.
Ya de allá nos refponden.
Voces dentro.
　　　　　　Guerra, guerra !
Soldad.
¡ Ay, Arfidas, advierte,
Que á morir nos trajifte !

Arfidas.
　　　　　De qué fuerte ?
Soldad.
Dijifte, que no habia
Armas, ni gente en efta felva umbria,
Y apenas tus foldados
Han falido del mar, cuando embofcados
En efa felva vieron
Infantes y caballos, que falieron

By that fair planet's rofy light I vow—
That planet which when feen ftrikes
　　blind the fight,
And which unfeen ftill fills the world
　　with light—
To leave thee not until thy wrathful
　　mood
Strikes down each tree of this enchanted
　　wood,
This bower of love,—where we to-day
　　revere
Love, as the greateft of enchantments
　　here,—
Like as when on the April-painted meads
The fouth-wind roars, the ftrong boughs
　　bend like reeds.
　　　　　Arfidas.
This war of love allied with jealoufy
Shall wake the fear, the wonder of the
　　fky.
　　　　Voices within.
On ! for Trinacria's right !
　　　　　Lyfidas.
Yonder they anfwer.
　　　　Voices within.
　　　　　　To the fight, the fight !
　　　　A Soldier.
Oh ! hear me, Arfidas, oh ! hear and
　　ftay,
You lead us but to death here.
　　　　　Arfidas.
　　　　　　In what way ?—
　　　　Soldier.
You told us that we fhould
Nor men nor arms here meet within
　　this fhadowy wood,
And fcarce your foldiers made
A landing from their fhips, when from
　　an ambufcade

A defender la entrada
Del monte.

Arſidas.
     No temais, no temais nada ;
Que eſos monſtruos incultos
Son fantáſticas formas, que no bultos.
No hay que temer eſtragos,
Que ſus heridas ſolo ſon amagos ;
Que tarde ejecutadas,
Se quedan en el aire ſeñaladas.

Liſidas.
Y tan cobardes fueron,   [hirieron.
Que, amenazando ſiempre, nunca
    Soldad.
¿ Cómo, ſi ya, cauſando al ſol deſmayos,
Truenos abortan, y deſpiden rayos ?

Arſidas.
Yo he de ſer el primero,
Que eſe pavor os quite ; altivo y fiero
Penetraré la ſierra.

Liſidas.
Todos te ſeguiremos.
    Todos.
        Guerra, guerra !
  Arſidas.
¡ Ha cauteloſo Griego,
Sal á apagar retórico eſte fuego !

Salen CIRCE *y las mugeres con
eſpadas.*
    Circe.
No ſaldrá, ſino yo ; que la memoria

Within the wood they ſaw
Horſemen and footmen to its outſkirts
    draw,
The entrance to defend
That to the mountain leads.
    Arſidas.
    Fear naught, fear naught, my friend,
For all theſe monſtrous ſwarms
Are bodileſs ſhapes, are falſe fantaſtic
    forms ;
No need to fear ſuch foes
Whoſe very ſwords can deal but phan-
    tom blows,
Which ſlowly dealt,
But by the yielding air are only felt.
    Lyſidas.
And coward-like,
Who threaten ever, but who never ſtrike.
    Soldier.
How, if already the ſcared ſunlight dies
And thunders rattle and the lightning
    flies ?
    Arſidas.
I will be firſt this panic to ſubdue,
And with undaunted daring to burſt
    through
This magic mountain's marge.
    Lyſidas.
We all ſhall follow where you lead.
    All.
        Charge ! charge !—
    Arſidas.
Ha ! wily Greek,   [rhetoric !
Forth, and appeaſe this fire with all thy

CIRCE *and her women enter with
drawn ſwords.*
    Circe.
He comes not forth, but I ; it were amiſs

No le ha de embarazar tan breve gloria.

Astrea.
Ninguno quede vivo.
　　　　Flérida.
Ni un amante, que vuelve vengativo
Sin zelos.

　　　Lisidas.
　　　Tú me ofendes, y yo te ofendo,
Que mas mi fama que tu amor pretendo.

　　　Circe.
Segur de vuestros cuellos
Hoy serán nuestras armas.　¡ A ellos !

　　　Todos.
　　　　　　¡ A ellos !
　　Arsidas.
En batalla tan dura
No atienda hoy el respeto á la hermosura.
Presto, Circe, serás tu mi trofeo.

　　　Libia.
¡ O qué bonitamente lo peleo !
　　*[Dase la batalla y retiranse los
　　　　　hombres.*

PALACIO DE CIRCE.

Sale LEBREL, *y* CLARIN *de mona.*
　　　Lebrel.
Pues nos dejó Circe, y pues
A puerta cerrada estamos,
Y tan solos nos hallamos,
Tiempo, Doña Marta, es
De tomar una licion.
Ya la vuelta os enseñé

To have his thoughts disturb'd for glory
　such as this.
　　　Astrea.
Spare not their lives !
　　　　Flerida.
Not even a lover's, who for vengeance
　strives,
Though jealousy-cured.
　　　　Lysidas.
　　　Thou *me* dost, and I thee offend,
For more than to thy love I to my fame
　pretend.
　　　Circe.
Before the day is gone
Your necks shall stain our swords.　On
　them !
　　　All.
　　　　　　On ! on !
　　Arsidas.
In such a battle and with such a foe
Beauty to-day its homage must forego :
Soon, Circe, soon thy trophy crowns
　my might.
　　　Libia.
Just look, how very prettily I fight.
　　*[The battle is joined and the men
　　　　give way.*

CIRCE'S PALACE.

Enter LEBREL, *and* CLARIN *as a monkey.*
　　　Lebrel.
Now that Circe's gone, and we
Here are left, both you and I,
With closed doors, and no one by,
'Tis an opportunity
For a lesson ; so, my pet,
As I lately taught you, tumble,

Del rodezno ; cómo fue ?
      [Voltea.
¡ Así bien, teneis razon !
   Clarin.
¡ Que aquesto pase por mí !
¡ Y que en fin haya de ser,
O voltear, ó no comer !
Desdichado hablador fui.
   Lebrel.
Ahora, Marta, ponte en pie.
   Clarin.
Ello en fin no hay replicar,
O no comer, ó voltear.   *[Voltea.*
   Lebrel.
¡ Lindamente, por mi fe !
Ahora, porque si yo
No tengo quien de vestir
Me dé, uced me ha de servir ;
Tome aqueste espejo, y no
Le quiebre, porque es azar,
Y véngase tras mí en pie.
   Clarin.
Qué cara tengo veré
De mona. Hay mayor pesar ?
¡ Válgame Júpiter santo,
Qué hocico !
  [En mirándose al espejo se le cae
   el vestido de mona.
   Lebrel.
    Quién aqui habló ?
   Clarin.
¿ Quién ha de ser, sino yo ?
   Lebrel.
De verte, Clarin, me espanto.
   Clarin.
Yo Clarin ? muy bueno es eso !
Mona soy.
   Lebrel.
  ¿ Dónde escondido ? . . .

Try the wheel-trick—do not grumble—
    [Clarin tumbles.
Pretty well, you'll do it yet.
   Clarin.
What a fate is mine ! thy laws
Nature thus to so maltreat—
I must tumble or not eat !
Wretched babbler that I was.
   Lebrel.
Jocko, now on hands and feet.
   Clarin.
All remonstrance being past,
I must tumble or must fast. *[Tumbles.*
   Lebrel.
By my faith, you're quite complete !
Now, as here I hav'n't got
An attendant when I dress,
You your worship can't do less
Than be valet on the spot.
Take the glass, don't break it though,—
On your hind legs ! that's the place.
   Clarin.
Now at length my monkey face
I can have a peep at. Oh !
Holy Jove, above who eyes me,
What a snout !
  [At seeing himself in the mirror, he
   loses the appearance of a monkey.
   Lebrel.
    Who speaks so nigh ?
   Clarin.
Why, who *could* it be, but I ?
   Lebrel.
Clarin here ? you quite surprise me.
   Clarin.
Clarin I ? that's good of you !
I'm a monkey.
   Lebrel.
  Where were you hidden ? . . . .

Mas la mona fe me ha ido.
        Clarin.
Ya otra admiracion confiefo.
        Lebrel.
¿Sabes por donde fe fue
La mona, que aqui tenia?
        Clarin.
Yo foy.
        Lebrel.
        Linda bobería!
Por la mona pregunté.
        Clarin.
Pues yo foy.

   Salen ANTÍSTES *y los Griegos con
      unas armas.*
        Antíftes.
        Quién eftá aqui?
        Clarin.
Los dos.
        Lebrel.
        ¡Que, porque viniefe
Clarin, la mona fe fuefe!
Tiempo y trabajo perdí.
        Antíftes.
Dime, Lebrel, ¿dónde eftá . . . .
        Lebrel.
La mona? No fé, ay de mí!
        Antíftes.
Ulífes? te digo.
        Clarin.
        Alli.

Defcúbrefe un trono, donde eftá ULÍSES
      durmiendo.
        Antíftes.
Entrar podeis todos ya;
Que pues aqui retirado
A Ulífes Circe dejó,

But the monkey off has flidden.
        Clarin.
This my wonder wakes anew.
        Lebrel.
Did you fee what way retired
The pet monkey that I had?
        Clarin.
I am he.
        Lebrel.
        That's not fo bad,—
'Twas for the monkey I inquired.
        Clarin.
I am he, I fay.

   Enter ANTISTES, *and the* GREEKS
      bearing pieces of armour.
        Antíftes.
        Who's here?
        Clarin.
We two.
        Lebrel.
        Plague on't! for this flunky
Turning up, I've loft my monkey—
Time and trouble too, I fear.
        Antíftes.
Do you know, Lebrel, where is . . . . ?
        Lebrel.
My poor monkey? no, ah! me.
        Antíftes.
Tut! I meant Ulyffes.
        Clarin.
        See.

A throne is difcovered, and on it
      ULYSSES *fleeping.*
        Antíftes.
Softly tread this room of his:—
Since remote from any hum
Circe left Ulyffes here,

Cuando al mar á ver falió
Las naves que habian llegado,
Efte es el tiempo mejor,
Para vencer fus extremos;
Y puefto que no podemos
Avifarle con rumor
De armas, hoy de Aquíles fea
El arnes fu trompa.   Aqui
Le dejemos, porque afi,
Cuando defpierte, le vea.
                Timántes.
Acuérdele mudo él
Las battallas, que venció,
Cuando en campaña fe vió
Coronado de laurel,
Para que defpertador
De tantos olvidos fea.
                Arquelao.
Quien no creyó la voz, crea
Las infignias del valor.
        [*Pónenle á los pies las armas.*
                Polidoro.
Trofeos, que foberanos
Troya entre cenizas llora,
Y aun eftais fudando ahora
La fangre de los Troyanos,
Volved por vos, y entre viles
Amores no os permitais
Empañar, pues aun guardais
El muerto calor de Aquíles.
        [*Vanfe, y defpierta* ULÍSES.

                Ulífes.
Pefado letargo ha fido
Efte á que rendido eftuve,
Ni bien vida, ni bien fueño,
Sino letal pefadumbre
De los fentidos, que torpes,
Ni defcanfan, ni difcurren,

When fhe went to fee anear
The great navy that had come,
'Tis the time to triumph o'er
Charms that fo his foul have bow'd,
And fince we are not allow'd
To advife him by the roar
Of the drums, his trumpet be
Now, Achilles' harnefs bright,—
Place it there within his fight,
That when waking he may fee.
                Timantes.
Mute may it recall the round
Of the battles that he won,
Of the fields he ftood upon,
With the victor laurel crown'd,
May it from delufive charms,
Wake him foon to manlier deed.
                Archelaus.
He who heeds no voice, may heed
The reproachful ruft of arms.
        [*They place the armour at his feet.*
                Polydorus.
Trophies of a realm fubdued,
Trophies Troy in afhes weeps,
Since along your bright mail creeps
Still the fweat of Trojan blood;
No bafe ftain of low defire
Let difgraceful love fling o'er you,
Wake, by thoughts of him who bore
        you,
Dead Achilles' martial fire.
                        [*Exeunt all.*
                Ulyffes (awaking.)
Lead-like lethargy, it furely
Muft have been that I lay under,—
Neither wholly life, nor fleeping,
But a dark lethean dulnefs
Of the fenfes, which, grown torpid,
Neither moved, nor wholly flumber'd.

Crepúsculos fon del alma,
Pues obran entre dos luces.
Quién eftá aqui ? Solo eftoy.
¿ Pues comó fin Circe pude
Vivir un inftante ? Bien,
Que eftaban fin luz, prefumen
Mis fentidos, pues fin fol
Aun todo el cielo no luce.
Circe! Circe! mi feñora!
¡ Qué mal tanta aufencia fuple
Tu memoria!—Mas qué veo ?
El grabado arnes iluftre
De Aquíles á mis pies yace,
Torpe, olvidado é inútil.
Bien eftá á mis pies, porque
Rendido á mi amor fe juzgue,
Y fegunda vez en mí
Amor de Marte fe burle.
Tarde, olvidado trofeo
Del valor, á darme acudes
Socorro contra mí mifmo ;
Que aunque contra mí me ayudes,
Hoy colgado en efte templo
Quedarás, donde fepulten
Sus olvidos tus memorias.

Twilights of the foul were they,
That 'twixt day and darknefs ftruggled.
Who is here ? I am alone.
Ah! how can I live one flutter
Of the heart without my Circe ?
Well my thoughts divined the murky
Dark near, fince without the fun
Heaven itfelf difplays no luftre.
Circe ! Circe ! my feñora,
For thy abfence, all I fuffer
Memory poorly pays for.   But,
What is this ? the graved refulgent
Armour of Achilles lieth
At my feet forgot, unufed.
Rightly at my feet, becaufe
To my love it deems it fubject,
And a fecond time in me
Victor Love o'er Mars exulteth.
All too late, forgotten trophy
Of true valour, doft thou come here
Succour 'gainft myfelf to give me ;
Since though 'gainft myfelf thy fuccour
Giv'ft thou, in this fane fufpended
Must thou here remain, where buried
Shall thy memory be forgotten.

El Efpiritu de Aquíles, *defde el centro*
de la tierra.

Aquíles.
¡ No le ofendas, no le injuries !
Ulifes.
¿ Qué voz es efta, que en mí
Tan nuevo pavor infunde ?
    [*Tocan dentro cojas deftempladas y*
        una fordina.
¿ A quién deftempladas trompas,
Exequias figuen lúgubres ?
¿ Quién caufa efte efecto ?

The fhade of Achilles *from below.*

Achilles.
Mock them not ; do not infult them.
Ulyffes.
Ah! what voice is this that makes me
In my inmoft heart to fhudder ?
    [*A mournful march of muffled drums*
        and trumpets is heard from below.
Ah ! for whofe fad obfequies
Play thefe mournful drums and trumpets?
Who occafions this ?

Aquíles (debajo de tierra).
        Quien
A fus venganzas acude.
      Ulifes.
Si ojos tengo con que mire,
Si oidos tengo con que efcuche,
En el centro de la tierra
Sonó la voz, y no fufre
Ella aun de fu grave faz
La arrugada pefadumbre;
Pues abre para quejarfe
Una boca, y de ella efcupe
Pardas nubes de humo y fuego,
¿Cuando, contra la coftumbre,
En el centro de la tierra
Forjan fus rayos las nubes?
       [Abrefe una boca, y fale fuego.

A mas el afombro pafa;
Trifte un monumento fube
De fu abifmo, haciendo un caos
De vapores y viflumbres.

  Va fubiendo un fepulcro, y en él
  Aquíles, *cubierto de un velo.*

O tú, que en leves cenizas,
Que aun el viento no facude,
En efe fepulcro yaces,
Quién eres?
      Aquíles.
        Porque no dudes
Quien foy, efte negro velo
Corre, y mi afpecto defcubre.
      [Defcúbrele Ulíses.
Conócefme?
      Ulifes.
      Si me deja
Efpecies con que te juzgue
Lo pálido de tu faz,

Achilles (from below).
        One who
To take ftern revenge doth come here.
      Ulyffes.
If I can believe my eyes,
If my hearing can be trufted,
From the centre of the earth
Came that voice, the earth that fuffers
Not upon its heavy face
Even the movement of a mufcle;
Since a mouth is open'd wide
For complaint, from which is fputter'd
Denfeft clouds of fmoke and fire.
When, againft all ufual cuftom,
In the centre of the earth,
Have the clouds forged flafhing thunders?
      [An abyfs opens from which fire burfts
           forth.
Higher ftill my terror rifes;
From the abyfs, a fad fepulchral
Tomb arifes, making chaos   [wreaths.
With its fteams and glimmering dun-

A tomb arifes from the abyfs, and in it
  is Achilles *covered with a veil.*

O dread fhape, that in light afhes,
Which not even the wind difturbeth,
Lieft in this fepulchre,
Say, who art thou?
      Achilles.
        That all further
Doubt fhould end, this black veil lift,
And my countenance difcover.
      *[*Ulysses *raifes the veil.*
Doft thou know me?
      Ulyffes.
        If I may
Truft the tefts wherewith to judge the
Afhy palenefs of thy face,

Que no hay vista que no turbe,
Lo yerto de tu esqueleto.
Que aun desfigurado luce,
Aquíles, Aquíles eres.

Aquíles.
Su espíritu soy ilustre,
Que de los elisios campos,
Donde eterna mansion tuve,
Volví á pasar de Aqueronte
Las verdinegras y azules
Ondas, derretidas gomas
Del salitre y del azufre.
A cobrar vengo mis armas,
Porque el amor no las juzgue
Ya de su templo despojo,
Torpe, olividado é inútil ;
Porque no quieren los dioses,
Que otro dueño las injurie,
Sino que en mi sepultura
A par de los siglos duren.
Y tú, afeminado Griego,
Que, entre las delicias dulces
Del amor, de negras sombras
Tantos esplendores cubres,
No entre amorosos encantos
Las tengas y las deslustres,
Sino rompiendo de amor
Las mágicas inquietudes,
Sal de Trinacria, y hollando
Al mar los vidrios azules,
A discrecion de los vientos
Sus pavimentos discurre ;
Que en la curia de los dioses
Quieren, que otra vez los sulques,
Hasta que de mi sepulcro
Las muertas aras saludes,
Y en él esas armas cuelgues.
No lo ignores, no lo dudes,

Which no sight can see untroubled,
And thy stiffen'd skeleton,
Which, though maim'd, retains such
     lustre,
Thou Achilles art, Achilles.

Achilles.
I his spirit am, so bruited,
Who from the Elysian fields, my
Everlasting home and country,
Have pass'd through the green and azure
Waves of Acheron, thick gummy
Molten mires of fire and brimstone,
Pools of nitre and of sulphur,
To reclaim once more my arms,
So that Love may never judge them
Of his temple the proud spoil,
Idle, all forgot, and useless ;
For the gods no longer wish
That another lord should rust them,
But that buried in my tomb
They should last while years are num-
     ber'd.
And, O thou effeminate Greek,
Who, amid the soft indulgence
Of weak love, so many splendours
In thick ebon shades dost cover,—
Not in amorous enchantments
Shouldst thou let them lose their lustre,
But the magic-woven web
Of love's passionate joys and troubles
Breaking, fly Trinacria, and
Treading the sea's glass-blue surface,
At the winds' discretion scud
O'er its level lawns unruffled.
For it is the gods' decree
That once more your curved prow cuts
     them,
Till the funeral altars standing
By my far tomb thou salutest,

O harás, que un rayo, con voces
Que horrible un trueno pronuncie,
Segunda vez te lo mande,
Cuando en abortada lumbre
Defatadas fus cenizas,
Aun, antes que ardan, ahumen.
[Húndefe.

Ulifes.
Efpera, helado cadáver,
Que afombro y horror infundes,
Que yo poftrada te doy
Palabra . . . . Todo fe hunde.
Pefada imaginacion
Fue la que en mis fueños tuve;
Pero, aunque foñada, es bien
Que la crea, y no la dude.

Salen los Griegos.
Antiftes.
Señor, qué es efto?
Timántes.
Que tienes?
Polidoro.
¿ Qué accidente hay, que te turbe?
Arquelao.
¿ De qué das voces al aire?
Floro.
¿ Qué temor hay, que te ocupe?
Lebrel.
¡ Que no parezca la mona,
Aunque todo el monte anduve!

Antiftes.
De qué te afombras?
Clarin.
¿ De qué
Te rezelas?

And in it thefe arms fufpend.
Be not doubtful or reluctant,
If thou wouldft not that a flafh,
Lightning-red, with voice of thunder,
This command fhould give once more,
When in the fwift-born refulgence
Shall its fcatter'd afhes fteam,
Ere to burning duft they crumble.
[He finks down.

Ulyffes.
Stay, oh! ftay, cold frozen corfe,
Thou that with fuch fear doft ftun me,
For my promife I now give thee
Proftrate here . . . . But all hath funken.
Some oppreffive fearful fancy
Was it that difturb'd my flumbers;
But although mere dreams, 'twere well
Not to doubt them, but to truft them.

Enter the Greeks.
Antiftes.
What is this, my lord?
Timantes.
What wouldft thou?
Polydorus.
What hath happen'd, that difturbs thee?
Archelaus.
Why fill all the air with outcries?
Florus.
Whence this fear that fo ufurps thee?
Lebrel.
Though I've gone through all the moun-
tain,
Ah! I cannot meet my monkey!
Antiftes.
What doth fright thee fo?
Clarin.
At what
Doft thou fhake?

Lebrel.
De quién huyes?
Ulíses.
De mí mismo.
Antístes.
Pues ¿ qué tienes?
Ulíses.
Nada tengo, mucho tuve.
¡ Ay amigos! tiempo es ya,
Que á los engaños me usurpe
Del mayor encanto, y hoy
El valor del amor triunfe.
¿ Dónde está, dónde se ha ido
Circe ?
Antístes.
A esa ribera acude,
Despues que aqui nos dejó,
A ver, qué bajeles surgen
A este golfo.
Ulíses.
Pues en tanto
Que descuidada presume,
Que los encantos de amor
Firmes en mi pecho duren,
Por esta parte, que el mar
Siempre repetido surte
Altas montañas, de quien
Turbante han sido las nubes,
Salgamos, y por no hacer
Ruido, y que ella nos escuche,
No el bajel, sino el esquife
Tomemos, y en él . . . .

Antístes.
No dudes.
Ulíses.
Huyamos de aqui; que hoy
Es huir accion iluftre,
Pues los encantos de amor

Lebrel.
From whom wouldſt run here?
Ulyſſes.
From myſelf.
Antiſtes.
Oh! ſay, what haſt thou . . .
Ulyſſes.
I had much, I now have nothing.
Ah! my friends, it now is time
To ſubdue the greateſt, ſubtleſt
Of enchantments, and this day
To crown valour love's triumpher.—
Where is ſhe, ſay, where has gone
Circe ?
Antiſtes.
To the ſhore ſhe hurried,
When ſhe left us here, to ſee
Whoſe the ſhips that in the gulf there
Had dropp'd anchor.
Ulyſſes.
Then while thus
She ſo careleſsly preſumeth
That the witchery of love
Still within my heart endureth,
By this path, to where the ſea
Heaves inceſſantly and ſurges
Up the lofty mountains, whoſe
Heads the dark clouds crown with tur-
bans,
Let us go, and for leſs noiſe,
Leſt ſhe hear and mar our purpoſe,
Not the veſſel, but the boat
Let us take, and in it . . . .
Antiſtes.
Truſt thee.
Ulyſſes.
Fly from here; for flight to-day
Is an act as brave as prudent,
Since the ſorceries of love,

Los vence aquel que los huye.
     Antiſtes.
Las lágrimas te reſpondan.
     Uliſes.
Hermoſa Juno, no culpes
El mayor encanto amor ;
Pues, aunque tus flores tuve,
Pude vencer mil encantos,
Y aqueſte ſolo no pude.
     Lebrel.
Al fin me voy ſin mi mona.
     Clarin.
¿ Que haſta ahora, que fui, dades ?
            [*Vanſe.*

ORILLAS DEL MAR, FRENTE AL PALACÍO
       DE CIRCE.

Salen, marchando, CIRCE *y ſus Damas,
que traen preſos á* ARSIDAS *y* LÍSIDAS.

     Circe.
Hagan ſalva á mis palacios
Los animados clarines,
Las cajas y las trompetas,
Porque ſus voces publiquen,
Que de Arſidas victorioſa
Hoy, y de Líſidas, Circe
Coronada de trofeos,
Vuelve á los brazos de Ulíſes.
     Arſidas.
Bien, Circe, podré negarte,
Que valiente me venciſte,
Mágica no, que mis gentes
A tus apariencias rindes,
Pues huyeron de las hueſtes,
Que aparentemente finges.
     Líſidas.
A ſacar de tu poder

He alone who flies, ſubdueth.
     Antiſtes.
Let theſe tears of ours be anſwer.
     Ulyſſes.
Lovely Juno, oh ! excuſe the
Greateſt of enchantments, Love,
Since although thy flowers I flouriſh'd,
Which a thouſand ſpells could conquer,
This one only was above me.
     Lebrel.
So in fine I loſe my monkey.
     Clarin.
Doubt you ſtill 'twas I, you dullard ?
            [*Exeunt.*

THE SEA-SHORE IN FRONT OF CIRCE'S
       PALACE.

Enter CIRCE *and her ladies, marching
with* ARSIDAS *and* LYSIDAS *as priſoners.*

     Circe.
Hail my palace-walls, ye clarions,
With your proud notes wake its ſilence !
Drums and trumpets, with your powers
All the liſtening world enlighten,
That o'er Arſidas victorious,
And o'er Lyſidas, comes Circe
Back again, encrown'd with trophies,
To the fond arms of Ulyſſes !
     Arſidas.
That 'twas valour that ſubdued me,
Circe, I could well deny thee,
That 'twas magic, no ; my people,
By thy apparitions frighten'd,
Fled before the hoſts of phantoms
That thy ſubtle ſkill depicted.
     Lyſidas.
To withdraw fair Flerida

A Flérida hermosa vine ;
¿Cómo pude defenderme,
Si ella misma es quien me rinde ?
    Circe.
Pues si preso estás por ella,
Tambien por ella estás libre.—
Ulises, invicto Griego,
Sal de esos ricos jardines,
Porque de zelos y amor
Las caducas pompas pises.
Advierte, que victoriosa,
Llena de aplausos insignes,
Vuelvo á tus brazos, porque
Triunfe en ellos.—Mas ay triste !
        [*Suena un claron.*
¿Qué bastarda trompa es esta,
Aspid de metal, que gime
Al aire ?
      Flérida.
      En el mar, señora,
Sonó la voz.
      Libia.
        Y el esquife
De ese griego bajel, hecho
Al mar, sus campañas mide.
      Astrea.
Ulises desde él te habla;
Escucha lo que te dice.
      Ulises (dentro).
Asperos montes del Flegra,
Cuya eminencia compite
Con el cielo, pues sus puntas
Con las estrellas se miden,
Yo fui de vuestros venenos
Triunfador, Teseo felice
Fui de vuestros laberintos,
Y Edipo de vuestra esfinge.
Del mayor encanto amor
La razon me sacó libre,

From thy power came I hither ;
How could I defend myself
When 'twas she contended with me ?
    Circe.
If for her thou'rt here in chains,
Then for her be free this instant.
From these rich-rosed gardens fair,
Come, unvanquish'd Greek ! Ulysses !
And tread down the fallen pomps
Love and jealousy once lit here.
See with what a victor air,
Led by plausive trumps and timbrels,
I reseek thy arms, for only
There I triumph ; but why thrills me
        [*A trumpet sounds.*
So this boding bugle, this
Snake of metal, whose throat hisses
On the air ?
      Flerida.
       From sea, Señora,
Comes the sound.
      Libia.
        And see the skiff there
Of the Grecian vessel, making
From the shore across the still sea.
      Astrea.
And Ulysses from it speaks ;
Hearken to his words, oh ! listen.
      Ulysses (within).
Rugged mountains of wild Phlegra,
Whose excessive heights are pitted
'Gainst the sky, because their proud peaks
With the stars of Heaven are mingled,
I was o'er your many poisons
The triumpher, of your circled
Labyrinth the happy Theseus,
Œdipus of all your sphinxes ;
From thy greatest of enchantments
Love, hath reason me deliver'd,

Trasladando esos palacios
A los campos de Anfitrite.
      Voces (*dentro*).
Buen viage !
      Flérida.
        Buen viage,
Todos los vientos repiten.
      Circe.
Escucha, tirano griego,
Espera, engañoso Ulíses,
Pues te habla, no cruel,
Sino enamorada Circe.
Cuando victoriosa yo
Triunfos arrastro, que pises,
¿ Quieres, que vencida llore ?
¿ Quieres, que me queje humilde ?
Escucha !—Mas ¡ay triste !
No llore quien te pierde, ni suspire,
Si te dan, para hacer mejor camino,
Agua mis ojos, viento mis suspiros.

      Flérida.
Señora, en vano te quejas ;
Que sordo el ingrato Ulíses,
Desbocado bruto, corre
A vela y remo el esquife.
      Libia.
Ya, perdiéndose de vista,
Un atomo es invisible.
      Astrea.
Y ya entre el agua y las nubes
Un pájaro apenas finge.
      Circe.
Ya estás, Arsidas, vengado.
Pero mal dije, mal dije ;

All your palaces exchanging
For the fields of Amphitrite.
      Voices within.
Pleasant voyage!
      Flerida.
        Pleasant voyage
All the winds appear to wish them.
      Circe.
Listen, listen, tyrant Greek!
Stay, deceitful, false Ulysses,
Since 'tis not the cruel queen
Calls thee, but the love-lorn Circe.
When, that thou might'st tread them
    down,
Triumphs for thy feet I bring thee,
Wouldst thou, conquering, I should
    weep,
Wouldst thou weakly I should whimper?
Hear me !—But, O bitter woe !
She must not weep or sigh from whom
    thou fliest,
If she must give thee for thy speedier
    flight,
Water her eyes, and wind the sobs she
    sigheth.
      Flerida.
Vainly, lady, thou lamentest,
Since the deaf ingrate Ulysses
Flies with rudder and with sail
On his ship as on a swift steed.
      Libia.
Almost lost to sight, 'tis now
To the smallest atom dwindled.
      Astrea.
And betwixt the wave and cloud
Like a tiny sea-bird wingeth.
      Circe.
Arsidas, thou art avenged ;
But my words are false and idle,—

Que nunca se venga un noble
En mirar un infelice.
Si lo eres, ese acero
En mi roja sangre tiñe;
Que no es venganza, piedad
Sí, darle la muerte á un triste.
Y sea antes que traspuesto
Ese neblí, que describe
Las ondas, ese delfin,
Que el campo del aire mide,
Ese caballo, que corre,
Ese escollo, que se rige,
Ese peñasco, que nada,
Se esconda, y no se divise;
Porque, perdido de vista,
Tardará tu acero insigne,
Y no será menester
Mas muerte, que no seguirle.
¡Escucha! Mas ¡ay triste!
No llore quien te pierde, ni suspire,
Pues te dan, para hacer mejor camino,
Agua mis ojos, viento mis suspiros.—
¿Mas qué me quejo á los cielos?
¿No soy la mágica Circe?
¿No puedo tomar venganza
En quien me ofende y me rinde?
Alterados estos mares
A ser pedazos aspiren
De los cielos; que si lleva,
Porque de encantos se libre,
El ramillete de Juno,
Que trajo del cielo Iris,
No de tormentas del mar
Le librarán sus matices.
Llamas las ondas arrojen,
Fuego las aguas espiren.
            [*Sale fuego del agua.*
Arda el azul pavimento,
Y sus campañas turquíes

True hearts ne'er can vengeance find
In the sight of one afflicted.
If thou art so, take this sword,
And with my red heart's blood tinge it,
Since to kill a wretch like me
Is not vengeance, but true pity:
And do this, or ere, fast fading,
Yon fleet falcon, that swift swimmeth
Ocean's waves, yon white-wing'd dol-
     phin,
'Mid the fields of air uplifted,
Yonder sea-steed gently flowing,
Yonder rudder'd rock that drifteth,
Yonder loosen'd cliff that floateth,
Undescried is wholly hidden;
For when it is lost to sight,
Then too late will fall thy swift steel,
Since no other death I'll need;
Then the thought I can't go with him.
Hear me! But, O bitter woe!
She must not weep or sigh from whom
     thou fliest,
If she must give thee for thy speedier flight,
Water her eyes, and wind the sobs she
     sigheth.
But why wail thus to the skies,
Am I not the sorceress Circe?
Cannot I take vengeance on
Him who wrongs me? who afflicts me?
Let the roused-up seas aspire,
As it were, to be the splinters
Of the broken heavens: and though
He that charm against bewitchments
Bears—the beauteous flowers of Juno,
Which from heaven were brought by
     Iris,—
From the tempests of the sea
Him shall not their tints deliver;
Flame, be darted from the billows,

Mieſes de rayos parezcan,
Que cañas de fuego vibren,
A ver, ſi hay deidad, que tanta
Tormenta le facilite.

*Serénaſe el mar, y ſale por él, en un carro
triunfal tirado de dos delfines, GA-
LATEA, y al rededor muchos Tritones
y Sirenas con inſtrumentos.*

Galatea.

Sí habrá, y quien, ſereno el mar,
Manſo, quieto y apacible,
Le dé paſo en ſus esferas.
Circe.
¿ Quién eres tú, que ſaliſte
De eſas húmidas alcobas
En triunfal carro ſublime,
A ſerenar de mi enojo
Las iras deſapacibles ?
Galatea.
Yo, que en eſte hermoſo carro,
A quien tiran dos delfines,
De Sirenas y Tritones
Tan acompañada vine,
Galatea ſoy, de Dóris
Hija, y de Nereo, invencible
Dios marino, y la que amante
De Acis, jóven infelice,
Murió á los bárbaros zelos
De Polifemo, terrible
Monſtruo, que el tálamo dulce
De nueſtras bodas felices
Cubrió de un peñaſco, que hoy
Túmulo es, que nos aflige :

Fire, from out the waves be ſpirted ;
    [*Fire riſes from the water.*
Let the azure pavement burn,
And its plains of turquoiſe gliſten,
Like a harveſt field of lightning,
Vibrating innumerous fire-ſtems,
To find out if any goddeſs
Can ſo great a ſtorm extinguiſh.

The ſea grows ſerene, and upon it GA-
LATEA *is ſeen advancing in a triumphal car drawn by two dolphins, and
ſurrounded by many Tritons and
Sirens bearing muſical inſtruments.*

Galatea.

There is one, who ſmooths the ſea
To a peaceful path of ſilver
For his paſſage through its ſpheres.
Circe.
Who art thou that hath ariſen
From the deep ſea's damp receſſes,
In triumphal chariot driven,
To appeaſe the unappeaſed
Anger of the wrath I've kindled ?
Galatea.
I, who in this beauteous car,
Which two dolphins move ſo lightly,
Come accompanied and circled
By the Tritons and the Sirens,
Galatea am, the daughter
Of fair Doris, and the mighty
Sea-god Nereus, and the loved once
Of young Acis, hapleſs ſtripling,
Victim of the jealous fury
Of wild Polyphemus, grimmeſt
Of all monſters, who the ſweet bed
Of the happy vows we plighted
Cover'd with a rock, which ever
Like a dark tomb o'er us riſes,

Cuya pirámide, cuanta
Sangre de los dos exprime,
Criftal es, que defatado
Nueftro fin llorando dice.
Defte rúftico jayan
Vengada me dejó Ulífes,
A cuya caufa mi voz
Al amparo fuyo afifte;
Y pidiendo á las deidades
De Neptuno y de Anfitrite,
Que ferenafen los mares,
Y que fus claros viriles
Efpejos fuefen del fol,
Mientras los Griegos los pifen.
Como á Ninfa de fus ondas,
Que difcurra me permiten
El mar, apagando cuanto
Fuego en él introdujifte;
Y afi ondas de plata y vidrio
Veloz mi carro defcribe,
Haciendo á fu hermofa efpuma,
Que á las rodadas fútiles,
O como plata fe entorchen,
O como vidrio fe ricen.

Circe.

Si deidad eres del mar,
Cuando en él mis fuerzas quites,
No en la tierra; y fi no puedo
Vengarme en quien huye libre,
En mí podré.　Eftos palacios,
Que mágico el arte finge,
Defvanecidos en polvo,
Sola una voz los derribe.
Su hermofa fábrica caiga
Defhecha, rota y humilde;
Sean páramo de nieve
Sus montes y fus jardines.
Un Mongibelo fuceda
En fu lugar, que vomite

Prefs'd beneath whofe pyramid
All the blood that from us trickles,—
So to weep our tragic end—
Turns to cryftal murmuring ripples.
'Gainft this ruftic giant rude
Vengeance gave to me Ulyffes,
On account of which my voice
In his caufe has been uplifted,
Afking of the deities
Neptune and fair Amphitrite,
That they would make fmooth the feas,
And that they, tranflucent mirrors,
Should outfpread them for the fun,
While the Greek fhip fail'd amidft them.
I, as being a fea-nymph born,
Am to run their realm permitted,
In the fea the fire appeafing,
Which your vengeful anger flings here;
And my fwift car thus o'er-rideth,
Sparkling waves of glafs and filver,
Making with its beauteous foam
'Neath its wheels the waves to gliften,
Now in curling wreaths of glafs,
Now in filvery twine entwifted.

Circe.

If thou'rt of the fea a goddefs,
Thou may'ft of my might deprive me
There, but not on land; if vengeance
I can't have on him who flies me,
On myfelf I can.　This palace,
Which by magic art I builded,
Let it vanifh into duft,
Let a fingle word, to fhivers
Shake this beauteous fabric down,
Ruin'd, broken, rent, made little.
O'er its mountains and its gardens
Let the dreary fnow be drifted,
And where now it ftands in beauty,
Be a wild volcano kindled,

Fuego, que á la luna abrase,
Entre humo, que al sol eclipse.
   [*Húndese el palacio de Circe, y
     aparece un volcan, arrojando
     llamas.*
         Aſtrea.
¡ Qué confuſion tan notable !
         Libia.
¡ O qué aſombro tan terrible !
         Flérida.
Huyamos, Libia !   [*Vaſe.*
         Libia.
      Huye, Aſtrea ! [*Vaſe.*
      Aſtrea.
¿ Dónde eſtar podemos libres ?
           [*Vaſe.*
       Circe.
Cuantos eſpíritus tuve
Preſos, ſujetos y humildes,
Inficionando los aires,
Huyan á ſu centro horrible.
Y yo, pues de mis encantos
A ſaber que es mayor vine
El amor, pues el amor,
A quien no rindieron, rinde,
Muera tambien, y ſuceda
A mi fin la noche triſte. [*Húndeſe.*

       Galatea.
Pues ſeguro el mar por donde
Venturoſo corre Ulíſes,
Tormentas vé de la tierra,
El mar con fieſtas publique
Su vencimiento, y haciendo
Regocijos y feſtines,
Sus Tritones y Sirenas
Lazos formen apacibles ;
Pues fue el agua tan dichoſa,
En eſta noche felice,

Belching fire, the pale moon burning,
And with ſmoke the ſea eclipſing.
   [*The palace of Circe ſinks into the
     earth, and a volcano riſes in its
     place, darting out flames.*
         Aſtrea.
O confuſion ſo unequall'd !
         Libia.
O the horror ſo terrific !
         Flerida.
Libia, fly !   [*Exit.*
        Libia.
     Oh ! fly, Aſtrea !   [*Exit.*
      Aſtrea.
Where for ſafety ? ſay, oh ! whither ?
           [*Exit.*
       Circe.
All the ſpirits that I held
Captive, ſubject to my ſway, and willing,
Flying on the poiſon'd air,
Seek the horrid homes that hide them.
And ſince I of my enchantments
Have now come to know the chief is
Love, ſince love it was that conquer'd
Him, whom all the reſt left victor,
Let me alſo die, and let
Mournful night's dark gloom engird me.
         [*She ſinks down.*
       Galatea.
Since the ſea, upon whoſe breaſt
Flies the fortunate Ulyſſes,
Views unmoved the ſtorms of land,
Let it now in joy and mirth here
Publiſh to the world his triumph,
And its Tritons and its Sirens,
Making *fêtes* and glad rejoicings,
Dance in many mazes mingled ;
And ſince on this happy night
Has the water been permitted

Que mereció ſer teatro
De ſoles, á quien humilde
El Poeta, entre otras honras,
Perdon de las ſaltas pide.
    [Hiciéron un bailete Tritones
         y Sirenas.

The proud theatre to be
Of two ſuns, the Poet wiſhes
Humbly, 'mid his other honours,
For his faults to aſk forgiveneſs.
    [The ſcene cloſes with a Ballet of
         Tritons and Sirens.

THE SORCERIES OF SIN.

AN AUTO.

FROM THE SPANISH OF CALDERON.

INTRODUCTION.

HE *Sorceries of Sin* is the only attempt that has ever been made in Englifh to prefent even one of Calderon's *Autos* in its integrity. Indeed, with the exception of the fcenes introduced into Dean Trench's analyfis of *The Great Theatre of the World*, not a fingle line of thefe remarkable dramas has ever previoufly been prefented in Englifh verfe. Writers in Reviews and Magazines have occafionally drawn attention to a few of the fecular dramas of Calderon; but the *Autos*, the moft wonderful of all his productions, and the only ones (with but two exceptions) which the great poet himfelf thought worthy of his revifion,* have been paffed over, I may fay, in almoft utter filence.† One of them has been admirably ana-

---

* Vera Taffis mentions that Calderon corrected the proofs of the two dramas which he allowed to be printed in the forty-fixth volume of the *Comedias de Varios Autores*. A fmall number out of one hundred and twenty. The *Autos* which he prepared for the prefs are contained in the volume of 1690 alluded to in the text.

† Even German enthufiafm, which has done fo much for the *Comedias* of Calderon, has fhrunk from the difficult tafk of dealing with the *Autos*. I know of but two writers who have given a tranflation of any of them. The firft is J. F. von Eichendorff, who publifhed eleven of them in his *Geiftliche Schaufpiele von Don Pedro Calderon de la Barca*, Stuttgart, 1846-53. The other is Ludwig Braunfels, who publifhed two little volumes of tranflations from Lope de Vega, Tirfo de Molina and Calderon, at Frankfort-on-the-Main in 1856. The fecond volume contains the Auto *La Cena de Balthafar*, previoufly tranflated by Eichendorff in the original *afonantes*, which Braunfels

lyfed in profe by Mr. Ticknor ;* another in the Rambler :† two or three have been meagrely and frigidly condenfed into a few lines by Southey ; ‡ and Sifmondi, who condefcended only to read one of them out of feventy three, has favoured us with an outline of that one, which is characterized by his ufual want of fympathy or appreciation. This neglect, perhaps, is not to be wondered at, confidering how very flight, after all, if we take into account their number and variety, has been the notice which his fecular dramas have as yet received from Britifh writers. Though it is not at all improbable, that, had the fame attention, fuch as it is, been devoted to the *Autos*, which has been given to the *Comedias*, a far greater amount of curiofity and intereft would be felt towards Calderon than any prefentation of his merely fecular dramas has yet fucceeded in awakening. This opinion, expreffed in different language in the introductory remarks which I prefixed to *The Sorceries of Sin* as originally publifhed in the Atlantis,§ has received the ftrongeft confirmation from an obfervation of Mr. Ticknor's, contained in a letter which he had the kindnefs to addrefs to me fhortly after the appearance of *The Sorceries of Sin* in the fcientific and literary journal to which I have alluded. Contrafting my former labours upon Calderon with my later, and encouraging me to proceed in the new path, Mr. Ticknor fays :—" With the two volumes of your tranflations from Calderon's plays, which you publifhed in 1853, I have been familiar from their firft appearance, and very thankful that you ventured on the bold undertaking. But this verfion of the *Encantos*

---

rejects as being unfuited to the genius even of the German language. *Los Encantos de la Culpa* is tranflated by Eichendorff under the title *Der Sünde Zauberei*, in the fecond volume (p. 315) of his work. The German tranflations of the *Comedias* are numerous. I have in my own poffeffion excellent ones by Auguftus Schlegel, Schach the hiftorian, Gries, Malfburg, Martin, Barman, Schmid, Schumacher, and others.

 * *The Divine Orpheus.* Hiftory of Spanifh Literature, v. ii. p. 323.

 † *Poifon and Antidote*, Rambler, Dec. 1855.

 ‡ Common Place Book, fecond feries, p. 253.

 § No. iv. July, 1859.

de la Culpa, with its *afonantes*, is much more interefting as a work of art, and more important. Allow me, then, to exprefs the hope that you will go on and tranflate more of the *Autos*. Nothing can, I think, give a clearer idea of what is moft charaćteriftic in Spanifh literature, or give foreigners a more juft idea of its peculiar power." This important teftimony to the attraćtivenefs of the *Autos* in themfelves, and to a certain fuccefs which has attended my attempt to transfer one of them, with its peculiar and varied verfification, into Englifh, I confefs I print here with great, and, I think, not unjuftifiable pride. Though the time and labour neceffary to complete the long dramas contained in this volume have not left me leifure to include another *Auto* in this collećtion, I truft that what is here prefented, by its ftrićt and rigid adherence to thofe principles of tranflation which in the fmaller piece have obtained the approval of fo eminent an authority, will fhow how highly I value it, and how earneftly I have again ftruggled to deferve it.

The precife time at which the firft volume of the *Autos* was publifhed appears to be a matter of fome uncertainty. But two collećted editions have been made in Spain, one in 1717, in fix volumes, 4to., the other in 1759-60, alfo in 4to. On the title-pages of both editions they are called *Obras Pofthumas*, and are reprefented as being then firft publifhed. This is true no doubt of the greater number of them, the manufcripts of all having been preferved in the archives of the corporation of Madrid, whofe property, for the purpofes of the Corpus Chrifti feftivities, they were. This property the municipality parted with on the 31ft of May, 1717, to Don Pedro de Pando y Mier, for the fum of fixteen thoufand reals, and it was by him that the firft collećtion was made.* Although the preface which Calderon prepared himfelf for the firft volume of the

---

* The *Autos* have never been republifhed out of Spain. The edition of Keil contains only the vague allufion of Vera Taffis as to their number. In Spain itfelf they have not yet been included in the valuable *Biblioteca de Autores Efpañoles* ftill in courfe of publication, though promifed by Señor Hartzenbufch in the preface to his edition of the *Comedias*, (p. xx.) and more recently by Don Jufto de Sancha in the notice prefixed

Autos is given in the two editions above mentioned, the volume itſelf is not alluded to, and ſeems to be unknown in Spain, if I may judge from the ſilence obſerved towards it in one of the lateſt publiſhed volumes of the *Biblioteca de Autores Eſpañoles*,* where the uſual ſtatement is made of the *Autos* being *firſt* publiſhed in 1717. Having picked up a few years ago, on a Dublin book-ſtall, a volume of the *Autos* publiſhed in 1690,† I took the liberty, in my paper in the Atlantis, of calling the attention of Mr. Ticknor to the faƈt, he having ſtated, in his Hiſtory of Spaniſh Literature (v. ii. p. 319, *note* 25), that " the *Autos*, being the property of the city of Madrid, and annually repreſented, were not permitted to be printed for a long time (Lara Prólogo). They were firſt publiſhed in 1717, in 6 volumes, 4to., and they fill the ſame number of volumes in the edition of 1759-60, 4to." This correƈtion, if I may call it ſo, I made with very great diffidence and deference, and I was relieved beyond meaſure at finding Mr. Ticknor not only received my obſervations with indulgence, but favoured me with the following moſt intereſting and valuable information upon the ſubjeƈt :—

 " What you ſay of the confuſion that you find in my notice of the firſt publication of the Autos is partly true. When I wrote my Hiſtory of Spaniſh Literature, I had not ſeen the twelve Autos publiſhed in 1690 from a MS. that ſeems to have been prepared by Calderon as early as

---

to his *Romancero y Cancionero Sagrados*, Madrid, 1855, p. vi. If well edited, this volume would form one of the moſt intereſting of the ſeries. The date " 31ſt of May, 1717," in the text, I have taken from the work referred to in the next note. Mr. Ticknor, in his letter, gives the date, 31ſt *of March*, 1716. The name of the aſſignee of the copyright in that work is given *Prado* (inſtead of *Pando*) y Mier. The correƈt name is ſupplied in Mr. Ticknor's letter, and is found at the bottom of the fly-leaf of each volume of the edition of 1759-60, containing the *Fee de erratas*.

 * *Dramaticos Poſteriores a Lope de Vega*, t. i. Note to *Chronological Catalogue of Dramatic Authors from Calderon to Canizares*, p. xxxvii.

 † *Autos Sacramentales Alegoricos y Hiſtoriales. Dedicados al Patriarca San Juan de Dios, compueſtos por Don Pedro Calderon de la Barca, &c.* En Madrid : por Juan Garcia Infanzon, año 1690.

1676; but a few years ago, at Florence, I picked up a copy, together with a copy of the Comedias publiſhed by Vera Taſſis in nine volumes between 1683 and 1694. From theſe ſources and from odd volumes of the Comedias *de Diferentes Autores*, going back to 1633, and the volumes publiſhed by Calderon's brother Joſeph, I intend to give as good an account as I can of the firſt editions, whether ſpurious or genuine, of all Calderon's dramas, religious and ſecular, in the third American edition of my Hiſtory, now in the preſs. Of courſe, I ſhall uſe in it what Hartzenbuſch has ſo well done.

" But there ſtill remains ſome obſcurity about the matter..... When Calderon, in July, 1680, gave the Duke de Veraguas the liſt of his dramas, which was publiſhed in the *Obeliſco* of Lara in 1683, the twelve Autos are marked as *impreſos*. But I know of no edition of them earlier than that of 1690, where they all appear, but *in a different order* from the one to which they ſtand in the liſt, which is, after all, the true foundation for all diſcuſſions about Calderon's dramas. It is plain, that, when he collected them for publication, he had the purpoſe of making more than one volume. The prefatory matter ſhows this, as you have well obſerved. But I know of nothing of the ſort, except the volume of 1690, until the 31ſt of March, 1716, when the City of Madrid—Como legataria del Doctor D. Pedro Calderon de la Barca—gave or ſold the right of printing them *all* to Pedro de Pando y Mier, after which everything is plain. Now can you give me any indication of the publication of any of Calderon's Autos earlier than the laſt date, except that of the twelve in 1690? If you can you will add another obligation to the many I owe you already.

" My only conjecture in relation to the matter is, that the twelve *Autos* of 1690 were *printed* in 1676; but that the prefatory matter in the firſt four leaves was not printed until the volume was *publiſhed* in 1690, where the title-page ſhows that no ſubſequent volume was likely to be added; the city of Madrid having then the right of property in them, which it did not part with until nineteen years later. But I do not much rely on this. Calderon was very loofe in his ftatements about his dramas and his unwillingnefs to have them publifhed."

The information afked for by Mr. Ticknor, in the above valuable bibliographical note, it is fcarcely neceffary to fay I was unable to fupply; and to the few obfervations I ventured to make upon the fubject, Mr. Ticknor was good enough to refer in a fubfequent letter which he favoured me with, a paffage from which I here fubjoin, as all that is likely to be ever known about the matter.

" The queftion of the firft publication of the *Autos* is, as you fay, a puzzling one, and I think will never be fettled to abfolute certainty. I rely little on Lara's Obelifco Funebre, becaufe there are certainly feveral grofs miftakes in it. Calderon's ftatements, too, I have found are not always to be trufted, and as for Taffas, aprohaciones &c., I have many times had as much trouble with them in other cafes as in this. My general impreffion, therefore, is that the Autos of 1690 were the firft publifhed, and that nothing was done earlier except to prepare them for the prefs, and get the needful permiffions to print them, beginning this work in 1676."

An allufion has been made in one of the notes to the *Catalogo Crono-logicoy Alfabetico* by Don Ramon de Mefonero Romanos (prefixed to his *Dramaticos Pofteriores a Lope de Vega*, t. i. pp. xxxvii. to liii.) of dramas and dramatifts in Spain from 1635 to 1740. The number of Calderon's *Comedias* fet down in this lift is 126, which includes thofe dramas in which Calderon was affifted by other poets, as well as thofe of which no copies are now known to exift; among others the *Don Quixote de la Mancha*, the lofs of which is fo much to be regretted. The names of 84 *Autos* are given, being eleven more than the number contained in the fix quarto volumes of 1717 or 1759-60, which I have mentioned as being but 73. There is certainly fome confufion in this lift, which contains the names of fourteen *Autos* not to be found in the fix quartos juft alluded to, omits two which thofe volumes contain, and alters the names of two others, if, indeed, thefe laft are not different *Autos* altogether.

Among the *new Autos* is one called *Devocion de la Cruz*, which muft not be confounded with the terrible tragedy of that name which Bouterwek fo ftrangely miftook for an *Auto*, as mentioned in the introduction to my tranflation of *The Devotion of the Crofs* in this volume. Another is called *Cruz en la Sepultura*, the very name under which *The Devotion of the Crofs* was firft publifhed in the edition of Huefca, 1633, as fully defcribed in the fame introduction. The expectation of new treafure, however, which this lift awakens adds greatly to the anxiety which Spanifh fcholars feel for the long-promifed republication of them in the *Library of Spanifh Authors.*

It only remains for me to add that my reafon for felecting *Los Encantos de la Culpa* in preference to others of at leaft equal, if not fuperior, brilliancy, was its connection with *El Mayor Encanto Amor*, and the intereft I felt, and which I am fure others will feel, at tracing the ingenuity and marvellous frefhnefs with which Calderon takes up the fame theme, which one would think he had exhaufted in the longer drama, and reprefenting it anew in a more wonderful and original manner than at firft. The remarks of Dean Trench on this fubject, in his admirable effay on the genius of Calderon, are fo appofite, that I make no fcruple of transferring them here :—

" The manner in which Calderon ufes the Greek Mythology is exceedingly interefting. He was gifted with an eye fingularly open for the true religious element, which, however overlaid and debafed, is yet to be detected in all inferior forms of religion. Thefe religions were to him the veftibules through which the nations had been guided till they reached the temple of the abfolute religion, where God is worfhipped in Chrift. The reaching out and feeling after an unknown truth, of which he detected fomething in the fun-worfhip of the Peruvians,* he

---

* See his *Daybreak in Copacabana.*

recognized far more diſtinctly in the more human, and therefore more divine, mythology and religion of ancient Greece. It may be that the genuine Caſtilian alienation from the Jew, which was not wanting in him, may in part have been at work when he extols, as he often loves to do, the ſuperior readineſs of the Gentile world, as contraſted with the Jewiſh church, to receive the proffered ſalvation, its greater receptivity of the truth. But whether this may have had any ſhare in the matter or not, it is a theme to which he is conſtantly in theſe *Autos* recurring, and which he loves under the moſt various aſpects to preſent. And generally he took a manifeſt delight in finding or making a deeper meaning for the legends and tales of the claſſical world, ſeeing in them the ſymbols and unconſcious prophecies of Chriſtian truth. He had no miſgivings, therefore, but that theſe would yield themſelves freely to be moulded by his hands. He felt that in employing them he would not be drawing down the ſacred into the region of the profane ; but elevating that which had been profaned into its own proper region and place. Theſe legends of heathen antiquity ſupply the allegorical ſubſtratum for ſeveral of his *Autos*. Now it is *The True God Pan*, or Perſeus reſcuing Andromeda, or Theſeus deſtroying the Labyrinth, or Ulyſſes defying the Enchantments of Circe, or the exquiſite mythus of Cupid and Pſyche. Each in turn ſupplies him with ſome new poetical aſpect under which to contemplate the very higheſt truth of all." *

---

* *Life's a Dream : The Great Theatre of the World.* From the Spaniſh of Calderon. With an Eſſay on his Life and Genius. By Richard Chenevix Trench. London, 1856, p. 96.

PERSONS REPRESENTED.

EL HOMBRE.	THE MAN.
LA CULPA.	SIN.
LA LASCIVIA.*	VOLUPTUOUSNESS.*
LA LISONJA.	FLATTERY.
EL ENTENDIMIENTO.	THE UNDERSTANDING.
LA PENITENCIA.	PENANCE.
EL OLFATO.	THE SMELL.
EL OÍDO.	THE HEARING.
EL TACTO.	THE TOUCH.
EL GUSTO.	THE TASTE.
LA VISTA.	THE SIGHT.
Músicos.	*Muficians.*
Acompanamiento.	*Chorus, &c.*

---

* This character, though taking a part in the *Auto*, is not included in the lift of *Perfonas* in the edition of 1759-60, from which I print.

INTITULADO

LOS ENCANTOS DE LA CULPA.

Suena un Clarin, y se descubre una Nave, y en ella el HOMBRE *el* ENTENDIMIENTO, *y los* CINCO SENTIDOS.

El Entendimiento.

EN la anchurosa Plaza
Del mar del Mundo, oy hombre te amenaza
Gran tormenta.

El Oído.

Yo he sido
De tus cinco sentidos el Oido,
Y assi el primero siento
Bramar las ondas, y gemir el viento.

La Vista.

Yo, que he sido la Vista,
Que al Sol los rayos perspicáz conquista,
Desde lexos diviso
Uno, y otro uracán, á cuyo viso
En esta cristalina
Campaña te previene fatál ruina.

El Tacto.

El Tacto soy, á horrores te provoco,
Pues yá cercanos los peligros toco.

THE SACRAMENTAL ALLEGORICAL AUTO,

ENTITLED

THE SORCERIES OF SIN.

A Trumpet founds, and a Ship is difcovered at fea.   In it are the
Man, *the* Understanding, *and the* Five Senses.

The Underftanding.

UPON the boundlefs plain of the world's wide fea,
O Man ! this day doth darkly threaten thee
A mighty tempeft.

The Hearing.

I who am the Hearing
'Mong thy five Senfes call'd, perceive the nearing
Of the impending ftorm; to me is known
Firft when the waves grow hoarfe and winds begin to groan.

The Sight.

I who am call'd the Sight—
Swift victor of the great Sun's golden light,—
With power to look between
Each whirlwind wild that breaks the blue ferene,
Forefeeing, can behold the coming woe
That on this cryftal plain this day thou'rt doom'd to know.

The Touch.

The Touch am I, harrowing thy foul fo much,
That dangers clofing round thee feem to touch.

El Olfato.
El Olfato te dice, que se crea
El humedo vapor de la maréa.
El Gusto.
Yo en trance tan injusto,
Con ser el Gusto, estoy aqui sin gusto.
El Oído.
Gran tormenta corremos.
El Entendimiento.
En el Mar de la vida nos perdémos.

El Tacto.
Larga aquella mayor.
El Olfato.
Iza el Trinquete.
El Gusto.
A la Triza.
El Oído.
A la Escolta.*
La Vista.
Al Chafaldete.
El Entendimiento.
En alterados hielos
Corre tormenta el hombre.
Todos.
Piedad, Cielos!
El Hombre.
En el Texto Sagrado,
Quantas veces las aguas se han nombrado,
Tantos doctos Varones
Las suelen traducir tribulaciones,
Con que la humana vida
Navega zozobrada, y sumergida.
El Hombre soy, á astucias inclinado,
Y por serlo, oy Ulíses me ha nombrado,
Que en Griego decir quiere
Cauteloso: y assi, quien oy quisiere

---

* Should obviously be *Escota.*

The Smell.
Smell, too, proclaims how near doth ruin glide,
Even by the humid vapours of the tide.
The Taſte.
For ſuch a tumult of the ſea and ſky
No taſte I feel, though Taſte itſelf am I.
The Hearing.
We run before the wind.
The Underſtanding.
Storm-toſt,
Upon the ſea of life our bark is loſt.
The Touch.
Looſen the mainſheet!
The Smell.
Hoiſt the foreſail, ho!
The Taſte.
To the cable!
The Hearing.
To the tack-rope!
The Sight.
Let the clew-lines go!
The Underſtanding.
Over the waves by mighty tempeſts driven,
Man ſtruggles on.
All.
Have pity, gracious Heaven!
The Man.
In the ſacred text do we
Find frequent mention of the waves of the ſea,
Which learnèd doctors all tranſlate
The tribulations of this mortal ſtate,
Through which in ſtormy ſtrife
Struggles ſubmerged and toſt the bark of human life.
I then am Man, to craft and cunning prone,
And therefore by Ulyſſes' name am known,
As if a Grecian ſynonym it were
For cautious ſenſe; therefore if any here
Wiſh to track well the ſtraits my fate goes through,
Let him Ulyſſes' ſtory keep in view:

Correr las lineas de la ſuerte mia,
De Ulíſes ſiga en mí la Alegoría :
Y los que en una parte
Me llamaron viador, viendo mi arte,
Y en otra navegante, que el camino
Del Mar diſcurro ſiempre peregrino,
Dando ocaſion á que ningun viviente
Se admire de peligro tan urgente :
Y aſſi nadie ſe eſpante,
Que Ulíſes peregrino, y navegante,
Con inquietud violenta,
Corra tanta tormenta,
Confuſos, y perdidos
En mis tribulaciones mis ſentidos.

El Oído.

Solo ſe eſcuchan en la ſelva fria
Ráfagas, que nos dán por travesía.

La Viſta.

Solo ſe vén en eſſos orizontes
Montes, que ſe deſhacen ſobre montes.

El Taƈto.

Solo ſe tocan ondas, con quien ſube
El mar, que nace mar, á morir nube.

El Olfato.

Uno ſon yá los dos azules velos.

El Guſto.

Qué nos vamos á pique.

Todos.

Piedad, Cielos !

El Entendimiento.

Si los llamais, ſerenidades crea
Vueſtro temor cobarde, y que no ſea
Eſte Baxél, que en pielagos ſe mueve,
Sepulcro de criſtal, tumba de nieve,
Que el Cielo, á humildes voces ſiempre abierto,
Al naufragio Piloto es felíz Puerto.

El Guſto.

Acordemonos dél, aora que eſtamos
En rieſgo los que el Mundo navegamos.

Then thofe who call me at one part
Of my courfe a wayfarer, feeing my art,
A mariner at another, day by day
Pilgrim-like treading over the fea's falt way,
Will wonder not at th' extremity
Of danger, which none living 'fcaped but he ;
And thus without a fear,
A pilgrim and a voyager,
You may behold Ulyffes braving
The fea's unreft, the tempeft's raving,—
See him in me confufed and loft,
And by my Senfes girded like a hoft.

The Hearing.
The wild gufts on this frozen foreftry
Of mafts fide-ftriking lift alone to thee.
The Sight.
Nought can be feen on the horizon wild,
But mountains upon yielding mountains piled.
The Touch.
Nought can be touch'd but waves, if waves they be
Which die in the air a cloud, though born a fea.
The Smell.
Commingled are their veil's deep azure dyes.
The Tafte.
We ftrike ! we fink !
All.
Have pity, O ye fkies !
The Underftanding.
If upon Heaven you call, your prayers, though weak,
Will of themfelves create the calm we feek,
Bringing this bark, which through the waves doth·go,
A cryftal fepulchre, a tomb of fnow,
Safe to that holy haven it lays bare
To fhipwreck'd pilot's eyes—fo ftrong is humble prayer.
The Tafte.
Oh ! may it grant it foon, for here are we
Toft in extremeft rifk upon the world's wide fea.

El Entendimiento.
Dadle voces en tales defconfuelos,
Pues él fiempre refponde.
    Todos.
        Piedad, Cielos!
    El Oído.
Yá efcucho, que fe llena
De paz la vaga habitacion ferena.
    El Gufto.
Y el Mar tranquilo, yá con ira fuma
No riñe, fino juega con la efpuma.
    El Entendimiento.
Todo el ayre es cambiantes, y reflexos.
    La Vifta.
Todo es ferenidad, y yá no lexos,
Antes que todos miro
Cumbres, que tocan al azul Zafiro,
Del Mar burlando la fañuda guerra.
    El Entendimiento.
Zelages fe defcubren : tierra, tierra.
    El Hombre.
Prudente Entendimiento,
Piloto, que al govierno eftás atento
De aquefta humana Nave,
Que nadar, y bolar á un tiempo fabe,
Siendo en manfiones de atomos de efpumas,
Sin efcamas Delfin, Cifne fin plumas,
Pón la Proa en aquella
Montaña, en quien la mas luciente Eftrella
Peligra, pues fu cumbre
Es en donde fe roba al Sol la lumbre :
Y affi fus puertas inconftantes cierra
A efte humano Baxél.
    Todos.
A tierra, á tierra.

   Defembarcan, y defaparece la Nave.
    El Hombre.
Humanos fentidos mios,

The Underſtanding.
In ſuch affliction let its vault be riven
Still with your cries, 'twill anſwer.
                    All.
                              Save us, Heaven.
                The Hearing
Already calm comes on, the wild winds ceaſe,
And o'er our heaving home glides the ſoft breath of peace.
            The Taſte.
The ſea grows tranquil—ſmoothly ſilver'd o'er,
It plays with the foam with which it fought before.
                The Underſtanding.
Bright grows the air with many a changeful hue.
                The Sight.
All grows ſerene, and lo! not far I view—
I firſt of all—the bare
Peaks of tall hills, which touch the azure air,
Now mocking the far wave-war on the ſtrand.
                The Underſtanding.
Now the clouds part—it is the land! the land!
                The Man.
O prudent pilot Underſtanding!
Thou who haſt been ſo long commanding
This bark of human life, this boat,
That at the ſelf-ſame time can fly or float,
Being upon the foam-flakes it reſts on,
A ſcaleleſs dolphin, and a plumeleſs ſwan,
Beneath yon mountain turn its prow,
Beneath yon peak which on its brow
Wears a ſtar of brighteſt ray—
That point whoſe light is filch'd even from the God of Day—
There where it ſeems to ſtretch a curvèd hand
To claſp this human bark.
                    All.
                    To land! to land!

        [*All diſembark and the veſſel diſappears.*
                The Man.
Human Senſes mine, my vaſſals,

Vaſſallos, que componeis
La Republica del Hombre,
Que mundo pequeño es.
Generoſo Entendimiento,
Piloto de eſſe Baxél,
Que ſobre el campo del mar
Monſtruo ſe alimenta, pues
Quanto bate el viento es ave,
Quanto baña el agua es pez.
Compañeros de mi vida,
Dexad el mar, no porque
Nueſtra peregrinacion
En la tierra, que aora veis,
Aya de ceſſar, ſupueſto
Que ſiempre tengo de ſer
Yo Peregrino del Mar,
Y de la Tierra tambien :
Dexad fiada eſſa Nave
A la diſcrecion cruel
De un embate, y otro embate,
De un baybén, y otro baybén.
Seguramente amarrada
Con las Ancoras eſté,
Que de quien Piloto ha ſido
El Entendimiento, aunque
Aora le dexe, quizá
Le avré meneſter deſpues :
Y entremos á examinar
Eſtos montes, que han de ſer
Puerto de nueſtra fortuna.

Who together all compoſe*
Man's Republic, he a little
World himſelf, as all do know.
Generous Underſtanding, thou ↙
Pilot of this myſtic boat,
Changeful monſter, paſturing well
Over the ſea-way, ſwift or ſlow,—
Being a bird when winds it play'd
    with,
Being a fiſh when ſeas waſh'd o'er.
Ye, companions of my life,
Leave the ſea, but not therefóre
Think that our long wandering ceaſes
In the land that you behold—
Since ſtill moving onward ever
Muſt my fate be, I ſuppoſe—
Over the earth to move a pilgrim—
Over the ſea likewiſe to go :—
Leave this bark awhile entruſted
To the cruel care and cold
Of waves daſhing wildly together,
Of foam writhing in hoſtile foam,
But let anchors firm and ſtrong
Safely ſtill the veſſel hold,
For the pilot Underſtanding,
Though he leaves her for the ſhore,
May perchance again require her :—
Let us enter now, and go
Curious through theſe hills which
    Heaven
Gives our fortunes as their port.

---

* The metre changes here to one which is ſeldom found in Calderon's ſecular dramas, but frequently in the Autos. It is a *ſingle* aſonante vowel rhyme in the laſt ſyllable of each alternate line, which, as in the more uſual *double* aſonantes, is kept up through the entire ſcene. It appears to be the oldeſt form of the aſonante, being found in the earlieſt primitive ballads, ſuch as that of *Vergilios*, of *Count Arnaldos*, of *The Infanta of France*, &c. (See Duran's *Romancero General*, Madrid, 1849, t. i. p. 151.) In the original of this ſcene, the vowel uſed is *e*, which is an effective one in Spaniſh ; for this, which is comparatively weak in Engliſh, I have ſubſtituted the ſtronger *o*. The laſt ſcene of *The Devotion of the Croſs* is in this *ſingle* aſonante vowel rhyme.

El Gusto.
Qué tierra es esta?
      El Tacto.
           No sé;
Mas quiera el Cielo que sea
Tiro, para que aya en él
Olandas, sedas, y ropas,
Donde regalado esté
Mi tacto.
     El Olfato.
       ¿ Mejor no fuera,
Que fuera á tanta altivéz
La gran India de Sabá,
Donde huviera para oler
Yo, suavissimas Aromas?
     El Oído.
Ninguno ha pedido bien,
Pedid la India Oriental,.
Porque habitan su vergél
Dulces Aves, cuyos cantos
Sonora musica dén,
Que regalen mis oídos.
     La Vista.
¿ Necios sois, pues no quereis
Que sea Tiro, y que aya aqui
Oro, y diamantes, en que
Mi vista halle mas reflexos,
Que el Sol en su rosicler?

     El Gusto.
Mal aveis deseado todos
En no desear, y creer,
Que sea la Tierra de Egypto
Essa tierra, para que
En ella hallémos las ollas,
Que en ella déxo Moysés,
Pues no ay en el Mundo gusto
Sin comer, y sin beber.

The Taste.
What land's this?
     The Touch.
         I cannot say.
Heaven but grant 'tis Tyre: if so
I shall find abundant here—
Silks, fine linen, purple robes,
Things my touch delights to feel.

     The Smell.
Were it not better then to hope
That 'twill prove some Arab plain—
Some Sabæan scented shore,
Where the sweetest odours may
Glad the happier sense I own ?—
     The Hearing.
No one yet has wish'd aright :
Wish the land through which we roam
May be beauteous eastern Ind,
In whose vocal bowers and groves
Sweet birds' songs may fill my ears
With melodious music tones.
     The Sight.
Idle are your wishes all,
Since you wish not for the zone
Where the diamonds glisten bright
And the land is rich with gold :
Sweeter to the sight are gems
Than the morn on roses throned.
     The Taste.
Badly have you all desired
In not wishing this alone,—
That this land should prove to be
Egypt's comfortable coasts,
Where perchance we'll find the flesh-pots
Left by Moses long ago,
Since the world hath little better
Than good drink and meat to show.

El Entendimiento.
¡Qué como humanos fentidos
Todos defeado aveis
Hallar cada uno el objeto,
Que mas conviene á fu fér!
¡No fuera mejor que fuera
La tofca Tebayda, en quien
La penitencia fe hallára,
Riyendofe del poder
De las Cortes populofas,
Puefto que tan cierto es,
Que fin pena de efta vida
No aya en la eterna placer?
El Hombre.
¡Y qué como Entendimiento
Has hablado tú! ¿Qué eftés
Siempre aconfejando penas
A mis fentidos? ¿No vés,
Que fon fentidos humanos,
Y que al fin es menefter
Alivios, que los diviertan
De las fatigas en que
Han nacido?

El Entendimiento.
     ¿Cómo tú,
Siendo fu Señor, y Rey,
Buelves por ellos? ¿Yá olvidas
Aquel paffado baybén
De la fortuna, en quien vifte
La Troya del Mundo arder,
De adonde te faqué yo?
¿Yá te olvidas, que defpues
En una tormenta vifte
Tus fentidos padecer
Con tantas tribulaciones?
¿Yá no te acuerdas de que
El Cielo te libró de ellas?

The Underſtanding.
Human Senfes, oh! how each,
Each and all are prompt and prone
To defire this land may offer
What its inftinct longs for moft!
Were it not better that it prove
The Thebais wild and lone,
Deferts where pale Penance may
Trample down the pride of courts—
Since there's nought more fure than
    this—
We through temporal pain alone
Can expect th' eternal blifs?
The Man.
Why for ever words of woe
Speak'ft thou, Underftanding, thus?
Why for ever fhadows throw
On the path my Senfes take?
Doft thou not their nature know,
That they're human, and require
Something foothing to confole—
Something fweet to eafe the pangs
That from birth-time they have
    known?
The Underſtanding.
Canft thou fpeak in their defence,
Thou who art their King and Lord?
Can it be thou haft forgot
That late peril fcarcely flown,
When from out the world's dread Troy
Wrapp'd in finful flames, alone
Thou wert refcued, and by me?—
Haft thou too forgot the roar
Of the wild waves, and the plight
Of thy fenfes fuffering fore,
And that Heaven it was that drew
Them and thee from their control?

El Gusto.
No tienes que responder,
Yo responderé por tí.
Prudentissima vejez,
Que aunque somos de una edad,
Solo tú cano te vés,
Porque te ha hecho tu podrida
Condicion encanecer :
¿ Aora sabes tú, que el hombre,
Quando en peligro se vé
De la enfermedad prolija,
Del enemigo cruel,
De la perdida de hacienda,
De la esperanza del bien,
Solo se acuerda del Cielo,
Y que se olvida despues,
Que lo uno esté mejorado,
U essotro alcanzado esté ?

El Entendimiento.
Essa ingratitud le pienso
Quitar yo, que aqueste fue
Del Entendimiento oficio.
El Hombre.
Mi Gusto os ha dicho bien :
Sentidos, seguid al Gusto,
Y no arguyais mas con él,
Sino esta tierra á que avemos
Llegado, á reconocer
Entrad.   Pues eres la Vista,
Delante de todos vé,
Mira si acaso descubres
Poblacion.   Tú, que eres fiel,
Oído, mira si oyes
Voces, que noticia dén
De gente, ó ganado.   Tú,
Del suavissimo placer

*The Taste.**
Do not *thou* reply : to *me*
Leave the answer and the tone.—
O thou cautious eld and wise,
Thou whose hair is white and hoar,
Thou alone of all our band,
Though thine age is not more old—
'Tis thy colder constitution
Doubtless caps thy head with snow,—
Hast thou yet to know that Man,
When some peril he beholds,
When some tedious sickness threatens,
Or some more malicious foe,
Or the loss of worldly wealth,
Or perchance the hope of gold,
Only then remembers Heaven,
And remembers it no more,
When his health he hath recover'd,
Or hath reach'd the wish'd-for goal ?
The Understanding.
Be it mine, O Man, to free thee
From ingratitude so low,—
'Tis thy Understanding's duty.
The Man.
Taste, thy words are wise and bold :—
Follow Taste, my Senses all,
And with *him* dispute no more,—
But this land to reconnoitre,
On whose bosom we are thrown,
Enter now : since thou, O Sight,
Seest many a mile before,
Look if thou, by any chance,
Canst the dwellers here behold.
Hearing, thou my faithful friend,
List if thou canst catch the tones
Of human voices borne afar,
Or the pasturing herd's deep low.

---

* *To the Man.*

Con que eſſas flores reſpiran
El raſtro ſigue con él.
Mira ſi puedes topar
Algun blando lecho en quien
Deſcanſe.   Y tú, Guſto, al fin,
Mira ſi hallas que comer,
Y todos buſcad delicias
Para mí.

El Entendimiento.
          Aunque deſee,
Que halles, penitencia, yendo
A eſſo, la Culpa hallaréis.
          La Viſta.
Yo veré ſi ay publacion.   [*Vaſe.*
          El Hombre.
Y yo me quedo ſin vér.
          El Oído.
Yo eſcucharé ſi oygo voces.   [*Vaſe.*
          El Hombre.
Yo, auſente tú, nada oiré.
          El Tacto.
Yo, ſi ay lecho en quien deſcanſes.
          El Hombre.   [*Vaſe.*
Yá yo no le he meneſter.
          El Olfato.
Yo, ſi hallo blandos aromas.   [*Vaſe.*
          El Hombre.
Yá no tienes para qué.

El Guſto.
Yo, ſi hallo dulces manjares. [*Vaſe.*
          El Hombre.
Aora no quiero comer,
Porque mientras vais voſotros
El Mundo á reconocer,
Al pie de eſte Cyprés quedo
Echado á dormir.
          [*Echaſe al pie de un Cyprés.*

Thou whoſe rapture riſes ſweet
From each ſcented flower that blows,
Follow too the track with them :—
Some ſoft bed for my repoſe
Thou by gentle preſſure find,—
And the taſk, O Taſte, I'll throw
Upon thee of finding food.
All on ſeparate miſſions go,
Seeking ſweet delights for me.
          The Underſtanding.
By another path I hoped
Thou wouldſt Penance find : purſuing
That, thou'lt find Sin's ſyren door.
          The Sight.
I depart to look for people.   [*Exit.*
          The Man.
Blind I ſtay, ſince Sight hath flown.
          The Hearing.
I to liſt if ſounds can reach me. [*Exit.*
          The Man.
Since thou'rt gone, I hear no more.
          The Touch.
I a bed in which to reſt thee.   [*Exit.*
          The Man.
None I need now for repoſe.
          The Smell.
I to find delicious odours.   [*Exit.*
          The Man.
Now they're naught, how ſweet they
  blow.
          The Taſte.
I ſweet ſavoury food to ſeek for. [*Exit.*
          The Man.
Now the thoughts of food I loathe.
Wherefore, whilſt you all depart
To explore this land unknown,
I, in ſleep, my weary body
At this cypreſs' foot ſhall throw.
          [*He lies down.*

El Entendimiento.
　　　Qué bien,
Para dormir, los fentidos
Apartas de tí; pues es
Cierto, que queda fin ellos
El que duerme : y qué bien fue
Cyprés el Arbol, que aqui
Tomafte para tí, pues
Viene á fer Arbol de muerte,
De quien el fueño tambien
Es fombra ; y aunque dorados
Los ricos Catres eftén,
En que defcanfen los hombres,
Defde el mendígo, hafta el Rey,
Aunque fean de otras maderas,
Son Arboles de Cyprés.
Quedó el hombre fin fentido,
Y durmió ; ¿ yá qué he de hacer?
Que aunque potencia del alma
Soy, y ella, que mortal no es,
Dormir no puede, efte tiempo
Que yáze el hombre, tambien
Eftoy yo fin difcurrir,
Sin percibir, ni entender.
Vaga mi imaginacion
Confufas vifiones vé ;
Y todo es tiniebla, y fombras
Para mí el Mundo, porque
Sin los fentidos no puedo
Aélos de razon hacer:
Seguirélos, pues fin mí
Se queda el hombre la vez
Que duerme, y que fepultado
Temporal cadaver es.　　　*[Vafe.*
　　　El Hombre.
Ay de mí ! pefado fueño,
No tanto me aflijas, ten
La violencia de las fombras.
¿ Qué es lo que mis ojos vén

The Underftanding.
Yes ; 'tis right that thou fhouldft fleep,
Since apart from thee, there prone,
Are thy Senfes ; for 'tis certain
That the man who fleeps doth hold
Them no longer in his keeping :
And the tree thou fleep'ft below,
Rightly hath thy choice felećted,
Since the cyprefs long hath grown
Death's efpecial tree ; and fleep
Is death's fhadow as we know.
Thus though weary man may flumber
In rich couches gilded o'er,
Call the wood of which they're made
What you pleafe, to king and clown
Cyprefs is it all the while.
Here then Man, by fleep o'erthrown,
Lies infenfate : this being fo,
What remains for me to do?
Since although I am the foul's
Manifefted power, and *that*
Deathlefs fpark no fleep can know,
Still while man thus lies, am I
Likewife left without difcourfe,
Powerlefs to perceive or think.
Now my fantafy beholds
Vifions all confufed and dim,
Darknefs o'er the world is thrown,
Since without the Senfes, I
Lofe all reafon and control :
I fhall follow them, fince Man,
While his eyes in fleep are clofed,
Without *me* remains, and buried
Thus, is for the while a corfe. *[Exit.*
　　　The Man (afleep).
Woe is me ! oppreffive dream,
Pain me not fo much ! withhold
Thefe thy fhadows' violent rage.
What is this my eyes behold,

Sin vifta? Mas digo mal,
Que mis fentidos cobré;
Si bien informes, y brutos,
En el punto que llegué
A vér eftos fieros monftruos,
Que me quieren defhacer;
Me pafma advertir, que quando
Efperaba, que cruel
Cada uno cebaffe en mí,
Todos fe echan á mis pies;
Por feñas dicen, que huya,
Que los quiero conocer
Parece; defefperados
Se entran al Monte otra vez.
Qué es efto, Cielos!

Al irfe fale el ENTENDIMIENTO *como
affombrado.*

El Entendimiento.
          Efcucha,
Ulífes, yo lo diré,
Que aunque eftás aora incapáz
De fentir, tocar, y vér,
Porque brutos tus fentidos,
Y entorpecidos fe vén,
Por los vicios, á que tú
Los difte licencia; bien
Me entiendes: mas los del alma
Fuerza es que velando eftén.
Apenas fuimos, Ulífes,
Vagando aquefte Orizonte
Tus compañeros, del Monte
Penetrando los Paífes,
Quando un Palacio eminente

Though my fight is gone?—Ah me!
Badly muft my thoughts be told
Till my fenfes I recover.
But I feem to fee a fwarm
Of mifshapen beafts approach me,
Bent on draining my heart's gore.
When their cruel fangs my fear
Seems to faften round my throat,
At my feet I fee them kneeling
With fubmiffive reverence low:
They by figns appear to fay,
Fly! oh! fly this fatal fhore!
Then when they perceive that I
This their hidden meaning know,
In defpair they all re-enter
The wild mountain wafte once more.
What is this? O Heavens!

As he ftarts up, the UNDERSTANDING
enters amazed.

The Underftanding.
          Ulyffes,
Hear me, and thou foon art told.
For although thou haft not now
Power to fee, or feel, or hold,
Since thy Senfes have become
Torpid, brutalifed, o'erthrown
By the vices that thou gav'ft them
Leave to feck, yet ftill I know
Thou canft underftand my meaning
Through the foul's inftinctive force.*
Scarce had we, Ulyffes, gone
This wild mountain's fummit over,
Hope, fome fair fields to difcover,
Thy companions leading on,
When our fight beheld with wonder

---

* The alternate vowel monorhymes terminate here, and the metre changes to the full confo-
nant rhyme as in the text.

Nueſtra viſta deſcubrió,
Cuya eminencia tocó
A las nubes con la frente.
Llegamos á ſus umbrales,
Y aviendo llegado á ellos,
En dos Eſquadrones bellos
De hermoſuras celeſtiales,
Vimos ſalirnos á hacer
Fieſtas á nueſtra fortuna,
Con varias muſicas una
Hermoſiſſima muger.
De paſſo la repetí
Nueſtra peregrinacion,
Que el uſo de la razon
Siempre me ha tocado á mí.
Ella, afablemente humana,
Dulcemente liſonjera,
A entender nos dió, que era
De eſtos Campos la Diana.
Mas yo, como Entendimiento
Soy, y á mi divino ſér
Siempre le toca tener
Natural conocimiento,
Conocí al inſtante, que era
La Culpa fiera, y cruel,
Que á habitar en un Verjél
Fue deſde la edad primera.
Aqui damas ſuyas ſon
Los vicios con que ella lidia,
Laſcivia, Gula, y Embidia,
Liſonja, y Murmuracion.
Mandonos agaſſajar
De eſtas damas, y ellas luego
Al mandato, ſi no al ruego,
Quiſieron executar :
Y con vicioſos placeres
Al momento nos brindaron ;
Tus ſentidos, que ſe hallaron
Servidos yá de mugeres

A proud palace rich and fair,
For whoſe lofty roofs the air
Bade the gold clouds part aſunder.
We its beauteous threſholds nearing,
Reach'd them, and beheld, delighted,
Two fair ſquadrons diſunited
Of celeſtial nymphs appearing,
And with ſmiling looks of human
Sympathy for our diſtreſſes—
Muſic mingling its careſſes—
After them one beauteous woman.
Of our perils on the ſea,
Of our journeyings ending never,
Brief I ſpoke, ſince Reaſon ever
Throws that duty upon me.
Then her voice ſo ſoftly bland,
Yielding ſwift to pity's law,
Let us know, in her we ſaw
The Diana of this land.
I, the Underſtanding, who
To that part which is divine
Add a wit ſo keen and fine,
By my natural inſtinct knew
She was Sin, that fierce and fell
Monſter full of ravening rage,
She who when of earlieſt age
In a garden loved to dwell,
And her dames, to whoſe addreſs
All her wiles entruſteth ſhe,
Are Envy, Calumny, Gluttony,
Flattery, and Voluptuouſneſs.
Theſe, her ladies, then ſhe bade
To regale us,—a beheſt
Scarcely needed ; the requeſt
Seem'd to make them but too glad,
Since upon the inſtant they
Flung their vicious wiles around them,
And thy Senſes, who thus found them
Served in this ſeductive way

Tan hermosas, y tan bellas,
Sin vér que el Entendimiento
Alli se hallaba, al momento
Se conformaron con ellas.
La Embidia, que es toda enojos
Del bien que en los otros vé,
Viendo á la Vista, porque
La Embidia, al fin, toda es ojos.
La Lascivia, que se ofrece
En los alhagos cruel,
Brindó al Tacto, porque él
Las blanduras apetece.
La Murmuracion, que es quien
Lo malo vé, y no lo bueno,
Brindó al Olfato, que lleno
De este defecto le vén.
Solo por esso le igualo
Con causa al murmurador,
Que no alaba lo mejor,
Y hace lo malo mas malo.
La Gula al Gusto brindó,
Probarlo no es menester;
Porque bien se dexa vér,
Que el Gusto á la Gula amó.
La Lisonja, mortal fiera
De las Cortes, al Oído
Brindó, que él objeto ha sido·
De toda voz lisonjera.
La Sobervia, con intento
De que el veneno que esconde
Passasse á mí, porque es donde
Peligra el Entendimiento,
Me brindó; mas sin el fruto,
Que de mí estaba esperando,
Por saber yo, que en pecando
Se convierte el hombre en bruto.
David lo diga, que atento
Este sentir en él hallo,
Que el que peca es un cavallo,

By such lovely ladies fair,
(Neither wishing nor demanding
Aid from me, the Understanding),
Yielded all, without a care.
Envy, who with agonies
Sees another's merit shine,
Pledged the Sight, because in fine
Envy is herself all eyes.
Wantonness, that ever were
Cruel most when most caressing,
Tempted Touch by her addressing,
Since he loves soft lures like her.
Calumny that doth reject
Good for bad, and false for true,
Smell selected, since he too
Labours 'neath the same defect:
If on this account alone,
He with Calumny should mate,
That he ne'er doth celebrate
The better and the worse makes known.
Gluttony the Taste allured,
Little proof this needs from me,
Since that Taste loves Gluttony
All the world is well assured.
Flattery was Hearing's choice,—
Flattery, that mortal pest,
Known to courts, where he's the quest
Of each false and flattering voice.
Pride, with full intent that I
Should her hidden poison drink,
(Understanding, Danger's brink
Neareth, when that nymph is nigh),
Came and pledged me, but the fruit
Hoped for so, she fail'd in winning,
Since I know that man, by sinning
Is transmuted to a brute.
David's song the sinner tells,
If in sin persisteth he,
Comes a beast of earth to be,

En quien no ay entendimiento.
Y fue aſſi, que como fueron
Bebiendo, todos mudados
En fieras, y transformados
En varias formas ſe vieron.
Mas atencion deſde aqui,
Hombre, te pide mi acento;
Eſcucha á tu entendimiento,
Que es el que te habla.

       El Hombre.

             Dí.

    El Entendimiento.
La Viſta, en Tigre cruel
Fue de la Embidia deſpojos,
Que eſte animal todo es ojos,
Bien lo publica ſu piel
Manchada de ellos; y quando
No baſte eſto, baſtará,
Que el Tigre muerte ſe dá,
Si oye múſica, rabiando.
Y el embidioſo, en ſus penas
Se dá muerte cada dia,
Si oye la dulce harmonia
Que hacen las dichas agenas.
El Taĉto, que fue el objeto
Que á la Laſcivia creyó,
En Oſſo ſe convirtió,
Que eſte animal, imperfeĉto.
Sin forma, y ſin ojos nace:
Y el Apetito, á creer llego,
Que nace ſin forma, y ciego,
Pues tantos errores hace.
El Guſto (gloton hambriento)
En un bruto inmundo fue
Transformado; eſto porque
Solo á ſu comida atento
Vive, ſin que de ſu pecho
El hombre ſervicio adquiera,
Pues ha meneſter que muera

In whoſe ſoul no reaſon dwells.
Thus it was, as each, the bowl
Drank of poiſon'd bliſs deranged,
Quick to grovelling beaſts they changed,
Reft of ſenſe, of ſhape, of ſoul.
Thy attention, O thou weak
Man! my voice is ſtill demanding;
Liſten to thy Underſtanding,
Who doth ſpeak to thee.

       The Man.

             Still ſpeak.

    The Underſtanding.
Sight, a tiger fierce did grow.
He, the keen-eyed Envy's prize,
Since an animal all eyes,
As its ſpotted ſkin doth ſhow,
Is the tiger, and we may
This additional reaſon add,
That the tiger dieth mad,
If he hears ſweet muſic play.
Thus the envious man doth feel
Every day the pangs of death,
If he heareth rumour's breath
Sweetly ſpeak another's weal.
Touch, that ſoon became the thrall
Of Deſire's laſcivious air,
Was transform'd into a bear—
An imperfeĉt animal,
At its birth unform'd and blind—
As is Appetite, that makes,
Therefore, all its dread miſtakes
Sightleſs, formleſs, undefined.
Taſte, the hungry glutton, grew
Eaſily a filthy ſwine—
It a beaſt that doth incline
But to eat and eat anew,—
Long delaying to conduce
To man's benefit thereby,
Since 'tis needful he muſt die

Para ferle de provecho.
El Olfato, que entregado
Se vió á la murmuracion,
Se convirtió en un Leon,
Que es quien rugidos ha dado.
Y finalmente, el Oído,
Que falfedades creyó
Lifonjeras, fe miró
En Camaleon convertido :
Y el bruto, que vivir quiere
Del viento folo fiado,
Es el mas vivo traflado
De la lifonja en que muere.

El Hombre.

Doéto Entendimiento mio
En gran peligro me veo,
A mis fentidos defeo
Refcatar con mi alvedrio,
Para vivir, pues que yo
No puedo de aqui aufentarme,
Que no tengo de dexarme
Compañeros, que me dió
Mi mifma naturaleza.
Y fupuefto que perdidos
Todos mis cinco fentidos
Eftán en efta afpereza
De la culpa, entrar intento
A libertarlos, porque
Bien de la empreffa faldré,
Si voy con mi Entendimiento.

El Entendimiento.

Pues que conmigo has de ir
A cobrarlos, ha de fer
Con tres cofas que has de hacer.
Primeramente, pedir
Al Cielo perdon de que
Tan mal los aconfejafte,
Que al riefgo los entregafte.
Otra, confeffar que fue

Ere he turns to any ufe.
Calumny, that had thrown out
Lures to Smell, converted him
Into a lion, gaunt and grim,
Who, loud roaring, roams about.
Laftly, Hearing, that had grown
But to live on what it heard,
Trufting every idle word,
Changed to a chameleon ;
Since the being that but needs
For its life the air, be fure
Is a lively portraiture
Of the fenfe that Flattery feeds.

The Man.

O my guide in every ill !
'Mid the rifks that round me hover,
I my Senfes would recover
By the ranfom of my will,
If 'twere but to live, fince I
Have no power by flight to fave me,
If all thofe whom Nature gave me,
As companions, forth not fly
With me from this fatal coaft.
And fuppofing that within
This enchanted wild of fin
My five Senfes may be loft,
Still I'll enter, notwithftanding,
Them to free, becaufe I know
I to victory muft go,
Going with my Underftanding.

The Underftanding.

Since then to this dangerous tafk,
Led by me, you mean to run,
There are three things to be done.
In the firft place, you muft afk
Heaven to pardon the exprefs
Sanction and unwife advice
Given by you, that they to Vice
Should entruft them : next, confefs

Tuya la culpa que ha avido,
Aunque ellos fueron, Ulíses,
Los que entregarſe quiſieron.
Y otra, averſe arrepentido.
    El Hombre.
Digo, que pido perdon
Del mal exemplo, (ay de mí !)
Que á mis ſentidos les dí:
Digo, que hago confeſſion
De la culpa que he tenido
De que ſe ayan entregado
A las manos del pecado,
Y que voy arrepentido.

*Tocan Chirimías, y deſcubreſe un Arco
Iris en un Carro, y en él la* PENI-
TENCIA, *y canta la Múſica.*

    La Múſica.
Yá que el Hombre confieſſa ſu culpa,
Y arrepentido me pide perdon,
(O Penitencia !) pues eres el Iris,
Acude bolando á darle favor.

    Penitencia.
Yá corro veloz
En el arco de Paz, en quien haces
Las amiſtades del hombre, y de Dios.

    El Hombre.
¿ Qué múſica tan ſonora
Es la que oímos los dos ?
    El Entendimiento.
Auxilio es que te dá Dios.
    El Hombre.
¿ Y aquel bello Arco, que aora
Sobre las nubes ſe aſſienta ?
    El Entendimiento.
Arco es, que la Paz abona,

That the fault was thine that caſt
Them into the ſnares of ſin,
They not loath to enter in,—
Let repentance be the laſt.
    The Man.
I declare, for ſuch tranſgreſſion,
For the bad example given
To my Senſes, I aſk Heaven
To forgive me : next, confeſſion
For the fault, by whoſe event
Into Sin's foul hands they fell,
I declare aloud as well :
And that truly I repent.

*There is a peal of Clarions, and a
Rainbow appears ; beneath it is a
Chariot, and in it is* PENANCE; *the
Muſic ſings.*

    The Muſic.
Now that Man his ſinful fault confeſſes,
And repenting aſks to be forgiven,
Fly, O Penance ! fly, celeſtial Iris,
Grace to grant him once again from
    Heaven !
    Penance.
Yes, adown the ſky,
On the arch of Peace I fly—
On the arch whoſe myſtic ſpan
Amity proclaims 'twixt God and man.
    The Man.
Ah ! that muſic ſo ſonorous
Which we hear, what may it be ?—
    The Underſtanding.
God's aſſiſtance aiding thee.
    The Man.
And that beauteous Bow, that o'er us
Reſts on clouds its radiant form ?
    The Underſtanding.
Is the Bow that bringeth Peace—

Y que yá cessó pregona
El rigor de la tormenta.
Dios le puso por señal
De Paz entre sí, y el hombre,
Y assi el verle no te assombre.
   El Hombre.
¿Y la Ninfa Celestial,
Quién es, que saberlo espero?
   El Entendimiento.
La Iris, Embaxatriz
Mas solicita, y felíz
Del Jupiter verdadero,
La que á los hombres embia
A consolar su dolencia.
   El Hombre.
Pues quién es?
   El Entendimiento.
    La Penitencia;
Bien que en esta alegoría
Probado está con decir,
Que es la que con dulce nombre
Se pone entre Dios, y el hombre.

   El Hombre.
Su voz bolvamos á oír.
   La Música.
Pues el hombre confiessa, &c.
   Penitencia.
Yá corro veloz, &c.
Christiano Ulises, tus voces
En el Empyreo se oyeron,
Que ellas hasta él subir saben
Por las Escalas del viento.
Y viendo, que tus sentidos
Tan postrados, y deshechos
De la culpa están, y que es

Is the Bow that maketh cease
All the rigour of the storm.
God has placed it as a sign—
Peaceful sign—'twixt him and thee:
Therefore, Man, rejoice and see.
   The Man.
And the heavenly nymph divine,
Who is she? oh! make her known!
   The Understanding.
Iris, the Embassadress,
Who with happy haste doth press
Downward from the true Jove's throne,
Bears her hither, to console
Man in all his misery.
   The Man.
And her name?—
   The Understanding.
    Is Penance: see
How this allegoric whole
Proves what has been said before,—
She it is who comes in Heaven's high
 plan,
Mediating betwixt God and man.
   The Man.
Let us hear her voice once more.
   The Music.
Now that man, &c.
   Penance.
Yes, adown the sky, &c.
Christian-born Ulysses, higher
Than the heavens were heard thy ac-
 cents,*
They well knowing how to climb there
By the wind's invisible ladder,
When, beholding that thy Senses
Were by sin o'erthrown and scatter'd,

---

* The afonante vowels in the original are, *e, o,* as in Viento, Oyeron, &c.; for these I have
substituted, in this scene, *a, e,* as in accents, ladder, enchanted, &c.

El rescatarlos tu intento,
El gran Jupiter me embia
Con auxilios, y consuelos
A tí, para que la Culpa
Con sus hechizos sobervios
No pueda dañarte, y puedas
Tú postrarlos, y vencerlos.
Aquestas flores te traygo,

[Dale un Ramillete de flores.
Que es un Ramillete bello
De virtudes matizadas
Con la Sangre de un Cordero,
De quien Ara fue cruenta
La Inmensa crueldad de un Leño.
En virtud de sus virtudes
Postrar podrás sus venenos,
Que no tendrán fuerza alguna
En tocandolas á ellos.
Toma, y á Dios : y no temas
Que me ausente, aunque me ausento,
Porque siempre que me llames,
Verás, que á tus voces buelvo.
Ella, y Música.
Corriendo veloz
En el arco de Paz, en quien hace
Las amistades del hombre, y de Dios.

*[Tocan Chirimías, y desaparece el
Arco.*
El Hombre.
Iris bello, hermosa Ninfa,
No desvanezcas tan presto
Tanta multitud de Estrellas,
Tanta copia de Luzeros.
El Entendimiento
Rayo de Luz, que has corrido
Por las Campañas del viento,
Señal de Paz, que á Moysés

And that thy intention is
For their rescue to do battle,—
Me, to aid thee and to counsel,
Hath the mighty Jove despatchèd,
That from all Sin's proud bewitchments
Should to thee no evil happen ;
And that thou may'st wholly conquer
And undo her worst enchantments,
Take these flowers that I bring thee.

[Lets fall a bunch of flowers.
Beauteous bunch of flowers, all dappled
O'er with virtues from the life-blood
Of a Lamb, whose crimson altar
Was a tree's unmeasured hardness,
By whose mystic aid thou mayest
All her poison'd snares down trample ;
Touch them but with this—that moment
Shall they lose all power to harm thee—
Take it, and adieu ! Thou need'st not
Fear my absence ; for, though absent,
Ever when thou callest on me
Thou shalt see that I will answer.
Penance and Music together.
Yes, along the sky,
On the arch of Peace I fly—
On the arch whose mystic span
Amity proclaims 'twixt God and man.
*[While the Clarions play, the Rain-
bow and Penance disappear.*
The Man.
Beauteous Iris, lovely nymph,
Do not hide in such swift darkness
Such a host of starry splendours—
Such a crowd of meteor flashes.
The Understanding.
Ray of light, that through the wind-
swept
Plains of azure Heaven hath darted—

Dios señaló en el Defierto :

     El Hombre.
Tente, aguarda.
      El Entendimiento.
         Efcucha, efpera.
      El Hombre.
Fuefe, dexandome impreffo
Un renglon de tres colores
En el Papel de los Cielos.
¡ Ay Entendimiento mio,
Dichofo foy, pues que tengo
Con que vencer los encantos
De efta Circe !

      El Entendimiento.
        Alza del fuelo
Effas flores.
      El Hombre.
       Ay de mí !
      El Entendimiento.
Qué fientes ?
      El Hombre.
        Herirme fiento
Con fus efpinas.   [*Alza las flores.*
      El Entendimiento.
        Las flores
De la penitencia, es cierto
Que afperas fon al principio,
Quanto fon fragrantes luego.
      El Hombre.
Efpinas de mi pecado,
Con temor á alzaros llego.
Vamos, que aunque mis fentidos
Eftén cautivos, y prefos
De fu belliffimo encanto,
Affi libertad pretendo.
      El Entendimiento.
No tienes que ir á bufcarla,

Sign of peace, which in the defert
God to Mofes indicated—
      The Man.
Stay ! detain thee !
      The Underftanding.
         Liften ! wait !
      The Man.
She is gone, but in her paffage
Leaving me a line of greeting
Writ in triple-hued enamel,
On the fkies cerulean paper,—
Underftanding mine, how happy
Am I in a power poffeffing
Of fubduing the enchantments
Of this Circe !
      The Underftanding.
        From the ground
Raife the flowers.
     The Man (in doing fo).
        Oh !
      The Underftanding.
        What fmarts thee ?
      The Man.
By the fharp thorns round thefe rofes
I am wounded.
      The Underftanding.
        Yes ; the fharpnefs
Of the penitential flowers
Is the firft thing felt, but after,
Nought but their delicious fragrance.
      The Man.
Ah ! with fear I ftoop to handle
Ye, the fharp thorns of my fin.
Let us on ! for though this faftnefs
Keeps my captive Senfes chain'd,
Spell-bound by fuch fweet enchantment,
Still I hope to liberate them.
      The Underftanding.
Then to meet with the enchantrefs,

Que ella á buſcarte á eſte pueſto Ha ſalido, con las voces De muſicas, é Inſtrumentos.	Thou no farther need'ſt to go, Since to meet thee ſhe advances. See, ſhe comes with ſongs and muſic, And her ſiren train, to charm thee!
Salen la LASCIVIA, *y la* CULPA *detrás de todos, y traen una Salvilla, un Vaſo de plata, y otra una Toalla al Hombro.*	*Enter* SIN, *followed by* VOLUPTUOUSNESS, FLATTERY, *and others.* VOLUPTU-OUSNESS *bears a ſalver, on which is a ſilver goblet, and* FLATTERY *a napkin.*

La Múſica.
En hora dichoſa venga
A eſtos Jardines amenos
El Peregrino del Mar,
Donde halle ſeguro Puerto.

The Muſic.
Happy, happy, be the hour
That to theſe delicious gardens
Comes the Pilgrim of the Sea,
In a ſafe port happily landed.

La Culpa.
En hora dichoſa venga,
Digan los dulces acentos,
Una, y mil veces, ſin que
Nada les uſurpe el eco,
Vandolero de los Ayres,
Que ſe queda con los medios.
En hora dichoſa venga
El hombre, que por ſus hechos
Es aſſunto de la fama
Por ſu valor, y ſu ingenio,
Donde tengan ſus fortunas
Dulce Patria, amado centro,
Noble aſylo, illuſtre amparo,
Blando albergue, y felíz Puerto.
Apenas ſupe, inconſtante
Hueſped de dos Elementos,
Que ſobre tribulaciones
Baten las olas, ſurgiendo
Yá los embates del Mar,
Yá las rafagas del Viento.
Apenas ſupe, Señor,
Oy de vueſtros compañeros,
(A quien yá en Palacios mios
Bien agaſſajados tengo)

Sin.
Happy be the hour he cometh!
Sing again in ſofteſt accents—
Once, a thouſand times repeat it—
So that Echo, the freehanded
Robber of the air, may filch not
From the ſound his uſual largeſs.
Happy be the hour that cometh
Here the man to whom is granted,
For his wit and worth in warfare,
Fame the proudeſt and the ampleſt:
Here, wherein a home and country
Now his happier fate imparteth,—
A proud ſhelter—a high ſafeguard—
A ſoft reſt—a happy haven.
Scarcely had I heard, O ever
Changeful gueſt of air and water,
Of two elements the victor,
Since on troublous billows wafted,
Now the rude ſea's rage thou curbeſt—
Now the wild wind's mightier mad-
Scarcely had I heard, my lord, [neſs:—
From thy comrades, whom my palace
Entertaineth now and welcomes
In obedience to my mandate,—

Que erais el valiente Ulíses,
Que quiere decir en Griego
Hombre ingenioso (que al fin
No ay fin, cautelas ingenio)
Que de la Troya del Mundo
Huyendo venís al fuego,
A quien vos mismo en vos mismo
Alimentais en incendios,
Quando á recibiros salgo
Con todo esse Coro bello
De mis damas, celebrando
Tan noble recibimiento.
Llegad todas á sus plantas,
Y con corteses festejos
Le saludad ; y porque
El que en el Mar tanto tiempo
Fluctuó golfos de penas
En pielagos de tormentos,
Es la sed la que le aflije ;
Mas á quién no admira esto,
Que siendo el Mar todo agua,
Tenga á su huesped sediento?
Brindadle con esse Nectar,
Que está de dulzuras lleno,
En tanto que en mis Palacios
Mas regalos le prevengo.
   La Lascivia.
Bebe, Señor, el sabroso
Licor que yo te presento.
   El Entendimiento.
¡ Ay de tí, si le bebieres,
Que todo es lascivo fuego !
Qué haces?
   El Hombre.
    Para resistirme
Conmigo mesmo peleo.
   El Entendimiento.
¿ No le bebas, yá no sabes
Que es tosigo, y es veneno ?

That thou wert the brave Ulysses,
Which doth mean in Grecian parlance,
An astute-soul'd man (astuteness
Being, as 'twere, a twin with talent),
Who from flaming Troy escaping,
Hither to a fire hast wander'd,
Which within thyself thou feedest,
From internal quenchless ashes, —
When I hurried to receive thee
With this beauteous choir of damsels,
Celebrating with due honour
Such a noble stranger's advent.
At his feet then lowly kneeling,
Welcome in the costliest manner
His arrival, and, because
He who in the sea has tarried
Such a length of time, exchanging
Gulfs of gloom for waves of saltness,
Was by thirst afflicted mostly—
Strange, the sea, which is all water,
That it should its guests leave thirsty,
And the liquid store so ample !—
Pledge him with this honey'd nectar
Sweeten'd by celestial savours,
While within my palace yonder
Are prepared more festive banquets.
   Voluptuousness.
Drink, my lord, the sweetly-savour'd
Liquor, which I dare to hand thee.
   The Understanding.
Woe to thee, if thou dost drink it !
Liquid lust-fire fills that chalice !
What then wilt thou do ?
   The Man.
    I struggle
With myself in self-fought battle !—
   The Understanding.
Drink it not : the draught concealeth
Poison deadlier than the adder.

El Hombre.
Sí, Entendimiento, y tu aviſo
Ha llegado á muy buen tiempo.
Eſtoy cobarde, eſtoy mudo,
Tanto al cortés cumplimiento,
Que debo á vueſtra beldad,
Y á vueſtra hermoſura debo;
Que aunque retorico fui,
Al miraros enmudezco:
En fé de lo qual, el nectar
Con que me brindais acepto;
Mas por no ſer deſcortes
Haré la ſalva primero
Con eſtas flores, que no
Se atreven á ſer groſſeros
Tanto mis labios, que lleguen
Sin aqueſſe cumplimiento.
    [*Toca el Vaſo en el Ramillete, y
        ſale Fuego.*
    La Laſcivia.
Ay de mí! El Fuego que avia
En eſte Vaſo encubierto
Rebentó.
    El Hombre.
        Es verdad, que mal
Arde encendido tu fuego,
Vil Laſcivia.
    La Laſcivia.
        Ay infelíz!

    La Culpa.
Mortales furias!
    El Hombre.
        Qué es eſto?
    La Culpa.
Saber oy, que deſvanezcas
Mis encantos.
    El Hombre.
        Sí, que aviendo

The Man.
Yes, my Underſtanding, yes: [*Aſide.*
Timely come thy words to warn me:—
I am timid, I am mute,   [*To Sin.*
Thinking of the courteous favour
Which I owe to thy perfections,
Which I owe thy beauty, lady.
For, though ſkill'd in ſpeech were I,
Dumb I'd grow in gazing at thee:—
Therefore I thy proffer'd nectar
Take, and thus by taking thank thee;
But, that I may not be wholly
Wanting in more courteous manner,
I ſhall firſt ſalute and touch it
With theſe flowers, the groſſer advent
Of my lips preſuming only
Such ſweet tribute to come after.
    [*He dips the noſegay in the golet
        from which fire iſſues.*
    Voluptuouſneſs.
Woe is me! the ſecret fire
Which within this cup I ſcatter'd
Has burſt forth.
        The Man.
            'Tis true, for hard
Is't to hide the fire thou wakeſt,
Vile Voluptuouſneſs.
        Voluptuouſneſs.
            Ah! me,
Woe the day!—
        Sin.
            My fury mads me!
        The Man.
Why, O Sin?
        Sin.
            For now I know
You have conquer'd my enchantments.
        The Man.
Yes, for having ventured hither

Llegado aqui accompañado
De mi noble entendimiento,
Aunque llegué fin fentidos,
Porque tú me los has prefo,
Con efte ramo fabré
Defvanecer tus intentos,
Porque es el ramo de Iris,
Que eftá de virtudes lleno.

La Culpa.
Ay infelice de mí !
¿ Aviendo volado el fuego
De la mina, que ocultaba
Entre lifonja mi pecho,
Cómo foy yo, cómo foy
La que me abrafo ? Qué es efto ?
¿ Tú eres quien la mina enciende,
Y foy yo quien la rebiento ?
El Hombre.
Sí, que fabiendo que eres
Horror de aqueftos Defiertos,
Y Circe de eftas Montañas,
Que quiere decir en Griego
Maleficiofa Hechicera,
A darte la muerte vengo,
Y á refcatar mis fentidos
De la prifion de tus hierros.
         [*Saca la Daga.*
La Culpa.
Ten la Daga ; efpera, aguarda,
No manches tan noble acero
En mí, que foy inmortal,
Y yá fin morir me has muerto.
Yo bolveré tus fentidos
A fu fér, porque viniendo
Armado de las virtudes,
Que dió tu arrepentimiento,
No tengo yo poder, no,
Para guardarlos mas tiempo.

Companied and happily guarded
By my noble Underftanding,
Though I come here in the abfence
Of my Senfes, ftill kept captive
By thy wiles, to me is granted
Power to fruftrate thy intentions
By this little branch I carry—
Wonder-working branch of Iris—
Full of virtues and of marvels.

Sin.
Ah ! unhappy me ! the fire
Having from the mine departed,
Which beneath fair Flattery's feeming
Hid my heart within its caverns !
How am I ? Oh ! how am I
Still its victim ? How does't happen
That the mine for *thee* enkindled,
Burfts 'neath *me* and leaves me blafted ?
The Man.
Thus ; no fooner had I heard
That thou wert the fhame and fcandal
Of thefe deferts, the dread Circe
Of thefe mountains, the enchantrefs
That thy Grecian name exprefles,
Than I came here to defpatch thee,
And to liberate my Senfes
From the prifon of thy fhackles.
         [*Draws his dagger.*
Sin.
Hold thy hand ! Oh ! do not thou
Stain the bright fteel of thy dagger
With the blood of an immortal.
Deathlefs though I be, thou ftabbeft
Deep enough without fuch aidance.
Back, the Senfes thou demandeft
I fhall give thee, fince beholding
That thy penitence hath arm'd thee
So with virtues, I no longer   [them.
Have the ftrength or power to guard

Oído, que oíste lifonjas,
Que tu dulce encanto fueron,
Por quien te tuvo trocado
En Camaleon tu afecto.

Sale el Oído *como affombrado.*
El Oído.
¿ De qué letargo tan dulce
A efta nueva voz defpierto ?
La Culpa.
Olfato murmurador
De lo malo, y de lo bueno,
Que fuifte Leon, que difte
Dañado olor con tu aliento.

Sale el Olfato *affombrado.*
El Olfato.
¡ O nunca yo defpertara
De tan regalado fueño !
La Culpa.
Tacto, que lafcivamente
Empleado en tus defeos
Offo fuifte, pues que nace
Sin forma, fin vifta, y cuerpo.

Sale el Tacto *affombrado.*
El Tacto.
¡ Qué á mi pefar me levanto
De tan regalado lecho !
La Culpa.
Vifta, que manchado Tigre
Has pacido efte Defierto,
Pues embidiofo eres ojos
Que fientes bienes agenos.

Sale la Vista *como affombrado.*
La Vifta.
¿ Si noche han de fer los mios,
De qué firve lo que veo ?

Hearing ! thou to whom light words
Were a fource of fweet enchantment,
On account of which defect
A chameleon's fhape I gave thee !

Enter the Hearing, *amazed.*
The Hearing.
Ah ! from fuch fweet lethargy
Muft I at this new voice waken ?
Sin.
Smell ! that libelleft in turn
Equally all forms of matter,
Thou a lion late, whofe breath
Fetid odours round thee fcatter'd !

Enter the Smell, *amazed.*
The Smell.
Ah ! that I had never woken
From a fleep by dreams fo gladden'd !
Sin.
Touch ! that, by thy low defires
Wholly occupied and trammell'd,
Wert a bear, fince it is born
Sightlefs, formlefs, and unfhapen !

Enter the Touch, *amazed.*
The Touch.
Oh ! the forrow ! to arife
From a bed fo foftly padded !
Sin.
Sight ! that in thefe deferts here
Liveft like a fpotted panther,
Fleck'd with envious eyes to fee
Aught of alien good that happens !

Enter the Sight, *amazed.*
The Sight.
Of what fervice are mine eyes,
If I'm doom'd to dwell in darknefs?

La Culpa.
Gusto, que animal inmundo
Eres, porque siempre hambriento
Solo en esta vida cuidas
De sustentarte á tí mesmo.

Sale el GUSTO *assombrado.*
El Gusto.
Que era un gran puerco soñaba,
Nadie que ay que creer en sueños
Diga, ó si diga, pues oy
Lo soy dormido, y despierto.
La Culpa.
Yá están aqui tus sentidos,
Yá á tu poder te los buelvo.
Idos, que en mí no durais
Sino solamente el tiempo
Que tarda en venir el hombre
Por vosotros; pues es cierto,
Que está en su mano el cobraros,
Como en su mano el perderos.
El Entendimiento.
No esperas mas, vén á este
Baxél de tu Entendimiento.
El Oído.
¿ Dónde hemos de ir tan apriessa ?
¿ Apenas llegado avemos
A estos Palacios, y yá
Nos quieres ausentar de ellos ?
La Vista.
¿ Adónde quieres llevarnos
Por esse Mar padeciendo ?
El Olfato.
Dexa que de las passadas
Fortunas nos reparemos.
El Gusto.
Dexame, Señor, que sea
Puerco otro poco de tiempo,
Pues no ay mas seguridad

Sin.
Taste ! that art a beast unclean,
Since with hunger never sated,
The sole thought of thy existence
Is how best to feed and fatten !

Enter the TASTE, *amazed.*
The Taste.
What a hog I dream'd I was !
Dreams are fables though, what matter ?
Waking or asleep by me
Is the self-same part enacted.
Sin.
See, thy Senses all are here :
Back into thy power I hand them.
Go ! your stay with *me* endured
Only for the time your master,
Man, delay'd to come and claim you,
Since 'tis certain power is granted
Not alone to man to lose you,
But to regain you when you're absent.
The Understanding.
Stay no longer here, but come
To my bark in which we landed.
The Hearing.
Whither should we go so quickly ?
Scarce have we the beauteous gardens
Of this friendly palace enter'd,
And already we're debarr'd them.
The Sight.
Wouldst thou bring us back to sea,
There to suffer new disasters ?
The Smell.
Let us here recruit our strength
After all the ills we've master'd.
The Taste.
Let me be a hog, I pray,
Once again, good sir, I ask thee,
Since of all the lives I know

En el Mundo, que fer puerco.
    El Entendimiento.
En fin, fois brutos, fentidos,
Tan brutos, que holgais de ferlo.
    El Gufto.
¿No fabemos quan bueno es
Eftár comiendo, y gruñendo?
    El Entendimiento.
¿Vamos, qué efperes, Ulífes?
    El Hombre.
Vamos, pero no tan prefto,
Porque de aver vifto aqui
Mis fentidos mal contentos
De dexar eftas delicias,
No fé (ay de mí!) lo que fiento.
    El Entendimiento.
Yo te llevaré por fuerza.
    El Hombre.
No harás tal, que tu confejo
Arraftrarme no podrá,
Moverme sí, yá lo has hecho:
Vé á prevenir el Baxél,
Pues Piloto eres.
    El Entendimiento.
        Yá buelvo.   [*Vafe.*

    El Hombre.
Por poder mas libremente
Vér efta Deidad, le aufento
De mí aquefte breve inftante
Sin temor de fus preceptos.—
    La Culpa (aparte).
Aora podré hablarle, pues
Apartó fu entendimiento.
Ya Ulífes, que victoriofo
Te miras de mí, bolviendo
De effas incultas Montañas
Coronado de trofeos,
No tan prefto al Mar te entregues

A hog's life is the moft happy.
    The Underftanding.
Ah! fo brutifh are the Senfes,
To be brutes appears to glad them!
    The Tafte.
Have we not found out how pleafant
'Tis to eat and grunt untrammell'd?
    The Underftanding.
Come, Ulyffes, why delay?
    The Man.
Let us go,—but ftill there's ample
Time to fpare, for fince I fee
How my Senfes are diftracted
At abandoning thefe pleafures,
Ah! I know not how I falter.
    The Underftanding.
I muft drag you hence by force.
    The Man.
Ah! by force you cannot drag me,
But by counfel you may lead:
Even already you attract me;
Go, prepare the bark, for you
Are the pilot.
    The Underftanding.
        Yes, with gladnefs
To return here.   [*Exit.*
    The Man (afide).
        That this goddefs
I may fee with freer glances,
Undeterr'd by his fuggeftions,
I have thus contrived his abfence.
    Sin (afide).
I can tempt him now, fince his
Underftanding hath departed.
O Ulyffes! crown'd with trophies,
Vanquifher of my enchantments,
Flying from this lonely ifland,
From its mountains and moraffes,
Do not truft thyfelf fo quickly

En eſſe inconſtante leño,	To the wild and dangerous vaſtneſs
Que el Mar da la Vida ſurca,	Of the ſea of life, to plough it
Amenazado de rieſgos.	In a frail bark ſo unſtable.
Mira alterados los Mares,	See! its mighty breaſt upheaving,
Que con veloz movimiento	In its rapid movement ſparkles
En pyramides de eſpumas,	Now as pyramids of cryſtal,
Son Alcazares de hielo.	Now as ſnow-embattled caſtles.
Dexa que el Mar ſe ſerene ;	Wait the wild turmoil's abating,
Y pues te miras exempto	Wait until the ſea grows calmer ;
De la Magia de mi encanto,	And ſince thou haſt been exempted
En fé de eſſe ramo bello,	From the ſpell of my enchantment
Que te dió la Iris, no quieras	By the gift that Iris gave thee,—
Bolverte al afán tan preſto :	By that budding beauteous branchlet,—
Deſcanſa en mi albergue oy,	Oh! return not back ſo quickly
Que mañana ſerá tiempo	To its dangers and diſaſters :
Para dexar eſtos Montes	Reſt thee in my houſe to-day ;
De tantas delicias llenos.	In the morning will be ample
¿ Qué prieſſa te corre aora	Time for thee to fly theſe mountains
De auſentarte ; y mas ſabiendo,	And theſe joy-enfolding gardens.
Que yo, cada vez que quieras	Why ſo ſwiftly fly for ſafety,
Ir, detenerte no puedo ?	Knowing well thou art ſo guarded,
Entra en mis ricos Palacios,	That whenever thou wouldſt leave me
Donde ſon divertimientos	I am powerleſs to withſtand thee ?—
Todas ſus ocupaciones	Enter then my dazzling palace,
Para el aplicado Ingenio.	Where an intellectual banquet,
Verás mis grandes Eſtudios,	Graced by gladneſs and enjoyment,
Mis admirables portentos	Waits upon thy welcome advent.
Examinaras, tocando	Thou wilt ſee my deep reſearches,—
De mi Ciencia los efectos.	Thou my wonders wilt examine,—
¿ Por qué pienſas que me llaman	All the ſecrets of my ſcience
La·Circe de eſtos Deſiertos ?	Will be bared to give thee anſwer.
Porque Ciencias prohibidas,	Wherefore, thinkeſt thou, the Circe
Que ſon Leyes que yo tengo,	Of theſe deſert waſtes they call me ?
Con mis eſtudios alcanzo,	'Tis becauſe forbidden knowledge
Con mis vigilias aprendo.	(*That* ſole law I leave untrampled)
Verás apagado el Sol,	I, by application, reach to,—
Solo á un ſoplo de mi aliento ;	I, by mighty ſtudies, maſter.
Pues en la luciente edad,	By a breath from out my lips,
El dia yo le obſcurezco :	Thou wilt ſee the ſunlight blacken'd,

Bien digo, la fombra foy, [*Aparte.*
David lo dixo en un Verfo.
Verás, á folo una linea,
Que corran mis penfamientos,
Defclavadas las Eftrellas
Del octavo Firmamento :
Y es verdad, pues tercer parte
     [*Aparte.*
De ellas aparté del Cielo.
La Nigromancía verás
Executada, faliendo,
A mi conjuro obedientes,
De fus fepulcros los muertos.
Cadaver es el que peca, [*Aparte.*
Pues me obedece, no miento.
La grande Chiromancía
Verás, quando en vivo fuego,
En los papeles del humo
Caracteres de luz leo.
¿ Qué fuego no enciendo yo ?
     [*Aparte.*
No es engaño, pues le enciendo.
Titubear verás caducos
Uno, y otro Polo, haciendo
Que defplomados fe caygan
Sobre todo el Univerfo.
No ferá la vez primera, [*Aparte.*
Que yo eftremecí fu Imperio.
El idioma de las aves
Verás, que yo fola entiendo,
Siendo el canto vaticinio,
Y fiendo el graznido aguero,
De las flores te leerá
Eftos efcritos quadernos,
Donde la naturaleza
Efcrivió raros myfterios.
A todas horas tendrás
Dulces muficas, oyendo
Suaves cantos de las aves,

Since in all its perfect prime,
Can I the bright noon-day darken ;
I may fay fo, fince a fhadow [*Afide.*
David calls me in the Pfalter.—
Thou wilt fee that my mere thought,
Even my wifh in filence wafted,
From the Heaven beyond the feventh
Will the mighty ftars unfaften.
True, a third of Heaven's bright hoft
     [*Afide.*
Thus my primal fall brought after.—
Necromancy fhalt thou fee,
Tried and tefted to the fartheft ;—
So that, yielding to my fpells,
From their graves the dead will an-
  fwer :—
Yes ; for dead in fin is he [*Afide.*
Who doth yield to my advances.—
Pyromancy, too, will fhow thee
How upon the red flames' fparkles,
How upon the curling fmoke-wreaths,
Knowledge there infcribed I gather :
I deceive not here—the fire [*Afide.*
Lit by me doth ever crackle.—
Thou wilt fee the poles of Heaven
Tremble at my dread commandments,
As if down about to fall
On the world's difturbèd axes :—
Not the firft time will it be [*Afide.*
That its kingdom I have fhaken.—
All the language of the birds
Wilt thou learn, by *me* fole mafter'd—
Both their fweet prophetic warble
And their harfher augural cackle.
On the flowers, too, wilt thou read,
As upon illumined parchment,
Written characters revealing
Nature's myfteries and marvels.
Every moment wilt thou have

De los hombres dulces verfos,
Sabrofifimos manjares
Te fervirán con affeo
Tal, que el Olfato, y el Gufto
Se eften lifongeando á un tiempo.
La vifta divertirás
En effos jardines bellos,
Que fon nueftros paraífos,
De varias delícias llenos.
Dormirás en regalada
Cama, donde el Tacto atento
A tu defcanfo, en mullidas
Flores, tendrá blando lecho.
A todas horas tendrás
Damas, que te eftén firviendo,
Que, como foy en comun
La Culpa, conmigo tengo
Y en particular á todas
Las que fe precian de ferlo.
 [*Vá dexando caer el* Hombre *las*
  Flores del Ramillete poco á poco.
Y fobre todo tendrás
Los regalos de mi pecho,
Las caricias de mis brazos,
Los alhagos de mi afecto,
Las finezas de mi amor,
La verdad de mi defeo,
La atencion de mi alvedrio,
De mi vida el rendimiento:
Y finalmente, delicias,
Guftos, regalos, contentos,
Placeres, dichas, favores,
Muficas, bayles, y juegos.

  El Hombre (*aparte*).
No fé qué he de refponder,
Porque divertido, oyendo

Sweeteft ftrains to greet and glad thee,—
Now the nightingale's lone ditty,
Now the poet's lovelier anthem.
Food the daintieft fhall be fpread
For thee with fuch nice exactnefs,
So that fmell and tafte together
Shall at once thy fenfes flatter.
Thy enraptured fight fhall revel
In thefe fweet delicious gardens,
Which to us are bowers of Eden,
Full of every form of gladnefs.
In a foft bed fhalt thou fleep,
Where the Touch, that looketh after
Thy repofe, on downieft flower-leaves
Shall outfpread thy pleafant pallet.
Lovely ladies every hour
Shall their various fervice grant thee,
Whom, as Sin fupreme, I keep
Here at once my flaves and partners,
Specially all thofe who are
To my fervice felf-attracted.
 [*During the latter part of this ad-*
  drefs, the Man *has let fall the*
  flowers of his nofegay one by one.
But, above all other joys,
Wilt thou have my heart's free largefs,
The delight of my embraces,
The fweet proof of my attachment,
All the fondnefs of my love,
All the truth defire implanteth,
The devotion of my will;
Of my life the fweet enthralment:
In a word, delicious joys,
Raptures, ravifhments, entrancements,
Pleafures, bliffes, fondeft favours—
Sports and plays, and fongs and dances.
  The Man (*afide*).
Ah! I know not what to fay!
Ah! I know not what to anfwer!

La retorica fuave
De fu voz, fui defhaciendo
El Ramo de las Virtudes,
Que defperdiciadas veo,
Y ajadas entre mis manos;
¿ Pero qué mucho, fi advierto,
Que para que ella me hablaffe
Aparté mi Entendimiento ?
Sin él hablaré.   Gallarda
Circe, á tus voces atento,
De mí me olvido, y yá folo
De tu hermofura me acuerdo.
A tus Palacios me guia,
Porque fer tu huefped quiero
Defde oy, eftimando humilde
Tan cortefes cumplimientos.

La Culpa.
Vencí.   La Mufica buelva
A repetir fus acentos;
Y effos gallardos Palacios,
Que eftán en el duro centro
Del Monte, fus puertas abran,
Que vá gran huefped á ellos.
    [*Defcubrefe un Palacio muy viftofo.*
        El Oído
Al Entendimiento aguarda
Antes, Señor, que entres dentro,
Porque fepas donde eftás.

El Hombre.
Para qué ? pues es tan cierto
Que no entrára, fi fupiera
(Ay de mí !) mi Entendimiento.
        El Gufto.
Dices bien, vamos fin él ;
¿ Para qué acá le querémos,
Que es un Miniftro canfado,

Since, oblivious of myfelf,
Liftening to her fweet-toned accents,
I have been, ah me! deftroying
All the beauty of this branchlet.
Wither'd in my hand it lies,
At my feet its leaves lie fcatter'd.
But what wonder, when I think,
In my Underftanding's abfence
Has fhe fpoken to me thus ?
Thus without him, then, I anfwer:—
Circe fair, in mute attention
I unto thy fweet voice hearken,
Self-forgetting, loft in dreaming,
By thy wondrous beauty dazzled.
Lead me to thy long'd-for palace ;
As thy gueft, thy flave command me ;
Let my humble acquiefcence
For thy courtefy thus thank thee.
        Sin.
I have conquer'd !—once again,
Mufic, fing your fweeteft accents,
And my beauteous palace home,
Which amid thefe mountains ftandeth,
Open wide your dazzling doors
For the great gueft who advanceth.
        [*A magnificent palace appears.*
        The Hearing.
Oh ! my lord, before thou goeft
Where thou know'ft not what may
        happen,
Here await thy Underftanding.
        The Man.
Wherefore ? fince if thus I acted,
Ah ! I know to well that *he*
Ne'er would fanction my advances.
        The Tafte.
Right ! without him let us go :—
What's the ufe of being faddled
With a pig and pleafure-hating

Todo limpio, y nada puerco ?
       Música.
En hora dichofa venga
A eftos jardines amenos
El Peregrino del Mar,
Donde halle feguro puerto.

  Vanfe, dadas las manos, y fale el
    Entendimiento.

     El Entendimiento.
Hombre, efpera, efcucha, aguarda,
No entres en effe fobervio
Alcazar, porque no fabes
Los peligros que eftán dentro.
Mas ay de mí! con las voces,
Que le han tenido fufpenfo,
No me oye : ¡ Qué bien (ay trifte !)
Se echa de vér, pues pudieron
Los alhagos de la Culpa,
Los hechizos, y venenos
Moverle, que me tenía
Retirado ! porque es cierto
Que á tenerme á mí configo,
No fe rindiera tan prefto.

    Sale la Penitencia.

     La Penitencia.
¿ Entendimiento, qué voces
Son eftas que dás al viento ?
     El Entendimiento.
Laftimas fon de aver dado
Mala cuenta de un fugeto
Que Dios me entregó : Oy el Hombre
Me ha dexado, de mí huyendo
Se ha entrado en effe Palacio,
Poblado de Encantamientos.
Las Virtudes que adquirió,
Con un arrepentimiento

Cool cantankerous old carper ?—
    The Mufic.
Happy, happy be the hour
That to thefe delicious gardens
Comes the Pilgrim of the fea
In a fafe port happily landed !

Exeunt all hand in hand.   The Under-
  standing *enters from the oppofite*
  fide.
    The Underftanding.
Hear ! weak Man, oh ! liften ! ftay !
Enter not that pride-built caftle,
Since thou knoweft not the quickfands
On whofe dangerous top it ftandeth :
But, ah me ! their flattering fongs
Keep his fenfes fo abftracted,
That he hears me not !   How foon
Can it now be feen, O fadnefs !
That the luftful lures of fin,
That her philtres and enchantments
Have the power to overwhelm him
In his Underftanding's abfence,
Since with *me*, he would not have
His confent fo freely granted.

    Enter Penance.

     Penance.
Why thefe outcries, Underftanding,
That thou to the winds imparteft ?
     The Underftanding.
Wailings are they for difcharging
Towards my human ward fo badly
Duties trufted me by God.
Man has left me, hath departed,
Fled me but juft now, and enter'd
This enchantment-peopled palace ;
All the virtues which by thee
Were to him repentant granted,

Que tuvo, defperdiciadas
En el ayre las encuentro.
La Penitencia (mira á las Flores).
Pues yo las recogeré,
Guardandolas para el tiempo
Que arrepentido me bufque,
De fu culpa, y de fu yerro.
    El Entendimiento.
Sin mí eftá, que no eftuviera,
Conmigo (ay de mí!) tan ciego,
Que fe olvidára de tí.
    La Penitencia.
Darte yo una induftria quiero,
Para facarle de aqueffe
Encanto; toca en fu pecho
Al arma, pues efcuchando
Efte belicofo eftruendo,
(Haciendole de sí mifmo
Siempre mortales acuerdos)
Verás, que con tal temor
Creera advertido, y atento
A fu Entendimiento, donde
Eftá fin Entendimiento.

Salen la Culpa, *y el* Hombre, *y los*
  Sentidos, *y canta la Múfica.*

    La Múfica.
Compitiendo con las felvas,
Donde las flores madrugan,
Los paxaros en el viento
Forman Abriles de plumas.

    La Culpa.
Vén por aqueftos jardines,
Adonde critica, y culta
La naturaleza, ha hecho,

As I enter'd here, I found
By the wanton breezes fcatter'd.
    Penance (feeing them on the ground).
I fhall re-collect them all,
And preferve them 'till he afk me
For them once again, when he
Feels repentant for his lapfes.
    The Underftanding.
Ah! without me is he now!
With me never had fuch hardnefs
Steel'd his heart forgetting *thee!*
    Penance.
I fhall fhow thee in what manner
Thou may'ft yet perchance releafe him
From the chains of this enchantment.
Touch the key-note of his foul,—
Sound to arms! the martial clatter
(For of death and deathfulleft omens
Ever breathes the call to battle!)
Soon will wake him from the ftupor
That his memory now doth darken:—
Then he will attend to *thee,*
Now without thee he advanceth.

Enter Sin, *the* Man, *and the* Senses;
  the Mufic fings.

    The Mufic.
With the bloffom'd boughs competing,
When the fweet flowers rife from
    flumber,*
Birds an April of the air
Fafhion with their painted plumage.
    Sin.
Come unto thefe gardens fair,
Where rich Nature's careful culture
With her beds and myrtle buds

---

* In this fcene the afonante vowels of the original are, *u, a:* in the tranflation, *u, e,* or their equivalents in found, are ufed.

Entre jardines, y murtas,
Alardes de fus primores,
Pues fu varia compoftura
Academia es, donde el Mayo
De un año para otro eftudia.
    El Hombre.
Tan hermofa es efta eftancia,
Que el mifmo Sol que la alumbra,
Su esfera dexára, á precio
De que fuera esfera fuya.
Digalo el Cielo, que al vér
Las flores que la dibujan,
Arreboló las Eftrellas,
Porque compitan las unas
Con las otras: Y affi, eftán
Defde la tiniebla obfcura,
Hafta la luciente Aurora,
Effas Eftrellas ceruleas,
Donde en brazos de la noche
Duermen las esferas mudas,
    El, y Mufica.
Compitiendo con las felvas,
Donde las flores madrugan.

    La Culpa.
Todo el jardin es delicias;
No ay planta, no ay hoja alguna,
Que verde aroma, los mas
Blandos perfumes no fupla.
Y porque Vifta, y Olfato
La pompa no fe atribuyan
Para sí folos, objetos
Son del Oído las puras
Fuentes, fiendo en el ruido,
Compás que á coros fe efcucha,
Apacibles porque parlan,
Y alegres porque murmuran.
Embidiofo todo viento,
Al ver por la tierra, en una

Maketh fuch a dazzling mufter,
That united they appear
Like a fair collegiate ftructure,
Whither comes the young-eyed May,
Year by year, an eager ftudent.
    The Man.
Yes, fo lovely is this place,
That the fun that flames refulgent
Would his own bright fphere abandon
For the fairer flower-fphere under ;
And the Heavens, the flowers beholding
Radiant in their rofy clufters,
Would paint red their own pale ftars,
That with thefe they might be number'd.
Thus it is from evening's grey
To the morn's glad gleams of umber,
Thefe cerulean ftars appear,
Twinkling each with trembling luftre,
When within the arms of Night
Sleep the filent fpheres of Summer,
    He and the Mufic together.
With the bloffom'd boughs competing,
When the fweet flowers rife from flum-
    ber.
    Sin.
All the garden is one joy :
Not a plant that here hath budded,
Not a leaf but breathes from out it
Fragrance that no tongue can utter :
And that Sight and Smell fhould boaft
    not,
That this Eden hath refulted
Solely from their aidance, lift !
Limpid fountains, leap and bubble,
Breaking with melodious beat
Songs whofe never-ceafing burden
Seemeth fad when moft they laugh,
Mirthful moft when moft they murmur.
And the envious Nymph of Air,

Primavera folamente,
Tantas Primaveras juntas,
De otras flores fe ha poblado,
Que aladas fus golfos furcan,
Siendo ramilletes vivos :
Y affi, quanto entre efta fuma
Deydad, las flores, y fuentes
De la tierra, con induftria,
Paxaros forman de rofas,
Por igualar fu hermofura :

Ella, y Múfica.
Los paxaros en el viento
Forman Abriles de plumas.
La Múfica.
De una belleza engañados,
Por Aurora la faludan,
Y viendo fus bellos ojos,
Quedan vanos de fu culpa.
El Hombre.
Toda effa belleza, toda
Effa varia compoftura
De vientos, y quadros, que
Emulos fiempre fe ufurpan
La alabanza, dignamente
Sus trofeos affegura,
Quando al faludar tu vifta
A todas horas te juzga
Aurora de effas Montañas,
Haciendo que fe confundan
En los tormentos del dia
Salpicadas las purpureas
Hojas ; pues aunque haya Aves,
Y flores del dia en la cuna,
Bebiendo á la Aurora el llanto,
Que cendales de oro enjuga,
El verte fegunda vez,

Seeing earth fo richly ftudded
With the flowers of many fprings,
Join'd in *this* that is the youngeft,
Has unto her azure plains
Flowers of other kinds conducted,
Which, upborn on myriad wings,
Living nofegays float and flutter.
And as earth's young goddefs fair
With her flowers and founts conftructeth
Spring's fweet Paradife below,
So the other in her upper
Beauteous realm of birds makes rofes
Rivalling the rich ones under :
    She and the Mufic together.
Birds an April of the air
Fafhion with their painted plumage.
    The Mufic.
By her lovelinefs deceived,
For Aurora they falute her,
And beholding her bright eyes,
Love the fweet miftake they fuffer.
    The Man.
All this fair variety,
All this lovelinefs that furgeth
Up from billowy buds of bloom,
By the wandering zephyrs ruffled,
All this realm of fpring, whofe crown
Earth and fky in turn ufurpeth,
When it looks upon thy face,
Every moment doth it judge thee
The Aurora of thefe hills,
Blending hours that erft were funder'd,
Streaking in the noontide's glow
All the leaves with rofeate purple,
So that birds and flowers that drank
Morning's pearly tears unnumber'd
Round the cradle of the day,
Tears that from her eyes fhe brufhes
With the golden-threaded clouds,

Con nueva salva segunda :

     El, y Música.
De tu belleza engañados
Por Aurora la saludan.
     La Culpa.
Culpa fuera de las aves,
Y las flores, porque nunca
Para equivocar deydades
Hallar pudieran disculpa.

     El Hombre.
Si es culpa, ó acierto, no
Es justo que yo lo arguya ;
Pero bien sé, que mi amor
Oy de su parte assegura ;
Que aunque culpa decir sea,
Que por Aurora te anuncian
Flores, y aves ; ni las aves,
Ni las flores se disculpan
De essa culpa, porque antes
Sé, que con causa mas justa,
     El, y Música.
En viendo tus bellos ojos,
Quedan vanos de su culpa.
     El Gusto.
Yá que me ha tocado á mí,
(Que en efecto soy la Gula)
Preveniros las viandas,
En cuya alegre dulzura,
Quanto corre, nada, y buela
Registro entre mil dulzuras
Su sabor, desnudo yá
De piel, de escama, y de pluma,
Mirad adonde quereis
Comer oy.
     La Lisonja.
     Sea con una

Seeing on the horizon under
Thee arise a second time,
Hail thee with new matin music ;
     He and the Music together.
By thy loveliness deceived
For Aurora they salute thee.
     Sin.
This were wrong in bird and flower.
Bird and flower are both excuseless
For confounding goddesses,
Whom their separate shapes have sun-
   der'd.
     The Man.
If 'tis right or no, the point
It were wrong I argued further.
This though know I well, my love
Is of *one* thing well assurèd,—
That, although 'twere wrong to say
That the flowers and birds misjudge thee
For Aurora, bird and flower
Would not wish to be excusèd
For that fault, since they, I feel,
Acting with impulsive justness—
     He and the Music together.
In beholding thy bright eyes,
Love the sweet mistake they suffer.
     The Taste.
Now since it devolves on me
(I who am thy Taste), the duty
Of providing for thy need
Viands cull'd from out the number
Of the things that swim or fly,
Or possess the earth's green surface,
'Mid whose thousand varied forms,
Stript of skin, of scale, and plumage,
I their hidden favours seize,—
Think where art thou to have supper ?
     Flattery.
Here, with all due service fair,

Ceremonia lifongera.
     El Gufto.
La Lifonja es muy aftuta,
Pues que fabe fembrar mefas
Tan candidas, y purpureas.

Sale por debaxo del Tablado una Mefa
  con muchas viandas, y fientafe la
  Culpa, *y* Ulíses, *y los demás firveu,*
  y los Sentidos *fe fient an en el fuelo.*

     La Culpa.
Sientate, y todos
Os fentad en la verdura
De effas flores.
     La Lafcivia.
       Pues yo quiero
Que no todas fe atribuyan
Las finezas, fin que á mi
El Huefped me deba una.
Aquella letra cantad,
Que yo hice.
     El Hombre.
      Pues fi es tuya
Será amorofa.
     La Lafcivia.
    Sí es.
     El Hombre.
No ay Dama aqui, que no acuda
A un Sentido.
     El Gufto.
     Si feñor,
Pero victor.
     El Hombre.
   Quién?
     El Gufto.
     La Gula.

Let it on the fpot be ufher'd.
     The Tafte.
What a clever lafs is this !
Since with fkill as fharp as fudden
Tables o'er the ground fhe fcatters
Gleaming all with plate and purple.

A table fumptuoufly provided with viands
  rifes from beneath. Sin *and* Ulysses
  place themfelves at the table, the Senses *on the ground : all are waited on*
  by the others.

     Sin.
Sit, Ulyffes, at my fide : —
On the foft and verdurous turf here
Let the reft recline.
     Voluptuoufnefs.
     Since I
Would not that our gueft fhould number
Every courtefy as thine,
One on my part thou wilt fuffer :
Sing that little canzonet
Made by me.
     The Man.
     Its gentle burden
Muft be love, if thine it be.
     Voluptuoufnefs.
So it is.
     The Man.
     Each Senfe is fuited
With a feparate lady.
     The Tafte.
      Yes ;
But there's one deferves a bumper.
     The Man.
Who is fhe ?
     The Tafte.
     Intemperance.

La Música.
Si quereis gozar florida
Edad entre dulce fuerte,
Olvidate de la muerte,
Y acuerdate de la vida.

*Tocan Caxas, y alborotanse todos, y
dicen dentro el* Entendimiento, *y
la* Penitencia.

La Culpa.
No canteis mas ; ¿ qué atrevida
Voz nuestros gustos divierte ?
     El Entendimiento.
Ulises, Capitan fuerte,
Si quieres dicha crecida.
     La Penitencia.
Olvidate de la vida.
     El Entendimiento.
Y acuerdate de la muerte.
     La Culpa.
¿ Quién, con tanto atrevimiento,
Trueca el gusto en confusion ?
     El Hombre.
Circe, las que escuchas son
Voces de mi Entendimiento,
El me ha llamado, é intento
Responderle.
     La Culpa.
       De él te olvida.
     El Hombre.
Suelta.
     La Culpa.
      Es accion atrevida.
Cantad, porque no se assombre
De oír aquella voz el Hombre.
     La Música.
Acuerdate de la vida.

The Music.
Wouldst thou, Man, to rapture give
Life's young hours that flower and fly,
Oh! forget that thou must die!
And but think that thou dost live!

*A sound of drums and voices is heard
from within : all start with surprise.
The* Understanding *and* Penance
answer from within.

     Sin.
Cease the song! What voice doth strive
Thus to mar our joy thereby ?
     The Understanding.
Valiant soldier! from on high
Wouldst thou lasting bliss receive ?
     Penance.
Oh! forget that thou dost live!
     The Understanding.
And remember thou must die!
     Sin.
Who is this whose bold voice breaketh
Rudely on my startled ear ?
     The Man.
'Tis my inner voice you hear—
'Tis my Understanding speaketh ;
Him my answering conscience seeketh.

     Sin.
Heed him not, no answer give.
     The Man.
Let me go.
     Sin.
      Thou goest to grieve.
Sing once more, lest Man should hear
That mysterious voice severe.
     The Music.
Oh! remember thou dost live !

El Hombre.
Sí haré, que bien larga es :
Y defpues tendré lugar
Para fentir, y llorar,
Pues me baftará defpues :
A tus brazos buelvo, pues,
Dulce dueño.
          La Culpa.
          Feliz fuerte !
          El Hombre.
Tu hermufura me divierte ;
Contigo ufano me nombre ;
No quiero mas dicha.
          El Entendimiento.
                    Hombre,
Acuerdate de la muerte.
                    [*Suena Caxa.*
          El Hombre.
¡ Fuerza es que me acuerde (ay trifte !)
Quando mi afecto fe mueve
De que es tan caduca, y breve,
Que en un inftante confifte !
Entendimiento, que hicifte
En mí tal efecto, advierte,
Que yá voy á obedecerte.
          La Culpa.
Vueftra voz fu paffo impida.
          La Múfica.   ·
Acuerdate de la vida.
          El Entendimiento.
Acuerdate de la muerte.
                    [*Suena Caxa.*
          El Hombre.
Aqui me eftán alhagando
Gufto, placer, y contento,
Quando alli mi Entendimiento
Al arma me eftá tocando.
          La Culpa.
Qué dudas ?

The Man.
Be it fo : the days extend ;
Life is long and full of joy :—
For contrition and annoy
Time enough ere comes the end.
To thine arms, then, deareft friend,
To thine arms once more I fly.
          Sin.
Happy fate !
          The Man.
          Felicity
Is it but thy face to fee :
Greater blifs there cannot be.
          The Underftanding.
Man ! remember thou muft die !
                    [*Drums found.*

          The Man.
Oh ! the woe, to be compell'd
This to think of even in blifs—
Rapture, oh ! how fleet it is,
Flying ere it fcarce is held :—
Underftanding mine, impell'd
By thy low voice whifpering nigh,—
See ! at thy beheft I fly !
          Sin.
Song, arreft the fugitive.
          The Mufic.
Oh ! remember thou doft live !
          The Underftanding.
Oh ! remember thou muft die !
                    [*Drums found.*
          The Man.
Here enjoyment round me draws
Nets of blifs, whofe woof enthrals me :
There my Underftanding calls me
To comply with valour's laws.
          Sin.
Canft thou waver ?

El Entendimiento.
　　Qué estás pensando?
　　La Culpa.
No de essa voz confundida
Tu memoria esté afligida.
　　El Entendimiento.
En aqueste encanto advierte:
Acuerdate de la muerte.
　　La Música.
Acuerdate de la vida.
　　El Hombre.
En dos mitades estoy
Partido, (passion tyrana!)
Entre el horror de mañana,
A la ventura de oy;
A aquel sigo, y á este voy;
Y uno, y otro en mal tan fuerte,
O me aflige, ó me divierte:
¿ Qual ha de ser preferida
De mis glorias?
　　　　La Música.
　　　　　Vida, vida.
　　El Hombre.
De mis penas?
　　El Entendimiento.
　　　　Muerte, muerte.
Y aunque me la dén á mí　　[*Sale.*
Los encantos de esta fiera,
He de entrar, porque no fuera
Entendimiento, si aqui
Temiera morir: ¿ assi,
Ulíses, te has olvidado
De tí mismo? ¿ Assi entregado
A unos placeres fingidos,
Que sin mí, y con tus sentidos
Aqui vives engañado?

　　La Culpa.
¿ Estará (dime) mejor,

The Understanding.
　　　　Canst thou pause?
　　Sin.
Oh ! no more attention give
To that voice, but bliss receive !
　　The Understanding.
Think, 'mid all this witchery—
Think that thou art doom'd to die.
　　The Music.
Only think that thou dost live.
　　The Man.
Oh ! to which, torn heart, give way—
Present bliss or future sorrow,
Or the anguish of to-morrow,
Or the rapture of to-day ?—
This I follow, that obey.
Wish the gladness, yet would fly
All the grief that comes thereby :—
Oh ! to which the preference give ?—
Which for my joy?
　　　　The Music.
　　　　That thou dost live !—
　　　The Man.
Which for my pain?
　　The Understanding.
　　　　That thou must die !—
Yes ; and though that fate be mine,
　　　　　[*He enters.*
By this monster's sorceries slain,
Here I enter : since 'tis plain,
I were not myself, or thine
God-given guide, should I resign
Death itself defending thee :
Hast thou lost all memory
Of thyself? that thus, Ulysses,
Thou wouldst live in phantom blisses
Here with thy senses, without *me ?*
　　Sin.
Were it better, then, that he,

Creído de tu prudencia,
Allá con la Penitencia,
Adonde todo es horror,
Todo tristeza, y pavor,
Que aqui, donde le divierte
Tanta gloria?
   El Entendimiento.
     Sí, si advierte,
Que aquesta gloria es fingida.
    La Culpa.
Cantad, cantad.
    La Música.
      Vida, vida.
   El Entendimiento.
Tocad, tocad: muerte, muerte.
    El Hombre.
Dices bien, á tí te creen
Los influxos de mi estrella.
    La Culpa.
Pues dexasme?
    El Hombre.
     ¿ Ay Culpa bella,
Que tú tambien dices bien?
   El Entendimiento.
Valor mis voces te dén.
    La Culpa.
Muevate el verme rendida.
   El Entendimiento.
Nada el seguirme te impida:
Tocad.
    La Culpa.
    Cantad.
    El Hombre.
      Pena fuerte!

    La Música.
Vida, vida.
    El Entendimiento.
    Muerte, muerte.

Following thy advice, should go,
Penance led, where all is woe,
All is grief and misery,
Than remain contentedly
Here, where on his every sigh
Pleasure waits?
   The Understanding.
     Undoubtedly,
If he knows she nought can give.
    Sin.
Sing! sing!
    The Music.
     'Tis sweet to live!
   The Understanding.
Peal! peal! Man needs must die!
    The Man.
True! oh true! my star to thee
Yields, oh voice! that speaks within.
    Sin.
Canst thou leave me?
    The Man.
     Beauteous Sin,
Ah! thy voice, too, moveth me.
   The Understanding.
May my voice thy soul's strength be!
    Sin.
May my tears thy love revive!
   The Understanding.
Follow me, be strong and strive;
Drums, rebeat.
    Sin.
    Sing sweet!
    The Man.
     I try
Suffering's depths!
    The Music.
     To live!
   The Understanding.
      To die!

(*Dentro La Penitencia*).
Muerte, muerte.
  La Música.
    Vida, vida.
  El Entendimiento.
Eſte es bien perecedero.
  La Culpa.
Aquella es pena cruel.
  El Entendimiento.
Por eſſo eſpera laurél.
  La Culpa.
Goza tu vida primero.
  El Entendimiento.
Mira que es encanto fiero.
  La Culpa.
Mira que es tormento fuerte.
  El Entendimiento.
En que eres mortal advierte.
  La Culpa.
No te acuerdes de eſſo, no.
  La Música.
Vida.
  La Penitencia.
 Muerte.
  Los dos.
    Quién venció?
  El Hombre.
La memoria de la muerte.
  La Culpa.
¿Qué importa que aya vencido,
Si eſcaparte no podrás
De mí? En mi poder eſtás,
Sin reſervarte un ſentido.
Las flores que avia texido
La Penitencia, que eran
Las virtudes que pudieran
Salvarte, yá las perdiſte,
Tú miſmo las deſhiciſte;
¿Pues qué alivio de mí eſperan

Penance (within).
To die ! to die !
  The Muſic.
    To live ! to live !
  The Underſtanding.
Life is but a dying day.
  Sin.
Death, a pang that ſtrikes thee down.
  The Underſtanding.
But it gives the laurel crown.
  Sin.
Life enjoy though, while you may.
  The Underſtanding.
Life's a dream that fades away.
  Sin.
Death's a pain that all would fly.
  The Underſtanding.
Think thy final hour draws nigh.
  Sin.
Think not ſo till life be done.
  The Muſic.
Life !
  Penance (within).
Death !
  The two.
    Say which has won ?
  The Man.
The remembrance I muſt die.
  Sin.
What imports it thus the gaining
Barren victory, if thou art
Powerleſs to eſcape my art?
Thou, with not a ſenſe remaining :
Since the potent flowers diſdaining,
Woven for thee by Heaven's hoſt,
Which the hands of Penance gave thee,
Virtues were they which could ſave thee,
Thou haſt ſcatter'd, thou haſt loſt;
Wherefore, therefore, canſt thou boaſt

Oy tus anfias ?
    El Entendimiento.
        No te dé
Aquefſo defconfianza,
Tén en el Cielo efperanza,
Que es columna de la Fé.
Eſſas virtudes, yo fé,
Que quando mas divertido
Las avias efparcido,
Para guardarlas llegó
A recogerlas . . . .
    La Culpa.
       Quién ?

    Sale la PENITENCIA.

    La Penitencia.
          Yo,
Que el Arco de paz he fido,
Que fi oy en Carro Triunfal
Me llegas á vér fentada,
Subſtituyendo Dofél
De oro, de purpura, y nacar,
Es, porque á triunfar de tí
Vengo, que quando me llama
Del hombre el Entendimiento,
No puedo yo hacerle falta.
Las virtudes, que fin él
Defperdició fu ignorancia,
Yo recogí ; pues es cierto,
Que fi fe adquieren en Gracia,
Siempre que buelva por ellas,
En depofito las halla.
Y para que el Hombre vea,
Que folas á vencer baſtan
Tus Encantos, oy verás
Todas aqueſtas viandas,

Thou art free from me to-day ?
    The Underſtanding.
Do not, therefore, Man, miſtruſt thee,
Hope in Heaven, to *that* entruſt thee—
Hope, the Faith's beſt prop and ſtay,
All thofe virtues flown away,
Scatter'd in thy wantonnefs—
One, I know, doth hither prefs
To reſtore them ; from the ſky
Comes ſhe hither now.

    Sin.
       Who ?

    PENANCE *enters.*

    Penance.
          I,
Erſt who wore the rainbow's drefs :
Who if in a car triumphal
Thou to-day behold'ſt me ſeated *
'Neath a canopy, wherein
Purple, pearl, and gold are blended,
'Tis becaufe I come to triumph
Over thee, for whenfoever
Calleth me Man's Underſtanding,
Never is the call negleéted.
All the virtues which he ſquander'd
In his ignorance, demented,
I have here re-gather'd, fince
Certain 'tis that when prefented
By the hand of Grace they've been,
He who turneth back repentant
Ever findeth them again,
Safely guarded and prefervèd.
And that Man may know that they
Can alone thy forceries render

---

* The metre in the original changes to afonante alternate vowel rhymes in *a, a.* For thefe I
have fubſtituted correfponding ones in *e, e.*

Del viento defvanecidas,
En humo, en polvo, y en nada,
Moftrando con efte exemplo
Lo que fon glorias humanas,
Pues el Manjar folamente,
Que es eterno, es el del alma :
Efte es el Pan Soberano,
Que veís yá fobre efta Tabla :
La Penitencia os le ofrece,
Que fin ella (cofa es clara)
Que verle no merecia
El hombre con glorias tantas.
Sentidos efto no es Pan,
Sino mas noble fubftancia :
Carne, y Sangre es, porque huyendo
Las efpecies, que aí eftaban,
Los accidentes no mas
Quedaron en Hoftia blanca.

La Culpa.
¿ Como quieres que te crean
Los Sentidos con quien hablas,
Si todos conocerán
Que los ofendes, y agravias ?
¿ Llega, Olfato, llega á oler
Effe Pan : en él qué hallas,
Pan, ó Carne ?

    Van llegando los SENTIDOS.
      El Olfato.
         De Pan es
El olor.
      La Culpa.
       ¿ Llega, qué aguardas,
Gufto ?
      El Gufto.
      Efte gufto es de Pan.

Powerlefs, thou wilt now behold
All the viands here collected
Vanifh into air, and leave
Nought behind to tell their prefence :
Showing thus how human glory
Is as falfe as evanefcent ;
Since the only food that lafteth
Is the food for fouls intended—
Is the eternal Bread of Life
Which now fills this table's centre.
It is Penance that prefents it,
Since without her (nought more certain)
Man deferveth not to witnefs
So much glory manifefted.
Yet, ye Senfes, 'tis not Bread,
But a fubftance moft tranfcendent :
It is Flefh and Blood ; becaufe,
When the fubftance is diffever'd
From the fpecies, the White Hoft then
But the accidents preferveth.
           Sin.
How canft thou expect to gain
Credence from thy outraged Senfes,
When they come to underftand
How you wrong them and offend them ?
Smell, come here, and with thy fenfe
Teft this bread, this fubftance,—tell me,
Is it bread or flefh ?

      The SENSES *approach.*
      The Smell.
           Its fmell
Is the fmell of bread.
         Sin.
           Tafte, enter ;
Try it thou.
      The Tafte.
       Its tafte is plainly
That of bread.

La Culpa.
¿ Llega, Tacto, qué te efpantas,
Dí lo que tocas ?
     El Tacto.
       Pan toco.
La Culpa.
¿ Vifta, á vér qué es lo que alcanzas ?

    La Vifta.
Pan folamente.
    La Culpa.
      Tú, Oído,
Rompe effa Forma, que llama
Carne la Fé, y Penitencia,
Y luego las defengaña
Al ruido de la fraccion :
¿ Qué refpondes?
     El Oído.
      Culpa ingrata,
Aunque la fraccion fe efcucha
Ruido de Pan, cofa es clara,
Que en fé de la Penitencia,
A quien digo que la llaman
Carne, por Carne la creo,
Pues que ella lo diga bafta.
    El Entendimiento.
Effa razon me cautiva.

    La Penitencia.
¿ Ea, Hombre, pues qué aguardas ?
Cautivo tu Entendimiento
Eftá yá de la Fé Santa
Por el Oído, á la Nave
De la Iglefia Soberana
Buelve, y dexa de la Culpa
Las delicias momentaneas.
Ulífes cautivo ha fido
De efta Circe injufta, y falfa :
Huye, pues, de fus encantos,

Sin.
    Touch, come, why tremble ?
Say what's this thou toucheft ?
    The Touch.
          Bread.
    Sin.
Sight, declare what thou difcerneft
In this object ?
    The Sight.
      Bread alone.
    Sin.
Hearing, thou, too, break in pieces
This material, which, as flefh,
Faith proclaims, and Penance preacheth ;
Let the fraction, by its noife,
Of their error undeceive them :
Say, is it fo?
    The Hearing.
      Ungrateful Sin,
Though the noife in truth refembles
That of bread when broken, yet
Faith and Penance teach us better
It is flefh, and what *they* call it
I believe : that Faith afferteth
Aught, is proof enough thereof.
    The Underftanding.
This one reafon brings contentment
Unto me.
    Penance.
    O Man! why linger ?
Now that Hearing hath firm-fetter'd
To the Faith thy Underftanding,
Quick, regain the faving veffel
Of the fovereign Church, and leave
Sin's fo briefly fweet exceffes.
Thou, Ulyffes, Circe's flave,
Fly this falfe and fleeting revel,
Since, how great her power may be,
Greater is the power of Heaven,

Yá que eftos fecretos hallas
En el Jupiter Divino,
Quien fus encantos defhagan.
    El Hombre.
Dices bien, Entendimiento,
De aquí mis Sentidos faca.
    Todos.
Vamos al Baxél, que aqui
Todo es fombras, y fantafmas.
    La Culpa.
¿ Qué importa, (ay de mí!) qué
    importa,
Que affi de mí poder falgas,
Si mis Encantos fabrán
Seguirte por donde vayas ?
Yo fabre alterar las ondas.
    La Penitencia.
Y yo fabré ferenarlas.

*Tocan Clarines, y defcubrefe la Nave, y
todos fe meten dentro.*

    La Culpa.
¿ Tribulaciones no fon
En la Efcritura las aguas ?
Luego á padecer le llevas
Trabajos, afanés, y anfias.
    La Penitencia.
Sí ; pero eftos fon regalos,
Con que mas merito alcanza.
    Dentro todos.
Buen viage, buen viage.
    La Culpa.
Aqueffas voces me matan.

    El Hombre.
Circe cruel, pues que fupe
Vencer prodigiofas Magias,
Quedate, donde te firva
De monumento tu Alcazar.

And the true Jove's mightier magic
Will thy virtuous purpofe ftrengthen.

    The Man.
Yes, thou'rt right, O Underftanding !
Lead in fafety hence my Senfes.
    All.
Let us to our fhip ; for here
All is fhadowy and unfettled.
    Sin.
What imports it—woe is me !—
What imports it that my fceptre
Thus you feem to 'fcape from, fince
My enchantments will attend ye ?
I fhall roufe the waves to madnefs.

    Penance.
I fhall follow and appeafe them.

*Trumpets peal. The fhip is difcovered,
and all go on board.*

    Sin.
Does not Holy Writ compare
Waves with woes that life engenders ?
Thither then ye go to fuffer
Toils, difcomforts, and diftreffes.
    Penance.
Yes, but thefe prove pleafures when
They to greater favour lead them.
    All (within).
Happy voyage ! happy voyage !
    Sin.
Oh ! with rage thefe cries o'erwhelm
    me !
    The Man.
Cruel Circe, now that all—
All thy wondrous wiles have ended,
Drag thy palace o'er thy head,
As thy monument and emblem.

La Culpa.
Ondas, que tanto Baxél
Sufris fobre las efpaldas,
En vueftros fenos de nieve
Le dad fepulcro de plata.

La Penitencia.
Ondas ferenas, al blando
Movimiento de las aguas,
Porque vueftros pavimentos
No fean montes, fino alcazar.
La Culpa.
Vientos que foplais del Norte
No le faqueis de Trinacria,
Y chocad, cafcado el pino,
En aquellas peñas altas.
La Penitencia.
Notos, que venís del Auftro,
Soplad con fuaves auras,
Porque hafta el Puerto de Hoftia
Oy á falvamento falga.
El Entendimiento.
Buen viage nos prometen
Las feñas de la bonanza.
La Culpa.
Haced, vicios, que velamen
Todo pedazos fe haga,
Y buelto el Barco, fea tumba
Con piramides, y jarcias.
El Hombre.
Haced, Virtudes, que rompa
La quilla fuave, y blanda,
Encrefpando las efpumas
Vidrios de nieve, y de plata.
Todos.
Buen viage, buen viage,
Que vientos, y ondas amaynan.
El Hombre.
Circe, poco tus Encantos

Sin.
Waves, that on your foam-white
    fhoulders
Bear the weight of fuch a veffel,
Give it fwift a filver tomb
In your bofom's fnowy centres.
Penance.
Halcyon waves, with filent fwell,
Roll your waters fmooth and level;
Like the bright floor of a palace,
Let your azure hills extend them.
Sin.
Winds, that from the black north blow,
Waft it not to feas ferener,
But upon Trinacrian rocks
Dafh its broken hull to pieces.
Penance.
Airs, that float from fouthern fkies,
Gently breathe with favouring breezes,
That it may the happy haven
Of the Hoft in fafety enter.
The Underftanding.
Friends, a profperous voyage promife
All the figns of fettled weather.
Sin.
Vices, tear the canvas down,
Rend the rifled fails in pieces,
Let the obelifcal mafts
Make the hull a tomb refemble.
The Man.
Virtues, for its curvèd keel
Make the fea-way fmooth and fettled,
Send its prow fwift-gliding through
Silvery foam, a fnow-fcaled ferpent.
All.
Happy voyage! happy voyage!
Sing the winds and waves together.
The Man.
Circe, now thy forceries vile

Han podido, pues me faca
(Ay de mí!) la Iris Divina,
Coronado de efperanzas.
La Penitencia.
Circe, yá fu Entendimiento
Va con él : poco las trazas
De tu Magia te han valido.
La Culpa.
Llena eftoy de pena, y rabia :
¿ Si yo foy vivora, cómo
No me rompo las entrañas ?
¿ Si foy afpid, cómo oy
Mi veneno no me mata ?
Pedazos del corazon
Me arrancaré con mis anfias
Para tirarlos al Cielo :
¿ Mas á mí, qué me acobarda ?
Si en la Nave de la Iglefia
Huyes de mí, fabré darla
Tormentas que la zozobren ;
Mas ay de mí ! que ya es vana
Mi Ciencia, pues que la veo
Navegar con tal bonanza :
Falten todos mis Sentidos,
Pues que yá poder me falta.

[*Suena Terremoto, y la ruido fe
bunde el Palacio.*
Confundanfe los Palacios,
Y bolviendofe montañas
Obfcuras, no viva en ellas
Sino yo, porque me faca
A quien encantado tuve
La Penitencia Sagrada,
En virtud de aquel Divino
Manjar, que dá por Vianda.

Todos.
A cuyo grande milagro

Harm me not, fince from thy mefhes
Faith, the heavenly Iris, leads me
With Hope's glory round my temples.
Penance.
Circe, now that as his guide
See his Underftanding wendeth,
Little can thy forceries wound him.
Sin.
Rage and anguifh overwhelm me !
If I am a viper, fay
Why, O heart ! doft thou not fever ?
If I am an afp, oh ! why
Does not my own poifon end me ?
In my anguifh I will tear
Out my heart in purple pieces
But to dafh them in Heaven's face.
Wherefore, though, fhould fear unnerve
   me ?
If thou flieft from me thus
In the Church's faving veffel,
Know, my ftorms can overwhelm it.
Idle boaft ! for all is ended,—
All my fcience now is o'er,
Since the fhip fails on fo fteady :
All my fenfes leave me too,
Since my magic power hath left me !
[*The found of an earthquake is heard,
and the palace difappears.*
Palaces fink down in ruin,
And the dark hills that upheld them,
Reappear in all their wildnefs—
I fole dweller in the defert :
For from me hath holy Penance
Him releafed, whom charm'd I held
   here,
By the virtue this divineft
Bread, this heavenly food, poffeffes.
All.
Let this mightieft miracle

El Mundo mil Fieſtas haga,
Principalmente Madrid,
Noble corazon de Eſpaña,
Que en celebrar á Dios Fieſta
Con la opinion ſe levanta.

*Con eſta repeticion, y al ſon de las
Chirimías, ſe dá* FIN AL AUTO.

Over all the world be fêted,
Specially within Madrid,
City where Spain's proud heart ſwelleth,
Which, in honouring God's Body,
Takes the foremoſt place for ever.

*With a repetition of this, and to the
ſound of clarions,* THE AUTO CON-
CLUDES.

THE DEVOTION OF THE CROSS.

FROM THE SPANISH OF CALDERON.

INTRODUCTION.

$\mathcal{L}$A *Devocion de la Cruz* was firſt printed at Hueſca, in 1634, in the twenty-eighth volume of the collection devoted to the dramatic works of various authors.* In the Introduction to *Love the Greateſt Enchantment*, I have already deſcribed this exceedingly rare collection, and enumerated the very few volumes of it that are now known to exiſt. The volume which contains *La Devocion de la Cruz*, under the name of *La Cruz en la Sepultura*, contains alſo another of Calderon's dramas, *Amor, Honor y Poder*, under the leſs conciſe title of *La Induſtria contra el Poder, y el Honor contra la Fuerza*, and both are ſtrangely attributed to Lope de Vega. *La Cruz en la Sepultura* is deſcribed as differing occaſionally from *La Devocion de la Cruz*, as ordinarily printed, and contains three characters and one entire ſcene which are not to be found in any of the editions of the drama publiſhed under that title. The *names* I have introduced, between brackets, into the liſt of *Perſons repreſented*, and the *ſcene*, ſimilarly marked, I have tranſlated at the proper place. Con-ſidering the power exhibited in this "wonderful and terrible drama," as

---

* *Parte Veinte y Ocho de Comedias de Varios Autores.* En Hueſca, por Pedro Bluſon, impreſor de la Univerſidad, año de 1634. A coſta de Pedro Eſcuer, mercader de libros. Señor Hartzenbuſch mentions his having ſeen *La Cruz en la Sepultura* printed as a ſeparate play, but without date, place, or name of printer. See his *Prologo*, t. I. p. xv. and his liſt of *Ediciones Conſultadas*, t. IV. pp. 654 and 659.

it has been well called by a diftinguifhed living writer,* and the celebrity which it has obtained in foreign countries, moft readers will be furprifed to learn that it was one of the earlieft productions of Calderon; written probably during his refidence at the Univerfity of Salamanca, which he left at nineteen, but certainly, as it is ftated, before 1620, when he had only completed his twentieth year.†   Like moft young dramatic writers, he appears to have freely made ufe of the labours of his predeceffors; and the following dramas are fuppofed to have had very confiderable influence upon him, both in the conception and working out of *The Devotion of the Crofs*.   The firft of thefe is *La Fundacion de la Orden de la nueftra Señora de la Merced*, by the Canon Tarrega, which is given in the exceedingly fcarce volume of Valencian Dramatifts, publifhed at Valencia in 1616, a copy of which I poffefs.‡   Another is Tirfo de Molina's *El Condenado por Defconfiado*, the *Enrico* of which fingularly refembles, both in his crimes and his love of relating them,§ the *Eufebio* of *The Devotion of the Crofs*, the *Ludovico Enio* of *The Purgatory of St. Patrick*, and other of Calderon's heroes of a fimilar ftamp.   Mira de Mefcua's *El Efclavo del Demonio* is, however, the play to which Calderon

---

* The Rev. Chenevix Trench, Dean of Weftminfter.   See his *Life's a Dream*, &c. p. 69.   London, 1856.

† " *La Devocion de la Cruz.*   Efcrita antes del año 1620, cenfurada ya para la imprefion en 3 de Abril de 1633." See CORRECCIONES at the end of *Comedias* de ALARCON; Madrid, 1852.

‡ *Norte de la Poefia Efpañola*, &c.   Año 1616 ; con privilegio.   Imprefo en Valencia ; en la Imprefion de Felipe Mey.   This and a preceding volume, *Doce Comedias famofas de cuatro Poetas naturales de la infigne y coronado Ciudad de Valencia*, año 1609, are among the fcarceft of Spanifh books, no copy being known to exift in any of the pubilc or private libraries of Madrid, or perhaps of all Spain, as Señor Ramon de Mefoneros Romanos fays, except that in the library of the Queen at Madrid, from which he has made his extracts in the firft volume of his *Dramaticos Contemporaneos a Lope de Vega* ; Madrid, 1857.   See his *Difcurfo Preliminar*, pp. xii. and xxi.

§ See *Comedias Efcogidas* de Fray Gabriel Tellez (el Maeftro Tirfo de Molina); Madrid, 1850, p. 189.

is more directly indebted, he having not only imitated the general action of that drama, but having transferred, according to Tieck, several passages of it, almost verbatim, to his own pages.* *The Devotion of the Crofs* has been admirably tranflated into German by Auguft Wilhelm von Schlegel, as has alfo *El Mayor Encanto Amor*, of which, in the preceding pages, a tranflation has been given.   In Englifh and French literature few writers have ever referred to Calderon without praifing the poetical power and beauty of this drama, and condemning it as " the very fublime of anti-nomianifm."   Like many other celebrated literary works, however, it has been more frequently referred to than read, and many writers have, either through careleffnefs or wilful hoftility, needlefsly mifreprefented and exaggerated its defects.†   Among critics who feem to have been actuated by the latter fpirit muft be placed Sifmondi, whofe analyfis of *The Devotion of the Crofs* is more than ufually inaccurate and unfair. One would think that there are crimes enough, either referred to or committed, in this drama, without the neceffity of adding to them ; and yet, by direct affertion and infinuation, he leaves on the mind of the reader a horrible impreffion of the almoft unutterable criminality of the two principal characters, which, if true, would of courfe render it unfit to be read, enacted, and, I need fcarcely fay, tranflated.   The fubject is difficult to be alluded to ; and yet, in juftice to a great poet, whofe defects, whatever they may have been, were certainly not thofe which might be

---

* See Schack's *Gefchichte der dramatifchen Literatur und Kunft in Spanien*, b. iii. p. 55.

† In defcribing the clafs of dramas to which *The Devotion of the Crofs* belongs, it is fingular that Bouterwek fhould have fallen into the miftake of calling it an *Auto ;* thereby leaving us to infer that he did not underftand the marked and impaffible diftance that feparates a religious *Drama (Comedia)* of Calderon, or any other Spanifh poet, from an *Auto*. *The Sorceries of Sin* in this volume will give the reader fome idea of what an *Auto* is, and how impoffible it is to confound it with a *Drama* in the ordinary fenfe, even when dealing with fpiritual or religious fubjects or things.   Mr. Longfellow has fallen into the fame miftake as Bouterwek, in his defcription of this drama.   See the chapter on *The Devotional Poetry of Spain*, in his *Outre Mer*.

inferred from the felection of fuch topics as thofe alluded to, I cannot avoid it altogether. Sifmondi, in fpeaking of this drama, calls the hero, Eufebio, " an inceftuous brigand ; " and, as if this were not enough, adds, further on, the phrafe, " His fifter, Julia, *who is alfo his miftrefs*," * &c. Now for the fhocking affertion contained in thefe two quotations there is not the flighteft fhadow of foundation. No criminal intercourfe whatever exifts between the hero and heroine of this terrible tragedy (how prevented the reader will learn in the powerful fcene, which, however faintly interpreted, muft rivet his attention), and the unfufpected relationfhip which exifts between them is never known to one of the parties until his laft moments, and to the other until after the death of her brother. How differently does another diftinguifhed French writer allude to this fubject. With the beautiful paffage to which I refer, I fhall leave the drama in the hands of the reader. " On devine fans peine," fays M. Philaréte Chafles, " que Julia eft la fœur d'Eufebe ; et cette invention dramatique augmentant d'intenfité irait coudoyer l'horrible et l'infoutenable, fi Calderon n'était doué de ce vrai genie dont l'effence eft pure. Nous allons le voir, dans une occafion fi difficile, retrouver la moralité qui lui eft propre, la fublime pudeur qui ne l'abandonne jamais. Ses ailes blanches et vierges trempent dans l'orage fans fe flétrir, et effleurent la foudre fans fe bruler."†

With regard to the locality in which the action of this fingular drama is fuppofed to take place, it may be right to add a few words. Neither in this, nor in any of the other dramas of Calderon, as given to us in the ordinary editions,‡ is the *fcene* ever mentioned, nor any of the ufual aids

---

* *Literature of the South of Europe.* I quote from Bohn's tranflation, v. II. p. 379, not having the original by me. Mr. Lewes, with equal inaccuracy, alfo adds the crime alluded to in the text to the category of Eufebio's offences. See his *Spanifh Drama* ; London, 1846, p. 110.

† *Etudes fur l'Efpagne*, par M. Philaréte Chafles ; Paris, 1847, p. 55.

‡ A remark which may be applied not only to all the Spanifh editions prior to that

to the reader's imagination fupplied, fuch as we generally find in the dramatic literature of other countries.   In the early Englifh drama, a board with the name of a town written upon it was fufficient for the lively imagination of the audience to waft the fpectators from London to York, or from Venice to Verona.   But in the Spanifh plays, as *printed*, this fignpoft information is wanting, and the reader is obliged to infer the fcene of the event from the language of the characters engaged.   This want, with many others, is fupplied in the edition of Señor Hartzenbufch, as well as in fuch German and French tranflations as I have feen.   In the prefent inftance "Sena" is the centre round which all the action of the drama revolves.   Señor Hartzenbufch prints the word "Sena" as in the text, leaving it doubtful whether he underftands it to mean Siena in Italy, or one of the three fmall towns in Spain that are called Sena. M. Damas Hinard, in his profe verfion of this play,* mentions two of thefe, one in Aragon, the other in Leon, and is uncertain which of them to decide on.   A third, near Santander, might be added, which, if we are to look at all in Spain for the locality, might be more likely, as the fea is mentioned more than once, as being in the neighbourhood of " the mountain," which is the fcene of fo many wonders.   This, however, would not be fufficient to decide the queftion, becaufe in matters of geographical precifion Calderon was as carelefs as Greene in his *Pandofto*, or Shakefpeare in his *Winter's Tale*.   But it feems to me that, notwithftanding the ftrong Spanifh colouring of the entire landfcape, the rude croffes, the *bandoleros*, and the *fierras*, Siena in Italy muft be confidered the centre round which all this wild and imaginary fcenery lies, Sena being the ancient Latin name of Siena, which Calderon probably adopted.   If proof were wanting, the facts of the ftory, either alluded to

---

of Señor Hartzenbufch's, but to all the foreign reprints that I have feen, including thofe of Ochoa (Paris, 1847), and of Keil (Leipzic, 1827-30).

* *Chefs-d'œuvre de Théâtre Efpagnol:* Calderon, 1re férie; Paris, 1841, p. 148, *note*.

or enacted, would be fufficient :—the miffion of Curcio from the Republic to the Pope; the journeying to and from Rome by Alberto, bifhop of Trent; his profefforfhip in the Univerfity of Bologna; and, laftly, the account which the Genoefe painter gives of himfelf, in the fcene taken from the Huefca edition of *La Cruz en la Sepultura,* of his bringing to Florence a painting ordered by one of his patrons there. Schlegel, in his *Die Andacht zum Kreuze,* adopts Siena without any remark, as does the writer of the very accurate paper on *The Devotion of the Crofs* in Blackwood,* and as moft other Englifh writers have done who have alluded to this play.

* Blackwood's Magazine, vol. xviii. p. 83.   July, 1825.

PERSONS REPRESENTED.

Eusebio.	Eusebio.
Curcio, *viejo.*	Curcio.
Lisardo.	Lisardo, *his son.*
Octavio.	Octavio, *in Curcio's service.*
Alberto, *viejo.*	Alberto, *an aged priest, bishop of Trent.*
Gil, *villano gracioso.*	Gil, *a peasant.*
Bras, Tirso, Toribio, *villanos.*	Tirso, Bras, Toribio, *peasants.*
Celio, Ricardo, *bandoleros.*	Celio, Ricardo, *bandits.*
[Un Pintor.	[A Painter.
Un Poeta.	A Poet.
Un Astrologo.]*	An Astrologer.]*
Julia, *dama.*	Julia, *Curcio's daughter.*
Arminda, *criada.*	Arminda, *her attendant.*
Chilindrina.	Chillindrina, *a follower of the bandits.*
Menga, *villana graciosa.*	Menga, *Gil's wife.*
Bandoleros y Villanos.	*Bandits and Peasants.*
Soldados.	*Soldiers.*

Scene, *Siena and its Neighbourhood.*

---

* From the edition of Huesca, 1634.

THE DEVOTION OF THE CROSS.

JORNADA I.

Dicen dentro Menga *y* Gil.

Menga.

VERÁ por dó va la burra.

Gil.

Jo dimuño; jo mohina.

Menga.

Ya verá por do camina :
Arre acá.

Gil.

¡ El diabro te aburra !
¿ No hay quién una cola tenga,
Pudiendo tenella mil ?

    [*Salen los dos.*

Menga.

¡ Buena hacienda has hecho, Gil !

Gil.

¡ Buena hacienda has hecho, Menga,
Pues tú la culpa tuviste !

ACT I.

A wild woody mountain district,
not far from the high road to
Siena.

Menga *and* Gil *behind the Scenes.*

Menga.

SEE ! the afs is going to turn
    her !

Gil.

Yo, dolt's dam ! yo, devil's
    daughter !

Menga.

There, fhe's ftuck ! you fhould have
    caught her ;
Yo ! geho !

Gil.

The devil burn her !
Had fhe fifty tails to tickle,
All were vain againft her will.

    [*They enter.*

Menga.

What a fix we're in, friend Gil !

Gil.

What the devil of a pickle !
All through fault of yours, I'm thinking,

Que como ibas caballera,
Que en el hoyo se metiera,
Al oido la dijiste,
Por hacerme regañar.
      Menga.
Por verme caer á mí,
Se lo dijiste, eso sí.
      Gil.
¿ Cómo la hemos de sacar ?
      Menga.
¿ Pues en el lodo la dejas ?
      Gil.
No puede mi fuerza sola.
      Menga.
Yo tiraré de la cola,
Tira tú de las orejas.
      Gil.
Mejor remedio seria
Hacer el que aprovechó
A un coche, que se atascó
En la corte esotro dia.
Este coche, Dios delante,
Que arrastrado de dos potros,
Parecia entre los otros
Pobre coche vergonzante.
Y por maldicion muy cierta
De sus padres (hado esquivo !)
Iba de estribo en estribo,
Ya que no de puerta en puerta ;
En un arroyo atascado,
Con ruegos el caballero,
Con azotes el cochero,
Ya por fuerza, ya por grado,
Ya por gusto, ya por miedo,
Que saliesen procuraban :
Por recio que lo mandaban,
Mi coche quedo que quedo.
Viendo que no importan nada
Cuantos remedios hicieron,

Since, my Menga, since you rode her,
You it must have been who show'd her
Just the very spot to sink in ;—
'Tis to vex me that you teaze her.
      Menga.
Since she threw me o'er her shoulder,
You it must have been who told her.
      Gil.
But the question, How release her ?
      Menga.
In the mud wouldst leave her here ?
      Gil.
All my strength, as nought, avails her.
      Menga.
I can pull her by the tail, sir ;
You can pull her by the ear.
      Gil.
No, I think a better way,
And a quicker to revive her,
Is to do, as did the driver
Of a coach the other day.
This same coach, the execration
Of the streets, in slow approaches
Slunk beside the other coaches,
Like a shabby poor relation ;
Or for some deep grief it bore,
(Who or what its grief can smother ?)
Went from one side to the other,
'Stead of *on* from door to door :—
In the kennel now 'tis stuck,
How the knight within doth growl !
Some try fair means, some try foul,
Coachee lashes, footmen chuck,
Cushions fly to make it lighter,
All is noise and cries and worrit ;
But the more they strive to stir it,
Seems my coach to stick the tighter.
Seeing thus 'twere best to parley,
Coachee takes the best of courses,

Delante el coche pusieron
Un harnero de cebada.
Los caballos, por comer,
De tal manera tiraron,
Que tosieron y arrancaron;
Y esto podemos hacer.
Menga.
¡Que nunca valen dos cuartos
Tus cuentos!
Gil.
Menga, yo siento
Ver un animal hambriento,
Donde hay animales hartos.
Menga.
Voy al camino á mirar
Si pasa de nuestra aldea
Gente, cualquiera que sea,
Porque te venga á ayudar,
Pues te das tan pocas mañas.
Gil.
¿Vuelves, Menga, á tu porfía?
Menga.
¡Ay burra del alma mia!　　[*Vase.*
Gil.
¡Ay burra de mis entrañas!
Tú fuiste la mas honrada
Burra de toda la aldea;
Que no ha habido quien te vea
Nunca mal acompañada.
No eres nada callejera;
De mijor gana te estabas
En tu pesebre, que andabas,
Cuando te llevaban fuera.

And before the half-starved horses
Holds outstretch'd a sieve of barley;—
The poor starvelings seek to swallow,
So they tug with might and main,
Drag the coach from out the drain,
And the example we may follow.*
Menga.
Tales like this you've now related
Ar'n't two farthings worth.
Gil.
　　　　　　　O'ercast
Am I, seeing one beast *fast*,
Where stand two quite satiated.
Menga.
I will to the road, the distance
Isn't far, to see some neighbour
Passing to his daily labour,
Who will come to give assistance:
Since 'tis little zeal you show.
Gil.
Menga mine, your wrath control.
Menga.
Oh! dear donkey of my soul!　[*Exit.*
Gil.
Donkey of my bowels, oh!
Thou that wert the most respected
Donkey of our village green,
Thou that never yet hast been
In bad company detected;
Thou that gadded not about,
But preferr'd domestic quiet,—
A snug manger and good diet—
To the joys of going out:

---

* Sydney Smith, in his amusing lecture "On the Conduct of the Understanding," condemning what he calls "the foppery of universality" in one's studies, says whimsically, that "he would exact of a young man a pledge never to read Lope de Vega!" Fortunately he does not include or exclude Calderon, who in this little story happens to have anticipated the witty canon in the anecdote which he tells us of himself and his horse "Calamity."—See *Life of* SYDNEY SMITH *by* LADY HOLLAND.

Pues ¿altanera y liviana?
Bien me atrevo á jurar yo,
Que ningun burro la vió
Aſomada á la ventana.
Yo ſé que no merecia
Su lengua deſdicha tal ;
Pues jamas para habrar mal
Dijo : Aqueſta boca es mia.
Pues como á ella la ſobre
De lo que comiendo eſtá,
Luego al punto ſe lo da
A alguna borrica pobre.
*   [Ruido dentro.*
Mas ¿qué ruido es eſte ? Alli
De dos caballos ſe apean
Dos hombres, y hácia mí vienen,
Deſpues que atados los dejan.
¡Deſcoloridos, y al campo
De mañana ¡ Coſa es cierta,
Que comen barro, ó eſtán
Opilados. Mas ¿ ſi fueran
Bandoleros ? ¡ Aqui es ello !
Pero lo que fuere ſea,
Aqui me eſcondo ; que andan,
Que corren, que ſalen, que entran.
*   [Eſcóndeſe.*

Salen LISARDO *y* EUSEBIO.
Liſardo.
No paſemos adelante,
Porque eſta eſtancia encubierta
Y apartada del camino,
Es para mi intento buena.
Sacad, Euſebio, la eſpada ;
Que yo, de aqueſta manera,
A los hombres como vos

Though thou'rt ſkittiſh, may be vain,
Yet I'll ſwear it, notwithſtanding,
No one ever ſaw you ſtanding,
Ogling at the window-pane.
True, that honeſt tongue of thine
Is a little rough, no matter,
You ſpeak truly, and don't flatter,
When you ſay, This voice is mine.
And you're generous, too, the graſs
Which your maw declines receiving,
I have often ſeen you leaving
To ſome poor and hungrier aſs.*
*   [A noiſe within.*
But what noiſe is this? Oh ! yonder
I behold two men who've ridden
Hard here, tie their panting horſes
To the trees, and wander hither ;—
Pale ! and in the fields ſo early !
Oh ! 'tis plain they've got green ſickneſs.
Should they prove, though, bandoleros !
'Gad ! that were a pretty buſineſs !—
Be they who they may, 'tis better
That I hide me here a little.
Here they come ; they reach, they enter,
Ere I've ſcarcely time to fix me.
*   [He conceals himſelf.*

Enter LISARDO *and* EUSEBIO.
Liſardo.
Let us then proceed no farther,
Since this thorny-tangled thicket,
Screen'd and ſever'd from the highway,
For my object is well fitted.
Draw then, draw your ſword, Euſebio,
As I mine, for thus ſuccinctly
Do I challenge men like you

---

* The humour of this addreſs will not unpleaſantly recall Goldſmith's " Elegy on the glory of her Sex, Mrs. Mary Blaize."

Saco á reñir.

Eufebio.
　　　　Aunque tenga
Baſtante cauſa en haber
Llegado al campo, quiſiera
Saber lo que á vos os mueve.
Decid, Liſardo, la queja,
Que de mí teneis.

Liſardo.
　　　　　Son tantas,
Que falta voz á la lengua,
Razones á la razon,
Y al ſufrimiento paciencia.
Quiſiera, Eufebio, callarlas,
Y aun olvidarlas quiſiera ;
Porque cuando ſe repiten,
Hacen de nuevo la ofenſa.
¿ Conoceis eſtos papeles ?

Eufebio.
Arrojadlos en la tierra,
Y los alzaré.

Liſardo.
　　　Tomad.
Qué os ſuſpendeis ? qué os altera ?

Eufebio.
Mal haya el hombre, mal haya
Mil veces aquel, que entrega
Sus ſecretos á un papel ;
Porque es diſparada piedra,
Que ſe ſabe quien la tira,
Y no ſe ſabe á quien llega.

Liſardo.
¿ Habéiſlos ya conocido ?

Eufebio.
Todos eſtán de mi letra,
Que no la puedo negar.

Liſardo.
Pues yo ſoy Liſardo, en Sena,

To the combat.

Eufebio.
　　　　Though ſufficient
Cauſe have I in having come
To the field here, yet my wiſhes
Are to know what thus has moved you.
Say, Liſardo, ſay what hidden
Charge againſt me have you ?

Liſardo.
　　　　　　　　I
Have ſo many, that to hint them
Would my tongue want words, my
　　　reaſon
Utterance, and all patience quit me.
I, Eufebio, would in ſilence,
Nay, in dark oblivion ſink them,
Since an inſult when repeated
Is a ſecond time committed.
Do you recognize theſe papers ?

Eufebio.
Throw them down, and I will lift them
From the ground.

Liſardo.
They're *there* then, take them :—
Why thus tremble ?　Why thus ſhiver ?

Eufebio.
Woe unto the man ! a thouſand
Woes to him, who hath committed
His heart's ſecrets to a letter !
'Tis a random ſtone, a miſſile,
Which the hand that flings it knoweth,
But is ignorant whom it hitteth.

Liſardo.
Have you ſcrutiniſed them fully ?

Eufebio.
That theſe letters were all written
By my hand, I muſt acknowledge.

Liſardo.
Well, Siena is my birth-place,

Hijo de Lifardo Curcio.	And my fire Lifardo Curcio.
Bien excufadas grandezas	The unfparing, the unftinted
De mi padre confumieron	Habits of my father wafted
En breve tiempo la hacienda,	Soon the wealth to him tranfmitted
Que los fuyos le dejaron ;	By more prudent predeceffors ;
Que no fabe cuánto yerra	Ignorant how much he finneth,
Quien, por excefivos gaftos,	Who by wild and wafteful outlay
Pobres á fus hijos deja.	Maketh paupers of his children.
Pero la necefidad,	But although neceffity
Aunque ultraje la nobleza,	May a noble name disfigure,
No excufa de obligaciones	It exempts not from their duties
A los que nacen con ellas.	Thofe whofe birth is burthen'd with
Julia pues, (¡ faben los cielos,	them.
Cuanto el nombrarla me pefa !)	Julia then . . . . (ah me! Heaven knows
O no fupo confervarlas,	How to name her name afflicts me !)
O no llegó á conocerlas.	Knew not rightly to obferve them,
Pero al fin, Julia es mi hermana ;	Or not knowing them could omit them.
¡ Pluguiera á Dios no lo fuera !	But ftill Julia (would to God
Y advertid, que no fe firven	That fhe were not!) is my fifter,
Las mujeres de fus prendas	And you know, when wooing women
Con amorofos papeles,	Of her rank, 'tis not permitted
Con razones lifonjeras,	To indite perfuafive flatteries,
Con ilícitos recados,	To addrefs love-laden billets,
Ni con infames terceras.	To fend meffages in fecret,
No os culpo en el todo á vos ;	And hire go-betweens to bring them.
Que yo confiefo, que hiciera	I for this don't wholly blame you,
Lo mifmo, á darme una dama	Since I will confefs, in this way
Para fervirla licencia ;	Would I act too, if a lady
Pero cúlpos en la parte	Leave to woo her would but give me ;
De fer mi amigo, y en efta	But I blame you, from the fact of
Con mas culpa os comprehende	Being my friend, and fo, from *this*, fee
La culpa que tuvo ella.	How through you the fault is doubled,
Si mi hermana os agradó	That by her has been committed.
Para mujer (que no era	If my fifter pleafed your fancy
Pofible, ni yo lo creo	As a wife (I cannot bring me
Que os atreviérais á verla	To believe it poffible,
Con otro fin, ni aun con efte ;	That you ever hoped to win her
Pues ¡ vive Dios ! que quifiera	Otherwife, or even as this ;
Antes, que con vos cafada,	Since, as God lives! I would wifh her,

Mirarla á mis manos muerta):
En fin, si vos la elegísteis
Para mujer, justo fuera
Descubrir vuestros deseos
A mi padre, antes que á ella.
Este era término justo,
Y entonces mi padre viera,
Si le estaba bien el darla,
Que pienso que no os la diera;
Porque un caballero pobre,
Cuando en cosas como estas
No puede medir iguales
La calidad y la hacienda,
Por no deslucir su sangre
Con una hija doncella,
Hace sagrado un convento;
Que es delito la pobreza.
Aqueste á Julia mi hermana
Con tanta prisa la espera,
Que mañana ha de ser monja,
Por voluntad, ó por fuerza.
Y porque no será bien,
Que una religiosa tenga
Prendas de tan loco amor,
Y de voluntad tan necia,
A vuestras manos las vuelvo,
Con resolucion tan ciega,
Que no solo he de quitarlas,
Mas tambien la causa dellas.
Sacad la espada, y aqui
El uno de los dos muera;
Vos, porque no la sirvais,
O yo, porque no lo vea.

Eusebio.
Tened, Lisardo, la espada,
Y pues yo he tenido flema
Para oir desprecios mios,

Ere with you I saw her married,
Dead, although my own hands kill'd
   her):
In a word, if you selected
Her to be your wife, 'twere fittest
That, before herself, my father
Were acquainted with your wishes.
That were the correct proceeding.
Then my father would consider
If 'twere right to give her to you,
And I think he would not give her;
For a gentleman grown poor,
When a case like this arises,
If he finds he cannot equal
Fortune with his rank's requirements,
Lest through an unmarried daughter
On his blood should fall defilement,
Seeks the safeguard of a convent;
Such a crime is want of riches.
This fate now so soon awaiteth
Upon Julia, on my sister,
That she must the veil to-morrow
Take, though force control her wishes!
And because it were not right
That a novice should have with her
Proofs of such a foolish passion,
And of a desire so silly,
I return them to your hands,
With a blind resolve and fixèd,
To destroy not only them,
But the very hand that writ them.
Draw then, draw your sword, for now
Either of us twain must die here;
You, that you may cease your service,
I, that service not to witness.

Eusebio.
Sheathe your sword awhile, Lisardo,
And since I have deign'd to listen
With such phlegm to my dispraises,

Efcuchadme la refpuefta ;
Y aunque el difcurfo fea largo
De mi fucefo, y parezca
Que, eftando folos los dos,
Es demafiada paciencia,
Pues que ya es fuerza reñir,
Y morir el uno es fuerza ;
Por fi los cielos permiten,
Que yo el infelice fea,
Oíd prodigios que admiran,
Y maravillas que elevan ;
Que no es bien, que con mi muerte
Eterno filencio tengan.
Yo no fé quien fue mi padre ;
Pero fé, que la primera
Cuna fué el pie de una Cruz,
Y el primer lecho una piedra.
Raro fué mi nacimiento,
Segun los paftores cuentan,
Que defta fuerte me hallaron
En la falda de efas fierras.
Tres dias, dicen, que oyeron
Mi llanto, y que á la afpereza,
Donde eftaba, no llegaron
Por el temor de las fieras,
Sin que alguna me ofendiefe :
Pero ¿ quién duda que era
Por refpeto de la Cruz,
Que tenia en mi defenfa ?
Hallóme un paftor, que acafo
Bufcó una perdida oveja
En la afpereza del monte,
Y trayéndome á la aldea
De Eufebio, que no fin caufa
Eftaba entónces en ella.
Le contó mi prodigiofo
Nacimiento, y la clemencia
Del cielo afiftió á la fuya.
Mandó en fin, que me trajeran

Hear the anfwer that I give them :—
And although my life's ftrange ftory
May feem long, and the recital
Out of reafonable patience
Weary you, we ftanding pitted
Breaft to breaft thus for the combat,
In which one of us muft die here,
And left Heaven perchance permitteth
Me to be the haplefs victim,
Hear the wonders moft aftounding,
Hear the marvels moft furprifing,
Which 'twere wrong my death fhould
    hide here
In its everlafting filence.
Who my father was I know not ;
But I know this, I, an infant,
Had a crofs's foot for cradle,
And a hard ftone for my firft bed.
Strange my birth, and ftrange the ftory
Which the fhepherds oft recited,
Who had found me thus abandon'd
In a gorge of thefe wild hills here.
For three days, they faid, they heard me
Crying, but to reach the cliffs where
I was placed they could not venture,
Through the terror of the wild beafts,
One of whom nor hurt nor touch'd me;
Who can doubt through certain inftincts
Of refpect unto the Crofs
Which in my defence ftood nigh me ?
There by accident, a fhepherd,
Seeking a loft lamb, defcried me
In the wildnefs of the mountain,
And who brought me to the village
Of Eufebio, who had caufe then
Doubtlefs to be dwelling in it.
Him he told of my prodigious
Birth, and pitying Heaven affifted
By its own, to wake his pity.

A su casa, y como á hijo
Me dió la crianza en ella.
Eusebio soy de la Cruz,
Por su nombre, y por aquella,
Que fue mi primera guia,
Y fue mi guarda primera.
Tomé por gusto las armas,
Por pasatiempo las letras;
Murió Eusebio, y yo quedé
Heredero de su hacienda.
Si fue prodigioso el parto,
No lo fue menos la estrella,
Que enemiga me amenaza,
Y piadosa me reserva.
Tierno infante era en los brazos
Del ama, cuando mi fiera
Condicion, bárbara en todo,
Dió de sus rigores muestra;
Pues con solas las encías,
No sin diabólica fuerza,
Partí el pecho de quien tuve
El dulce alimento; y ella,
Del dolor desesperada,
Y de la cólera ciega,
En un pozo me arrojó,
Sin que ninguno supiera
De mí.   Oyéndome reir,
Bajáron á él, y cuentan,
Que estaba sobre las aguas,
Y que con las manos tiernas
Tenia una Cruz formada,
Y sobre los labios puesta.
Un dia que se abrasaba
La casa, y la llama fiera
Cerraba el paso á la huida,
Y á la salida la puerta,
Entre las llamas estuve
Libre, sin que me ofendieran:
Y advertí despues, dudando

Finally he bade them bring me
To his house, and as his son
To be rear'd, and cared, and christen'd.
Thus, Eusebio of the Cross
Am I call'd; a name that mingles
His with that one which to me
Was my guide first, and my first friend.
Arms I took to as a passion,
As a pastime books enticed me.
Then Eusebio died, and left me
The sole heir of all his riches.
If my birth was so prodigious,
Nothing less so was my life's star,—
Now a threat'ning foe to fright me,
Now a pitying friend to guide me.
Still a tender infant, lying
In my nurse's arms, my wicked
Nature, which was wholly savage,
Gave a sample of its wildness;
Since but with my gums, their weakness
By a demon's power assisted,
I cut through the tender bosom
Out from which my sweet food
    trickled:—
She, made desperate by the anguish,
And by sudden anger blinded,
Down into a deep well threw me,
Unperceived by any witness.
Thence my laugh being heard, they ventured
To the bottom, and the finders
Said they found me on the water,
And that with my little fingers
I a natural Cross had fashion'd,
And had placed it on my lips there.
On a certain day when fire had
Seized our dwelling, and the wild flame
Barr'd all entrance or all exit
From the outside or the inner,

Que haya en el fuego clemencia,
Que era dia de la Cruz.
Tres luſtros contaba apenas,
Cuando por el mar fui á Roma,
Y en una brava tormenta,
Defefperada mi nave
Chocó en una oculta peña,
En pedazos dividida,
Por los coſtados abierta :
Abrazado de un madero
Salí venturoſo á tierra,
Y eſte madero tenia
Forma de Cruz.   Por las fierras
De eſos montes caminaba
Con otro hombre, y en la ſenda
Que dos caminos partia,
Una Cruz eſtaba pueſta.
En tanto que me quedé,
Haciendo oracion en ella,
Se adelantó el compañero ;
Y deſpues dándome prieſa
Para alcanzarle, le hallé
Muerto á las manos ſangrientas
De bandoleros.   Un dia,
Riñendo en una pendencia,
De una eſtocada caí,
Sin que hicieſe reſiſtencia,
En la tierra ; y cuando todos
Penſaron hallarla ajena
De remedio, ſolo hallaron
Señal de la punta fiera
En una Cruz que traia
Al cuello, que en mi defenſa
Recibió el golpe.   Cazando
Una vez por la aſpereza
Deſte monte, ſe cubrío
El cielo de nubes negras,
Y publicando con truenos
Al mundo eſpantoſa guerra,

I among the flames was able
To paſs free, untouch'd, uninjured ;
And 'twas thought of then, while wonder
At the fire's forbearance fill'd them,
That it was the Day of the Croſs !
Scarce three luſtres had I circled,
When by ſea to Rome I journey'd ;
And a wild ſtorm having riſen,
Drove my hapleſs bark with fury
On a ſharp rock lying hidden ;
And the open bulwarks parting,
Soon the veſſel broke in ſplinters ;—
I, a paſſing plank embracing,
Safely to the ſhore was drifted !
And this plank, I found, was faſhion'd
Like a Croſs.   Among the ridges
Of theſe mountains once I travell'd
With a friend, and in the middle
Of the path where two roads parted
Was a ruſtic Croſs uplifted ;
To recite a prayer before it
While I ſtay'd behind a little,
My companion ſtill went forward ;
And when uſing double quickneſs
To o'ertake him, dead I found him,
By the red hands of banditti
Foully murder'd.   I one day
Mix'd up in a feud, was ſmitten
By the ſharp ſtroke of a dagger,
So that down I fell reſiſtleſs
On the ground, and when all round me
Reckon'd that my wound admitted
Of no help, they could but only
Find a ſlight mark of the fierce ſteel
On a Croſs I wore ſuſpended
From my neck, and which was dinted
Thus in my defence.   When hunting
Once amid the rougheſt diſtrict
Of this mountain, heaven had cover'd

Lanzas arrojaba en agua,
Balas diſparaba en piedras.
Todos hicieron las hojas
Contra las nubes defenſa,
Siendo ya tiendas de campo
Las mas ocultas malezas ;
Y un rayo, que fue en el viento
Caliginoſo cometa,
Volvió en ceniza á los dos
Que de mí eſtaban mas cerca.
Ciego, turbado y confuſo
Vuelvo á mirar lo que era,
Y hallé á mi lado una Cruz,
Que yo pienſo que es la meſma,
Que aſiſtió á mi nacimiento,
Y la que yo tengo impreſa
En los pechos ; pues los cielos
Me han ſeñalado con ella,
Para públicos efectos
De alguna cauſa ſecreta.
Pero aunque no ſé quien ſoy,
Tal eſpíritu me alienta,
Tal inclinacion me anima,
Y tal ánimo me fuerza,
Que por mí me da valor
Para que á Julia merezca ;
Porque no es mas la heredada,
Que la adquirida nobleza.
Eſte ſoy, y aunque conozco
La razon, y aunque pudiera
Dar ſatisfaccion baſtante
A vueſtro agravio, me ciega
Tanto la paſion de veros
Hablando de eſa manera,
Que ni os quiero dar diſculpa,
Ni os quiero admitir la queja ;
Y pues quereis eſtorbar,
Que yo ſu marido ſea ;
Aunque ſu caſa la guarde,

Itſelf o'er with black clouds thickly,
And in thunder-claps proclaiming
'Gainſt the world a war terrific,
Shot its bullets in the hail-ſtones,
In the rain its lances tilted.
We all flying from the cloud-guſts,
Shelter ſought beneath the thick leaves,
Where, like tents of an encampment,
Arch'd the thickets dark and prickly ;
When a bolt, that on the ſwift wind
Like a vaporous comet glitter'd,
Into aſhes burn'd the two
Who were ſtanding cloſe beſide me !
Blind, diſtracted, in confuſion
Round I turn'd to ſee what hid me,
And I then perceived a Croſs,—
It the ſame, in my opinion,
Which ſtood o'er me on my birth-day,
And of which I bear the impreſs
On my breaſt ; ſince Heaven hath
    mark'd me
With that ſymbol's myſtic image,
Thus to publiſh the effects
Of a cauſe that yet lies hidden.
Thus though ignorant who I am,
Such a ſpirit doth incite me,
Such an impulſe animates me,
Such a glow of courage fires me,
That I feel I'm not unworthy
To love Julia, and to win her ;
Since nobility is equal
Whether ſelf-born or tranſmitted.
This I am, and though the reaſon
I well know, and though ſufficient
Satisfaction I could make you
For your wrong, ſuch paſſion blinds me,
Seeing that you have adreſs'd me
In a way ſo cold and ſlighting,
That I'll neither make excuſes,

Aunque un convento la tenga,
De mí no ha de estar segura ;
Y la que no ha sido buena
Para mujer, lo será
Para dama ; así desea
Desesperado mi amor,
Y ofendida mi paciencia,
Castigar vuestro desprecio,
Y satisfacer mi afrenta.

Lisardo.
Eusebio, donde el acero
Ha de hablar, calle la lengua.
   [*Sacan las espadas y riñen, y* Li-
     sardo *cae en el suelo, y procu-*
     rando levantarse, torna á caer.
¡ Herido estoy !
     Eusebio.
       ¿ Y no muerto ?
     Lisardo.
No, que en los brazos me queda
Aliento para . . . . ¡ Ay de mí !
Faltó á mis plantas la tierra.
     Eusebio.
Y falte á tu voz la vida.
     Lisardo.
No me permitas que muera
Sin confesion.
     Eusebio.
       ¡ Muere, infame !
     Lisardo.
No me mates, por aquella
Cruz en que Cristo murió.
     Eusebio.
Aquesa voz te defienda

Nor admit the quarrel right here ;
And since my desire of being
Married to her you would hinder,
Though her father's house should guard
   her,
Though a convent's walls may hide her,
Neither shall ensure her safety ;
She, too good to be permitted
To become my wife, shall serve me
As a mistress :—thus desireth
The despair of my affection,
Thus my patience now extinguish'd,
To chastise your proud despisal,
And my honour's stain outwipe here.
     Lisardo.
When the sword can speak, Eusebio,
Let the tongue at least be silent.
       [*They draw and fight.*

Ah ! I'm wounded !   [*He falls.*
     Eusebio.
          And not dead ?
     Lisardo.
No ! for in these arms surviveth
Strength enough . . . . But woe is me,
'Neath my feet the firm earth sinketh !
     Eusebio.
And in life's last gasp thy voice sinks.
     Lisardo.
Oh ! allow me not unshriven
Here to die !
     Eusebio.
      Die ! miscreant, villain !
     Lisardo.
I implore you not to kill me,
By the Cross on which Christ suffer'd.
     Eusebio.
Ah ! that solemn word unfits me

De la muerte.   Alza del fuelo ;
Que cuando por ella ruegas,
Falta rigor á la ira,
Y falta á los brazos fuerza.
Alza del fuelo.
   Lifardo.
     No puedo ;
Porque ya en mi fangre envuelta
Voy defpreciando la vida,
Y el alma pienfo que efpera
A falir, porque entre tantas
No fabe cual es la puerta.
   Eufebio.
Pues fíate de mis brazos,
Y anímate ; que aqui cerca
De unos penitentes monjes
Hay una ermita pequeña,
Donde podrás confefarte,
Si vivo á fus puertas llegas.
   Lifardo.
Pues yo te doy mi palabra,
Por efa piedad que mueftras,
Que fi yo merezco verme
En la divina prefencia
De Dios, pediré que tú
Sin confefarte no mueras.
   [*Llévale* Eusebio *en brazos.*
    Gil.
¡ Han vifto lo que le debe !
La caridad eftá buena ;
Pero yo fe la perdono.
¡ Matarle, y llevarle á cueftas !

  Salen Bras, Tirso, Menga y
    Toribio.

   Toribio.
¡ Aqui dices que quedaba ?
   Menga.
Aqui fe quedó con ella.

For the death-ftroke.   Rife, Lifardo,
Since when you through it afk pity,
From my arm the ftrength departeth,
From my anger flies its rigour.
Rife, then, from the ground.
   Lifardo.
      I cannot ;
For already the red river
Of my life is paft all ftaying,
And I think the foul but lingers
To go forth, becaufe it knows not
Which, 'mid many, is the right door.
   Eufebio.
Then entruft thee to my arms,
And take courage ; for hard by here
Stands the little hermitage
Of fome penitential friars,
Where thou may'ft confefs, if haply
Thou to reach their doors furviveft.
   Lifardo.
For the pity thou doft fhow me,
I my folemn promife give thee,
That if e'er to God's divineft
Prefence I fhall be admitted,
I fhall afk for thee the grace
Likewife not to die unfhriven.
   [Eusebio *carries him out in his arms.*
    Gil.
Whoe'er faw the like of this ?
Charity in faith's a fine thing ;
But I'll rather you'd excufe me :—
Firft to kill him, then to lift him !

  Enter Menga, Bras, Tirso, *and*
    Toribio.

   Toribio.
Was it here you faid he waited ?
   Menga.
Here it was I left him with her.

Tirso.
Mírale alli embelesado.
      Menga.
Gil, ¿qué mirabas?
         Gil.
            ¡ Ay Menga !
      Tirso.
¿ Qué te ha sucedido?
         Gil.
            ¡ Ay Tirso !
      Toribio.
¿ Qué viste? Danos respuesta.

         Gil.
¡ Ay Toribio !
      Bras.
          Di, ¿ qué tienes,
Gil, ó de qué te lamentas ?
         Gil.
¡ Ay Bras, ay amigos mios !
No lo sé mas que una bestia :
Matóle, y cargó con él,
Sin duda á salar le lleva.
      Menga.
¿ Quién le mató ?
         Gil.
          ¿ Que sé yo ?
      Tirso.
¿ Quién murió ?
         Gil.
         No sé quien era.
      Toribio.
¿ Quién cargó ?
         Gil.
         ¿ Que sé yo quien ?
      Bras.
¿ Y quién le llevó ?
         Gil.
         Quien quiera.

Tirso.
See him, how he stares and gapes there.
      Menga.
What do you gaze at, Gil ?
         Gil.
           Ah, Menga !
      Tirso.
What has happen'd to you ?
         Gil.
           Ah, Tirso !
      Toribio.
What have you seen ? come, tell us
    quickly.
         Gil.
Ah, Toribio !
      Bras.
         Say, what ails you,
Gil, or wherefore do you sigh so ?
         Gil.
Ah ! friend Bras, ah ! all my neighbours,
Ass that I am, I know not *why* so :
Him he kill'd, and raised and carried
Off, I hav'n't a doubt, to pickle.
      Menga.
Who was it kill'd him ?
         Gil.
           How do *I* know ?
      Tirso.
Who was kill'd ?
         Gil.
         I know not either.
      Toribio.
Who raised him up ?
         Gil.
         How know I who did ?
      Bras.
Who carried him off ?
         Gil.
         Whoe'er you like then :

Pero porque lo fepais,
Venid todos.

    Tirfo.
   ¿Do nos llevas?
    Gil.
No lo fé; pero venid,
Que los dos van aqui cerca.
     [*Vanfe todos.*

Sala en Casa de Curcio, en Sena.

  Salen Julia y Arminda.

   Julia.
Déjame, Arminda, llorar
Una libertad perdida,
Pues donde acaba la vida,
Tambien acaba el·pefar.
¿Nunca has vifto de una fuente
Bajar un arroyo manfo,
Siendo apacible defcanfo
El valle de fu corriente;
Y cuando le juzgan falto
De fuerza las flores bellas,
Pafa por encima dellas,
Rompiendo por lo mas alto?
Pues mis penas, mis enojos
La mifma experiencia han hecho;
Detuviéronfe en el pecho,
Y falieron por los ojos.
Deja que llore el rigor
De un padre.

   Arminda.
    Señora, advierte . . .
    Julia.
¿Qué mas venturofa fuerte
Hay, que morir de dolor?
Pena que deja vencida
La vida, fer gloria ordena;

But to find out all about it
Come with me.

    Tirfo.
  But where will you bring us?
    Gil.
I don't know, but come along
For the two are not far diftant.
     [*Exeunt.*

A room in Curcio's house at Siena.

  Enter Julia *and* Arminda.

   Julia.
Let me weep, my faithful friend,
Liberty's laft hope that leaves me,
Since till death's cold hand relieves me,
Can my forrow have no end.
Haft thou ne'er, its fount outgrowing,
Seen a gentle ftreamlet fleeing,
Its fmooth peaceful pathway being
The fweet valley of its flowing;
And when all the lovely flowers
Think it fcarce has ftrength to move them,
Lo! the pent-up ftream above them
Sweeps their lovelieft from the
   bowers?—
This, whereby the fair flower dies,
Have my pains, my griefs effected:
In my breaft they were collected,
And they burft forth from mine eyes.
Let me weep the cruelty
Of a father.

   Arminda.
  Lady, fee . . . .
    Julia.
But what happier deftiny
Is there, than of grief to die?
Pain that, victor of the ftrife,
Conquers life is a glorious fate,—

Que no es muy grande la pena,
Que no acaba con la vida.
      Arminda.
¿ Qué novedad obligó
Tu llanto ?
      Julia.
     ¡ Ay, Arminda mia !
Cuantos papeles tenia
De Eusebio, Lisardo halló
En mi escritorio.
      Arminda.
      ¿ Pues él
Supo que estaban alli ?
      Julia.
Como aqueso contra mí
Hará mi estrella cruel.
Yo, (¡ ay de mi !) cuando le via
El cuidado con que andaba,
Pensé que lo sospechaba,
Pero no que lo sabia.
Llegó á mí descolorido,
Y entre apacible y airado,
Me dijo, que habia jugado,
Arminda, y que habia perdido ;
Que una joya le prestase
Para volver á jugar.
Por presto que la iba á dar,
No aguardó á que la sacase :
Tomó él la llave, y abrió
Con una cólera inquieta,
Y en la primera naveta
Los papeles encontró.
Miróme y volvió á cerrar.
Y sin decir nada (¡ ay Dios !)
Buscó á mi padre, y los dos
(¿ Quién duda es para tratar
Mi muerte ?) gran rato hablaron
Cerrados en su aposento ;
Salieron, y hácia el convento

Since the pain cannot be great,
Unto which succumbs not life.
      Arminda.
But what *new* grief is the ground
Of these tears ?
      Julia.
     Arminda mine,
Of Eusebio, every line,
By Lisardo has been found
In my escritoir.
      Arminda.
      Did hé
Know that they were there conceal'd ?
      Julia.
This my cruel star reveal'd
Shining balefully on mé ;
I (ah me !) because he grew,
Plainly, hourly, more dejected,
Thought indeed that he suspected,
But I did not think he knew.
Thus he came, his hair was tost,
Pale his cheek, his eye betray'd
Peace and wrath, he said he play'd
Deep and long, that he had lost ;
Luck was bad, and, to retrieve it,
Ask'd me for some trinkets' loan,
Which to give I would have flown
Had he waited to receive it ;
But he, with an angry air,
Seized the key, unlock'd the drawer,
And within the escritoir
Found Eusebio's letters there.
Coldly eyeing me, he straight
Lock'd the drawer, said naught,
    withdrew
(God !) to seek my sire, the two,
(Oh ! who doubts that the debate
Turn'd up on my death ?) discourse
Held there long within his room,

Los dos fus pafos guiaron,
Segun Octavio me dijo.
Y fi lo que eftá tratado
Ya mi padre ha efectuado,
Con jufta caufa me aflijo;
Porque fi de aquefta fuerte,
Que olvide á Eufebio, defea,
Antes que monja me vea,
Yo mifma me daré muerte.

Sale EUSEBIO.

Eufebio (aparte).
Ninguno tan atrevido,
Si no tan defefperado,
Viene á tomar por fagrado
La cafa del ofendido.
Antes que fepa la muerte
De Lifardo Julia bella,
Hablar quifiera con ella,
Porque á mi tirana fuerte
Algun remedio configo,
Si, ignorado mi rigor,
Puede obligarla el amor
A que fe vaya conmigo;
Y cuando llegue á faber
De Lifardo el hado injufto,
Hará de la fuerza gufto,
Mirándofe en mi poder.—
Hermofa Julia.

Julia.
     ¿ Qué es efto ?
¿ Tú en efta cafa ?
Eufebio.
      El rigor
De mi defdicha, y tu amor
En tal peligro me ha puefto.

Then came forth, and through the gloom
To the convent bent their courfe,
As Octavio has told me.
If then what was there projected
By my father is effected,
Juftly you in tears behold me;
For if thus he feeks to try
From Eufebio's love to free me,
Ere a nun he lives to fee me,
By my own hands fhall I die.

EUSEBIO *enters unfeen.*

Eufebio (afide).
No one ever dared before,
Defperate though his cafe might be,
Thus to fly for fanctuary
To the injured party's door;
But my urgent fate compels me,
Ere Lifardo's death be known,
Ere fair Julia's love be grown
Into hate and fhe repels me,
Quickly to anticipate
Rapid rumour's dread revealings,
And by both our mutual feelings
Urge her to embrace my fate,
And to fly with me this hour:—
Then, although his death muft pain her,
She will feel fhe muft reftrain her,
Seeing that fhe's in my power:—
         [He advances.
Beauteous Julia!
Julia.
     Can it be
Thou art in this houfe?
Eufebio.
       To prove
My misfortune and thy love,
I have run this rifk for thee.

Julia.
Pues ¿cómo has entrado aqui,
Y emprendes tan loco extremo?
Eusebio.
Como la muerte no temo.
Julia.
¿Qué es lo que intentas afi?
Eusebio.
Hoy obligarte defeo,
Julia, porque agradecida
Des á mi amor nueva vida,
Nueva gloria á mi defeo.
Yo he fabido cuanto ofende
A tu padre mi cuidado,
Que á fu noticia ha llegado
Nueftro amor, y que pretende
Que tú recibas mañana
El eftado que defea,
Para que mi dicha fea,
Como mi efperanza, vana.
Si ha fido gufto, fi ha fido
Amor el que me has moftrado,
Si es verdad que me has amado,
Si es cierto que me has querido,
Vente conmigo; pues ves
Que no tiene refiftencia
De tu padre la obediencia,
Deja tu cafa; y defpues
Que habrá mil remedios pienfa;
Pues ya en mi poder, es jufto
Que haga de la fuerza gufto,
Y obligacion de la ofenfa.
Villas tengo en que guardarte,
Gente con que defenderte,
Hacienda para ofrecerte,
Y un alma para adorarte.
Si darme vida defeas,
Si es verdadero tu amor,
Atrévete, ó el dolor

Julia.
Oh! why haft thou ventured here,
Such a wild attempt to try?
Eusebio.
I am not afraid to die.
Julia.
What's thy object?—O my fear!
Eusebio.
Julia, I have grown ambitious
That this happy day at length
Should my love give newer ftrength,
Newer glory to my wifhes.
I have learn'd how much offended
Is your father by my fuit,
That to him has come the bruit
Of our love, that 'tis intended,
Ere fhall come to-morrow's e'en,
Thou a ftate of life muft take,
Which, he thinks, my blifs will make
Vain as all my hopes have been.
If with favour thou haft heard me
Speak my love, nor yet reproved me,
If 'tis certain thou haft loved me,
If 'tis true thou haft preferr'd me,
Come then with me: fince 'tis plain
Thou canft never make refiftance
To thy father's ftrong perfiftence,
Leave thy houfe; thy ftrength will gain
Thoufand aids when thou art hence;
When thou'rt in my power 'twill be
Beft to yield to fate's decree,
And to pardon the offence.
Villas have I to rife o'er thee,
Vaffals have I to defend thee,
Wealth and all its aids to tend thee,
And a true heart to adore thee.
Wouldft thou ftay this life nigh fled,
Doft thou worth a true love deem me,
Dare this ftep, or thou wilt fee me

Hará que mi muerte veas.
      Julia.
Oye, Eufebio.
        Arminda.
           Mi feñor
Viene, feñora.
      Julia.
         Ay de mí !
      Eufebio.
¿ Pudiera hallar contra mí
La fortuna mas rigor ?
      Julia.
¿ Podrá falir ?
        Arminda.
         No es pofible
Que fe vaya; porque ya
Llamando á la puerta eftá.
      Julia.
¡ Grave mal !
      Eufebio.
        ¡ Pena terrible !
¿ Qué haré ?
      Julia.
      Efconderte es forzofo.
      Eufebio.
¿ Dónde ?
      Julia.
      En aquefe apofento.
      Arminda.
Prefto, que fus pafos fiento.
      [*Efcóndefe* Eusebio.

    Sale Curcio.

    Curcio.
Hija, fi por el dichofo
Eftado, que tú codicias,
Y que ya feguro tienes,
No das á mis parabienes
La vida y alma en albricias,

Slain by grief, here lying dead.
      Julia.
Oh ! Eufebio, hear . . . .
      Arminda.
          My mafter
Comes, feñora.
      Julia.
        Woe is me !
      Eufebio.
Oh ! with what perfiftency
Fortune dogs me with difafter !
      Julia.
Can he not go forth ?
      Arminda.
           'Tis vain
To attempt it ; 'tis too late,
For he's calling at the gate.
      Julia.
Dread mifchance !
      Eufebio.
        Terrific pain !
What remains ?
      Julia.
      Concealment folely.
      Eufebio.
Where ?
      Julia.
      Within this chamber here.
      Arminda.
Quick ! his fteps are drawing near.
      [Eusebio *conceals himfelf.*

    Enter Curcio.

    Curcio.
Daughter, if for that moft holy
State thou long'ft for, that calm goal
Which now crowns thy expectations,
Thou, as my beft gratulations,
Yield'ft not up thy heart and foul,

Del defeo que he tenido
No agradeces el cuidado.
Todo queda efectuado,
Y todo tan prevenido,
Que folo falta ponerte
La mas bizarra y hermofa,
Para fer de Crifto efpofa ;
Mira ¡ que dichofa fuerte !
Hoy aventajas á todas
Cuantas fe ven envidiar,
Pues te verán celebrar
Aqueftas divinas bodas.
¿ Qué dices?
       Julia (aparte).
          ¿ Qué puedo hacer ?
      Eufebio (aparte).
Yo me doy la muerte aqui,
Si ella le dice que sí.
        Julia.
No fé como refponder.—   [*Aparte.*
Bien, feñor, la autoridad
De padre, que es preferida,
Imperio tiene en la vida;
Pero no en la libertad.
¿ Pues, que fupiera antes yo
Tu intento, no fuera bien ?
¿ Y que tú, feñor, tambien
Supieras mi gufto?

      Curcio.
         No ;
Que fola mi voluntad,
En lo jufto, ó en lo injufto,
Has de tener tú por gufto.
        Julia.
Solo tiene libertad
Un hijo para efcoger
Eftado ; que el hado impío
No fuerza el libre albedrío.

Then my zeal will be derided,
By thy ingrate heart eluded.
Everything has been concluded,
I have everything provided ;
There's but one thing to await,
In a rich robe to be clothèd
As Chrift's veftal bride betrothèd ;
See now, what a happy fate !
All the friends thy feaft invites
Will be envious of thy mating,
Since they'll fee thee celebrating
Thefe divineft marriage rites.
What then fay'ft thou ?
       Julia (afide).
          Woe the day !
      Eufebio (afide).
Here I'll give myfelf my death
If the fatal " Yes " fhe faith.
        Julia.
(Ah ! I know not what to fay !)
           [*Afide.*

Though a fire's authority
So endow'd, fo richly rife,
Hath dominion over life,
It hath none o'er liberty.
Wer't not right that I fhould know
Earlier what thou tell'ft me now ?
Wer't not proper, too, that thou
Knew my wifhes likewife ?
      Curcio.
          No ;
For my will alone fhould be
Ever facred in thy fight,
Be the matter wrong or right.
        Julia.
Sir, the only liberty
That a child has is to choofe
In the world its fitting ftate ;
This no law or impious fate

Déjame penſar y ver
De eſpacio eſo ; y no te eſpante
Ver que término te pida ;
Que el eſtado de una vida
No ſe toma en un inſtante.
　　　　Curcio.
Baſta que yo lo he mirado,
Y yo por tí he dado el ſí.
　　　　Julia.
Pues ſi tú vives por mí,
Toma tambien por mí eſtado.
　　　　Curcio.
¡ Calla, infame ! ¡ calla, loca !
Que haré de aqueſe cabello
Un lazo para tu cuello,
O ſacaré de tu boca
Con mis manos la atrevida
Lengua, que de oir me ofendo.
　　　　Julia.
La libertad te defiendo,
Señor, pero no la vida.
Acaba ſu curſo triſte,
Y acabará tu peſar ;
Que mal te puedo negar
La vida que tú me diſte.
La libertad, que me dió
El cielo, es la que te niego.
　　　　Curcio.
En eſte punto á creer llego
Lo que el alma ſoſpechó,
Que no fue buena tu madre,
Y manchó mi honor alguno ;
Pues hoy tu error importuno
Ofende el honor de un padre,
A quien el ſol no igualó
En reſplandor y belleza,
Sangre, honor, luſtre y nobleza.
　　　　Julia.
Eſo no he entendido yo,

E'er ſhould hinder or refuſe.
Let me think awhile, nor fear
For this pauſe to be petition'd,
For a moment's inſufficient
To decide a life's career.
　　　　Curcio.
'Tis enough that I've decided,
And have given the " Yes " for thee.
　　　　Julia.
Since my life thou liv'ſt for me,
Take the ſtate, too, thou'ſt provided.
　　　　Curcio.
Silence, rebel ! ſilence, fool !
Leſt around thy neck I twine
Laſſo-like thoſe locks of thine,
Or permit my hands to pull
Out thy tongue, that like a knife
Cuts me to the heart to hear.
　　　　Julia.
'Tis the freedom I hold dear
I defend, but not the life :—
Finiſh its unhappy courſe,
And thy grief conclude thereby,
Since 'twere ſinful to deny
That to thee who art its ſource ;
What I wiſh to have reſpected
Is my freedom—Heaven's ſole gift.
　　　　Curcio.
Now aſſurance doth uplift
Doubt from that I've long ſuſpected,
That my wife, your mother rather,
Stain'd my life's elſe ſpotleſs mirror,
Since to day thy obſtinate error
Wounds the honour of a father,
Who hath not the ſun for equal,
In its light and lovelineſs,
For blood, birth, and nobleneſs.
　　　　Julia.
Ere I ſpeak, I wait the ſequel,

Por eso no he respondido.
            Curcio.
Arminda, salte allá fuera.—
            [*Vase* ARMINDA.
Y ya que mi pena fiera
Tantos años he tenido
Secreta, de mis enojos
La ciega pasion obliga
A que la lengua te diga
Lo que te han dicho los ojos.
La Señoría de Sena,
Por dar á mi sangre fama,
En su nombre me envió
A dar la obediencia al Papa
Urbano Tercio.   Tu madre,
Que con opinion de santa
Fue en Sena comun ejemplo
De las matronas romanas,
Y aun de las nuestras, (no sé
Como mi lengua la agravia;
Mas, ¡ay infelice! tanto
La satisfaccion engaña)
En Sena quedó, y yo estuve
En Roma con la embajada
Ocho meses; porque entonces
Por concierto se trataba,
Que esta Señoría fuese
Del Pontífice; Dios haga
Lo que á su estado convenga,
Que aqui importa poco, ó nada.
Volví á Sena, y hallé en ella . . . .
(Aqui el aliento me falta,
Aqui la lengua enmudece,
Y aqui el ánimo desmaya)
Hallé (¡ay injusto temor!)
A tu madre tan preñada,
Que para el infeliz parto,
Cumplia las nueve faltas.
Ya me habia prevenido

As thy meaning is not clear.
            Curcio.
Wait without, Arminda, go!
            [*Exit* ARMINDA.
Seeing that my bitter woe,
Which I've held so many a year
Hidden, from its centre flies,
And by passion render'd bold,
Makes thee by the tongue be told
What's been told thee by the eyes.
This proud seigniory Siena,
To my blood to add new honour,
Sent me once to pay obedience,
In its name, unto the Pontiff,
The third Urban; and thy mother,
Who, reputed and acknowledged
As a saint, was through Siena
Thought the universal model,
The bright copy and exemplar,
Of all matrons, of the Roman,
And even of our own: (I know not
How my tongue can dare to wrong her,
But alas! the satisfaction
That seems fair deceives too often !)
She remain'd behind; I tarried
Eight months at the sacred college
With the embassy, at that time
The idea being in progress
'Bout the giving of Siena
To the Pontiff, which same project
May God settle as beseems him !
For 'tis here of slight importance.
On returning home, I found her . . . .
(Here the breath doth fail my body,
Here my tongue grows mute in silence,
Here my frighten'd courage falters,)
Found her . . . (hence, O coward fear!)
In her pregnancy so forward,
That for her unhappy burden

Por sus mentirosas cartas
Esta desdicha, diciendo,
Que, cuando me fui, quedaba
Con sospecha; y yo la tuve
De mi deshonra tan clara,
Que discurriendo mi agravio,
Imaginé mi desgracia.
No digo que verdad sea;
Mas quien tiene sangre hidalga
No ha de aguardar á creer,
Que el imaginar le basta.
¿Qué importa que un noble sea
Desdichado, (¡ oh ley tirana
De honor! ¡ oh bárbara fuero
Del mundo!) si la ignorancia
Le disculpa? Mienten, mienten
Las leyes; porque no alcanza
Los misterios al efecto
Quien no previene la causa.
¿Qué ley culpa á un inocente?
¿Qué opinion á un libre agravia?
Miente otra vez; que no es
Deshonra, sino desgracia.
¡ Bueno es, que en leyes de honor
Le comprenda tanta infamia
Al Mercurio que le roba,
Como al Argos que le guarda!
¿Qué deja el mundo, qué deja,
Si así al inocente infama,
De deshonra, para aquel
Que lo sabe y que lo calla?
Yo entre tantos pensamientos,
Yo entre confusiones tantas,
Ni ví regalo en la mesa,
Ni hice descanso en la cama.
Tan desabrido conmigo
Estuve, que me trataba
Como ajeno el corazon,
Y como á tirano el alma.

She her nine months had accomplish'd;
She already had forewarn'd me,
In false lines of seeming fondness,
Of this great misfortune, saying,
When I left her, that the prospect
Seem'd most likely : and so patent
Thought I then was my dishonour,
That, deep brooding on my insult,
I imagined my misfortune :
That 'twas real I assert not,
Since what man whose blood is noble
Waits for proof, when 'tis sufficient
To imagine it as proven?
What imports it that a noble
Is unhappy (oh! despotic
Law of honour! oh! stern edict
Of the world!) when want of knowledge
Exculpates him? Lying, lying
Laws are they, because the mortal
Should be blamed not for the issues
Who the cause hath not foreboded.
What law proves the innocent guilty?
Blameless, what opinion wrongs them?
Lying laws once more : for then 'twere
Not dishonour but misfortune.
Is it right, by the laws of honour,
That an equal infamy follows
Him, the Argus who doth guard it,
And the Mercury who robs it?
I, involved in such dark fancies,
I, in such a maze involvèd,
Found no solace at the table,
No repose upon the soft bed.
And I grew so discontented
With myself soon, that my cold heart
Came to treat me as a stranger,
And my soul as not its owner.
And though many a time I reason'd
With myself, and well-nigh proved her

Y aunque á veces difcurria
En fu abono, y aunque hallaba
Verisímil la difculpa,
Pudo en mí tanto la inftancia
Del temer que me ofendia,
Que con faber que fue cafta,
Tomé de mis penfamientos,
No de fus culpas, venganza.
Y porque con mas fecreto
Fuefe, previne una caza
Fingida, porque á un zelofo
Ficciones folo le agradan.
Al monte fui, y cuando todos
Entretenidos eftaban
En fu alegre regocijo,
Con amorofas palabras,
(¡ Qué bien las dice quien miente !
¡ Qué bien las cree quien ama !)
Llevé á Rofmira, tu madre,
Por una fenda apartada
Del camino, y divertida
Llegó á una fecreta eftancia
Defte monte, á cuyo albergue
El fol ignoró la entrada ;
Porque fe la defendian
Rúfticamente enlazadas,
Por no decir que amorofas,
Arboles, hojas y ramas.
Aqui pues, adonde apenas
Huella imprimió mortal planta,
Solos los dos . . . .

Sale ARMINDA.

Arminda.

           Si el valor,
Que el noble pecho acompaña,
Señor, y fi la experiencia,
Que te han dado honrofas canas,
En la defdicha prefente

Innocent, I ftill was haunted
With the fear fhe might have wrong'd me.
And though thus with full affurance
She was chafte, I yet refolvèd
To avenge not her offences
But the dark thoughts that engroff'd me.
And more fecretly and fafely
That this fhould be done, I order'd
A fictitious hunt, for fictions
Are the jealous man's fole comfort.
We departed to the mountain,
And while all our friends difported
In the joyous recreation,
I, with words of amorous fondnefs,
(Ah ! how eafily by falfehood
Can fuch treacheries be fpoken !
Ah ! how eafily be trufted
By the fond heart of a lover !)
Led thy mother, led Rofmira,
By a path, that, through the copfes
Winding, from the roadway brought us
To a lone and diftant corner
Of the mountain, to whofe entrance
Scarce the fun reveal'd a portal,
It was fo completely hidden
By the ruftic running over,
Not to fay the amorous twining
Of leaves, trees, and thorns, and rofes.
Here, then, here, where human footftep
Scarce was planted till that moment,
We two only . . . .

Enter ARMINDA.

Arminda.

           If the firmnefs
Which to noble breafts belongeth,
If, fir, the dear-bought experience
Which has given thee honour'd hoar
    hairs,

No te niega ó no te falta,
Exámen será el valor
De tu ánimo.

       Curcio.
        ¿Qué causa
Te obliga á que así interrumpas
Mi razon?
       Arminda.
      Señor . . . .
       Curcio.
           Acaba;
Que mas la duda me ofende.
       Julia.
¿Por qué te suspendes? Habla.

       Arminda.
No quisiera ser la voz
De mi pena y tu desgracia.
       Curcio.
No temas decirla tú,
Pues yo no temo escucharla.
       Arminda.
A Lísardo, mi señor . . . .
       Eusebio.
Esto solo me faltaba.
       Arminda.
Bañado en su sangre traen
En una silla por andas
Cuatro rústicos pastores,
Muerto (¡ay Dios!) á puñaladas;
Mas ya á tu presencia llega:
No le veas.

       Curcio.
      ¡Cielos, tantas
Penas para un desdichado!
¡Ay de mí!

In the presence of this sorrow
Fail thee not nor fly thee wholly,
It will be the test and trial
Of thy strength of mind.
       Curcio.
          What object
Forces thee to interrupt me
Thus unsummon'd?
       Arminda.
        Sir . . . .
       Curcio.
         Say shortly
What it is, for doubt is worse still.
       Julia.
Speak! Why pause thus? What doth
    stop thee?
       Arminda.
That I may not be the voice
Of my pain, and thy misfortune.
       Curcio.
Be not thou afraid to tell
What I fear not to have told me.
       Arminda.
Sir, oh! sir, thy son Lisardo . . . .
       Eusebio (at the side).
This remain'd to overthrow me!
       Arminda.
Bathèd in his blood, and lying
On a litter stretch'd, is borne here
By four rustic shepherd swains,
Dead (O God!) from cuts and sword-
    stabs;
But already he is here:—
Look not on him.
       Curcio.
      Heavens! what torments
Numberless for one poor wretch here!
Woe is me!—

Salen los Villanos con Lisardo *muerto en una silla.*

Julia.
Pues ¿ qué inhumana
Fuerza enſangrentó la ira
En ſu pecho ? ¿ qué tirana
Mano ſe bañó en mi ſangre,
Contra ſu inocencia airada ?
¡ Ay de mí !

Arminda.
Mira, ſeñora . . . .

Bras.
No llegues á verle.

Curcio.
Aparta.

Tirſo.
Detente, ſeñor.

Curcio.
Amigos,
No puede ſufrirlo el alma.
Dejadme ver eſe cadáver frio,
Depóſito infeliz de heladas venas,
Ruina del tiempo, eſtrago del impío
Hado, teatro funeſto de mis penas.
¿ Qué tirano rigor (¡ ay hijo mio !)
Trágico monumento en las arenas
Conſtruyó, porque hicieſe en quejas
vanas
Mortaja triſte de mis blancas canas ?
¡ Ay amigos ! decid ; ¿ quién fue homicida
De un hijo, en cuya vida yo animaba ?

Enter Gil, Menga, Bras, Toribio, *and others, bearing a bier, upon which is the body of* Lisardo.

Julia.
Unpitying monſter,
Who art thou whoſe wrath is written
Blood-red on this breaſt ? What horrid
Hand is bathèd in my heart's blood ?
Anger'd by his innocence only ?
Woe is me !

Arminda.
Reflect, ſeñora . . . .

Bras.
Come not nearer !

Curcio.
Hence ! nor ſtop me.

Tirſo.
Do hold back, ſir.

Curcio.
Friends, my heart
Leaves me powerleſs to withhold me.
Let me behold this corſe, ſo coldly lying,
The ſad depoſit now of frozen veins—
Ruin of time, dead fruit of fate undying,
The fatal theatre of all my pains.
What tyrant wrath, a demon's wrath
outvying,
Raiſed, O my ſon, upon theſe crimſon'd
plains,
This tragic pile, o'er which in ſorrow
bow'd
My white hairs ſtreaming ſerve thee
as a ſhroud ?
Tell me, my friends, what hand to
mercy ſteel'd
Slew this dear ſon, in whom my life's
blood lay ?

Menga.
Gil lo dirá; que, al verle dar la herida,
Oculto entre unos árboles estaba.

Curcio.
Di, amigo, di, ¿quién me quitó esta
    vida?

Gil.
Yo solo sé, que Eusebio se llamaba,
Cuando con él reñia.
    Curcio.
          ¿ Hay mas deshonra ?
Eusebio me ha quitado vida y honra.
Disculpa ahora tú de sus crueles
             [A Julia.
Deseos la ambicion ; di que concibe
Casto amor, pues, á falta de papeles,
Lascivos gustos con tu sangre escribe.

Julia.
Señor . . . .
    Curcio.
    No me respondas como sueles ;
A tomar hoy estado te apercibe,
O apercibe tambien á tu hermosura
Con Lisardo temprana sepultura.
Los dos á un tiempo el sentimiento
    esquivo
En este dia sepultar concierta,
El muerto al mundo, en mi memoria
    vivo,

Menga.
Gil, who was present, 'mong some
    trees conceal'd,
Saw him fall wounded in a desperate
    fray.

Curcio.
Say, who was he who sent him
    unanneal'd
Before his God, and snatch'd from
    me to-day
My life's best life ?
    Gil.
    But this alone I know,
He call'd himself, I think, Eusebio.
    Curcio.
Eusebio ! thus my honour and my life
    He robs relentless in his sateless mood!
             [To Julia.
Excuse him, prithee, thou his would-
    be wife ;
Say the chaste eagerness with which
    he wooed
Caused the slight error that produced
    this strife,
He wanted ink, and so he wrote in
    blood!
    Julia.
Oh! sir . . . .
    Curcio.
    Reply not in thy usual way ;
Hear my commands and study to obey.
Prepare to-day to seek the cloister's gloom,
    Or else prepare in beauteous death
    to lie
With young Lisardo in his early tomb:
At one sad moment both my children
    die ;
Both share the same and yet a different
    doom ;

Tú, viva al mundo, en mi memoria
 muerta.
Y en tanto que el entierro os apercibo,
Porque no huyas, cerraré esta puerta.
Queda con él, porque de aquesa suerte
Lecciones al morir te dé su muerte.

Both leave me lone, and yet how
 differently,—
One lives in memory, though his soul
 has fled,
And one, though living, seems to meas
 dead.
Here, by thy brother's bloody bier, think
 o'er
  The choice I give thee; think what
   thou hast done;
  Look on these tears and on that
   innocent gore,—
A sire dishonour'd and a murder'd son!
Thou canst not fly, for I shall lock this
 door.
Here I shall leave thee by this couch
 alone;
  Look on this pallid form that here
   doth lie,
And learn from it the way that thou
 shalt die.

[*Vanse todos, y queda* JULIA *en medio de*
LISARDO *y* EUSEBIO, *que sale por otra
puerta.*

[*Exeunt all but* JULIA, *who stands in
the middle of the stage, between
the dead body of* LISARDO *and*
EUSEBIO, *who comes forth from his
place of concealment.*

Julia.
Mil veces procuro hablarte,
Tirano Eusebio, y mil veces
El alma duda, el aliento
Falta, y la lengua enmudece.
No sé, no sé como pueda
Hablar; porque á un tiempo vienen
Envueltas iras piadosas
Entre piedades crueles.
Quisiera cerrar los ojos
A aquesta sangre inocente,
Que está pidiendo venganza,
Desperdiciando claveles:

Julia.
I attempt a thousand times,
Dread Eusebio, to address thee,
And a thousand times my breath
Fails me, and my tongue is fetter'd.
Ah! I know not, know not how
To address thee, since together
Pious anger steels my heart,
And unnatural pity melts me.
I would wish to close mine eyes
To this innocent blood here present,
Which, in asking vengeance, sheds
Purple pinks o'er all this death-bed:

Y quisiera hallar disculpa
En las lágrimas que viertes;
Que al fin heridas y ojos
Son bocas que nunca mienten.
Y en una mano el amor,
Y en otra el rigor presente,
A un mismo tiempo quisiera
Castigarte y defenderte.
Y entre ciegas confusiones
De pensamientos tan fuertes
La clemencia me combate,
Y el sentimiento me vence.
¿ Desta suerte solicitas
Obligarme ? ¿ desta suerte,
Eusebio, en vez de finezas,
Con crueldades me pretendes ?
Cuando de mi boda el dia
Resuelta esperaba, ¿ quieres
Que, en vez de apacibles bodas,
Tristes obsequias celebre ?
Cuando por tu gusto era
A mi padre inobediente,
¿ Lutos funestos me das,
En vez de galas alegres ?
Cuando, arriesgando mi vida,
Hice posible el quererte,
¿ En vez de tálamo (¡ ay cielos !)
Un sepulcro me previenes ?
Y cuando mi mano ofrezco,
Despreciando inconvenientes
De honor, ¿ la tuya bañada
En mi sangre me la ofreces ?
¿ Qué gusto tendré en tus brazos,
Si para llegar á verme,
Dando vida á nuestro amor,
Voy tropezando en la muerte ?
¿ Qué dirá el mundo de mí,
Sabiendo que tengo siempre,
Si no presente el agravio,

And I would find some excuse
In the tears I see thou sheddest:
Since but tears and eyes alone
Are the mouths that lie not ever.
Thus on one hand here is love,
And on the other is resentment,
And I would at one time wish
Both to punish and defend thee;
And amid the wild confusion
Of the passionate thoughts that press me,
Now with clemency contend,
Now to sterner duty nerve me.
Is it in this way, Eusebio,
Thou wouldst show thy wish to serve me ?
Is it in this way thou giv'st me
Cruelties and not caresses ?
When resolved, my marriage day
I awaited, wouldst thou let me,
'Stead of peaceful bridal feasts,
Celebrate but sad interments ?
When I was, to make thee happy,
To my father disobedient,
Wouldst thou give me mourning robes
In the place of gala dresses ?
When at risk of life I made it
Possible perchance to wed thee,
Is it not a bride-bed, (heavens !)
But a tomb thou wouldst present me ?
When I offer thee my hand,
Scorning all the fears suggested
By my honour, thine deep-dyed
In my blood thou wouldst extend me !
In thine arms what bliss were mine,
If to reach them I beheld me
Giving life unto our love,
Struggling with death's hand that led me?
What would say the world of me,
Knowing that I kept for ever,
If not present, the deep wrong,

Quien le cometió presente?
Pues cuando quiera el olvido
Sepultarle, solo el verte
Entre mis brazos será
Memoria con que me acuerde.
Yo entonces, yo, aunque te adore,
Los amorosos placeres
Trocaré en iras, pidiendo
Venganzas; pues ¿cómo quieres
Que viva sujeta un alma
A efectos tan diferentes,
Que esté esperando el castigo,
Y deseando que no llegue?
Basta, por lo que te quise,
Perdonarte, sin que esperes
Verme en tu vida, ni hablarme.
Esa ventana, que tiene
Salida al jardin, podrá
Darte paso; por ahí puedes
Escaparte; huye el peligro,
Porque, si mi padre viene,
No te halle aqui.   Vete, Eusebio,
Y mira que no te acuerdes
De mí; que hoy me pierdes tú,
Porque quisiste perderme.
Vete, y vive tan dichoso,
Que tengas felicemente
Bienes, sin que á los pesares
Pagues pension de los bienes.
Que yo haré para mi vida
Una celda prision breve,
Si no sepulcro, pues ya
Mi padre enterrarme quiere.
Alli lloraré desdichas
De un hado tan inclemente,
De una fortuna tan fiera,
De una inclinacion tan fuerte,
De un planeta tan opuesto,
De una estrella tan rebelde,

The wrong-doer ever present?
Since if in forgetfulnefs
I would hide it, but to fee thee
In my arms alone would be
A dread memory and remembrance.
I then, I, though I adore thee,
Will love's joys fo fweet and tender
Change to anger, fternly calling
For revenge; fince wouldft thou, tell me,
Have a foul live on and be
To fuch different moods fubjected,
As to hope the chaftifement
And yet wifh it not effected?
'Tis enough that I forgive thee,
Since I loved thee: but hope never
In your life-time to fpeak with me,
Or to fee me.   Look, this trellis,
Opening on the garden, gives thee
A free exit: fly the peril,
That when back returns my father,
Here he find thee not.   In mercy
Go, Eufebio, and no thought have
More of me; to-day for ever
Haft thou loft me.   Since, to lofe me,
Thus for ever thou preferreft.
Go, then, go, and live fo happy,
So ferenely be poffeffor
Of life's bleffings, as to pay not
Sorrow's toll for being bleffed.
I fhall make my narrow cell
As a life-long prifon ferve me,
If not as a grave; my father
So defiring to inter me:
There I'll weep o'er the misfortunes
Of a hard fate fo inclement,
Of a fortune fo ungenial,
Of a liking fo exceffive,
Of a ftar fo unpropitious,
Of a planet fo averted,

De un amor tan desdichado,
De una mano tan aleve,
Que me ha quitado la vida,
Y no me ha dado la muerte,
Porque entre tantos pesares,
Siempre viva, y muera siempre.
   Eusebio.
Si acaso mas que tus voces
Son ya tus manos crueles
Para tomar la venganza,
Rendido á tus pies me tienes.
Preso me trae mi delito,
Tu amor es la cárcel fuerte,
Las cadenas son mis yerros,
Prisiones que el alma teme,
Verdugo es mi pensamiento;
Si son tus ojos los jueces,
Y ellos me dan la sentencia,
Por fuerza será de muerte.
Mas dirá entonces la fama
En su pregon: "este muere,
Porque quiso;" pues que solo
Es mi delito quererte.
No pienso darte disculpa;
No parezca que la tiene
Tan grande error, solo quiero
Que me mates y te vengues.
Toma esta daga, y con ella
Rompe un pecho que te ofende,
Saca un alma que te adora,
Y tu misma sangre vierte.
Y si no quieres matarme,
Para que á vengarse llegue
Tu padre, diré que estoy
En tu aposento.

   Julia.
    ¡Detente!
Y por última razon,

Of a life's love so unhappy,
Of a hand whose treacherous sternnesss
Takes away my life indeed;
Yet my death doth not present me,
Since I must amid such sorrows
Live for ever, die for ever.
   Eusebio.
If by any chance thy hands
Can more cruelly avenge thee
Than already have thy words,
At thy feet, see, I surrender.
Here my crime has led me captive,
Love for thee is my strong cell here,
Mine own failings are my chains,
Bonds at which the scared soul trembles;
The stern headsman is my thought:
If the judges are presented
By thine eyes, my doom must be
Death, if they pronounce the sentence.
But then Fame, my fate proclaiming,
Will declare, "This man met death here
For his love"—because in loving
Thee alone have I offended.
I attempt not to excuse me,—
Vain, it seems, would such attempt be,
For so great a fault: I only
Wish thou'dst kill me, and avenge thee.
Take this dagger, and with it
Pierce a bosom that offends thee,
Break a fond heart that adores thee,
And in mine thine own blood shed
  here.
If to kill me thou declinest,
That thy father for his vengeance
May return, I'll say I'm hid here
In thy chamber.
   Julia.
    Oh! arrest thee!
Stay! and as the last request

Que he de hablarte eternamente,
Has de hacer lo que te digo.
   Eufebio.
Yo lo concedo.
   Julia.
    Pues vete
Adonde guardes tu vida;
Hacienda tienes, y gente
Que te podrá defender.
   Eufebio.
Mejor ferá que yo quede
Sin ella; porque fi vivo,
Será impofible que deje
De adorarte, y no has de eftar,
Aunque un convento te encierre,
Segura.
   Julia.
   Guárdate tú;
Que yo fabré defenderme.
   Eufebio.
¿ Volveré yo á verte ?
   Julia.
    No.
   Eufebio.
¿ No hay remedio ?
   Julia.
    No le efperes.
   Eufebio.
¿ Que al fin me aborreces ya ?
   Julia.
Haré por aborrecerte.
   Eufebio.
¿ Olvidaráfme ?
   Julia.
   No fé.
   Eufebio.
¿ Veréte yo ?
   Julia.
Eternamente.

I may make of thee for ever,
Grant the favour that I afk thee.
   Eufebio.
I concede it.
   Julia.
    Flee, oh! flee hence,
Where thou may'ft preferve thy life:
Thou haft property and people
Who for thy defence are able.
   Eufebio.
It were better that I ftay'd here
Without *it :* for if I live,
From adoring thee I never
Can defift; nor fhalt thou be
Safe, although a convent's fhelter
Seem to guard thee.
   Julia.
    Guard thou thee;
I fhall know how to defend me.
   Eufebio.
Once more fhall I fee thee ?
   Julia.
     No.
   Eufebio.
No refource ?
   Julia.
   Do not expect it.
   Eufebio.
Am I then detefted fo ?
   Julia.
I have reafon to deteft thee.
   Eufebio.
Wilt forget me ?
   Julia.
   I don't know.
   Eufebio.
Shall I fee thee ?
   Julia.
   Never, never.

Eusebio.
Pues ¿aquel pasado amor . . . . ?
   Julia.
Pues ¿esta sangre presente . . . . ?
La puerta abren ; vete, Eusebio.
   Eusebio.
Iré por obedecerte.
¡ Que no he de volverte á ver !
   Julia.
¡ Que no has de volver á verme !
  [*Suena ruido, vanse los dos, cada
   uno por su parte, y entran el cuerpo
   algunos criados.*

Eusebio.
What then of our fond love past ?—
   Julia.
What then of this red blood present?—
Lo! the door! Eusebio, fly !
   Eusebio.
I shall go, but through obedience :—
Oh ! to see thee never more !
   Julia.
Oh ! that thou no more must see me !
  [*A noise is heard outside; they go out
   at opposite doors, and servants enter
   and remove the body.*

<table>
<tr><td>

JORNADA II.

MONTE.

Diſparan dentro un arcabuz, y ſalen RICARDO, CELIO y EUSEBIO *en trage de bandoleros, con arcabuces.*

       Ricardo.

ASÓ el plomo violento
    Su pecho.
        Celio.
           Y hace el golpe mas
ſangriento,
Que con ſu ſangre la tragedia imprima
En tierna flor.
        Euſebio.
          Ponle una Cruz encima,
Y perdónele Dios.

</td><td>

ACT II.

THE MOUNTAIN. A RUDE CROSS AT ONE SIDE, WITH SEVERAL OTHERS IN THE DISTANCE.*

A ſhot is heard within: enter RICARDO, CELIO, *and* EUSEBIO, *dreſſed as bandits, and armed with arquebuſes.*

       Ricardo.

HAT ball of wingèd lead
    Paſs'd through his breaſt.
        Celio.
          And made a wound ſo red,
That the ſad tale o'er all the tender moſs
Is writ in blood.

       Euſebio.
          Put over him a croſs,
And God be merciful to his ſoul.

</td></tr>
</table>

* M. Philarète Chaſles greatly aſſiſts the imagination in its efforts to realize the externals of this ſcene :—

"Dans une gorge de montagne, au ſein d'une ſolitude âpre et ſauvage, loin de tous les chemins fréquentés, au milieu de rocs bronzés par la pluie, jaunis ſous le ſoleil, et de grands blocs de pierre ſuperpoſés, aux arêtes aiguës qui ſe deſſinent durement à l'horizon, il y a une grande croix, formée de deux débris de chêne que l'outil du charpentier n'a pas même equarrês. C'eſt un de ces payſages aux couleurs tranchées, aux lignes aiguës, qui s'accordent avec toutes les penſées terribles, et toutes les fureurs de l'âme. Là doivent ſe réfugier les *bandoleros ;* là des ennemis acharnés doivent commencer et finir un combat mortel.

"C'eſt là auſſi que Calderon place ſes aêteurs."—*Etudes ſur l'Eſpagne,* p. 43.

Ricardo.
            Las devociones
Nunca faltan del todo á los ladrones.

    [*Vanse* Ricardo *y* Celio.
    Eusebio.
Y pues mis hados fieros
Me traen á capitan de bandoleros,
Llegarán mis delitos
A fer, como mis penas, infinitos.
Como fi diera muerte
A Lifardo á traicion, de aquefta fuerte
Mi patria me perfigue,
Porque fu furia y mi defpecho obligue
A que guarde una vida,
Siendo de tantas bárbaro homicida.
Mi hacienda me han quitado,
Mis villas confifcado,
Y á tanto rigor llegan,
Que el fuftento me niegan.
No toque pafagero
El término del monte, fi primero
No rinde hacienda y vida.

    Salen Ricardo *y* Bandoleros con
    Alberto.

    Ricardo.
Llegando á ver la boca de la herida,
Efcucha, Capitan, el mas extraño
Sucefo.

    Eusebio.
    Ya defeo el defengaño.
    Ricardo.
Hallé el plomo defhecho
En efte libro que tenia en el pecho,
Sin haber penetrado,
Y al caminante folo defmayado:

Ricardo.
            Right notions,
Thieves though we be, we've got of
    our devotions.
    [*Exeunt* Ricardo *and* Celio.
    Eusebio.
Since then by fate's command
I now am captain of a robber-band,
Be my offences from this day
Great as my griefs, and infinite as they.
Treating Lifardo's death as if it were
By treachery caufed and not in duel fair,
My country fo purfued me with its hate,
So great its fury, and my wrath fo great,
I was compell'd, a barbarous murderer
    grown,
Full many a life to take to fave my own.
My property they fequeftrated,
My villas all they confifcated,——
Their rigour fo increafed, that they
My very means of fuftenance took away;
Therefore no traveller more
Shall pafs the mountain's boundary before
Money and life he yield me on the fpot.

    Enter Ricardo *and bandits leading*
    in Alberto.

    Ricardo.
Going to fee the place where he was
    fhot,——
Oh! liften, captain, nothing has come
For downright wonder.   [near it
    Eusebio.
    Then I wifh to hear it.
    Ricardo.
I found the bullet prefs'd
Againft this book he carried in his breaft;
The book unpierced, his breaft without
    a wound,

Veſle aqui ſano y bueno.

Euſebio.
De eſpanto eſtoy, y admiraciones lleno.
¿ Quién eres, venerable
Caduco, á quien los cielos admirable
Han hecho con prodigio milagroſo?

Alberto.
Yo ſoy, o Capitan, el mas dichoſo
De cuantos hombres hay; que he
    merecido
Ser Sacerdote indigno, y he leido
En Bolonia ſagrada Teología
Cuarenta y cuatro años con deſvelo;
Dióme ſu Santidad, por eſte zelo,
De Trento el Obiſpado,
Premiando mis eſtudios ; y admirado
Yo de ver, que tenia
Cuenta te tantas almas,
Y que apenas la daba de la mia,
Los laureles dejé, dejé las palmas,
Y huyendo ſus engaños,
Vengo á buſcar ſeguros deſengaños
En eſtas ſoledades,
Donde viven deſnudas las verdades.
Paſo á Roma, á que el Papa me conceda
Licencia, Capitan, para que pueda
Fundar un órden ſanto de eremitas.
Mas tu ſaña atrevida
Quita el hilo á mi ſuerte y á la vida.

For the ſcared traveller had only
    ſwoon'd ;—
Here ſee him ſafe and ſound once more.
Euſebio.
Terror and wonder thrill me to the
    core!—
Who art thou, venerable ſage,
Whom Heaven hath made the wonder
    of the age,
Working for thee a miracle ſo great?
Alberto.
I am, O captain, the moſt fortunate
Of all mankind, although in worth the
    leaſt,
Since I have merited to be a prieſt.
For four-and-forty years I read with
    care
Sacred theology from Bologna's chair.
His Holineſs, for all the years thus ſpent,
Gave me the Biſhopric of Trent,
Rewarding thus my ſtudious zeal long
    ſhown ;
But I afraid, from conſcious qualms,
To account for others' ſouls that ſcarce
    can ſave mine own,
Fled its laurels, fled its palms,
And the world's deceits rejecting,
Sought ſecurer peace, ſelecting
Theſe remote and lonely dells,
Where nought but naked truth auſterely
    dwells.
I was going to Rome, with hope
Of obtaining licence from the Pope
To found, O captain, 'mid theſe heights,
A holy order of lone eremites,
When thy rage ſo deſperate
Sever'd my thread of life, and changed
    my fate.

Eusebio.
¿ Qué libro es este, di ?
    Alberto.
           Este es el fruto,
Que rinde á mis estudios el tributo
De tantos años.

    Eusebio.
     ¿ Qué es lo que contiene ?
    Alberto.
El trata del orígen verdadero
De aquel divino y celestial madero,
En que animoso y fuerte,
Muriendo, triunfó Cristo de la muerte.
El libro, en fin, se llama
" Milagros de la Cruz."

    Eusebio.
         ¡ Qué bien la llama
De aquel plomo inclemente,
Mas que la cera, se mostró obediente !
¡ Pluguiera á Dios, mi mano
Antes, que blanco su papel hiciera
De aquel golpe tirano,
Entre su fuego ardiera !
Lleva ropa y dinero
Y la vida, solo este libro quiero ;
Y vosotros salidle acompañando,
Hasta dejarle libre.

    Alberto.
        Iré rogando
Al Señor, te dé luz para que veas
El error en que vives.

Eusebio.
Tell me, what book is this?
    Alberto.
             It is the fruit
Which many a year's hard study in
   pursuit
Of truth has given me.
    Eusebio.
      What does it contain ?
    Alberto.
It treats of the true history
Of that divine and holy tree
On which by yielding up his mighty
   breath
Christ died, and, dying, triumph'd over
   death.
The book is call'd by the appropriate
   name,
" The Miracles of the Cross."
    Eusebio.
         How well the flame
Of the fierce bullet knew what to obey,
When, soft as wax, the stubborn lead
   gave way !
Oh! would to God! that ere my hand's
   wild rage
Had dared to do a deed so dire,
As to deface this spotless page
By that rude shot, 'twere burn'd in its
   own fire !
Keep thou thy money, life, and dress,
This book alone is all I would possess :
Do you, my comrades, guide him on
   his way
Till you can set him free.
    Alberto.
         And I shall pray,
Each step I take, that God may thee
   inspire

Eufebio.
                          Si defeas
Mi bien, pídele á Dios, que no permita
Muera fin confefion.

Alberto.
                          Yo te prometo,
Seré miniftro en tan piadofo efeto,
Y te doy mi palabra,
(Tanto en mi pecho tu clemencia labra)
Que fi me llamas en cualquiera parte,
Dejaré mi defierto,
Por ir á confefarte :
Un Sacerdote foy, mi nombre Alberto.

Eufebio.
¿Tal palabra me das?
          Alberto.
                          Y la confiefo
Con la mano.
          Eufebio.
                    Otra vez tus plantas befo.
[*Vafe* ALBERTO *con* RICARDO *y los*
          Bandoleros.

Sale CHILINDRINA.

Chilindrina.
Hafta venir á hablarte,
El monte atravefé de parte á parte.

Eufebio.
Qué hay, amigo?
          Chilindrina.
                    Dos nuevas harto malas.
          Eufebio.
A mi temor el fentimiento igualas.
Qué fon?

To know thy finful life.
          Eufebio.
                          Doft thou defire
My welfare? Then afk God that I may
          not
Without confeffion die.
          Alberto.
                          I promife thee
Thy helper in that pious wifh to be ;
Yes, I pledge to thee my word,
(So much thy clemency my heart hath
          ftirr'd,)
That in whatever place thou wilt addrefs
          me,
In my defert I fhall own thy claim,
And haften to confefs thee :
I am a prieft, Alberto is my name.
          Eufebio.
Thy word doft give me ?
          Alberto.
                          Let my hand repeat
The promife thus.
          Eufebio.
                    Once more I kifs thy feet.
[ALBERTO *is led out by* RICARDO
          and the other bandits.

Enter CHILLINDRINA.

Chillindrina.
Up this wild mountain's fteep acclivity
I've roam'd through every part to fpeak
          with thee.
          Eufebio.
What brings thee, friend ?
          Chillindrina.
                          Two bits of evil news.
          Eufebio.
Terror and grief my feelings interfufe :
What are they ?

Chilindrina.
Es la primera,
(Decirla no quifiera)
Que al padre de Lifardo
Han dado . . . .

Eufebio.
Acaba, que el efecto aguardo.
Chilindrina.
Comifion de prenderte ó de matarte.

Eufebio.
Efotra nueva temo
Mas, porque en un confufo extremo
Al corazon parece que camina
Toda el alma, adivina
De algun future daño.
¿ Qué ha fucedido ?

Chilindrina.
A Julia . . . .
Eufebio.
No me engaño
En prevenir triftezas,
Si para ver mi mal, por Julia empiezas.
¿ Julia no me dijifte ?
Pues efo bafta para verme trifte.
¡ Mal haya amen la rigurofa eftrella,
Que me obligó á querella !
En fin, Julia . . . . profigue.

Chilindrina.
En un convento
Seglar eftá.

Chillindrina.
The firft is,
(I would that I had not to tell thee
this,)
Unto Lifardo's father by the ftate
Is given . . . .
Eufebio.
Conclude, the whole refult I wait.
Chillindrina.
Commiffion or to feize thee or to flay
thee.
Eufebio.
Thy fecond news I fear
More than the firft ; becaufe, on ftretch
to hear,
My troubled foul flies to my trembling
heart
Confufed, difturb'd, divining that thou
art
The bearer of bad tidings of worfe pain :
What then has happen'd ?
Chillindrina.
Julia . . . .
Eufebio.
Not in vain
My boding forrows whifper'd from
within,—
If thou haft evil news, with Julia thou'lt
begin :
Saidft thou not Julia ? more thou need'ft
not add,
For that is quite enough to make me
fad.
Accursèd be the baneful ftar above her
That forces me to love her !
Julia in fine . . . . proceed.
Chillindrina.
Is by her friends
Placed in a convent.

Eufebio.
 ¡ Ya falta el fufrimiento !
¡ Que el cielo me caftigue
Con tan grandes venganzas
De perdidos defeos,
De muertas efperanzas,
Que de los mifmos cielos,
Por quien me deja, vengo á tener zelos !
Mas ya tan atrevido,
Que viviendo matando,
Me fuftento robando,
No puedo fer peor de lo que he fido :
Defpéñefe el intento,
Pues ya fe ha defpeñado el penfamiento.
Llama á Celio y Ricardo. (Amando
 muero !)

Chilindrina.
Voy por ellos.   [*Vafe.*
  Eufebio.
 Ve, y diles, que aqui efpero.—
Afaltaré el convento que la guarda.
Ningun grave caftigo me acobarda ;
Que por verme feñor de fu hermofura,
Tirano amor me fuerza
A acometer la fuerza,
A romper la claufura,
Y á violar el fagrado ;
Que ya del todo eftoy defefperado.
Pues fi no me pufiera
Amor en tales puntos,
Solamente lo hiciera
Por cometer tantos delitos juntos.

Eufebio.
 My endurance ends !
Oh ! that Heaven fhould have decreed
Its vengeful bolts to launch at me fo
 faft !
My loft defires—
My hopes all paft—
And now the heaven fhe leaves me for
 requires
I fhould be jealous even of heaven at
 laft.
But fo bold am I, fo changed my mien,
Who in murder can difport me,
Who by robbing can fupport me,
Worfe I cannot be than I have been.
Let then the daring deed be wrought,
In fact, fince I have dared it in my
 thought :
Call Celio and Ricardo. (Ah ! love
 leads me to my bier !)
  Chillindrina.
I go to call them.   [*Exit.*
  Eufebio.
 Go, and fay I wait them here.—
I fhall fcale the convent that doth hold her,
No fear fhall fright me, till thefe arms
 enfold her ;
Since to fee me mafter of her charms
Tyrant love's tumultuous courfe
Forces me to truft to force ;
To fill her cloifter with alarms,
To violate a confecrated place,
Since defperate have I grown and loft
 to every grace ;
Though if love that brings me to it
Were not enough to make this deed be
 done,
I for this alone would do it, [in one.
That all poffible crimes I might commit

Salen GIL *y* MENGA.

Menga.

¡ Mas que encontramos con él,
Segun mezquina nací!

Gil.

¿ Menga, yo no voy aqui?
No temas efe cruel
Capitan de buñuleros,
Ni el hallarlo te alborote,
Que honda llevo yo, y garrote.

Menga.

Temo, Gil, fus hechos fieros ;
Si no, á Silvia á mirar ponte,
Cuando aqui la acometió ;
Que doncella al monte entró,
Y dueña falió del monte,
Que no es peligro pequeño.

Gil.

Conmigo fuera cruel,
Que tambien entro doncel,
Y pudiera falir dueño.

[*Reparan en* EUSEBIO.

Menga.

¡ Ah feñor ! que va perdido,
Que anda Eufebio por aqui.

Gil.

No eche, feñor, por ahí.

Eufebio (aparte).

Eftos no me han conocido,
Y quiero difimular.

Gil.

¿ Quiere que aquefe ladron
Le mate ?

Eufebio (aparte).

Villanos fon.——

¿ Con qué podré yo pagar
Efte avifo ?

Enter GIL *and* MENGA.

Menga.

But if we fhould meet him here !
Born to all bad luck am I !

Gil.

Don't you fee that I am by,
Menga mine ? So do not fear
This bold captain of banditti,
This cantankerous curmudgeon,
While I carry fling and bludgeon.

Menga.

Ah ! I fear, and more's the pity,
Left, like Silvia, fuch another
Trick in my cafe fhould be play'd,
Who to the mountain came a maid,
And went out of the mount a mother;
'Tis no trifling rifk to run.

Gil.

Mine will be the danger rather
To come out, perchance, a father,
Having gone in but a fon.

[*They perceive* EUSEBIO.

Menga.

Ah ! fir, you are loft ! this fpot
Is Eufebio's haunt, they fay.

Gil.

Do not venture, fir, that way.

Eufebio (afide).

It is plain they know me not:
I'll diffemble in their prefence.

Gil.

Would you have the robber flay you ?
Stop, fir !

Eufebio.

How can I repay you
[*afide.*
For this good advice ? (But peafants
Are they).

Gil.
    Con huir.
De ese bellaco.
     Menga.
         Si os coge,
Señor, aunque no le enoje
Ni vuestro hacer, ni decir,
Luego os matará; y creed,
Que con poner, tras la ofensa,
Una Cruz encima, piensa,
Que os hace mucha merced.

    Salen Ricardo *y* Celio.

     Ricardo.
¿Dónde le dejaste?
     Celio.
        Aqui.
     Gil.
Es un ladron, no le esperes.
     Ricardo.
Eusebio, ¿qué es lo que quieres?
     Gil.
¿Eusebio le llamó?
     Menga.
       Sí.
     Eusebio.
Yo soy Eusebio; ¿qué os mueve
Contra mí? ¿No hay quien responda?
     Menga.
Gil, ¿tienes garrote y honda?
     Gil.
Tengo el diabro que te lleve.
     Celio.
Por los apacibles llanos,
Que hace del monte la falda,
A quien guarda el mar la espalda,
Ví un escuadron de villanos,
Que armado contra tí viene,
Y pienso que se avecina;

Gil.
    Just by simply flying
From the rascal.
     Menga.
        If he catch you,
In a moment he'll dispatch you,
Though you ne'er, his temper trying,
Wrong'd him, or provoked his slaver
By a word or deed. When dead
He'll a cross place at your head,
Thinking he confers a favour.

    Enter Ricardo *and* Celio.

     Ricardo.
Here you left him?
     Celio.
        Here, I say.
     Gil (to Eusebio).
Quick! don't wait the robber, go!
     Ricardo.
What's your wish, Eusebio!
     Gil.
Eusebio did he call him?
     Menga.
        Yea.
     Eusebio.
That's my name: what ails you? pooh!
In a moment why so still?
     Menga.
Where's the sling and bludgeon, Gil?
     Gil.
Where's the devil except in you?
     Celio.
Where the peaceful vales expand
At this mountain's foot, that swelleth
O'er the sea which it expelleth,
I have seen a shepherd band
Coming in a well-arm'd crowd,
Seeking thee, nor long it tarries,

Que aſi Curcio determina
La venganza que previene.
Mira qué pienſas hacer;
Junta tu gente, y partamos.
       Euſebio.
Mejor es que ahora huyamos;
Que eſta noche hay mas que hacer.
Venid conmigo los dos,
De quien juſtamente fio
La opinion y el honor mio.
       Ricardo.
Muy bien puedes; que por Dios,
Que he de morir á tu lado.
       Euſebio.
Villanos, vida teneis,
Solo porque le lleveis
A mi enemigo un recado.
Decid á Curcio, que yo
Con tanta gente atrevida
Solo defiendo la vida,
Pero que le buſco no.
Y que no tiene ocaſion
De buſcarme deſta ſuerte,
Pues no dí á Liſardo muerte
Con engaño, ó con traicion.
Cuerpo á cuerpo le maté,
Sin ventaja conocida,
Y antes de acabar la vida
En mis brazos le llevé
Adonde ſe confeſó,
Digna accion para eſtimarſe;
Mas que ſi quiere vengarſe,
Que he de defenderme yo.——
       [*A los Bandoleros.*
Y ahora, porque no vean
Aqueſtos por donde vamos,
Atadlos entre eſtos ramos:
Vendados ſus ojos ſean,
Porque no aviſen.

Since 'tis here: thus Curcio carries
Out the vengeance he hath vow'd.
Think now what is beſt to do,
Summon all the troop and try . . . .
       Euſebio.
It is beſt that now we fly,
Since to-night there's much to do.
Come with me, ye two, whom I
With a confidence ſo juſt
Honour and my fame entruſt.
       Ricardo.
So you may, for we would die
At your ſide our zeal to ſhow.
       Euſebio.
Peaſants, know I let you live
But for this, that you may give
A brief meſſage to my foe;
This from me to Curcio ſpeak:—
With the brave bands that attend me
I will for my life defend me;
But that his I do not ſeek.
And that he hath got no reaſon
For purſuing me in this way,
Since if I his ſon did ſlay
'Twas not foully or by treaſon;
Arm'd as he I ſtood before him,
Vantage none on either ſide.
True, he fell, but, ere he died,
In theſe very arms I bore him
Where his ſins he might confeſs,
Act more worthy praiſe than blame;
But if vengeance be his aim,
I'll defend me ne'ertheleſs.
       [*To the Robbers.*
Now that theſe two may not ſee
By what road our troop is wending,
Tie them to theſe boughs here bending;
Let their eyes, too, bandaged be,
That they may not tell aught.

Ricardo.

    Aqui
Hay cordel.
    Celio.
      Pues llega presto.
    Gil.
De San Sebastian me han puesto.
    Menga.
De San Sebastiana á mí.
Mas ate cuanto quisiere,
Señor, como no me mate.
    Gil.
Oye, señor, no me ate,
Y puto sea yo, si huyere.
Jura tú, Menga, tambien
Este mismo juramento.
    Celio.
Ya estan atados.
    Eusebio.
      Mi intento
Se va ejecutando bien ;
La noche amenaza obscura,
Tendiendo su negro velo.
Julia, aunque te guarde el cielo,
He de gozar tu hermosura.
    [*Vanse los Bandoleros, dejando á*
      GIL *y* MENGA *atados.*
    Gil.
¿ Quién habrá que ahora nos vea,
Menga, aunque caro nos cueste,
Que no diga, que es aqueste
Peralvillo de la aldea ?
    Menga.
Vete llegando hácia aqui,

Ricardo.

            Try
This good cord, 'twill do.
    Celio.
        Make fast then.
    Gil.
See me tied like Saint Sebastian !
    Menga.
Saint Sebastiana am I.
Tightly as you like, sir, tie,
Only don't quite crucify me.
    Gil.
Ah ! sir, listen, do not tie me,
And I'll swear I will not fly :
Menga, too, will swear pell-mell
All the oaths that you can mention.
    Celio.
Now they're fasten'd.
    Eusebio.
      My intention
Has been carried out right well.
Now night threatens, and its sooty
Veil draws o'er the face of even.
Julia, spite of hell or heaven,
Soon I shall possess thy beauty.
    [*The Bandits depart, leaving* GIL
      and MENGA *tied.*
    Gil.
Who that saw us to this willow
Tied here, Menga, wouldn't say,
Here's a pair condemn'd to-day
By the parish Peralvillo ?*
    Menga.
Gil, as I can't get near *you,*

---

* Peralvillo is the name of a small town near Ciudad-Rodrigo, where the archers of the Holy Brotherhood were accustomed to execute without trial all criminals found in the act of committing their offences. From this circumstance, very rapid justice in Spain went by the name of *La justice de Peralvillo.*—M. DAMAS-HINARD.

Perhaps " Lynch Law" would best express its meaning in English.—TR.

Gil; que yo no puedo andar.
     Gil.
Menga, venme á defatar,
Y te defataré á tí
Luego al punto.
     Menga.
         Ven primero
Tú, que ya eftás importuno.
     Gil.
¿ Es decir, que vendrá alguno ?
Pondré que falta un arriero,
Las tres ánades cantando,
Un caminante pidiendo,
Un eftudiante comiendo,
Una fantera rezando,
Hoy en aquefte camino,
Lo que á ninguno faltó :
Mas la culpa tengo yo.
     Una voz (dentro).
Hácia efta parte imagino
Que oigo voces ; llegad prefto.
     Gil.
Señor, en buena hora acuda
A defatar una duda
En que ha rato que eftoy puefto.
     Menga.
Si acafo bufcais, feñor,
Por el monte algun cordel,
Yo os puedo fervir con él.
     Gil.
Efte es mas gordo y mejor.
     Menga.
Yo, por fer muger, efpero
Remedio en las anfias mias.
     Gil.
No repare en cortesías,
Desáteme á mí primero.

You come here, now don't deny me.
     Gil.
Menga, come here and untie me,
And I'll then untie you too,
In a twinkling.
     Menga.
         Come you firft,
Since you are fo *hafty*, you know.
     Gil.
Come, come, anyone, high or low !
Would to God that at the worft
Some gay muleteer loud trolling
A light lilt, fome nun her pfalms,
Some poor fcholar afking alms,
Some foot-traveller flowly ftrolling,
Would but take this road to-day,
So that help may fail not wholly !—
Oh! my loofe tongue and my folly !
     A voice within.
It appears to me this way
Voices I can hear, quick! fee !
     Gil.
At a lucky time, Sir Traveller,
Have you come to be th'unraveller
Of this knotty point for me.
     Menga.
If you're feeking, fir, along
This wild road a rope to tie you,
I'm the one that can fupply you.
     Gil.
Mine is better and more ftrong.
     Menga.
As a woman, from my pains
I fhould firft deliver'd be.
     Gil.
Oh! a fig for courtefy !
Loofe me firft, fir, from my chains.

Salen Curcio, Octavio, Tirso, Bras,
    y soldados.

      Tirso.
Hácia aquesta parte suena
La voz.
      Gil.
    ¡ Qué te quemas !
      Tirso.
            Gil,
¿ Qué es esto ?
      Gil.
      El diabro es sútil ;
Desata, Tirso, y mi pena
Te diré despues.
      Curcio.
       ¿ Qué es esto ?
      Gil.
Venga en buen hora, señor,
A castigar un traidor.
      Curcio.
¿ Quién desta suerte os ha puesto ?
      Gil.
¿ Quién ? Eusebio, que en efeto
Dice : . . . . Pero ¿ qué se yo
Lo que dice ? El nos dejó
Aqui en semejante aprieto.
      Tirso.
No llores pues, que no ha estado
Hoy muy poco liberal
Contigo.
      Bras.
    No lo ha hecho mal,
Pues á Menga te ha dejado.
      Gil.
¡ Ay Tirso ! no lloro yo,

Enter Curcio, Octavio, Tirso, Bras,
    and others.

      Tirso.
From this place doth sound again
That same voice.
      Gil.
      You burn.*
      Tirso.
        How ? why ?
What's this, Gil ?
      Gil.
      The devil is sly :—
Loose me first, and I'll explain
All about it.
      Curcio.
      What's this ? say.
      Gil.
Sure you're sent, sir, by the skies
A vile traitor to chastise.
      Curcio.
Who has tied you in this way ?
      Gil.
Who ? Eusebio : and the scamp
Said . . . . but hang me ! if I know
What he said ; he left us, though,
Tied up tight here with the cramp.
      Tirso.
Well, don't cry ! 'twas well to find him
Act so generously, Gil,
Towards you to-day.
      Bras.
      He meant no ill,
Menga to have left behind him.
      Gil.
Ah ! I do not shed a tear,

---

* Gil, who it is to be recollected is the *gracioso* or buffoon of the drama, treats the advancing party as if they were playing the game of hide-and-seek, and makes use of the exclamation generally employed to attract or divert the attention of the seeker.—M. Damas-Hinard.

Porque piadofo no fue.
       Tirfo.
Pues ¿por qué lloras?
       Gil.
               ¿Por qué?
Porque á Menga me dejó:
La de Anton llevó, y al cabo
De feis, que no parecia,
Halló á fu muger un dia;
Hicimos un baile bravo
De hallazgo, y gaftó cien reales.

       Bras.
¿Bártolo no fe cafó
Con Catalina, y parió
A feis mefes no cabales?
Y andaba con gran placer
Diciendo: ¡Si tú le viefes!
Lo que otra hace en nueve mefes,
Hace en cinco mi muger.

       Tirfo.
Ello, no hay honra fegura.
       Curcio.
¿Que efto llegue á efcuchar yo
Defte tirano? ¿quién vió
Tan notable defventura?
       Menga.
Como deftruirle pienfa;
Que hafta las mifmas mugeres
Tomaremos, fi tú quieres,
Las armas para fu ofenfa.
       Gil.
Que aqui acude es lo mas cierto;
Y toda efta procefion
De Cruces que miras, fon,
Señor, por hombres que ha muerto.

Tirfo, for his illiberality.
       Tirfo.
Why then weep?
       Gil.
           For the fatality
Of his *leaving* her with me here.
Anton's bride when he took away,
Six days long fhe was out of our fight,
On the feventh fhe came to light;—
Oh! what a feaft we had that day
On the hundred reals fhe brought in
    her pocket!
       Bras.
Yes, and didn't Bartolo wed
Catalina, and wafn't fhe brought to bed
In fix months of a boy, and didn't he
    rock it,
Feeling the happieft man alive,
And telling his friends triumphantly, too,
What takes other women nine months
    to do
Mine is able to do in five?
       Tirfo.
Honour's nothing in his fight.
       Curcio.
Still am I condemn'd to hear
Of this villain's vile career?—
Oh! my wretched, wretched plight!
       Menga.
Think this monfter of feduction
How to capture, how to kill.
Even the women, if you will,
All will arm for his deftruction.
       Gil.
That we're on his track is plain,
For thefe croffes, far projected
O'er the horizon, are erected
O'er the men that he hath flain.

Octavio.
Es aqui lo mas secreto
De todo el monte.
     Curcio (aparte).
            Y aqui
Fue ¡cielos! donde yo vi
Aquel milagroso efeto
De inocencia y castidad,
Cuya beldad atrevido
Tantas veces he ofendido
Con dudas, siendo verdad
Un milagro tan patente.
     Octavio.
Señor, ¿qué nueva pasion
Causa tu imaginacion?
     Curcio.
Rigores, que el alma siente,
Son, Octavio; y mis enojos,
Para publicar mi mengua,
Como los niego á la lengua,
Me van saliendo á los ojos.
Haz, Octavio, que me deje
Solo esa gente que sigo,
Porque aqui de mí y conmigo
Hoy á los cielos me queje.
     Octavio.
Ea, soldados, despejad.
       Bras.
¿Qué decis?
        Tirso.
        ¿Qué pretendeis?
         Gil.
Despiojad,* ¿no lo entendeis?
Que nos vamos á espulgar.
    [*Vanse todos, menos* Curcio.
     Curcio.
¿A quién no habrá sucedido

Octavio.
'Tis the most secluded spot
Of the mountain.
     Curcio (aside).
          And 'twas here,
Heavens! I saw with awe and fear
That stupendous wonder wrought
By the power of two magicians—
Innocence and Chastity—
Beauteous guardian powers by me
Wrong'd so oft through vile suspicions
Of one fair as she was pure.
     Octavio.
Ah! sir, what new form of pain
Thus disturbs your mind again?
     Curcio.
'Tis a pain no time can cure;
'Tis a grief that *will* arise;
'Tis a pang whose hidden cause,
Though to tell the tongue may pause,
Must be spoken by the eyes.
Lead aside, O friend! the train
Of my followers; in this lonely
Spot, and to the high heavens only,
Of me, *to* me, would I plain.
     Octavio.
Lads, our leader rest allows ye.
       Bras.
How allows ye?
       Tirso.
       What's that, pray?
       Gil.
Don't you see, as plain as day,
That he says to us, Lads, all louse ye?*
    [*Exeunt all but* Curcio.
     Curcio.
Doth it happen not in sorrow,

---

* This coarse pleasantry of mistaking the word *despejad* for *despiojad* I have ventured to imitate.

Tal vez, lleno de pesares,
Descansar consigo á solas,
Por no descubrirse á nadie?
Yo á quien tantos pensamientos
A un tiempo afligen, que hacen
Con lágrimas y suspiros
Competencia al mar y al aire,
Compañero de mí mismo
En las mudas soledades,
Con la pension de mis bienes
Quiero divertir mis males.
Ni las aves, ni las fuentes
Sean testigos bastantes;
Que al fin las fuentes murmuran,
Y tienen lengua las aves.
No quiero mas compañía,
Que aquestos rústicos sauces;
Pues quien escucha, y no aprende,
Será fuerza que no hable.
Teatro este monte fue
Del suceso mas notable,
Que entre prodigios de zelos
Cuentan las antigüedades
De una inocente verdad.
Pero ¿ quién podrá librarse
De sospechas, en quien son
Mentirosas las verdades?
Muerte de amor son los zelos,
Que no perdonan á nadie,
Ni por humilde le dejan,
Ni le respetan por grave.
Aqui pues, donde yo digo,
Rosmira y yo . . . De acordarme,
No es mucho que el alma tiemble,
No es mucho que la voz falte;
Que no hay flor, que no me asombre,
No hay hoja, que no me espante,
No hay piedra, que no me admire,
Tronco, que no me acobarde,

When the heart is full of sadness,
That one seeketh self-communion
Rather than confide in any?
I, afflicted at one moment
By the numerous thoughts that wrack me,
With my sighing and my weeping
Rivalling the air and water,
I, companion of myself,
'Mid these wilds that no voice gladdens,
Seek to while away my sorrows,
Thinking of the joys departed.
I would have nor birds nor fountains
Witnesses of this self-parley,—
For in fine the fountains murmur,
And the birds have tongues that warble;
I would only be companion'd
By these rough and rustling alders:
For who hears and understands not
Cannot speak of aught that passes.
This wild mountain was the scene
Of a more surprising marvel
Than antiquity relateth,
All through jealousy's strange annals,
Of an innocent woman's truth.
Ah! but who can break the shackles
Of suspicions, which to truths
Give the very air of falseness?
Jealousy is the death of love.
No love lives while that plague lasteth,
Nor the lowly is pass'd over,
Nor the lofty left unblasted.
Here then, here, where I am speaking,
I Rosmira led . . . . What marvel
That the thought doth make me shudder,
That the memory makes me falter!
Since there's not a flower but frights me,
Not a leaf but makes me startle,
Not a stone I see but shocks me,
Not a tree-trunk but unmans me,

Peñafco, que no me oprima,
Monte, que no me amenace;
Porque todos fon teftigos
De una hazaña tan infame.
Saqué al fin la efpada, y ella,
Sin temerme y fin turbarfe,
Porque en riefgos de honor* nunca
" El inocente es cobarde:
Efpofo, dijo, detente;
No digo que no me mates,
Si es tu gufto, ¿porque yo
Cómo he de poder negarte
La mifma vida que es tuya?
Solo te pido, que antes
Me digas por lo que muero;
Y déjame que te abrace."
Yo la dije: " En tus entrañas,
Como la víbora, traes
A quien te ha de dar la muerte.
Indicio ha fido baftante
El parto infame que efperas:
Mas no le verás, que antes,
Dándote muerte, feré
Verdugo tuyo y de un ángel."
" Si acafo," me dijo entonces,
" Si acafo, efpofo, llegafte
A creer flaquezas mias,
Jufto ferá que me mates.
Mas á efta Cruz abrazada,
A efta que eftaba delante,
Profiguió, doy por teftigo,
De que no fupe agraviarte,
Ni ofenderte; que ella fola
Será jufto que me ampare."
Bien quifiera entonces yo,
Arrepentido, arrojarme
A fus pies, porque fe via
Su inocencia en fu femblante.

  * Hartzenbufch reads " *amor.*"

Not a rock but feems to crufh me,
Not a mountain but o'erhangs me;
Since they all have been fpectators
Of fo infamous an act here.
I my fword drew, and fhe fhowing
Fear nor trouble in her manner,
Since in rifks of love and honour
Innocence is ne'er faint-hearted,—
" Hold!" fhe faid, " oh! hold, my
  hufband!
'Tis not for my life I afk thee,
Take it, if thou fo art minded,
Since I can't refufe to grant thee
That which is thine own already;
What I afk thee for, is rather
To fay *why* I die, then let me
Die, but die in thy embraces."
I replied, " Within thy body,
Like the viper, thou doft carry
That which is thine own deftruction,
Proved enough by that unhappy
Birth of fhame that thou awaiteft;
But that birth fhall never happen,
For in killing thee my vengeance
Seals thine own fate and an angel's."
" If by any chance, my hufband,—
If by any chance," fhe anfwer'd,
" Thou my frailty canft believe in,
It is juft that thou fhouldft ftab me;
But I call this crofs to witnefs,"
(Then, as now, the one here planted),
" This that I embrace, that never
Have I thought to wrong or harm thee
In thine honour, and I truft me
To its faving power to guard me."
I would then have almoft wifh'd,
In repentance, to have caft me
At her feet, her innocence
Shining in her eyes' pure glances.

El que una traicion intenta
Antes mire lo que hace ;
Porque una vez declarado,
Aunque procure enmendarfe,
Por decir que tuvo caufa,
Lo ha de llevar adelante.
Yo pues, no porque dudaba
Ser la difculpa baftante,
Sino porque mi delito
Mas amparado quedafe,
El brazo levanté airado,
Tirando por varias partes
Mil heridas ; pero folo
Las ejecuté en el aire.
Por muerta al pie de la Cruz
Quedó, y queriendo efcaparme,
A cafa llegué, y halléla
Con mas belleza que fale
El alba, cuando en fus brazos
Nos prefenta el fol infante.
Ella en fus brazos tenia
A Julia, divina imágen
De hermofura y difcrecion :
(¿Qué gloria pudo igualarfe
A la mia?) que fu parto
Habia fido aquella tarde
Al mifmo pie de la Cruz ;
Y por divinas feñales,
Con que al mundo defcubria
Dios un milagro tan grande,
La niña que habia parido,
Dichofa con feñas tales,
Tenia en el pecho una Cruz,
Labrada de fuego y fangre.
Pero ¡ay! que tanta ventura
Templaba el que fe quedafe
Otra criatura en el monte ;
Que ella, entre penas tan graves,
Sintió haber parido dos ;

He who treachery meditateth
Well at firft fhould weigh the matter :
For if once it is outfpoken,
Though he'd have it countermanded,
From his having own'd a caufe,
To the clofe it muft be acted.
I then, not becaufe I thought her
Exculpation lefs than ample,
But becaufe fome palliation
Wifh'd I for my guilty madnefs,
Raifed my angry arm, inflicting,
In a wild and furious manner,
Many a death-wound; but I dealt them
Only on the air that parted :—
At the foot of the Crofs, for dead,
She remain'd, and I, diftracted,
Flying thence, went home, and found
  her
Lovelier than in golden gladnefs
When day dawns, and, in its arms
Bearing the infant fun, advances.
For within her arms fhe held
Julia, image and example
Of all heavenly grace and beauty ;
(Oh! what rapture could be balanced
Againft mine then!) the birth having
On that very evening happen'd
At the foot of that fame Crofs.
And for proofs divinely patent,
By whofe means would God difcover
To the world fo great a marvel,
On the new-born baby's bofom,
Happy to be thus fo mark'd there,
Was a Crofs of blood and fire
Work'd in wonderful enamel.
But, alas! what moderated
So much joy was, that an after
Child was left upon the mountain.
Since fhe, in her painful travail,

Y yo entonces . . . .

Sale Octavio.

Octavio.

                    Por el valle
Atraviesa un escuadron
De bandoleros; y antes
Que cierre la noche triste,
Será bien, señor, que bajes
A buscarlos, no obscurezca;
Porque ellos el monte saben,
Y nosotros no.

Curcio.

                    Pues junta
La gente vaya adelante;
Que no hay gloria para mí,
Hasta llegar á vengarme.   [*Vanse.*

Vista exterior de un Convento.

Salen Eusebio, Ricardo y Celio *con una
escala.*

Ricardo.

Llega con silencio, y pon
A esa parte las escalas.

Eusebio.

Icaro seré sin alas,
Sin fuego seré Faeton:
Escalar al sol intento,
Y si me quiere ayudar
La luz, tengo de pasar
Mas allá del firmamento.
Amor ser tirano enseña.—
En subiendo yo, quitad
Esa escala, y esperad,
Hasta que os haga una seña.
Quien subiendo se despeña,

Felt she had given birth to two.
And I then . . . .

Enter Octavio.

Octavio.

                    Along the valley
Winds its devious way a squadron
Of banditti; and, ere darkness
In the night's sad gloom enfolds it,
It were well, sir, that you hasten'd
Down to seek them, lest you lose them:
For they know the mountain-passes,
And we know them not.

Curcio.

                    Combined,
Let our people all advance then;
Since no rest can I enjoy
Till my heart's revenge is granted.
                              [*Exeunt.*

Outside a Convent at Night.

Enter Eusebio, Ricardo, *and* Celio
with a scaling-ladder.

Ricardo.

Silently tread; a little nigher:—
Here fix the ladder with the slings.

Eusebio.

Icarus I'll be without his wings,
Phaëton without his fire;
I intend to scale the sun,
If then I would have its light
Aid me in my daring flight;
Mount I must till heaven is won,—
Tyrant love, watch over all!—
When I enter, from the grating
Take the ladder, and be waiting
Hereabouts until I call.—
Though proud Phaëton may fall,

Suba hoy, y baje ofendido,
En cenizas convertido;
Que la pena del bajar,
No será parte á quitar
La gloria de haber fubido.

      Ricardo.
¿ Qué efperas ?

         Celio.

            Pues ¿ qué rigor
Tu altivo orgullo embaraza ?

      Eufebio.
¿ No veis como me amenaza
Un vivo fuego ?

      Ricardo.

         Señor,
Fantafmas fon del temor.

      Eufebio.
¿ Yo temor ?

      Celio.

Sube.

      Eufebio.

         Ya llego,
Aunque á tantos rayos ciego,
Por las llamas he de entrar ;
Que no lo podrá eftorbar
De todo el infierno el fuego.

        [Sube y entra.

      Celio.
Ya entró.

      Ricardo.

      Alguna fantasía
De fu mifmo horror fundada,
En la idea acreditada,
O alguna ilufion feria.

      Celio.
Quita la efcala.

      Ricardo.

        Hafta el dia
Aqui le hemos de efperar.

Dazzled by the light furprifing,
In his afhes agonifing,
Still the pain of falling down
Cannot take away the crown,
Or the glory of the rifing.

      Ricardo.
What delays thee ?

      Celio.

         Say, what here
Can impede thy haughty aim ?

      Eufebio.
Saw you not a living flame
Flafh before my eyes ?

      Ricardo.

         A mere
Phantafy it was of fear.

      Eufebio.
I to fear ?

      Celio.

      Then up !

      Eufebio.

         Although
Lightnings blind me, I fhall go :
Through the very flames I'll enter ;
Powerlefs now as a preventer
Were the infernal fire below.

      [He afcends and enters.

      Celio.
Now he's in.

      Ricardo.

      Some phantafy
On its in-born horror founded—
Of ideal fears compounded,—
Some illufion it muft be.

      Celio.
Take the ladder down.

      Ricardo.

        Here we
Muft remain till morning's prime.

Celio.
Atrevimiento fue entrar,
Aunque yo de mejor gana
Me fuera con mi villana ;
Mas defpues habrá lugar.   [*Vanfe.*

CELDA DE JULIA.

Sale EUSEBIO.

Eufebio.
Por todo el convento he andado
Sin fer de nadie fentido,
Y por cuanto he difcurrido,
De mi deftino guiado,
A mil celdas he llegado
De religiofas, que abiertas
Tienen las eftrechas puertas,
Y en ninguna á Julia ví.
¿ Dónde me llevais afi,
Efperanzas fiempre inciertas ?
¡ Qué horror ! ¡ qué filencio mudo !
¡ Qué obfcuridad tan funefta !
Luz hay aqui ; celda es efta,
Y en ella Julia.   ¿ Qué dudo ?
    [*Corre una cortina, y ve á* JULIA
        durmiendo.
¿ Tan poco el valor ayudo,
Que ahora en hablarla tardo ?
Qué es lo que efpero ? qué aguardo ?
Mas con impulfo dudofo,
Si me animo temerofo,
Animofo me acobardo.
Mas belleza la humildad
Defte trage la afegura ;
Que en la muger la hermofura
Es la mifma honeftidad.
Su peregrina beldad,
De mi torpe amor objeto,

Celio.
'Twas a daring thing to climb,—
Though the hours I'd rather pafs
With my own dear village lafs,—
Better luck another time !   [*Exeunt.*

THE CORRIDOR OUTSIDE THE CELL
OF JULIA.

Enter EUSEBIO.

Eufebio.
All through the convent I have glided
Unperceived by any mortal,
And my path through porch and portal
By my deftiny feems guided.
To a thoufand cells, divided
By their narrow open doors,
Have I come on the corridors,
And have Julia feen in none.
Whither would ye lead me on,
Hopes that feek but phantom fhores ?
Oh ! what filent horror's here !
Oh ! what darknefs here doth dwell !
There's a light within this cell ;
Julia's in it !   Why this fear ?
    [*Draws a curtain, and* JULIA *is
        feen afleep.*
Does my courage difappear ?
Is't fo flight, that I delay
Now to advance ?   Why paufe ?   Why
    ftay ?
By an impulfe to and fro,
Trembling, I a boldnefs fhow,
Bold, a coward's heart betray.
Lovelier in the humblenefs
Of this drefs fhe feems to me,
For with women modefty
Is in itfelf a comelinefs.
Her furpafling lovelinefs,

Hace en mí mayor efeto ;
Que á un tiempo á mi amor incito
Con la hermofura apetito,
Con la honeftidad refpeto.
! Julia ! ¡ ah Julia !

Julia.
Quién me nombra ?
Mas ¡ cielos ! ¿ qué es lo que veo ?
¿ Eres fombra del defeo,
O del penfamiento fombra ?
Eufebio.
¿ Tanto el mirarme te afombra ?
Julia.
¿ Pues quién habrá que no intente
Huir de tí ?
Eufebio.
Julia, detente.
Julia.
¿ Qué quieres, forma fingida,
De la idea repetida,
Sola á la vifta aparente ?
¿ Eres, para pena mia,
Voz de la imaginacion ?
¿ Retrato de la ilufion ?
¿ Cuerpo de la fantasía ?
¿ Fantafma en la noche fria ?

Eufebio.
Julia, efcucha, Eufebio foy,
Que vivo á tus pies eftoy ;
Que fi el penfamiento fuera,
Siempre contigo eftuviera.
Julia.
Defengañándome voy
Con oirte, y confidero,
Que mi recato ofendido
Mas te quifiera fingido,
Eufebio, que verdadero,

Which I feek, unawed, uncheck'd,
Moves me with a twin effect ;
At one time it doth incite,
By its beauty, appetite,
By its modefty, refpect.
Julia ! Julia !
Julia (awaking).
Who doth call me ?—
But, O heavens ! what's this I fee ?
Art thou defire's dread phantafy ?
Art thou a dream that doth enthral me ?
Eufebio.
Does my prefence fo appal thee ?
Julia.
Who would not in dread difmay
Fly from thee ?
Eufebio.
Ah ! Julia, ftay !
Julia.
What's thy wifh, fictitious form,
Spectre that no life doth warm,
Sight-born fhape, what wouldft thou ?
fay.
Art thou, for my punifhment,
The expreffion of my thought ?
Image by illufion wrought ?
Phantafy's embodiment ?
Phantom on the cold night fent ?
Eufebio.
Thine Eufebio am I, fweet,
Living, lying at thy feet.
For if I thy thought could be,
I for ever were with thee.
Julia.
The delufion, the deceit,
Liftening thee, I'm labouring through,
And I think that my pride-pain'd
Honour would prefer the feign'd,
Falfe Eufebio, than the true,

Donde yo llorando muero,
Donde yo vivo penando.
¿Qué quieres? ¡estoy temblando!
¿Qué buscas? ¡estoy muriendo!
¿Qué emprendes? ¡estoy temiendo!
¿Qué intentas? ¡estoy dudando!
¿Cómo has llegado hasta aqui?

Eusebio.

Todo es extremos amor,
Y mi pena y tu rigor
Hoy han de triunfar de mí.
Hasta verte aqui, sufrí
Con esperanza segura ;
Pero viendo tu hermosura
Perdida, he atropellado
El respeto del sagrado,
Y la ley de la clausura.
De lo cierto, ó de lo injusto
Los dos la culpa tenemos,
Y en mí vienen dos extremos,
Que son la fuerza y el gusto.
No puede darle disgusto
Al cielo mi pretension ;
Antes desta ejecucion,
Casada eras en secreto,
Y no cabe en un sugeto
Matrimonio y religion.

Julia.

No niego el lazo amoroso,
Que hizo con felicidades
Unir á dos voluntades,
Que fue su efecto forzoso,
Que te llamé amado esposo ;
Y que todo eso fue así,
Confieso ; pero ya aqui,
Con voto de religiosa,
A Cristo de ser su esposa
Mano y palabra le dí.
Ya soy suya, ¿qué me quieres?

Here, where weeping I renew
Every day a living death.
What's your wish ? I gasp for breath !
What's your object ! Ah ! I die !
What's your aim ? an aspen I !
What's your end ? doubt answereth.
Here why have you dared to be ?

Eusebio.

'Tis but love's infensate daring,
Thy disdain and my despairing,
That have triumph'd over me.
Till I saw thee here, thy free
State my love with fond hopes fed ;
But, beholding thee as dead,
Lost to me, the cloister's law,
This asylum's sacred awe,
Have I crush'd beneath my tread.
Be the act unjust, or just,
We must bear the blame united.
By two powers am I incited—
Violence and pleasure's lust.
In the fight of Heaven disgust
My pretensions cannot rouse,
Since at heart thou wert my spouse
Ere thou cam'st this step to take,
And one tongue should never make
Marriage and monastic vows.

Julia.

I deny not the sweet bond
That in happiest unison
Join'd two separate wills in one ;
Nay, that, 'neath love's magic wand,
I bestow'd on thee the fond,
Sweet name of husband,—I confess
All this is true ; but ne'ertheless,
By a holier law invited,
Have I hand and promise plighted
Here to wear Christ's bridal dress ;
I am His : what wouldst thou ? Go !

Vete, porque el mundo afombres,
Donde mates á los hombres,
Donde fuerces las mugeres.
Vete, Eufebio; ya no efperes
Fruto de tu loco amor;
Para que te caufe horror,
Que eftoy en fagrado, pienfa.
   Eufebio.
Cuanto es mayor tu defenfa,
Es mi apetito mayor.
Ya las paredes falté
Del convento, ya te ví;
No es amor quien vive en mí,
Caufa mas oculta fue.
Cumple mi gufto, ó diré,
Que tú mifma me has llamado,
Que me has tenido encerrado
En tu celda muchos dias :
Y pues las defdichas mias
Me tienen defefperado,
Daré voces : Sepan . . . .
   Julia.
       Tente,
Eufebio, mira . . . . (¡ay de mí!)
Pafos fiento por aqui,
Al coro atraviefa gente.
¡ Cielos, no fé lo que intente !
Cierra efa celda, y en ella
Eftarás, pues atropella
Un temor á otro temor.
   Eufebio.
¡ Qué poderofo es mi amor !
   Julia.
¡ Qué rigurofa es mi eftrella ! [*Vanfe.*

Where with fear the world thou filleft,
Where unhappy men thou killeft,
Where thou work'ft weak women's woe.
Go ! nor hope, Eufebio,
Thy infenfate love's fruition,—
Think with horror and contrition
Of this facred place, and fly me.
   Eufebio.
Ah ! the more thou doft deny me,
Greater grows my love's ambition.
I have fcaled the walls, my way
Through the convent led to thee ;
Love no more impelleth me—
I fome fubtler law obey.
Grant my wifh, or I fhall fay,
That I came by thee here bidden ;
That thou here haft kept me hidden
In thy cell for many days ;
And, fince my misfortunes craze
This poor brain, defpairing, chidden,
I fhall cry out : Know . . . .
   Julia.
       Oh, ftay !
Hold, Eufebio ! . . . (woe is me !)
For the nuns' fteps, audibly,
To the choir approach this way.
Heavens ! I know not what to fay :—
Clofe the cell—the entrance bar—
Here remain : fince oft a far
Worfe fear doth a lefs remove.
   Eufebio.
Oh ! how powerful is my love !
   Julia.
Oh ! how rigorous is my ftar !
      [*Scene clofes.*

VISTA EXTERIOR DEL CONVENTO.

Salen RICARDO *y* CELIO.

Ricardo.
Ya fon las tres, mucho tarda.
Celio.
El que goza fu ventura,
Ricardo, en la noche obfcura,
Nunca el claro fol aguarda.
Yo apuefto que le parece,
Que nunca el fol madrugó
Tanto, y que hoy aprefuró
Su curfo.
Ricardo.
Siempre amanece
Mas temprano á quien defea,
Pero al que goza mas tarde.
Celio.
No creas, que al fol aguarde,
Que en el oriente fe vea.
Ricardo.
Dos horas fon ya.
Celio.
No creo,
Que Eufebio lo diga.
Ricardo.
Es jufto;
Porque al fin fon de fu gufto
Las horas de tu defeo.
Celio.
¿ No fabes lo que he llegado
Hoy, Ricardo, á fofpechar ?
Que Julia le envió á llamar.
Ricardo.
Pues fi no fuera llamado,
¿ Quién á efcalar fe atreviera
Un convento ?

OUTSIDE THE CONVENT.

Enter RICARDO *and* CELIO.

Ricardo.
'Tis three o'clock ; he tarries late.
Celio.
He for whom the dark night flies
With love's planet in its fkies,
Ne'er the fun's clear beams need wait.
I'll be bound, to him it feems
That the fun gets up to-day
Far too foon, his golden way
Thus foreftalling.
Ricardo.
Yes, it beams
Ever early for defire,
Ever late when love is bleft.
Celio.
Do not think, though, he will reft
In there till the eaft's on fire.
Ricardo.
Two hours gone.
Celio.
I would admire,
If he thinks fo.
Ricardo.
You are right,
For the hours of his delight
Are the hours of your defire.
Celio.
Do you know, that the fufpicion
I have form'd, Ricardo, is
'Tis the lady's wifh, not his ?
Ricardo.
If he had not got permiffion,
Who is there that thus would dare
Convent walls to fcale ?

Celio.
    ¿No has fentido,
Ricardo, á efta parte ruido?
    Ricardo.
Sí.
    Celio.
Pues llega la efcalera.

Salen por lo alto Julia *y* Eusebio.

    Eufebio.
Déjame, muger.
    Julia.
    ¿Pues cuando
Vencida de tus defeos,
Movida de tus fufpiros,
Obligada de tus ruegos,
De tu llanto agradecida,
Dos veces á Dios ofendo,
Como á Dios, y como á efpofo,
Mis brazos dejas, haciendo
Sin efperanzas defdenes,
Y fin pofefion defprecios?
¿Dónde vas?
    Eufebio.
    Muger, qué intentas?
Déjame, que voy huyendo
De tus brazos, porque he vifto
No fé qué deidad en ellos.
Llamas arrojan tus ojos,
Tus fufpiros fon de fuego,
Un volcan cada razon,
Un rayo cada cabello,
Cada palabra es mi muerte,
Cada regalo un infierno:
Tantos temores me caufa
La Cruz, que he vifto en tu pecho;
Señal prodigiofa ha fido,
Y no permitan los cielos,

Celio.
    Doft hear
Sounds, Ricardo, drawing near?
    Ricardo.
Yes.
    Celio.
Then place the ladder there.

Julia *and* Eusebio *appear at the window.*
    Eufebio.
Leave me, woman.
    Julia.
    How? when I,
By thy fond defirings conquer'd,
Moved to pity by thy fighings,
By thy warm entreaties foften'd,
Doubly have difpleafed the Godhead,
As my God and my efpoufed;
Flying from thefe arms that lock'd thee,
Doft thou without hope difdain me,
And without poffeffion fcorn me?
Whither goeft thou?

    Eufebio.
    Woman, leave me,
For I fly thofe arms that fold me,
Having feen but now within them
Some, I know not what, God's token;
In each glance a flame is darted,
In each figh a fire outbloweth,
A volcano every accent,
Lightning every fair trefs golden,
In each word my death is mutter'd,
At each fond carefs hell opens;
So much fear that Crofs hath caufed me
Which thy breaft reveal'd and fhow'd
    me:
Sign prodigious! facred fymbol!

Que, aunque tanto los ofenda,
Pierda á la Cruz el refpeto.
Pues fi la hago teftigo
De las culpas que cometo,
¿ Con qué vergüenza defpues
Llamarla en mi ayuda puedo ?
Quédate en tu religion,
Julia, yo no te defprecio,
Que mas ahora te adoro.

Julia.
Efcucha, detente, Eufebio.
        Eufebio.
Efta es la efcala.
        Julia.
              Detente,
O llévame allá.
        Eufebio.
              No puedo, [*Baja.*
Pues que, fin gozar la gloria
Que tanto efperé, te dejo.
Válgame el cielo ! caí.   [*Cae.*

        Ricardo.
Qué ha fido ?
        Eufebio.
              ¿ No veis el viento
Poblado de ardientes rayos ?
¿ No mirais fangriento el cielo,
Que todo fobre mí viene ?
¿ Dónde eftar feguro puedo,
Si airado el cielo fe mueftra ?
Divina Cruz, yo os prometo,
Y os hago folemne voto
Con cuantas cláufulas puedo,
De en cualquier parte que os vea,
Las rodillas por el fuelo,
Rezar un Ave Maria.

And the heavens allow me nowhere,
Though I fo offend, to fail in
Reverence for a fign fo holy.
Since if I a witnefs make it
Of the crimes I dare each moment,
With what fhame would I hereafter,
In my hour of need, invoke it ?
Stay, then, Julia, in religion ;
Ah ! indeed I do not fcorn thee,
I adore thee more than ever.
        Julia.
Oh ! Eufebio, hear me ! hold thee !
        Eufebio.
Here's the ladder.
        Julia.
              Oh ! remain,
Or elfe take me with you.
        Eufebio.
              Hopelefs [*He defcends.*
Is it ; no ; I leave thee here
With my fo long-figh'd-for glory
Unenjoy'd. But, heavens ! I fall.
                [*He falls.*
        Ricardo.
What has happen'd ?
        Eufebio.
              See you nowhere
Red bolts peopling all the night wind ?
Do you not behold the gory
Heavens that open to o'erwhelm me ?
Where can I be fafe, if o'er me
Heaven difplays its awful anger ?
Thee, O Crofs divine, I promife,
And a folemn vow I make thee,
With all ftrictnefs of devotement,
Wherefoe'er I fee thee ftanding,
Kneeling on the ground before thee,
To recite then a Hail Mary !

[*Levántase, y vanse los tres, de-*
jando la escala puesta.
Julia.

Turbada y confusa quedo.
¿ Aquetas fueron, ingrato,
Las firmezas ? ¿ Estos fueron
Los extremos de tu amor ?
¿ O son de mi amor extremos ?
Hasta vencerme á tu gusto,
Con amenazas, con ruegos,
Aqui amante, alli tirano,
Porfiaste ; pero luego
Que de tu gusto y mi pena
Pudiste llamarte dueño,
Antes de vencer huiste.
¿ Quién, sino tú, venció huyendo ?
¡ Muerta soy, cielos piadosos !
¿ Por qué introdujo venenos
Naturaleza, si habia,
Para dar muerte, desprecios ?
Ellos me quitan la vida ;
Pues que con nuevo tormento
Lo que me desprecia busco.
¿ Quién vió tan dudoso efecto
De amor ? Cuando me rogaba
Con mil lágrimas Eusebio,
Le dejaba ; pero ahora,
Porque él me deja, le ruego.
Tales somos las mugeres,
Que contra nuestros deseos,
Aun no queremos dar gusto
Con lo mismo que queremos.
Ninguno nos quiera bien,
Si pretende alcanzar premio ;
Que queridas despreciamos,
Y aborrecidas queremos.
No siento que no me quiera,
Solo que me deje siento.
Por aqui cayó, tras él

[*He arises, and the three go out, leav-*
ing the ladder in its place.
Julia (at the window).

In confusion I am lost here.
Was this then, O thou ungrateful !
Thy fix'd purpose ? This the whole,
  then,
Of thy love's excess ? Or is it
Mine own love's excess absorbs me ?
Till you conquer'd me to yield you
All your wish, by threats, by softness,
Now a lover, now a tyrant,
You persisted ; but, when wholly
Of your joy and of my sorrow
You could call yourself the owner,
You before the victory fled me ;
Who but you e'er fled that conquer'd ?
Ah ! I die ! ye pitying heavens !
Why has Nature's hand concocted
Poisons, when contempt she nurtures,
Which to kill is far more potent ?
It is *that* that takes my life :
Since, to add unto my torment,
That which shuns me I must seek.
Such effects of love, what mortal
Ever saw ? For when Eusebio
Ask'd me, in all forms of fondness,
Even with tears, I scorn'd him ; now
Him I ask, because he scorns me.
Such the nature of us women,
That against what most we covet,
We even would not wish to please
With what would delight our ownselves.
No one loves us well who seems
To over-value what he hopeth :
For when we are loved, we scorn,
When we're scorn'd, our love is strongest.
Me, his want of love moves not,
'Tis his leaving me that moves me.

Me arrojaré. ¿ Mas qué es esto ?
¿ Esta no es escala ? Sí.
¡ Qué terrible pensamiento !
Detente, imaginacion,
No me despeñes ; que creo,
Que si llego á consentir,
A hacer el delito llego.
¿ No saltó Eusebio por mí
Las paredes del convento ?
¿ No me holgué de verle yo
En tantos peligros puesto
Por mi causa ? ¿ pues qué dudo ?
¿ Qué me acobardo ? ¿ qué temo ?
Lo mismo haré yo en salir,
Que él en entrar ; si es lo mesmo,
Tambien se holgará de verme
Por su causa en tales riesgos.
Ya por haber consentido,
La misma culpa merezco ;
¿ Pues si es tan grande el pecado,
Por qué el gusto ha de ser menos ?
¿ Si consentí, y me dejó
Dios de su mano, no puedo
De una culpa, que es tan grande
Tener perdon ? ¿ pues qué espero ?
                [*Baja por la escala.*
Al mundo, al honor, á Dios
Hallo perdido el respeto,
Cuando á ceguedad tan grande
Vendados los ojos vuelvo.
Demonio soy que he caido
Despeñado deste cielo,
Pues sin tener esperanza
De subir, no me arrepiento.
Ya estoy fuera de sagrado,
Y de la noche el silencio
Con su obscuridad me tiene
Cubierta de horror y miedo.
Tan deslumbrada camino,

Here he fell, then after him
Shall I throw me.   But what holds
    here ?
Is not this the ladder ? Yes.
What a dreadful thought comes o'er me !
Stay, imagination, stay ;
Whelm me not, for faith has told me
That, when I consent in thought,
I commit the crime that moment.
Was it not for me Eusebio
Scaled the steep walls of my convent ?
Did I not feel pleased to see him
Running so much risk to show me
His regard ? Then what doth fright me ?
What doth cow me ? Why thus ponder ?
I will do the same in leaving,
As in entering, he ; if so then,
He too will be pleased to see me,
For his sake, like risks encounter.
By consenting, I already
With an equal guilt am loaded ;
If the sin has been committed,
Why not with the joy console me ?
If I've given consent, and God
Flings me from his hand, 'tis hopeless,
For a crime so great, to expect
Pardon ; then why wait ? What holds
    me ?   [*She descends the ladder.*
For the world, for God, for honour,
All respect I find I've lost here,
When I turn my hooded eyes
Round upon this darksome prospect ;
I'm a demon that has fallen
From this heaven serene and spotless,
Since, all hope being gone, to rise there
No repentant instinct prompts me.
I am out of sanctuary,
And the silent night involves me,
With its darkness, in a net-work

Que en las tinieblas tropiezo,
Y aun no caigo en mi pecado.
¿Dónde voy? ¿qué hago? ¿qué intento?
Con la muda confusion
De tantos horrores temo,
Que se me altera la sangre,
Que se me eriza el cabello.
Turbada la fantasía,
En el aire forma cuerpos,
Y sentencias contra mí
Pronuncia la voz del eco.
El delito, que antes era
Quien me animaba soberbio,
Es quien me acobarda ahora.
Apenas las plantas puedo
Mover, que el mismo temor
Grillos á mis pies ha puesto.
Sobre mis hombros parece
Que carga un prolijo peso,
Que me oprime, y toda yo
Estoy cubierta de hielo.
No quiero pasar de aqui,
Quiero volverme al convento,
Donde de aqueste pecado
Alcance perdon; pues creo
De la clemencia divina,
Que no hay luces en el cielo,
Que no hay en el mar arenas,
No hay átomos en el viento,
Que, sumados todos juntos,
No sean número pequeño
De los pecados que sabe
Dios perdonar.   Pasos siento,
A esta parte me retiro
En tanto que pasan; luego
Subiré, sin que me vean.

                       [Retirase.

Of intensest fear and horror.
So bereft of light I wander,
That, at every step I totter,
Stray from all things but my sin.
Whither go I? With what object?
I am fearful, in the silent
Throng of horrors that enfold me,
That my hair will stand on end soon,
That my heart's blood will be frozen.
On the air perturbèd fancy
Phantoms and strange spectres formeth;
And, in sentencing me, sounds
Echo's voice austere and solemn:
The offence, which was erewhile
That which so my pride embolden'd,
Makes a coward of me now.
I can scarcely move my footsteps,
Scarce can drag my feet, for fear
Hangs its heavy fetters on them.
An oppressive weight appears
To be placed upon my shoulders,
Which doth weigh me down; and I
All with ice am cover'd over.
No! I will not further go,
I will back unto my convent.
Where for this sin I may ask
Pardon, since such faith I foster
In the clemency divine,
That the stars that light heaven yonder,
That the sands upon the shore,
That the atoms of the mote-beams,
All together join'd, would be,
I believe, but a faint token
Of the number of the sins
God can pardon.—Steps approach here!
I shall to this side retire
Until they have pass'd and gone hence;
Then I shall ascend unseen.

                       [Retires.

Salen RICARDO *y* CELIO.

Ricardo.

Con el efpanto de Eufebio
Aqui fe quedó la efcala,
Y ahora por ella vuelvo,
No aclare el dia, y la vean
A efta pared.

[*Quitan la efcala y vanfe, y* JULIA
llega donde eftaba la efcala.

Julia.

Ya fe fueron ;
Ahora podré fubir,
Sin que me fientan.   Qué es efto ?
¿ No es aquefta la pared
De la efcala ? Pero creo,
Que hácia eftotra parte eftá.
Ni aqui tampoco eftá.   Cielos !
¿ Cómo he de fubir fin ella ?
Mas ya mi defdicha entiendo ;
Defta fuerte me negais
La entrada vueftra, pues creo,
Que, cuando quiero fubir
Arrepentida, no puedo.
Pues fi ya me habeis negado
Vueftra clemencia, mis hechos
De muger defefperada
Darán afombros al cielo,
Darán efpantos al mundo,
Admiracion á los tiempos,
Horror al mifmo pecado,
Y terror al mifmo infierno.

Enter RICARDO *and* CELIO.

Ricardo.

In Eufebio's fright, forgotten
Here the ladder has remain'd ;
And to take it, I now come here,
Left at dawn of day they fee it
On this wall.

[*Exeunt, taking the ladder.* JULIA
*returns to the place where it
ftood.*

Julia.

They've gone : now foftly,
Unperceived I may afcend.
How is this, though ? Is it not here,
In this part of the wall, the ladder
Stood this moment ? In this other
Place, I think, then it muft be :—
No, nor here 'tis.   Heavens above me !
How can I afcend without it ?
Ah ! I now know my misfortune ;
In this way you would all entrance
Bar againft me, fince it fhows me
That when I would wifh, repentant,
To afcend, the attempt were hopelefs.
Since then you have thus denied me
Your foft clemency, the bold deeds
Of a woman's defperation,
Shall the heavens fcare that behold
      them,
Make the world that fees them tremble,
Fill futurity with wonder,
Strike even fin itfelf with horror,
And fhock hell even to the loweft.

<table>
<tr><td>

JORNADA III.

MONTE.

Sale GIL *con muchas Cruces, y una*
muy grande al pecho.

Gil.

OR leña á este monte voy,
   Que Menga me lo ha man-
     dado,
   Y para ir seguro, he hallado
Una brava invencion hoy.
De la Cruz, dicen, que es
Devoto Eusebio; y así
He salido armado aqui
De la cabeza á los pies.
Dicho y hecho; ¡él es par diez!
No encuentro, lleno de miedo,
Donde estar seguro puedo;
Sin alma quedo.   Esta vez
No me ha visto, yo quisiera
Esconderme hácia este lado,
Mientras pasa; yo he tomado
Por guarda una cambronera
Para esconderme.   ¡No es nada!
Tanta pua es la mas chica:
¡Pléguete Cristo! mas pica,
Que perder una trocada,
Mas que sentir un desprecio
De una dama Fierabras,

</td><td>

ACT III.

A WILD FOREST IN THE MOUNTAIN.

Enter GIL, *having his dress covered*
with numerous Crosses, and with a
large one on his breast.

Gil.

HROUGH these wilds for
   wood I stray,
   Driven abroad by Menga's
     dunning;
So, to go secure, a cunning
Stratagem I've plann'd to-day.
This Eusebio is, I hear,
Still to the Cross devout, and so,
Thus all arm'd from top to toe,
Forth I venture without fear :—
Well and good.   He's there, by Jove!
Looking glum and this way striding,
And there's not a spot to hide in!
Oh! I cannot breathe or move!
But he sees me not, this thickly
Twisted thorn-bush here may screen
   me.
Oh! for something soft between me
And these sharp points bare and prickly!
Backwards, frontwards, under, over,
Where I stand the thorns are pricking,
Where I sit the thorns are sticking;
Ah! 'tis plain I'm not in clover,

</td></tr>
</table>

Que á todos admite, y mas
Que tener zelos de un necio.

Sale Eusebio.
    Eusebio.
No sé adonde podré ir;
Larga vida un triste tiene,
Que nunca la muerte viene
A quien le cansa el vivir.
Julia, yo me ví en tus brazos;
Cuando tan dichoso era,
Que de tus brazos pudiera
Hacer amor nuevos lazos.
Sin gozar al fin dejé
La gloria que no tenia;
Mas no fue la causa mia,
Causa mas secreta fue;
Pues teniendo mi albedrío,
Superior efecto ha hecho,
Que yo respete en tu pecho
La Cruz que tengo en el mio.
Y pues con ella los dos,
¡ Ay Julia! habemos nacido,
Secreto misterio ha sido,
Que lo entiende solo Dios.

    Gil (aparte).
Mucho pica, ya no puedo
Mas sufrillo.
      Eusebio.
      Entre estos ramos
Hay gente. ¿ Quién va?
      Gil.
      Aqui echamos
A perder todo el enredo.

Though the grass is thick about me.
Better bear with conscience gnawing,
Better bear a fool's hee-hawing,
Or a scolding woman flout me.
      [Conceals himself.

Enter Eusebio.
    Eusebio.
Still my days are dark and dreary,
Still along life's road I go,
Careless whither, death is slow
Only to the life-aweary.
Julia, O, my hoped-for wife!
When within thy arms I found me,
Then might love have twined around
    me
Garlands new to deck my life;
But the glory I repell'd,
Fled the untasted joy I sought,
Not through mine own strength me-
    thought,
No, some secret force compell'd,
Since my will I could resign
To that mightier power protecting,
On thy beauteous breast respecting
That same Cross that's stamp'd on mine.
Then, since Heaven was pleased to send
Thee and me thus sign'd to earth,
Some strange mystery marks our birth
God alone doth comprehend.
    Gil (aside).
Ah! I'm prick'd in every joint;
More I can't endure!
      Eusebio.
      Quite near
Sounds a voice:—Who's there?
      Gil.
      I'm here,
Quite made up on every point.

Eusebio (aparte).
Un hombre á un árbol atado,
Y una Cruz al cuello tiene;
Cumplir mi voto conviene
En el suelo arrodillado.

Gil.
¿ A quién, Eusebio, enderezas
La oracion, ú de qué tratas?
Si me adoras, ¿ qué me atas ?
Si me atas, ¿ qué me rezas?
            Eusebio.
¿ Quién es ?
            Gil.
            ¿ A Gil no conoces ?
Desde que con el recado
Aqui me dejaste atado,
No han aprovechado voces
Para que alguien (¡ qué rigor !)
Me llegase á desatar.
            Eusebio.
Pues no es aqueste el lugar
Donde te dejé.
            Gil.
            Señor,
Es verdad ; mas yo que ví
Que nadie llegaba, he andado,
De árbol en árbol atado,
Hasta haber llegado aqui.
Aquesta la causa fue
De suceso tan extraño.
            Eusebio (aparte).
Este es simple, y de mi daño
Cualquier suceso sabré.—
Gil, yo te tengo aficion,
Desde que otra vez hablamos,
Y aqui quiero que seamos
Amigos.

Eusebio (aside).
Ah ! a man to a tree is bound,
On his breast's a Cross, I now
Must fulfil my solemn vow,
Humbly kneeling on the ground.
                        [*Kneels.*
Gil.
Who, sir, do you kneel before ?
Do you mean to deify me ?
If you adore me, why do you tie me ?
If you tie me, why adore ?
            Eusebio.
Say, who *are* you ?
            Gil.
                        Not know Gil ?
Since the time you left me tied here
With the message, I have cried here
Without stint, out loud and shrill,
That some kind hand from this cord
Would release me.   (What a case !)
            Eusebio.
But then this is not the place
That I left you in.
            Gil.
                        My lord,
That is true ; but when 'twas clear
None would come, it seem'd to me
Best, thus tied, from tree to tree
On to glide, till I came here.
That's the simple explanation
Of so strange a circumstance.
            Eusebio (aside).
Through this simpleton perchance
I may get some information
Of my loss.—Gil, I was quite
Taken with your worth when we
Last time met, so let us be
Friends henceforth.

Gil.
Tiene razon;
Y quifiera, pues nos vemos
Tan amigos, no ir allá,
Sino andarme por acá,
Pues aqui todos feremos
Buñoleros, que diz que es
Holgada vida, y no andar
Todo el año á trabajar.
Eufebio.
Quédate conmigo pues.

Salen Ricardo *y* Bandoleros, *y traen
á* Julia *veftida de hombre y cubierto
el roftro.* [**Salen* Ricardo, *y*
Julia, *de hombre; un* Pintor, *un*
Poeta, *y un* Astrologo.†]

Ricardo.
En lo bajo del camino,
Que efta montaña atraviefa,
Ahora hicimos una prefa,
Que fegun es, imagino,
Que te dé gufto.
Eufebio.
                    Eftá bien,
Luego della trataremos.

Gil.
You fay quite right;—
And I'd wifh, fince friendfhip's tether
Binds us fo, to go not near
My old cabin, but ftay here
Bundoleering all together.
'Tis a pleafant life, they fay,
Not a ftroke of work or bother
From one year's end to the other.
Eufebio.
Then with me you here may ftay.

Enter Ricardo *and the other brigands,
leading in* Julia, *dreffed in man's
clothes, and having her face covered.*
[**Enter* Ricardo, *and* Julia *as a man;
a* Poet, *a* Painter, *and an* Astro-
loger.†]

Ricardo.
On the road that 'neath heaven's cope
O'er this rugged mountain rifes,
We to-day have made fome prizes
Of fuch value that I hope
They may pleafe you.
Eufebio.
                    Right, we'll fee
Soon to that, but now behold

---

* Commencement of the fcene in the edition of Huefca.

† As mentioned in the introduction to this drama, *La Devocion de la Cruz* was firft publifhed in the *Parte Veinte y Ocho de Comedias de Varios Autores* (Huefca 1634), under the title of *La Cruz en la Sepultura*, and as the work of Lope de Vega. Señor Hartzenbufch mentions that this, the earlieft impreffion, exhibits many variations from the received text, which are of greater or leffer importance. In this place an entirely new fcene is introduced, which is not to be found in the edition of Vera Taffis or in the later editions. This fcene he prints in the notes to his Calderon. It was probably omitted from the acted play, as needlefsly breaking the continuity of the plot. Though flightly imperfect, it is fufficiently curious to be preferved, and I have therefore introduced it [between brackets] into the text both of the original and tranflation. Señor Hartzenbufch alfo prints the portion of this fcene (in the edition of Huefca), which is nearly the fame as that in the later editions. A few of the verbal differences that exift between them, I have drawn attention to below.—See Hartzenbufch's "Calderon," *Notas y Iluftraciones,* t. iv. p. 701.

Sabe ahora, que tenemos
Un nuevo soldado.
>> *Ricardo.*
>>> ¿ Quién ?
>> *Gil.*
Gil ; ¿ no me ve ?
>> *Eusebio.*
>>> Este villano,
Aunque le veis inocente,
Conoce notablemente
Desta tierra monte y llano,
Y en él será nuestra guia :
Fuera desto, al campo irá
Del enemigo, y será
En él mi perdida espía.
Arcabuz le podeis dar,
Y un vestido.
>> *Celio.**
>>> Ya está aqui.
>> *Gil.*
Tengan lástima de mí,
Que me quedo á embandolear.†
>> [*Eusebio.*
¿ Quien eres tu ?
>> *Pintor.*
>>> Yo, señor,
Soy de nacion jinoves ;
A Florencia paso, y es
Mi ejercicio el de pintor.
Llevo a Celio Batistela,
Un florentin poderoso,
Aqueste retrato hermoso,
Que es de Madama Florela ;
Que el me mandó que lo hiciese.
>> *Eusebio.*
Muestra, a ver. ¡ Hermosa dama !
¿ Como dice qui ? *Madama*

A new comrade, just enroll'd
In our gallant troop.
>> *Ricardo.*
>>> Who's he ?
>> *Gil.*
Don't you see me ? Gil.
>> *Eusebio.*
>>> This swain,
Though so innocent appearing,
Knows each natural bound and mearing
Of this land here, hill and plain ;
He will be our guide by-and-by
Through it, nay, he will repair
To the enemy's camp, and there
Act the desperate part of spy.—
Give him then an arquebuss,
And a soldier's dress.
>> *Celio.**
>>> They're here.
>> *Gil.*
Woe the day that I appear
Robber-raw-recruited thus !
>> [*Eusebio.*
Who art thou ?
>> *Painter.*
>>> Sir, my confession
I can make to you with ease :—
I'm by birth a Genoese,
And a painter by profession.
I to Celio Batistela,
Of Florence, this fine picture bear
Of a lady young and fair,
Call'd Madama la Florela,
By him order'd, to him sold.
>> *Eusebio.*
Let me see it.   A fair dame
Truly ! but why write her name

---

* " *Ricardo.*"   Huesca Edition.

† " *á bandolear.*"   Huesca Edition.

Florela.

       Gil.
      Oye : el cuento es efe
De un pintor que hizo un retrato
De un gato ; y porque fupiefe
De quien era quien le viefe,
Pufo abajo : " Aquefte es gato."
      Pintor.
No es defeto en la pintura
Traer efcrito fu nombre ;
Que nadie habra a quien no afombre
Efta imitada figura.
Y yo foy el que pintar
Enfeño los naturales
Arboles y frutas, tales
Que fe pueden admirar
Los hombres ; pues cuando imito
La variedad, y la veo
Queda fin hambre el defeo,
Sin defeo el apetito.
      Eufebio.
Si en ti perfecion tan bella
Ha alcanzado la pintura,
Gran genero de locura
Es no aprovecharte della,
Atalde aqui ; y fi mirare
La variedad de las flores,
Dadle paleta y colores ;
Coma de lo que pintare.
      Ricardo.
Vamos.
      Gil.
      Llevad de camino
Aquefta epigrama brava
Que   *   *   *   *
Hizo un ingenio divino,—
" Galanes, damas hermofas,
Baratas fueles vender,
Saliendo de tu poder

'Neath it ?

      Gil.
      Lift ! a tale doth run
Of a painter to whom fat
For her picture Pufs : below her,
So that every one might know her,
He infcribed, " This is a cat."
      Painter.
No defect is't in a painting
That it fhould its own name bear ;
Here's a figure, howfoe'er,
One can gaze at without fainting.
I am he who taught the art
Of depicting fruits and trees
After Nature : they fo pleafe
Thofe that fee them, that they ftart,
Wondering at them.   My own fight,
Feeding on their fair variety,
Makes me furfeit to fatiety,
Takes the edge off appetite.
      Eufebio.
If to fuch extreme perfection
Painting hath progrefs'd with thee,
'Tis a great abfurdity
Not to ufe it for refection.
Tie him there : no fear he faints,
Flowers to him are like a falad ;
Give him fome colours and a pallet,
Let him eat of what he paints.
      Ricardo.
Let us go.
      Gil.
      And on the way,
Take with you this clever epigram,
Which   *   *   *   *
A great genius made one day :—
" Fabio, a many an hour,
To gallants and ladies fair,
Things you fell, nor rich nor rare

Eſtas y otras muchas coſas.
Fabio, con mano no eſcaſa
Pon tu mujer en la tienda,
Que aunque mil veces ſe venda
Siempre ſe te queda en caſa."
    Euſebio.
Tu, ¿ quien eres ?
    Aſtrologo.
        Señor, ſoy
Aſtrologo.
    Euſebio.
    Buen oficio.
    Aſtrologo.
Aunque ſe tiene por vicio ;
Pero ahora a Francia voy
A enſeñar aſtrologia.
    Euſebio.
¿ Y tu la ſabes ?
    Aſtrologo.
        Yo he ſido
Quien los paſos ha medido
Al ſol que ilumina el dia.
    Euſebio.
Si pudo tu ciencia ver
Tanto, ¿ por que no previno
Lo que en aqueſte camino
Te habia de ſuceder ?
    Aſtrologo.
Ya tenia yo mirado
Que en el camino que ſigo
Habia de topar contigo.
    Euſebio.
Pues dime que has alcanzado
De lo que he de hacer aqui.
    Aſtrologo.
Ya he viſto en efetos llanos
Que he de morir a tus manos.
    Euſebio.
Vete libre, porque aſi

Which muſt paſs from out your power.
Put into your ſhop your ſpouſe,—
Wondrous then will grow your pelf,
Since, though oft ſhe ſells herſelf,
Still ſhe never leaves your houſe.
    Euſebio.
Thou, who art thou ?
    Aſtrologer.
        Sir, I am
An aſtrologer.
    Euſebio.
    A good employment.
    Aſtrologer.
Yes, it's not without enjoyment:
I am going to France to cram
Pupils in the ſtarry art.
    Euſebio.
And you know it ?
    Aſtrologer.
        I am one
Who hath track'd the path of the ſun
Through the heavens as on a chart.
    Euſebio.
If your viſion is ſo clear,
Why did you foreſee not, ſay,
As you journey'd on your way,
What would happen to you here ?
    Aſtrologer.
Nought of that, ſir, was conceal'd,
For I knew by deſtiny
I was doom'd to meet with thee.
    Euſebio.
Tell me what has been reveal'd
Of thy fate here now with me.
    Aſtrologer.
I have learn'd my fate commands
That I periſh by thy hands.
    Euſebio.
Then, to prove fate wrong, go free.

Conozcas de tu ignorancia
El error, que defde el fuelo
No fe ha de medir el cielo,
Que es infinita diftancia.
            Gil.
Efcúcheme.   A un licenciado
En eftrellas, mató un dia
Una beftia : afi decia
Adonde eftaba enterrado :
" Yace un aftrólogo, cuya
Ciencia a todos anunciaba
La fuerte, y nunca acertaba
A pronofticar la fuya.
Un cadáver vió en cenizas
Su cadáver : que defvelo
Tal entender pudo el cielo
Mas no a las caballerizas."
            Eufebio.
¿Y tu ?
            Poeta.
       Efpanol ; mi ejercicio
Hacer verfos : foy poeta
En efeto ; que efta feta
Algunos la han hecho oficio.
            Eufebio.
Muchos he oido decir
Que ocupan aquefa parte.
            Gil.
Como fe efcriben fin arte,
Son fáciles de efcribir.
            Poeta.
¿ Que mas arte han de tener,
Señor, que haber de agradar
Entero á todo un lugar
Pues jueces vienen á fer
El difcreto, y ignorante,
Que juzgan fin atencion
De mirar a cuyos fon ;
Pues quieren que un principiante

Thus thou'lt know thine auguries
Are but error's monftrous birth,
Knowing little of the earth,
Knowing nothing of the fkies.
            Gil.
Hear me.   A licentiate, read
In all ftar-lore, by a horfe
Once was kill'd, and o'er the corfe
Where 'twas buried this was faid :—
" An aftrologer, o'erthrown
By his fteed, here lies : he told
Death-days round to young and old,
But could never tell his own.
The firft corfe (fo runs the fable)
That met *his* exclaim'd, ' My eyes !
You that underftood the fkies,
To know nothing of the ftable ! ' "
            Eufebio.
Thou art too . . . . ?
            Poet.
            A Spaniard : my
Bufinefs to write verfe ; in fact
I'm a poet : few can act
Better in that way than I.
            Eufebio.
There are many who, like you,
Try to play the poet's part.
            Gil.
Thofe who fcribble without art
Find it eafy work to do.
            Poet.
Why, what greater art can be
Than to tickle a whole town,
Pleafe the taftes of clerk and clown,
Since your judges they muft be—
Wife and foolifh, faint and finner,
Paffing fentence like omnifcience,
Heedlefs of their own deficience ;
Who require too a beginner

Tenga el mifmo eftilo y ciencia
Que un anciano, fin mirar
Que á efo fe han de aventajar
Ochenta años de experiencia ?
     Eufebio.
En tus razones fe ve
Que fiempre en vofotros lidia
Envidia y pafion.
     Poeta.
         Si envidia
Quien no tiene para qué
Dejen de envidiarme á mi.
     Eufebio.

*   *   *   *

Con irte vivo y dejarte.
     Gil.
Copla hay tambien para ti.
De la comedia es dudofo,
En fin : que indeterminado,
Lo que al ignorante agrado,
Canfa al fin al ingeniofo,
Bufca, Lifardo, otros modos,
Si fama quieres ganar ;
Que es dificil de cortar
Veftidos que venga á todos.]
     Eufebio.
¿ Quién es† efe gentil hombre,
Que el roftro encubre ?
     Ricardo.
         No ha fido
Pofible, que haya querido
Decir la patria, ni el nombre ;
Porque al Capitan no mas
Dice que lo ha de decir.

Should have the fame fkill and ftyle
Of one older in fuch matters,
Not reflecting on the latter's
Eighty years' ufe of the file ?
     Eufebio.
From your arguments 'tis feen
How for ever with you dwell
Spleen and envy.
     Poet.
         If to fwell
'Gainft injuftice be call'd fpleen,
I'm content it fo fhould be.
     Eufebio.

*   *   *   *

Go, I let thee live, be off!
     Gil.
Take this rhyme along with thee :—
Since, howe'er the poet tries,
Doubtful is his drama's fate,
For what may the crowd elate,
The judicious may defpife.
If you're feeking for fame's prizes,
Try fome method lefs remote,
For 'tis hard to cut a coat
That will fuit all forts of fizes.*]
     Eufebio.
Who's this gentleman, whofe aim
Is to hide his face ?
     Ricardo.
         In vain
Have we afk'd him to explain
What's his country or his name ;
To the captain of our band
Thefe he only will avow.

---

* " If this mutilated and erroneoufly attributed fragment," fays Señor Hartzenbufch, " is Calderon's, *The Devotion of the Crofs* muft be one of his earlieft dramas, written probably when he was a ftudent at Salamanca, where he remained till his nineteenth year."

† " *y quien es el gentil hombre,*" &c. Huefca Ed.

Eufebio.
Bien te puedes defcubrir,
Pues ya en mi prefencia eftás.*
    Julia.
¿ Sois el Capitan ?
    Eufebio.
        Sí.
    Julia (aparte).
          ¡ Ay Dios !
    Eufebio.
Dime quien eres, y á qué
Vínifte.
    Julia.
      Yo lo diré,
Eftando folos los dos.
    Eufebio.
Retiraos todos un poco.
    [Vanfe, y quedan los dos folos.
Ya eftás á folas conmigo,
Solo árboles y flores
Pueden fer mudos teftigos
De tus voces ; quita el velo
Con que cubierto has traido
El roftro, y dime : ¿ quién eres ?
¿ Dónde vas ? ¿ qué has pretendido ?
Habla.

    Julia.
    Porque de una vez
        [Saca la efpada.
Sepas á lo que he venido,
Y quien foy, faca la efpada ;
Pues defta manera digo,
Que foy quien viene á matarte.
    Eufebio.
Con la defenfa refifto
Tu ofadía y mi temor,
Porque mayor habia fido

  * " *Con el capitan eftas.*" Huefca Ed.

Eufebio.
Then you may declare them now,
Since before his face you ftand.
    Julia.
Are you the captain ?
    Eufebio.
        True.
    Julia (afide).
          Too true !
    Eufebio.
Tell me who you are, and why
You have come here.
    Julia.
        I'll reply
When we are alone, we two.
    Eufebio.
All of you retire awhile.
    [Exeunt all but Julia *and* Eusebio.
Now that thou'rt alone here with me,
Having only trees and flowers
Silently to look and liften
To thy words, remove the veil
With which cover'd thou haft hidden
Half thy face, and fay who art thou,
Whither goeft thou, here what brings
    thee ;—
Speak !
    Julia.
    That you may know at once
        [Draws her fword.
What it is that brings me hither,
Who I am too, draw thy fword ;
Since I mean to fay in *this* way
That to kill thee I have come here.
    Eufebio.
In defence I make refiftance
To thy daring and my doubt,
Since it feems to me that bigger

De la accion, que de la voz.
      Julia.
Riñe, cobarde, conmigo,
Y verás, que con tu muerte
Vida y confusion te quito.
      Eusebio.
Yo por defenderme mas,
Que por ofenderte, riño;
Que ya tu vida me importa,
Pues si en este desafío
Te mato, no sé por qué,
Y si me matas, lo mismo.
Descúbrete ahora pues,
Si te agrada.
      Julia.
        Bien has dicho,
Porque en venganzas de honor,
Sino es que conste el castigo
Al que fué ofensor, no queda
Satisfecho el ofendido. [*Descúbrese.*
¿Conócesme? ¿qué te espantas?
¿Qué me miras?

      Eusebio.
        Que rendido
A la verdad y á la duda,
En confusos desvaríos,
Me espanto de lo que veo,
Me asombro de lo que miro.
      Julia.
Ya me has visto.
      Eusebio.
        Sí, y de verte
Mi confusion ha crecido
Tanto, que si ántes de ahora
Alterados mis sentidos
Desearon verte, ya
Desengañados, lo mismo,
Que dieran antes por verte,

Is thine action, than thy voice.
      Julia.
Fight then, coward, fight then with me,
And thou'lt see that with thy death
Life and doubt at once shall quit thee.
      Eusebio.
I in my defence, much more
Than for thy least hurt, fight with thee,
Feeling even now an interest
In thy life; since if I kill thee
In this strife, I know not wherefore,
And 'tis so if me thou killest.
Then discover thyself now,
If it please thee.
      Julia.
        Thou speak'st wisely,
Since, when honour cries for vengeance,
If the hand of the chastiser
Is unknown unto the wronger,
Full revenge is not inflicted.
      [*She discovers herself.*
Dost thou know me? Whence this terror?
Why thus gaze?
      Eusebio.
        Because bewilder'd,
Lost in mingled truth and doubt,
In confusions so conflicting,
I am shock'd at what I see,
I am scared at what I witness.
      Julia.
Well, thou'st seen me.
      Eusebio.
        Yes, and seeing thee
So with new confusion fills me
That if but a moment hence
My disturb'd and doubting wishes
Long'd to see thee, even already
Disabused, they now would give here
The same price to see thee not,

Dieran por no haberte visto.
¿Tú, Julia, en aqeste monte?
¿Tú con profano vestido,
Dos veces violento en tí?
¿Cómo sola aqui has venido?
¿Qué es esto?
       Julia.
        Desprecios tuyos
Son, y desengaños mios.
Y porque veas, que es flecha
Disparada, ardiente tiro,
Veloz rayo, una muger,
Que corre tras su apetito,
No solo me han dado gusto
Los pecados cometidos
Hasta ahora, mas tambien
Me le dan, si los repito.
Salí del convento, fui
Al monte, y porque me dijo
Un pastor, que mal guiada
Iba por aquel camino,
Neciamente temerosa,
Por evitar mi peligro,
Le aseguré, y le di muerte,
Siendo instrumento un cuchillo,
Que él en su cinta traia.
Con este, que fue ministro
De la muerte, á un caminante,
Que cortesmente previno
En las ancas de un caballo,
A tanto cansancio alivio,
A la vista de una aldea,
Porque entrar en ella quiso,
Le pagué en un despoblado
Con la muerte el beneficio.
Tres dias fueron, y noches
Los que aquel desierto me hizo
Mesa de silvestres plantas,
Lecho de peñascos frios.

That to see thee they'd have given.
Thou here, Julia, in this mountain?
Thou, profanely dress'd, committest
Thus a two-fold sacrilege
'Gainst thyself: why hast thou hither
Come alone? What's this?
      Julia.
        Thy scorn
And my disillusion is it:—
And to show thee that an arrow
Shot in air, a burning missile,
A swift lightning-bolt's a woman
Who to passion doth submit her,
Not alone do I feel pleasure
In the sins I have committed
Until now, but I do even
Feel it in their repetition.
I my convent left, and fled
To the mountain, where a simple
Shepherd having said I was taking
The wrong pathway through the thicket,
Him, through foolish fearfulness,
And to silence thus a witness
Of my flight, I put to death,
A rude knife, which at his girdle
Hung suspended; being the weapon.
With this weapon, the inflicter
Thus of death, a traveller,
Who had courteously provided,
On the haunches of his horse,
Rest for my long-travell'd tiredness,
When we came in sight of a village,
Him, because he wish'd to bide there,
In a lonely place I paid
Back with death for all his kindness.
Three long days and nights I spent
In that desert, which provided
With its cold rocks for my bed,
For my scant food with its wild herbs.

Llegué á una pobre cabaña,
A cuyo techo pajizo
Juzgué pavellon dorado
En la paz de mis sentidos.
Liberal huéspeda fué
Una serrana conmigo,
Compitiendo en los deseos
Con el pastor su marido.
A la hambre y al cansancio
Dejé en su albergue rendidos
Con buena mesa, aunque pobre,
Manjar, aunque humilde, limpio.
Pero al despedirme dellos,
Habiendo antes prevenido,
Que al buscarme no pudiesen
Decir: "nosotros la vimos;"
Al cortés pastor, que al monte
Salió á enseñarme el camino,
Maté, y entré donde luego
Hago en su muger lo mismo.
Mas considerando entonces,
Que en el propio trage mio
Mi pesquisidor llevaba,
Mudármele determino.
Al fin, pues, por varios casos,
Con las armas y el vestido
De un cazador, cuyo sueño,
No imágen, trasunto vivo
Fué de la muerte, llegué
Aqui, venciendo peligros,
Despreciando inconvenientes,
Y atropellando designios.
        Eusebio.
Con tanto asombro te escucho,
Con tanto temor te miro,
Que eres al oido encanto,
Si á la vista basilisco.
Julia, yo no te desprecio,
Pero temo los peligros

I approach'd a lowly cabin,
Whose straw roof appear'd to glisten,
To my tired and languid spirits,
Lovelier than a gold pavilion.
There a shepherd's wife the part
Play'd of liberal hostess with me,
Rivalling the swain, her husband,
In all kindly acts and wishes.
Weariness and hunger long
Could not in that lodging linger,
With its food though lowly, clean,
With its fare so good, though simple;
But at leaving I determined,
With a fatal fix'd prevision,
That to my pursuers never
Should they say, "Yes, here we hid her."
So I slew the courteous shepherd
Who had come some way to guide me
Through the mountain, and returning,
Did the same thing to his wife there.
But considering that I carried
A detector and a spier
In mine own dress, I determined
In another to disguise me.
And at length, with various fortune,
In the arms and the equipment
Of a hunter, whose sound slumber
No mere fancied type or image
Was of death, I here have wander'd,
Conquering every risk and hindrance,
Every obstacle despising,
Trampling all that would resist me.
        Eusebio.
With such terror do I see thee,
With such horror do I listen,
To my sight thou art a basilisk,
To my hearing thou'rt bewitchment;
I do not despise thee, Julia,
But I fear the sure though hidden

Con que el cielo me amenaza,
Y por eſo me retiro.
Vuélvete tú á tu convento;
Que yo temeroſo vivo
De eſa Cruz tanto, que huyo
De tí.—¿ Mas qué es eſte ruido ?

Salen los Bandoleros.
Ricardo.
Preven, ſeñor, la defenſa ;
Que apartados del camino,
Al monte Curcio y ſu gente
En buſca tuya han ſalido.
De todas eſas aldeas
Tanto el número ha crecido,
Que han venido contra tí
Viejos, mugeres y niños,
Diciendo, que ha de vengar
En tu ſangre la de un hijo
Muerto á tus manos, y jura
De llevarte por caſtigo,
O por venganza de tantos,
Preſo á Sena, muerto ó vivo.
Euſebio.
Julia, deſpues hablaremos.
Cubre el roſtro, y ven conmigo ;
Que no es bien, que en poder quedes
De tu padre y mi enemigo.—
Soldados, eſte es el dia
De moſtrar aliento y brio.
Porque ninguno deſmaye,
Conſidere, que atrevidos
Vienen á darnos la muerte,
O prendernos, que es lo miſmo :
Y ſi no, en pública cárcel,
De deſdichas perſeguidos,
Y ſin honra nos veremos.

Dangers with which Heaven doth threat
   me,
Therefore muſt I not ſtay with thee.
Thou return unto thy convent ;
For ſuch holy awe doth give me
That ſtrange Croſs of thine, I fly
From thee.—But what noiſe comes
   hither ?

Enter RICARDO *and other bandits.*
Ricardo.
Sir, prepare for thy defence,—
For, departing from the highway,
Curcio and his people all
Up the mountain's ſides are climbing ;
For from all theſe villages
Hath increaſed ſo his enliſtment,
That againſt thee now come on
Even the old men, women, children,
Saying that he comes for vengeance
In thy blood, for a ſon death-ſtricken
By thy hands, and he has vow'd
For thy chaſtiſement to bring thee,
Or for his revenge, in chains
To Siena, dead or living.
Euſebio.
Julia, more we'll ſpeak anon,
Veil thy face now and come with me,
Leſt thou fall into the hands
Of my enemy and thy ſire here.—
Soldiers, this is now the day
To diſplay your ſtrength and ſpirit!
That no craven heart be here,
Think that theſe expeſtant viſtors
Hither come to give us death,
Or, what's worſe, to make us priſoners ;
If ſo in a public gaol,
By a thouſand ills affliſted,
Without honour we ſhall ſee us.

Pues fi efto hemos conocido,
¿ Por la vida, y por la honra,
Quién temió el mayor peligro ?
No pienfen que los tememos,
Salgamos á recibirlos ;
Que fiempre eftá la fortuna
De parte del atrevido.
            Ricardo.
No hay que falir ; que ya llegan
A nofotros.
            Eufebio.
            Preveníos,
Y ninguno fea cobarde ;
Que, vive el cielo ! fi miro
Huir alguno ó retirarfe,
Que he de efangrentar los filos
De aquefte acero en fu pecho
Primero que en mi enemigo.

        Dentro CURCIO.

            Curcio.
En lo encubierto del monte
Al traidor Eufebio he vifto,
Y para inútil defenfa
Hace murallas fus rifcos.
            Voces (dentro).
Ya entre las efpefas ramas
Defde aqui los defcubrimos.
            Julia.
¡ A ellos !   [*Vafe.*
            Eufebio.
        Efperad, villanos ;
Que ¡ vive Dios ! que teñidos
Con vueftra fangre los campos
Han de fer undofos rios.
            Ricardo.
De los cobardes villanos
Es el número excefivo.

If then this we have admitted,
Who is there for life, for honour,
That will fear the greater rifk here ?
Let them think not that we fear them ;
Let us forth and meet them firft then,
Since is fortune on the fide
Ever of the boldeft fpirits.
            Ricardo.
There's no need to go, for they
Are already here.
            Eufebio.
                Be firm then,
And let no one play the coward ;
For, as Heaven lives ! if I witnefs
One of you or fly or falter,
I my fword's edge fhall encrimfon
In his heart's blood, rather than
In the enemy's that I fight with.

        Curcio (within).

            Curcio.
In the heart here of the mountain,
I have feen Eufebio hidden,
And the wretch, in vain defence,
Makes a rampart of thefe cliffs here.
            Voices (within).
Through thefe thick o'erhanging boughs
We already can defcry them.
            Julia.
On them !   [*Exit.*
            Eufebio.
                Wait for us, bafe peafants !
For, as God doth live ! befprinkled
With your blood, the fields fhall run
Rippling red like wavy rivers.
            Ricardo.
Very numerous is the crowd
Of thefe craven herds and hinds here.

Curcio (dentro).	*Curcio (within).*
¿ Adónde, Eusebio, te escondes ?	Where, Eusebio, art thou hid ?
Eusebio.	*Eusebio.*
No me escondo, que ya te sigo.	Thee I seek, I am not hidden.
[Vanse todos, y disparan arcabuces dentro.	*[Exeunt all: shots are heard within.*
Sale JULIA.	*Enter* JULIA.
Julia.	*Julia.*
Del monte que yo he buscado	Scarcely have I trod the grass
Apenas las yerbas piso,	Of this mountain's sought-for ridges,
Cuando horribles voces oigo,	When I hear tumultuous cries,
Marciales campañas miro :	When the strife of war I witness ;
De la pólvora los ecos,	By the echoes of the powder,
Y del acero los filos,	By the gleam of swords that glitter,
Unos ofenden la vista,	Dazzled is the eye that sees them,
Y otros turban el oido.	Deafen'd is the ear that listens ;—
¿ Mas qué es aquello que veo ?	But, alas ! what's this I see ?
Desbaratado y vencido	Put to rout, and backward driven,
Todo el escuadron de Eusebio	All the squadron of Eusebio
Le deja ya al enemigo.	Leave him to the enemy's will there.
Quiero volver á juntar	I'll return and reunite
Toda la gente que ha habido	All the followers he had with him,
De Eusebio, y volver á darle	I'll return and give him aid ;—
Favor ; que si los animo,	For if them I thus inspirit,
Seré en su defensa asombro	I in his defence will be
Del mundo, seré cuchillo	The world's terror, the Fates' swift shears,
De la Parca, estrago fiero	The fierce ruin of their lives,
De sus vidas, vengativo	To the future times the symbol
Espanto de los futuros,	Of revenge, and th' admiration
Y admiracion destos siglos. *[Vase.*	Of the ages that we live in. *[Exit.*
Sale GIL *de bandolero.*	*Enter* GIL *dressed as a bandit.*
Gil.	*Gil.*
Por estar seguro, apenas	To preserve my skin, I scarcely
Fui bandolero novicio,	Have commenced my thieve's noviciate,
Cuando, por ser bandolero,	When the being a bandolero
Me veo en tanto peligro.	Is, I see, a dangerous business ;—
Cuando yo era labrador,	When I was a labourer,

Eran ellos los vencidos;
Y hoy, porque foy de la carda,
Va fucediendo lo mifmo.
Sin fer avariento traigo
La defventura conmigo;
Pues tan defgraciado foy,
Que mil veces imagino,
Que, á fer yo Judío, fueran
Defgraciados los Judíos.

Salen MENGA, BRAS, TIRSO *y otros*
villanos.

Menga.
¡ A ellos, que van huyendo !
Bras.
No ha de quedar uno vivo
Tan folamente.
Menga.
       Hácia aqui
Uno dellos fe ha efcondido.
Bras.
Muera efte ladron.
Gil.
       Mirad,
Que yo foy.
Menga.
      Ya nos ha dicho
El trage, que es bandolero.
Gil.
El trage les ha mentido,
Como muy grande bellaco.
Menga.
Dale tú.
Bras.
    Pégale digo.
Gil.
Bien dado eftoy y pegado :
Advertid . . .

My fide was it that was lick'd then,
And to-day, for being a tramper,
With the fame luck I'm afflicted !
Though no mifer, in my pocket
I misfortune carry with me ;
Since fo evil-ftarr'd am I,
That it ftrikes me many a minute,
That if ever I turn'd Jew,
Jews themfelves could be outwitted.

Enter MENGA, BRAS, TIRSO, *and*
other peafants.

Menga.
After them ! for they are flying !
Bras.
On ! no quarter muft be given,—
Let not one furvive !
Menga.
      See, here
One of them is flyly hidden !
Bras.
Kill the robber !
Gil.
      Ah ! now fee
Who I am.
Menga.
     That you're a brigand
Has your drefs already told us.
Gil.
Then my drefs lies like a villain
And a rafcal to have faid fo.
Menga.
Give it to him !
Bras.
     Pay him off quickly !
Gil.
I've been paid, and got it foundly,—
See, confider ! . . .

Tirſo.
No hay que advertirnos,
Bandolero ſois.
Gil.
Mirad
Que ſoy Gil, votado á Criſto!
Menga.
¿Pues no hablaras antes, Gil?
Tirſo.
Pues, Gil, ¿no lo hubieras dicho?
Gil.
¿Qué mas antes, ſi el yo ſoy
Os dije deſde el principio?
Menga.
¿Qué haces aqui?
Gil.
¿No lo veis?
Ofendo á Dios en el quinto,
Mato ſolo mas, que juntos
Un médico y un eſtio.
Menga.
¿Qué trage es eſte?
Gil.
Es el diablo.
Maté á uno, y ſu veſtido
Me puſe.
Menga.
¿Pues cómo, di,
No eſtá de ſangre teñido,
Si le mataſte?

Gil.
Eſo es fácil;
Murió de miedo, eſta ha ſido
La cauſa.
Menga.
Ven con noſotros,
Que victorioſos ſeguimos
Los bandoleros, que ahora

Tirſo.
We conſider
Only you're a thief.
Gil.
That *I* am
Gil, I call all Heaven to witneſs.
Menga.
Why not ſay ſo ſooner, Gil?
Tirſo.
Gil, why ſay not ſo at firſt, then?
Gil.
How, what ſooner, when I told you
From the firſt I was myſelf here?
Menga.
What are you doing?
Gil.
Don't you ſee?
I'm a-breaking juſt the fifth—tenth
Of the commandments, killing more
Than the ſummer and a phyſician.
Menga.
What's this dreſs?
Gil.
It is the devil,—
One of them I kill'd, and rigg'd me
In his dreſs then.
Menga.
But ſay, why
Is the dreſs not ſtain'd, if you kill'd
   him,
With his blood?
Gil.
Oh! that is eaſy
To explain, the cauſe is ſimple,
'Twas of fear he died.
Menga.
Come with us,
For victorious the banditti
We purſue, for now the cowards

Cobardes nos han huido.
   Gil.
No mas veſtido, aunque vaya
Titiritando de frio.   [*Vanſe.*

Salen peleando Eusebio *y* Curcio.
   Curcio.
Ya eſtamos ſolos los dos,
Gracias al cielo que quiſo
Dar la venganza á mi mano
Hoy, ſin haber remitido
A las agenas mi agravio,
Ni tu muerte á agenos filos.
   Euſebio.
No ha ſido en eſta ocaſion
Airado el cielo conmigo,
Curcio, en haberte encontrado ;
Porque ſi tu pecho vino
Ofendido, volverá
Caſtigado y ofendido.
Aunque no ſé qué reſpeto
Has pueſto en mí, que he temido
Mas tu enojo, que tu acero :
Y aunque pudieran tus brios
Darme temor, ſolo temo,
Cuando aqueſas canas miro,
Que me hacen cobarde.
   Curcio.
     Euſebio,
Yo confieſo, que has podido
Templar en mí de la ira,
Con que agraviado te miro,
Gran parte ; pero no quiero,
Que pienſes inadvertido,
Que te dan temor mis canas,
Cuando puede el valor mio.
Vuelve á reñir ; que una eſtrella,
O algun favorable ſigno

Fly before us panic-ſtricken.
   Gil.
Catch me dreſs'd again, although
With the cold I ſhake and ſhiver !
     [*Exeunt.*

Enter Eusebio *and* Curcio *fighting.*
   Curcio.
Now we are alone, we two,
Thanks to favouring Heaven that giveth
Vengeance to my own right hand
On this day, without tranſmitting
To another's arm my wrong,
To another's ſword thy ſwift death.
   Euſebio.
Curcio, on this occaſion
Heaven has not been angry with me,
In permitting me to meet thee ;
Since if thou haſt carried hither
An indignant breaſt, thou'lt bear it
Back both puniſh'd and indignant.
Though I know not what reſpect
Thou haſt cauſed in me, that gives me
More fear for thy wrath than ſword :
And although thy ſtrength and ſpirit
Well might fright me, I but fear
When I ſee thoſe locks of ſilver,
Which a coward make me.
   Curcio.
       I
Own, Euſebio, thou art gifted
With ſome power, to appeaſe a part
Of the wrath with which, afflicted,
I behold thee ; but I would not
Have thee careleſsly attribute
To theſe hoary hairs thy fear,
When my valour were ſufficient.
Come, renew the fight ! one ſtar
Or one planet's favouring ſignal

No es baſtante á que yo pierda
La venganza que conſigo.
Vuelve á reñir.

    Euſebio.

     ¿ Yo temor?
Neciamente has preſumido,
Que es temor lo que es reſpeto ;
Aunque, ſi verdad te digo,
La victoria que deſeo
Es, á tus plantas rendido,
Pedirte perdon ; y á ellas
Pongo la eſpada, que ha ſido
Temor de tantos.

    Curcio.

    Euſebio,
No has de penſar, que me animo
A matarte con ventaja ;
Eſta es mi eſpada. (Aſi quito
       [*Aparte.*
La ocaſion de darle muerte.)
Ven á los brazos conmigo.
  [*Abrázanſe los dos, y luchan.*
    Euſebio.
No ſé qué efecto has hecho
En mí, que el corazon dentro del pecho,
A peſar de venganzas y de enojos,
En lágrimas ſe aſoma por los ojos,
Y en confuſion tan fuerte,
Quiſiera, por vengarte, darme muerte.
Véngate en mí ; rendida
A tus plantas, ſeñor, eſtá mi vida.

    Curcio.
El acero de un noble, aunque ofendido,
No ſe mancha en la ſangre de un rendido ;
Que quita grande parte de la gloria

Muſt not make me loſe the hope
Of the vengeance I ambition.
Fight anew, then!

    Euſebio.

     I to fear?
Oh! thou haſt preſumed too ſimply
Fear in that that was reſpect ;
Though, if I the truth admitted,
The ſole victory I deſire
Is, thus kneeling, thy forgiveneſs
To implore ; and at thy feet
To lay down this ſword, that has given
Fear to many a heart.

    Curcio.

    Euſebio,
Do not think that I could kill thee
At ſuch diſadvantage. Here
Alſo is my ſword; (I rid me [*Aſide.*
Of the means thus of his death.)—
Arm to arm then ſtruggle with me.
  [*They cloſe, and ſtruggle together.*

    Euſebio.
I know not by what charm poſſeſs'd,
Thus with thy heart againſt my breaſt,
My wrath expires, my vengeance dies,
In tender tears that guſh from out mine
  eyes.
So I implore thee, thus with trembling
  breath,
Confuſed, amazed, to give me inſtant
  death ;
Take thy revenge, I terminate the
  ſtrife,
My lord, by laying at thy feet my life.
    Curcio.
A brave man's ſword, how wrathful
  be his mood,
Is never ſtain'd in the defenceleſs blood

El que con fangre borra la victoria.

Voces (dentro).
Hácia aqui eftan.
   Curcio.
    Mi gente victoriofa
Viene á bufcarme, cuando temerofa
La tuya vuelve huyendo.
Darte vida pretendo;
Efcóndete; que en vano
Defenderé el enojo vengativo
De un efcuadron villano,
Y folo tú, impofible es quedar vivo.

Eufebio.
Yo, Curcio, nunca huyo
De otro poder, aunque he temido el tuyo;
Que fi mi mano aquefta efpada cobra,
Verás, cuanto valor en tí me falta,
Que en tu gente me fobra.

Salen Octavio *y todos los villanos.*

Octavio.
Defde el mas hondo valle á la mas alta
Cumbre de aquefte monte no ha quedado
Alguno vivo; folo fe ha efcapado
Eufebio, porque huyendo aquefta tarde..

Eufebio.
Mientes; que Eufebio nunca fue cobarde.
   Todos.
¡Aqui eftá Eufebio? ¡Muera!
   Eufebio.
¡Llegad, villanos!

Of a fallen foe: for war's triumphant
  ftory,   [half its glory.
If writ in needlefs blood, is fhorn of
    Voices (within).
Here, here they are.
   Curcio.
    My victor troop comes here
To feek me, while thy followers in fear
Fly from the unfuccefsful ftrife.
I wifh to fave thy life;—
Conceal thyfelf, for I would vainly ftrive
Thee to defend againft a band
Of vengeful peafants fword in hand,
And thou againft fo many fcarce couldft
  live.
   Eufebio.
I, Curcio, never fly
From any power, though thine I've
  fear'd to try;
But if my hand this fword uplifts again,
Thou'lt fee the valour that 'gainft thee
  proved weak
Can act its wonted part ftill on thy men.

Enter Octavio *with a crowd of
  peafants.*

   Octavio.
From deepeft valley to the higheft peak
Of this vaft mountain, not a foul our
  wrath
Has left alive: Eufebio only hath
Efcaped, for flying as the evening
  lower'd ....
   Eufebio.
Thou lieft! Eufebio never was a coward.
   All.
Eufebio here? The monfter let us flay!
   Eufebio.
Villains, come on!

Curcio.
¡ Tente, Octavio, espera !
Octavio.
¿ Pues tú, señor, que habias
De animarnos, ahora desconfias ?

Bras.
¿ Un hombre amparas, que en tu sangre
　　y honra
Introdujo el acero y la deshonra ?

Gil.
¿ A un hombre, que atrevido
Toda aquesta montaña ha destruido ?
A quien en el aldea no ha dejado
Melon, doncella, que él no haya catado,
Y á quien tantos ha muerto,
¿ Cómo así le defiendes ?

Octavio.
¿ Qué es, señor, lo que dices ? ¿ qué pre-
　　tendes ?
Curcio.
Esperad, escuchad, (¡ triste suceso !)
¿ Cuanto es mejor que á Sena vaya preso ?
Date á prision, Eusebio ; que prometo,
Y como noble juro, de ampararte,
Siendo abogado tuyo, aunque soy parte.

Eusebio.
Como á Curcio no mas, yo me rindiera,
Mas como á juez, no puedo ;
Porque aquel es respeto, y este es miedo.

Curcio.
Oh ! hold, Octavio, stay !
Octavio.
How, sir, canst thou, that shouldst in-
　　spirit us,
Now interpose and check our vengeance
　　thus ?
Bras.
Canst thou defend a man whose bloody
　　aim
Thy name and blood has stain'd with
　　blood and shame ?
Gil.
A man whose daring no restraint e'er
　　bound,
Who ravaged all this mountain region
　　round,
Who left no village in the wild unwasted,
Nor melon's juice, nor maiden's lip
　　untasted ?
Is it for killing of so many people
Him thus you will defend ?
Octavio.
What is it, sir, you say ? What thus in-
　　tend ?
Curcio.
Oh ! listen, stay ! (unhappy fate !) to
　　me
Seems it far better in captivity
To lead him to Siena : yield, Eusebio,
　　yield,
I give my knightly word to guard thy
　　fate,
And though thy accuser, be thy advo-
　　cate.
Eusebio.
To thee, as Curcio, I perchance might
　　yield me,
But to a judge I cannot ; since 'tis clear

Octavio.

¡ Muera Eufebio !

    Curcio.

        Advertid . . . .

    Octavio.

            Pues qué, ¿ tú quieres

Defenderle ? ¿ á la patria traidor eres ?

    Curcio.

¿ Yo traidor ? Pues me agravian defta
    fuerte,

Perdona, Eufebio, porque yo el primero

Tengo de fer en darte trifte muerte.

    Eufebio.

Quítate de delante,

Señor, porque tu vifta no me efpante ;

Que viéndote, no dudo,

Que te tenga tu gente por efcudo.

        [Vanfe todos peleando con él.

    Curcio.

Apretándole van.   ¡ O quien pudiera

Darte ahora la vida,

Eufebio, aunque la fuya mifma diera !

En el monte fe ha entrado,

Por mil partes herido,

Retirándofe baja defpeñado

Al valle.   Voy volando,

Que aquella fangre fria,

Que con túmida voz me eftá llamando,

Algo tiene de mia ;

Que fangre, que no fuera

Propia, ni me llamara, ni la oyera.

              [Vafe.

The former were refpect, the latter fear.

    Octavio.

Eufebio, die !

    Curcio.

    Oh ! hear . . . .

    Octavio.

        What thus can move thee

Him to defend, and thus a traitor prove
    thee ?

    Curcio.

A traitor I ?—fince thus fufpicion durft

Wrong me fo much, Eufebio, forgive me,

That death's dark wound I'm doom'd
    to give thee firft.

    Eufebio.

Oh ! fir, ftand not before me,

At fight of thee, it is not fear comes
    o'er me ;

No, but I do not doubt thy face will be

A fhield betwixt thy followers and me.

        [Exit fighting with the peafants,
             who purfue.

    Curcio.

They prefs him hard.   Oh ! who is
    there thy life,

Eufebio, now can fave,

Though his for thine were offer'd in
    the ftrife ?

Through the mountain's rocky walls

Hath he enter'd wounded, bleeding

From a thoufand wounds.   He falls

Headlong to the vale ! I fly,

For that cold, cold blood outflown,

With its timid voice doth call me nigh,

As if it were a portion of mine own ;—

Were the blood not mine own, that
    voice fo clear

Then had not power to call, nor I
    have power to hear.   *[Exit.*

Baja despeñado EUSEBIO.

Eusebio.
Cuando, de la vida incierto,
Me despeña la mas alta
Cumbre, veo que me falta
Tierra donde caiga muerto:
Pero si mi culpa advierto,
Al alma reconocida,
No el ver la vida perdida
La atormenta, sino el ver
Como ha de satisfacer
Tantas culpas una vida.
Ya me vuelve á perseguir
Este escuadron vengativo;
Pues no puedo quedar vivo,
He de matar, ó morir:
Aunque mejor será ir
Donde al cielo perdon pida;
Pero mis pasos impida
La Cruz, porque desta suerte
Ellos me dén breve muerte,
Y ella me dé eterna vida.
Arbol, donde el cielo quiso
Dar el fruto verdadero
Contra el bocado primero,
Flor del nuevo paraiso,
Arco de luz, cuyo aviso
En piélago mas profundo
La paz publicó del mundo,
Planta hermosa, fértil vid,
Arpa del nuevo David,
Tabla del Moises segundo:
Pecador soy, tus favores
Pido por justicia yo;
Pues Dios en tí, padeció
Solo por los pecadores.

[*The wildest part of the mountain.*
EUSEBIO *is seen lying at the foot of a
cross.*]

Eusebio.
From this cliff so steep and tall
Falling headlong, almost dead,
Earth still fails beneath my tread,
Where a living corse I fall;
But when I my guilt recall,
Upward still my spirit climbs,
Unregretting vanish'd times,
But with hope before I die,
Means to find to satisfy
With one life so many crimes.
Hither the revengeful foe
Comes my life's last drops to drain,—
Here the hope of life is vain,
I must give or meet the blow;
Though 'twere better far to go
Where for pardon I may pray;—
But this Cross, athwart my way
Rising up, in silence saith,—
They indeed can give you death,
I, the life that lasts alway.
Tree, whereon the pitying skies
Hang the true fruit love doth sweeten,
Antidote of that first eaten,
Flower of man's new paradise,
Rainbow, that to tearful eyes
Sin's receding flood discloses,—
Pledge that earth in peace reposes,
Beauteous plant, all fruitful vine,
A newer David's harp divine,
Table of a second Moses;—
Sinner am I, therefore I
Claim thine aid as all mine own,
Since for sinful man alone,
God came down on thee to die:

A mí me debes tus loores;
Que por mí folo muriera
Dios, fi mas mundo no hubiera:
Luego eres tú, Cruz, por mí;
Que Dios no muriera en tí,
Si yo pecador no fuera.
Mi natural devocion
Siempre os pidió con fe tanta,
No permitiéfeis, Cruz fanta,
Muriefe fin confefion.
No feré el primer ladron,
Que en vos fe confiefe á Dios.
Y pues que ya fomos dos,
Y yo no le he de negar,
Tampoco me ha de faltar
Redencion que fe obró en vos.
Lifardo, cuando en mis brazos
Pude ofendido matarte,
Lugar dí de confefarte,
Antes que en tan breves plazos
Se defatafen los lazos
Mortales. Y ahora advierto
En aquel viejo, aunque muerto;
Piedad de los dos aguardo.
¡ Mira que muero, Lifardo ;
Mira que te llamo, Alberto!

Sale CURCIO.

Curcio.
Hácia aquefta parte eftá.
Eufebio.
Si es que venis á matarme,
Muy poco hareis en quitarme
Vida, que no tengo ya.
Curcio.
¡ Qué bronce no ablandará
Tanta fangre derramada!
Eufebio, rinde la efpada.

Praife through me thou haft won thereby,
Since for me would God have died,
If the world held none befide.
Then, O Crofs! thou'rt all for me,
Since God had not died on thee
If fin's depths I had not tried.
Ever for thy interceffion
Hath my faith implored, O Crofs!
That thou wouldft not to my lofs
Let me die without confeffion.
I, repenting my tranfgreffion,
Will not the firft robber be
Who on thee confefs'd to God;
Since we two the fame path trod,
And repent, deny not me
The redemption wrought on thee.
Thou, Lifardo, though I could
Slay thee in my angry mood,
Still thefe arms were prompt to prefs
      thee,
Still could bear thee to confefs thee,
Ere thy life flow'd out in blood.
And the reverend man, whom I
Now recall thus faint and weak:
Pity from ye two I feek,—
See, Lifardo, fee, I die!
Hear, Alberto, hear my cry!

Enter CURCIO.

Curcio.
Here he fell, adown this fteep.
Eufebio.
If thou feek'ft my life, 'twill be
Eafy now to take from me
That which I no longer keep.
Curcio.
Oh! an eye of bronze would weep,
So much blood to fee outpour'd!—
Yield, Eufebio, yield thy fword.

Eufebio.
¿ A quién ?
  Curcio.
  A Curcio.
  Eufebio.
    Efta es. [*Dáfela.*
Y yo tambien á tus pies
De aquella ofenfa pafada
Te pido perdon. No puedo
Hablar mas ; porque una herida
Quita el aliento á la vida,
Cubriendo de horror y miedo
El alma.

  Curcio.
  Confufo quedo.
¿ Será en ella de provecho
Remedio humano ?
  Eufebio.
    Sofpecho,
Que la mejor medicina
Para el alma es la divina.
  Curcio.
¿ Dónde es la herida ?
  Eufebio.
    En el pecho.
  Curcio.
Déjame poner en ella
La mano, á ver fi refifte
El aliento. (¡ Ay de mí trifte !)
 [*Regiftra la herida, y ve la Cruz.*
¿ Qué feñal divina y bella
Es efta, que al conocella,
Toda el alma fe turbó ?

  Eufebio.
Son las armas que me dió
Efta Cruz, á cuyo pie
Naci ; porque mas no fé

Eufebio.
Yield to whom ?
  Curcio.
  To Curcio.
  Eufebio.
    Yes ,
   [*He gives his fword*
And thy feet I likewife prefs
For that paft offence, my lord,
Afking thy forgivenefs. Here
Voice doth fail me, for a wound
Stops my breath, my fenfe hath fwoon'd
And a horror and a fear
Fill my foul.
  Curcio.
  Confufed I hear ;—
Cannot human aid arreft
Thy fwift-failing life ?
  Eufebio.
    The beft
Cure for foul fo fick as mine
Is, I feel it, the divine.
  Curcio.
Where's thy wound ?
  Eufebio.
    'Tis in my breaft.
  Curcio.
Let me then my hand place there,
Thus to learn, (oh ! woe the day !)
What its troubled throb doth fay ;—
  [*He examines the wound, and fee.*
    the Crofs.
But what mark, divine and fair,
Is this fign my hand lays bare,
Which to fee, my foul moves fo ?
  Eufebio.
'Tis my creft's emblazoned glow,
Given me by this Crofs, whofe bafe
Was my birth's myfterious place,

De mi nacimiento yo.
Mi padre, á quien no feñalo,
Aun la cuna me negó;
Que fin duda imaginó,
Que habia de fer tan malo.
Aqui nací.
Curcio.
Y aqui igualo
El dolor con el contento,
Con el gufto el fentimiento,
Efeétos de un hado impío
Y agradable. ¡ Ay hijo mio!
Pena y gloria en verte fiento.
Tú eres, Eufebio, mi hijo,
Si tantas feñas advierto,
Que para llorarte muerto
Ya juftamente me aflijo.
De tus razones colijo
Lo que el alma adivinó.
Tu madre aqui te dejó
En el lugar que te he hallado;
Donde cometí el pecado,
El cielo me caftigó.
Ya aquefte lugar previene
Informacion de mi error;
¿ Pero cual feña mayor,
Que aquefta Cruz, que conviene
Con otra que Julia tiene?
Que no fin mifterio el cielo
Os feñaló, porque al fuelo
Fuérais prodigio los dos.
Eufebio.
No puedo hablar, padre, ¡ á Dios!
Porque ya de un mortal velo
Se cubre el cuerpo, y la muerte
Niega, pafando veloz,
Para refponderte voz,
Vida para conocerte,
Y alma para obedecerte.

For of *it* no more I know,
Since my father, of whom ne'er
I knew more, denied to me
Even a cradle: doubtlefs he
Then divined my dark career.
Here I firft drew breath.
Curcio.
And here
Grief and joy contend in me,
Anguifh and delight agree,
Sad and fweet thoughts o'er me fteal;—
O my long-loft fon! I feel
Pain and pride in feeing thee.
Thou, Eufebio, art my fon,—
This a thoufand proofs have faid;
Ah! that I muft mourn thee dead,
Ere thy life hath well begun.
What my foul by brooding on
Had divined, thy words make clear,
That thy mother left thee here,
In the place where I ftand o'er thee;
Where I finn'd to her who bore thee,
Falls the wrath of Heaven fevere.
Yes, delufion difappeareth,
All the more this place I fee;
But what greater proof can be
Than that *thy* breaft alfo beareth
The fame Crofs that Julia weareth?
Not without fome myftery
Heaven has mark'd you out to be
The world's wonder thus, ye two.
Eufebio.
I can fpeak no more, adieu,
Ah! my father, for on me
Falls the fatal veil, and death,
In its fwift flight paffing by me,
Life to know thee doth deny me,
Time to live thy fway beneath,
And to anfwer thee even breath.

Ya llega el golpe mas fuerte,
Ya llega el trance mas cierto.
Alberto!

     Curcio.
     ¡ Que llore muerto
A quien aborrecí vivo!
     Eusebio.
¡ Ven, Alberto !
     Curcio.
      ¡ O trance esquivo !
¡ Guerra injusta !
     Eusebio.
      ¡ Alberto ! ¡ Alberto !
        [*Muere.*

     Curcio.
Ya al golpe mas violento
Rindió el último aliento;
Paguen mis blancas canas
Tanto dolor.

     [*Tirase de los cabellos.*

 Sale BRAS.

   Bras.
     Ya son tus quejas vanas ;
¡ Cuándo puso inconstante la fortuna
En tu valor extremos?
     Curcio.
      En ninguna
Llegó el rigor á tanto.
Abrasen mis enojos
Este monte con llanto,
Puesto que es fuego el llanto de mis ojos.
¡ O triste estrella ! ¡ o rigurosa suerte !
¡ O atrevido dolor !

   Sale OCTAVIO.

   Octavio.
     Hoy, Curcio, advierte

Now the final stroke draws nigh :—
O Alberto !

     Curcio.
     Strange that I
Mourn his death whose life I sought.
     Eusebio.
Come, Alberto !
     Curcio.
      Fight hard fought !

     Eusebio.
Haste, Alberto ! haste, I die !   [*Dies.*

     Curcio.
In that last convulsive groan
Hath his troubled spirit flown.
Let these gray hairs for such pain
Pay now the price.

     [*He pulls his hair distractedly.*

 Enter BRAS.

   Bras.
     Thy wailings all are vain :
Will fickle fate, relenting, ne'er give o'er
Trying thy courage thus?
     Curcio.
      I ne'er before
More keenly felt its ire ;
The griefs I cannot drown
With scalding tears could burn this
    mountain down,
For even the flood my tears let fall is fire.
O luckless star ! O destiny of woe !
O bitter pang !

   Enter OCTAVIO.

   Octavio.
     To-day doth fortune show

La fortuna en los males de tu estado,
Cuantos puede sufrir un desdichado.
El cielo sabe cuanto hablarte siento.

Curcio.
¿ Qué ha sido ?
        Octavio.
            Julia falta del convento.
        Curcio.
El mismo pensamiento, di, ¿ pudiera
Con el discurso hallar pena tan fiera ?
Que es mi desdicha airada,
Sucedida aun mayor, que imaginada.
Este cadáver frio,
Este que ves, Octavio, es hijo mio.
Mira si basta en confusion tan fuerte
Cualquiera pena destas á una muerte.
Dadme paciencia, cielos,
O quitadme la vida,
Ahora perseguida
De tormentos tan fieros.

Salen GIL, TIRSO, *y villanos.*
        Gil.
¡ Señor !
        Curcio.
    ¿ Hay mas dolor ?
        Gil.
                Los bandoleros,
Que huyeron castigados,
En busca tuya vuelven, animados
De un demonio de un hombre,
Que encubre de ellos mismos rostro y
    nombre.

In all thine ills, which vainly wait a cure,
How much one hapless mortal can
    endure :—
God knows I grieve to make the tidings
    known.
        Curcio.
What are they ?
        Octavio.
            Julia from her cell hath flown.
        Curcio.
Could wildest frenzy feign
A more o'erwhelming stroke or fiercer
    pain ?
Alas ! my hapless fate o'ercast
Makes each new sorrow greater than
    the last.
This cold corse here thou gazest on,
Octavio, is the body of my son ;
Think, 'mid the crowd of ill succeeding
    ill,
If one alone were not enough to kill.
Oh ! grant me patience, Heaven,
Or take this life away,
Afflicted day by day
With visitations from thy scourging
    hand.

Enter GIL, TIRSO, *and peasants.*
        Gil.
My lord !
        Curcio.
    Some newer grief?
        Gil.
                The robber band,
That but now chastised had fled,
Rallying, come to attack thee, led
By a man whom hell doth seem to
    inflame,   [and name.
Who hideth even from them his face

Curcio.
Ahora que mis penas fuéron tales,
Que son lisonjas los mayores males.
El cuerpo se retire lastimoso
De Eusebio, en tanto que un sepulcro
　　honroso
A sus cenizas da mi desventura.
Tirso.
¿Pues cómo piensas darle sepultura
Hoy en lugar sagrado,
Cuando sabes que ha muerto excomul-
　　gado?
Bras.
Quien desta suerte ha muerto,
Digno sepulcro sea este desierto.
Curcio.
¡O villana venganza!
¿Tanto poder en tí la ofensa alcanza,
Que pasas desta suerte
Los últimos umbrales de la muerte?
　　　　　　　　　　[*Vase llorando.*

Bras.
Sea en penas tan graves
Su sepulcro las fieras y las aves.

Otro.
Del monte despeñado
Caiga, por mas rigor, despedazado.

Tirso.
Mejor es darle ahora sepultura
Entre de aquestos ramos la espesura.*
　　　[*Colocan entre las ramas el cuerpo
　　　　　de Eusebio.*

* " Mejor es darle agora
　Rústica sepultura entre estos ramos."
　　　　　　　　HARTZENBUSCH's *Ed.*

Curcio.
Such sorrows rack my breast,
That now the greatest ills appear a jest.
Take hence the body of Eusebio,
And place it where in time a tomb
　　shall show
How o'er his ashes still my tears endure.
Tirso.
What! do you think of giving sepulture,
In holy ground, unto a desperate man,
Who died beneath the Church's heaviest
　　ban?
Bras.
For one who died in such a desperate case,
The desert seems a fitting burial-place.
Curcio.
O vengeance of a vulgar breast!
Has thy rude anger then no bounds,
　　no rest?
Must thy coarse appetite insatiate crave
For food beyond the threshold of the
　　grave?　　　　　[*Exit weeping.*
Bras.
Wild beasts and birds of prey should
　　limb from limb
Tear such a wretch, and so thus bury him.
Another.
Let's throw his body o'er the rocks,
　　that so
In fragments it may reach the sands
　　below.
Tirso.
No, since the time no other mode allows,
Let's make his rustic grave beneath
　　these boughs.
　　　[*They place the body of* EUSEBIO
　　　　　as described.
Now since the night, wrapp'd in her
　　mournful shroud,

Pues ya la noche baja,
Envuelta en efa lóbrega mortaja :
Aqui en el monte, Gil, con él te queda;
Porque fola tu voz avifar pueda,
Si algunas gentes vienen
De las que huyeron.   [*Vanfe.*

Gil.
          ¡ Linda flema tienen !
A Eufebio han enterrado
Alli, y á mí aqui folo me han dejado.
Señor Eufebio, acuérdefe, le digo,
Que un tiempo fuí fu amigo.
¿ Mas qué es efto? ó me engaña mi defeo,
O mil perfonas á efta parte veo.

Sale ALBERTO.

Alberto.
Viniendo ahora de Roma,
Con la muda fufpenfion
De la noche en efte monte
Perdido otra vez eftoy.
Aquefta es la parte adonde
La vida Eufebio me dió,
Y de fus foldados temo,
Que en grande peligro eftoy.
          Eufebio.
¡ Alberto !
          Alberto.
          ¿ Qué aliento es efte
De una temerofa voz,
Que, repitiendo mi nombre,
En mis oidos fonó ?

Finds too a grave in yonder murky
          cloud,
Let us away : thou on the mountain,
          Gil,
Hadft beft remain befide the body ftill;
Shouldft thou fee any of the troop that
          fled,
Call loud for aid, we'll hear.
                    [*Exeunt.*
          Gil.
          That's eafily faid :
Eufebio's corfe they bury out of fight,
And leave but me to watch it through
          the night.
Señor Eufebio, recollect, I pray,
How you and I were friends the other
          day.
But what is this? Unlefs my eyes betray
          me,
At leaft a thoufand perfons here waylay
          me.

Enter ALBERTO.

Alberto.
In the filent dark of night,
On my journey back from Rome,
I again have loft my way
In this wild and mountain road :
'Tis the place that robber chieftain
Spared my life fome time ago,
And new peril from his foldiers
Now again my fears forbode.
          Eufebio.
Oh ! Alberto !
          Alberto.
          What faint breath
Of a trembling voice here blown
Falls upon my ear, my name
Sadly fighing o'er and o'er ?

Eusebio.

¡ Alberto !

Alberto.
      Otra vez pronuncia
Mi nombre, y me pareció
Que es á esta parte ; yo quiero
Ir llegando.

Gil.
      ¡ Santo Dios !
Eusebio es, y ya es mi miedo
De los miedos el mayor.

Eusebio.
¡ Alberto !

Alberto.
      Mas cerca suena.
¿ Voz, que discurres veloz
El viento, y mi nombre dices,
Quién eres ?

Eusebio.
      Eusebio soy ;
Llega, Alberto, hácia esta parte,
Adonde enterrado estoy ;
Llega, y levanta estos ramos ;
No temas.

Alberto.
      No temo yo.
Gil.
Yo sí.

      [ALBERTO *le descubre.*
Alberto.
      Ya estás descubierto.
Dime de parte de Dios,
¿ Qué me quieres ?
      Eusebio.
      De su parte

Eusebio.

Oh ! Alberto !

Alberto.
      Ah ! that voice
Syllables my name once more !
Here it seems to sound from : nigher
Let me listen.

Gil.
      Holy God !
'Tis Eusebio ! fear like this
Have I never felt before.

Eusebio.
Oh ! Alberto !

Alberto.
      Now 'tis nearer :
Voice that fliest fleetly forth
On the wind, and call'st my name,
Say, who art thou ?

Eusebio.
      I was known
As Eusebio : oh ! Alberto !
Hither come where I am thrown,
Take away these boughs that hide me ;*
Do not fear.

Alberto.
      No fear I know.
Gil.
Not so *I.*

      [ALBERTO *discovers him.*
Alberto.
      Thou'rt now laid bare,—
Tell me, in the name of God,
What with me thou willest.
      Eusebio.
      I

---

* In Tirso de Molina's *El Condenado por Desconfiado,* the body of *Paulo* is also hidden under boughs, and laid bare in the same manner, with, however, a very different result.—See his *Comedias Ecogidas.* Madrid, 1850. p. 203. TR.

Mi fe, Alberto, te llamó,
Para que, antes de morir,
Me oyeſes de confeſion.
Rato ha que hubiera muerto,
Pero libre ſe quedó
Del eſpíritu el cadáver ;
Que de la muerte el feroz
Golpe le privó de uſo,
Pero no le dividió.   [*Levántaſe.*
Ven adonde mis pecados
Confieſe, Alberto, que ſon
Mas, que del mar las arenas,
Y los átomos del ſol.
¡ Tanto con el cielo puede
De la Cruz la devocion !

Alberto.
Pues yo cuantas penitencias
Hice haſta ahora, te doy,
Para que en tu culpa ſirvan
De alguna ſatisfaccion.
     [*Vanſe* Eusebio *y* Alberto.
          Gil.
¡ Por Dios, que va por ſu pie !
Y para verlo mejor,
El ſol deſcubre ſus rayos.
A decirlo á todos voy.

Salen por el otro lado Julia *y algunos*
     Bandoleros.

          Julia.
Ahora, que deſcuidados
La victoria los dejó
Entre los brazos del ſueño,
Nos dan baſtante ocaſion.
          Uno.
Si has de ſalirlos al paſo,
Por eſta parte es mejor ;
Que ellos vienen por aqui.

In his name, by faith made bold,
Call'd thee, ere my death, to hear
My confeſſion long untold.
I have been a brief while dead,
And my corſe without control
Of the ſpirit here has lain ;
But although death's mighty ſtroke
Took its active uſe away,
Still unſever'd was the ſoul.
               [*He ariſes.*
Come, Alberto, where my ſins
I to thee may tell, though more
Than the atoms of the ſun
Or the ſands upon the ſhore ;—
All ſo powerful is with Heaven
The devotion of the Croſs.
          Alberto.
Then on thee the various penance
Of my lifetime I beſtow,
That at leaſt to ſome extent
For thy ſins they may atone.
     [*Exeunt* Eusebio *and* Alberto.
          Gil.
There, by heavens ! away he walks ;
And to ſee him, I ſuppoſe,
See the ſun ſhines out on purpoſe.
Oh ! I burſt to have it told !

Enter on the other ſide Julia *and*
     ſome bandits.

          Julia.
Now that in the careleſſneſs
Of ſucceſs they lie here prone,
Buried in the arms of ſleep,
Let us make the time our own.
          A Bandit.
If thou wouldſt ſecure the paſs,
Better 'tis this way to go,
For in that way they advance.

Salen CURCIO *y villano.*

Curcio.

Sin duda que inmortal foy
En los males que me matan,
Pues no me mata el dolor.

Gil.

A todas partes hay gente;
Sepan todos de mi voz
El mas admirable cafo,
Que jamas el mundo vió.
De donde enterrado eftaba
Eufebio, fe levantó,
Llamando á un clérigo á voces.
¿ Mas para qué os cuento yo
Lo que todos podeis ver ?
Mirad con la devocion
Que eftá puefto de rodillas.

Curcio.

¡ Mi hijo es ! ¡ Divino Dios !
¿ Qué maravillas fon eftas ?

Julia.

¿ Quién vió prodigio mayor ?

Curcio.

Afi como el fanto anciano
Hizo de la abfolucion
La forma, fegunda vez
Muerto á fus plantas cayó.

Sale ALBERTO.

Alberto.

Entre fus grandezas tantas,
Sepa el mundo la mayor
Maravilla de las fuyas,
Porque la enfalce mi voz.
Defpues de haber muerto Eufebio,
El cielo depofitó
Su efpíritu en fu cadáver,
Hafta que fe confefó;

Enter CURCIO *and his followers.*

Curcio.

Oh ! I furely muft have grown
Deathlefs 'mid the deadlieft ills,
Since I die not of my woe.

Gil.

Folks are round on every fide,
Let my voice to all unfold
The moft wonderful event
That the world has ever known :—
From the place that buried lay
Dead Eufebio, he arofe,
Calling loudly on a prieft !
But what need of words to fhow
That which you yourfelves can fee ?
Look there yonder, bending low,
See with what refpeét he kneels.

Curcio.

'Tis my fon, divineft God,
What a miracle is this !

Julia.

What a wonder here is fhown !

Curcio.

And the faintly elder fcarce
O'er his head doth make the form
Of abfolution, when he falls
At his feet a corfe once more

Enter ALBERTO.

Alberto.

'Mid its greateft miracles
That the wondering world may know
Now the ftrangeft of them all,
Let my voice its praife extol.
After this Eufebio died,
Heaven was pleafed to let his foul
Still within his body ftay
Till he could confefs the whole

Que tanto con Dios alcanza
De la Cruz la devocion.
   Curcio.
¡ Ay hijo del alma mia !
No fue defdichado, no,
Quien en fu trágica muerte
Tantas glorias mereció.
Afi Julia conociera
Sus culpas.
   Julia.
   ¡ Válgame Dios !
¿ Qué es lo que eftoy efcuchando?
¿ Qué prodigio es efte ? ¿ Yo
Soy la que á Eufebio pretende,
Y hermana de Eufebio foy ?
Pues fepa Curcio, mi padre,
Sepa el mundo y todos hoy
Mis graves culpas ; yo mifma,
Afombrada á tanto horror,
Daré voces : fepan todos
Cuantos hoy viven, que yo
Soy Julia, en número infame
De las malas la peor.
Mas ya que ha fido comun
Mi pecado, defde hoy
Lo ferá mi penitencia ;
Pidiendo humilde perdon
Al mundo del mal ejemplo,
De la mala vida á Dios.
   Curcio.
¡ O afombro de las maldades !
Con mis propias manos yo
Te mataré, porque fea
Tu vida y tu muerte atroz.
   Julia.
Valedme vos, Cruz divina ;
Que yo mi palabra os doy,
De hacer, volviendo al convento,
Penetencia de mi error.

Of his fins, fuch power with God
Hath devotion to the Crofs.
   Curcio.
Ah ! my fon, my much-loved fon,
Thou wert not unlucky, no,
To obtain fo much of glory
By the ftroke that laid thee low ;
Would that Julia now could know
Her tranfgreffions !
   Julia.
   Help me ! God !
What is this that now I hear ?
What is this that fhocks me fo ?
I Eufebio's fifter ? I
Am the fame who fought his love !
Then let Curcio, let my father,
Let the world and all men know
My great guilt ! I will myfelf,
Frighten'd by this horrid blow,
Publicly proclaim it :——Now
Let all living men be told
I am Julia, 'mid the crowd
Of all reprobates the worft ;
But as my offence has been
Public, let my penance fhow
Publicly that I repent ;
Humbly pardon I implore
From the world for bad example,
For an evil life from God.
   Curcio.
Prodigy of wickednefs,
By my own right hand alone
Shalt thou die : that life and death
Be with thee atrocious both.
   Julia.
Aid me thou, O Crofs divine !
And I plight to thee my word,
Back unto my cell returning,
For my error to atone.

[*Al querer herirla* Curcio, *ſe abraza de la Cruz, que eſtaba en el ſepul- cro de* Eusebio, *y vuela.*

Alberto.
¡ Gran milagro !
             Curcio.
                 Y con el fin
De tan grande admiracion,
La Devocion de la Cruz
Felice acaba ſu autor.

[*As* Curcio *is about ſtriking her,* ſhe *embraces the Croſs that ſtands be- ſide the grave of* Eusebio, *which riſes into the air with her and diſ- appears.*

Alberto.
What a miracle !
             Curcio.
               And thus,
With ſo wonderful a cloſe,
Happily the author endeth
The Devotion of the Croſs.

THE END.

CHISWICK PRESS :—PRINTED BY WHITTINGHAM AND WILKINS,
TOOKS COURT, CHANCERY LANE.

A LIST

OF

Calderon's Dramas and Autos Sacramentales,

Translated into English Verse

BY DENIS FLORENCE MAC-CARTHY, M.R.I.A.

THE PURGATORY OF SAINT PATRICK.

"With the 'Purgatory of St. Patrick' especial pains seem to have been taken".

"Considerable license has been taken with the prayer of St. Patrick; but its spirit is well preserved, and the translator's poetry must be admired".

"If Calderon can ever be made popular here, it must be in the manner generally adopted by Mr. Mac-Carthy in the specimens, six in number, which are here translated, preserving, namely, the metrical form, which is one of the characteristics of the old Spanish drama. This medium, through which it partakes of the lyrical character, is no accident of style, but an essential property of that remarkable creation of a poetic age—remarkable, because while the drama so adorned was entirely the offspring of popular impulse, in opposition to many rigorous attempts in favour of classical methods, it was at the same time raised above the tone of common expression by the rhythmical mode which it assumed, in a manner decisive of its ideal tendency. It thus displays a combination rare in this kind of poetry: the spirit of an untutored will, embodied in a form the romantic expression of which might seem only congenial to choice and delicate fancies. . . . .

"In conclusion, what has now been said of Calderon, and of the stage which he adorned, as well as of the praise justly due to parts of Mr. Mac-Carthy's version, will at least serve to commend these volumes to curious lovers of poetry".

From an elaborate article in "The Athenæum", by the late eminent Spanish scholar, Mr. J. R. Chorley, on the first two volumes of Mr. Mac-Carthy's translations from Calderon.

THE CONSTANT PRINCE.

A Drama.

"In his dramas of a serious and devout character, in virtue of their dignified pathos, tragic sublimity, and religious fervour, Calderon's best title to praise will be found. In such, above all in his *Autos*, he reached a height beyond any of his predecessors, whose productions, on religious themes especially, striking as many of them are, with situations and motives of the deepest effect, are not sustained at the same impressive elevation, nor disposed with that consummate judgment which leaves nothing imperfect or superfluous in the dramas of Calderon. 'The Constant Prince' and 'The Physician of his own Honour', which Mr. Mac-Carthy has translated, are noble instances representing two extremes of a large class of dramas".

From the same article in "The Athenæum", by J. R. Chorley.

THE PHYSICIAN OF HIS OWN HONOUR.

"'The Physician of his own Honour is a domestic tragedy, and must be one of the most fearful to witness ever brought upon the stage. The highest excess of dramatic powers, terror and gloom has certainly been reached in this drama".

From an eloquent article in " The Dublin University Magazine" on " D. F. Mac-Carthy's Calderon".

THE SECRET IN WORDS.

A Drama.

"The ingenious verbal artifice of 'The Secret in Words', although a mere trifle if compared to the marvellous intricacy of a similar cipher in Tirso's 'Amar por Arte Mayor', from which Calderon's play was taken—loses sadly in a translation; yet the piece, even with this disadvantage, cannot fail to please".

J. R. Chorley in " The Athenœum".

THE SCARF AND THE FLOWER.

A Drama.

"The 'Scarf and the Flower', nice and courtly though it be, the subject spun out and entangled with infinite skill, is too thin by itself for an interest of three acts long; and no translation, perhaps, could preserve the grace of manner and glittering flow of dialogue which conceal this defect in the original".

J. R. Chorley in " The Athenœum".

LOVE AFTER DEATH.

A Drama.

"'Love after Death' is a drama full of excitement and beauty, of passion and power, of scenes whose enthusiastic affection, self-devotion, and undying love are drawn with more intense colouring than we find in any other of Calderon's works".

From an article in " The Dublin University Magazine" on D. F. Mac-Carthy's Calderon.

"Another tragedy, 'Love after Death', is connected with the hopeless rising of the Moriscoes in the Alpujarras (1568–1570), one of whom is its hero. It is for many reasons worthy of note; amongst others, as showing how far Calderon could rise above national prejudices, and expend all the treasures of his genius in glorifying the heroic devotedness of a noble foe".

Archbishop Trench.

LOVE THE GREATEST ENCHANTMENT.

A Drama.

"This fact connects the piece with the first and most pleasing in the volume, 'Love the greatest Enchantment', in which the same myth [that of Circe and Ulysses] is exhibited in a more life-like form, though not without some touches of allegory. Here we have a classical plot which is adapted to the taste of Spain in the seventeenth century by a plentiful admixture of episodes of love and gallantry. The adventure is opened with nearly the same circumstances as in the tenth *Odyssey:* but from the moment that Ulysses, with the help of a divine talisman, has frustrated all the spells (beauty excepted) of the enchantress, the action is adapted to the manners of a more refined and chivalrous circle".

" The Saturday Review" in its review of " Mac-Carthy's Three Plays of Calderon".

THE DEVOTION OF THE CROSS.

A Drama.

"The last drama to which Mr. Mac-Carthy introduces us is the famous 'Devotion of the Cross'. We cannot deny the praise of great power to this strange and repulsive work, in which Calderon draws us onward by a deep and terrible dramatic interest, while doing cruel violence to our moral nature. . . . Our readers may be glad to compare the translations which Archbishop Trench and Mr. Mac-Carthy have given us of a celebrated address to the Cross contained in this drama. 'Tree whereon the pitying skies", etc. Mr. Mac-Carthy does not appear to us to suffer from comparison on this occasion with a true poet, who is also a skilful translator. Indeed he has faced the difficulties and given the sense of the original with more decision than Archbishop Trench".

" The Guardian", in its review of the same volume.

THE SORCERIES OF SIN.

An Auto.

"The central piece, the 'Sorceries of Sin', is an 'Auto Sacramental', or Morality, of which the actors represent Man, Sin, Voluptuousness, etc., Understanding, and the Five Senses. The Senses are corrupted by the influence of Sin, and figuratively changed into wild beasts. Man, accompanied by Understanding and Penance, demands their liberation and encounters no resistance; but his free-will is afterwards seduced by the Evil Power, and his allies reclaim him with difficulty. Yet the plan of the apologue is embellished with many ingenious conceits and artifices, and conformed in the leading circumstances with an Homeric myth — the names of Ulysses and Circe being frequently substituted for those of the Man and Sin".

" The Saturday Review" on "Mac-Carthy's Three Plays of Calderon".

BELSHAZZAR'S FEAST.

An Auto.

"The first *auto* translated is "Belshazzar's Feast', a fortunate selection, for it is probably unsurpassed in dramatic effect and poetic description, and withal is much less encumbered with theology than most others".

From an article in " The New York Nation", by a distinguished professor of Cornell University, on " Mac-Carthy's Translations of Calderon".

THE DIVINE PHILOTHEA.

An Auto.

"'The Divine Philothea', probably the last work of the kind written by Calderon, and as such worthy of atten-

tion, inasmuch as it is the composition of an old man of eighty-one, is conceived with much boldness and executed with marvellous skill. No fewer than twenty personages are represented on the stage, and these have their several parts allotted to them with great discrimination, ingenuity, and judgment. The Senses, the Cardinal Virtues; Paganism and Judaism; Heresy and Atheism; the Prince of Light and the Power of Darkness, figure amongst the characters".

" The Bookseller", June 29, 1867, on Mac-Carthy's " Mysteries of Corpus Christi (Autos Sacramentales), from the Spanish of Calderon".

THE TWO LOVERS OF HEAVEN.

A Drama.

"Of these 'The Wonder-working Magician' is most celebrated; but others, as 'The Joseph of Women', 'The Two Lovers of Heaven', quite deserve to be placed on a level if not higher than it. A tender pathetic grace is shed over this last, which gives it a peculiar charm".

Archbishop Trench.

Calderon's *Autos Sacramentales*, or Mysteries of Corpus Christi. Duffy: Dublin and London, 1867.

From " The Irish Ecclesiastical Record".

"In conclusion, we heartily commend to our readers this most interesting and valuable specimen of Spanish thought and devotion, wrought, as it is, into such pure and beautiful English. . . . . When we remember the great literary advantages which Spain once possessed in the intellect and faith of her literary giants, we may well rejoice in the appearance among us of one of the greatest of that noble race in the person of Calderon, especially when introduced to us by a poet whose claim upon our consideration has been so emphatically made good by his own original productions as Denis Florence Mac-Carthy".